Praise for Shirley Dickson

OUR LAST GOODBYE

"[An] unputdownable and emotional World War II story.... Dickson is truly a gifted author who will pull every emotion out of you while reading her books."

—*Sinfully Wicked Book Reviews*

"Exceedingly well written. Shirley [Dickson] has written a story that will tug on even the toughest of heartstrings."

—*Ginger Book Geek*

THE ORPHAN SISTERS

"It was a heart-warming story of family, love and heartbreak which will undoubtedly pull at your heart-strings. Just make sure you have a box of tissues ready!"

—*Stardust Book Reviews*

"A book that will stay with me for many years to come and I urge you all to grab your nearest copy and start reading immediately you will not be disappointed."

—*Stacy Is Reading*

Our Last Goodbye

ALSO BY SHIRLEY DICKSON

The Orphan Sisters

SHIRLEY DICKSON

Our Last Goodbye

FOREVER

New York   Boston

Forever
Hachette Book Group
1290 Avenue of the Americas, New York, NY 10104
read-forever.com
twitter.com/readforeverpub

Originally published in 2019 by Bookouture
First U.S. Edition: December 2020

Forever is an imprint of Grand Central Publishing. The Forever name and logo are trademarks of Hachette Book Group, Inc.

The publisher is not responsible for websites (or their content) that are not owned by the publisher.

Library of Congress Cataloging-in-Publication Data
Names: Dickson, Shirley, author.
Title: Our last goodbye / Shirley Dickson.
Description: First U.S. edition. | New York : Grand Central Publishing,
    2020. | "Originally published in 2019 by Bookouture"—Title page verso.
Identifiers: LCCN 2020030158 | ISBN 9781538703731 (trade paperback)
Subjects: GSAFD: Historical fiction. | Love stories.
Classification: LCC PR6104.I29 O87 2020 | DDC 823/.92—dc23
LC record available at https://lccn.loc.gov/2020030158

ISBN: 978-1-5387-0373-1 (trade paperback)

Printed in the United States of America

LSC-C

Printing 1, 2020

For Wal and all the rest of my wonderful family.

CHAPTER ONE

North East town of South Shields

October 1943

As the cinema house lights went up and the strains of the National Anthem filled the hall, May Robinson and her mam rose from their seats and stood to attention. May began to sing but the cigarette smoke that fogged the air caught in her throat. She coughed before trying to carry on, "God save our gracious king... long live our noble king..."

Mam, standing at her side, turned to her daughter and her plump face split into a fond smile. She too sang along, "God save the king..."

When the music faded, folk began collecting their possessions—mackintoshes, umbrellas, handbags—and made for the aisles. May helped Mam on with her black woollen coat, which reeked of mothballs, and, checking they'd left nothing behind, they joined the throng heading to the Regal's front of house, where they waited with the rest for the doors to open. The lights went out and the foyer was plunged into darkness. May and her mam followed the queue for the exit.

"Eee, that film did me the power of good," Mam said in an enthralled undertone, "I've never laughed so much in an age. Mind you, not that I've had anythin' to laugh about lately... not with that lazy sod drivin' us to distraction. I swear your da's getting worse..." Mam continued, "Those two—Mickey Rooney and Judy Garland—with their dancing and singing, were just the tonic I needed."

Mam began to hum, "I Got Rhythm," as the pair of them inched forward, into the damp air wafting in from the open doorway.

Today was Mam's birthday. She didn't expect a fuss, and as far as Dad was concerned, neither did she get one. But May always tried to make her mother's birthdays special and today was no exception. She'd planned this trip to the flicks and had used her sweet coupons on two ounces of aniseed balls—Mam's favourite—from the sweetie shop. Sweets, like most household goods, were in short supply and at times simply unobtainable.

"And another thing... did you know you resemble yon lass in the film? You've got the same look about you."

May was startled and felt her cheeks flush in the dark. Folk all around were absorbed in their own conversations, but she would die if anyone overheard her mother. Fancy being compared to a famous star!

"Mam... that's ridic—"

"Have you looked in the mirror lately?" May heard the smile in Mam's voice. "With your bonny wavy hair, dark brown eyes and those Cupid's bow lips, you're the image of her." Mam sniffed indignantly. "And though I say so mesel'... with those high cheekbones, you're far prettier."

May sensed folk listening in, and looked around shyly, hoping no one was paying too much attention.

"I've got a ma just the same," an amused male voice piped up from behind. "She's never happier than when she's embarrassin' us."

Just then May was swept forward by the queue and the moment mercifully passed. Leaving the cinema, she stepped out into the dark and foggy night.

*

As she waited for Mam, beside her, who fumbled in her battered leather handbag, May heard the voices of the rest of the picture-goers as they receded into the distance.

"I know I brought it," she despaired. There was more rustling as she searched in the seemingly bottomless bag. "D'you know I've even found me compact that's been lost for months?" She let out a troubled sigh. "But no torch."

The night was foggy and claustrophobic. May felt disorientated and Mam's disembodied voice only helped to increase the illusion. She felt somehow unreal, like when she was a kid and needed to fling her arms around Mam to be comforted by the warmth of her ample body. The blackout had been introduced so that enemy planes wouldn't realise they flew over built-up areas. Householders hung heavy curtains over their windows; no welcoming light shone from street lamps, and torches, if used, were masked with tissue paper. Bus and car headlamps were also fitted with black discs with a narrow slit arranged to point downward.

"We'll manage without." May hoped her voice conveyed more conviction than she felt.

"I know we will, pet, but what use is a torch if I can never find the damn thing?" Mam's frustration was clear as she berated herself for leaving such a vital piece of equipment at home. "And what use is it painting white stripes on kerbs and lines in the middle of the road if folk can't damn well see a hand in front of them in this fog..."

That moment a crackle sounded in the air, before a blue spark from the overhead wire of a trolleybus flashed from the roadway.

"A trolleybus!" Mam cried. "Can you see its number? Hopefully it's goin' our way."

The smell of sulphur lingered in the atmosphere, like just before a thunderstorm, and May thought that it might be caused by the trolley's spark.

She squinted into the fog but couldn't see any light from the trolley's number box. "It's too far away."

"I'll put a hand out," Mam called. "Maybe the driver might see us and stop."

King Street, with shops closed and no one about, resembled a ghost town. And in the eerie silence, Mam's moderately high-heeled shoes clip-clopped as she edged towards the road. She never wore heels, May thought, with a pang. So excited had she been about tonight's treat, she'd worn her Sunday best rig-out for the occasion, though it was a shabbier Sunday attire than in days past; an aged, dark green felt hat, worn at the heel black lace-up shoes and a limp floral scarf.

The trolley whirred nearer and, sensing it looming in the dark fog, a feeling of foreboding gripped May.

"Where are you, Mam?" Like the blind, arms outstretched, she groped into the void ahead.

"I cannot see a thing, hinny," Mam said. "But I'm stayin' put till we catch a trolley... It's madness to walk home in these conditions."

Before they'd set out the weather had been fine but it had changed for the worse while they were inside the cinema.

A noise in the air she couldn't identify caught May's attention, then a cry of pain.

"Bugger me..." came Mam's perturbed voice. "I've fallen over the kerb... me ankle hurts like blazes."

Before May could move, a trolley, its diffused beam a hazy light, silently loomed large out of the wall of fog.

"My God... Help!"

There was a sickening muffled thud.

"Mam! Are you all right?"

As May catapulted forward, she knew, with heart-wrenching clarity, that this was the last birthday she and her mother would ever celebrate together.

CHAPTER TWO

November 1943

May was the last to receive a brown pay packet from the floral tray.

"There you go, pet," the lady from the wages section said. "The princely sum of forty-two shillings. Divvent spend it all at once, mind." Cackling, she handed the pay packet to May and hurried away.

The factory hooter blew then; the time was half-past five and it was the end of the ten-hour day shift. Switching off her machine, May collected her bait box, flask and knitting and filed with the rest of the machinists down to the basement cloakroom. She shrugged out of navy overalls and took off her peaked hat whose fishnet covered her glossy, chestnut-brown hair. She put on her coat and checked her handbag for her identity card. She knew her number off by heart.

Following the rest of the lasses to the exit, May punched her time card and made her way outside into the night's oppressive darkness to the bicycle shed where, by the light of a dim torch, she unlocked her bicycle chain. She manoeuvred the Raleigh past the low, camouflaged buildings and made her way down to the plant's main gate.

As she waited in the snaking queue, a voice beside her piped up, "Is that you, May? How you gettin' on, hinny?"

May recognised the voice of Bertha Cuthbertson, someone she used to work with. Bertha, who'd worked at the factory since the beginning of the war, was now supervisor on a different production line.

May, forever truthful, was stuck for what to say. Since Mam's accident, life had been one long day of sorrow after another.

She managed to mutter, "I miss Mam."

"Aw! Of course. How insensitive can a body be?" Bertha whispered, her tone exuding sympathy, "You'll still be floored after the tragedy."

"Yes. I am."

Bertha squeezed her arm.

May's thoughts turned to the one person she wanted to be here to comfort her. But Billy was away abroad fighting for his country.

"Next," the Local Defence Volunteer on the gate barked.

As she stood before the LDV's cabin, the dim light from his torch waved her past, and May relaxed. She constantly worried she might be searched and that somehow she might have made a ghastly mistake—a lapse of concentration, maybe—and some item from work would be found in her possession. She could only guess what the LDV bloke searched for—a precision instrument, cutlery pinched from the canteen or an important document someone could plant on her person to retrieve once she was safely outside the factory gates—and if found, May would forever more be labelled a thief, or worse still, an enemy spy.

"One of these days, lass, your imaginin's will get you into trouble," Mam's voice spoke in her head. May's chin trembled. She sorely missed Mam and couldn't bear to think back to the day of the accident, and what her mother might have suffered.

Once outside the sprawling factory grounds, May mounted her bike and made for home. These dark days before Christmas she craved natural light but, like a mole underground, she felt she lived her life in darkness.

May's work at the factory was making precision instruments for aeroplanes. The job was monotonous, and she worked in a dungeon-like machine room beneath mercury vapour lamps that shed misty greenish-white light that hurt her eyes.

"Speed is what's important," the foreman had informed May when she trained. "It takes fifteen people working flat out to keep a pilot flying."

May was proud to be one of those fifteen, but since Mam had died she had a hankering to do something more meaningful. Something that would make a real difference to people's lives.

As she pedalled in the half-light, May was reluctant to go home. This was the time of day when she had to face reality. Mam wouldn't be there with a pot of tea to greet her. Mam was gone—dead and buried—never to be seen again. The finality of it left May with a panicky, powerless feeling. She couldn't face another evening alone in the house reminiscing about Mam and of course... Billy. She constantly worried for his safety and knew that in her present forlorn state she'd rake up not the good times she'd spent with him but the upset and heartache. The trouble was, with no one else in the house, May had too much time to think.

May was worried about Dad because it was only weeks after Mam died and he was never home, his whereabouts a mystery. When Mam was alive, he'd sit in the bay window, jug of ale at his side, expecting to be waited on hand and foot.

"If you ask me," Mam confided on more than one occasion, "it's boxing in his younger days that addled your da's brain."

Dad was up and out first thing these days and usually late home at night, but to be truthful May preferred he was getting on with his life to the drunken state he was in when Mam was alive.

Her mind made up, May decided she'd visit her good friend Etty Milne to pass away the evening. She cycled towards the dark and dripping Tyne Dock arches. In the gloom, May's spirits took a nosedive as scenes from her mam's funeral played in her mind's eye.

She remembered the huddle of neighbours that stood at their front door in Templeton Street as May climbed into the black limousine by the kerbside; the whisperings she tried not to hear.

"Poor lass, did yi' hear her mam was run over by a corporation trolleybus?"

"I did. And what I heard was the bus had to be jacked up so's the workmen could reach the corpse…"

As she was driven to the cemetery, all May could think of was what state a body would be in after being run over by a trolleybus.

The cortège proceeded at a snail's pace through the cemetery gates and along the pathways and came to a halt at a newly dug grave surrounded by a mound of brown earth. As folk stood like black statues circling the graveside, May recognised the faces of neighbours and friends, seafaring gentlemen that had once boarded at the lodging house Mam ran, and ladies from the Women's Voluntary Service where Mam helped twice a week at the clothing depot.

Mr. Newman, the funeral director, presided over the burial. Dapper in a black suit and bowler hat, he was accompanied, surprisingly, by his wife Ramona Newman—Mam's sister. The two sisters didn't get along, but they were relatives, and Mam, after all, believed in family, so maybe it was right that Ramona should be there.

The thought of family brought May's brothers to mind. Serving abroad in the forces, they couldn't attend Mam's funeral. Thanks be to the Lord, May silently prayed, as, under the circumstances, with emotions running high, there'd no doubt be trouble. Both brothers detested Dad for the way he'd treated their Ma over countless years.

The vicar said prayers then gave, in a detached voice, a speech about Mam. As she listened May was appalled; the person he spoke about wasn't the Mam she knew but someone humourless and proper who would never use a word of bad language. May's nerves were in such tatters she almost giggled at the saintly person Mam had become.

Halfway through the ceremony, Dad's emaciated figure staggered up to the graveside. Dressed in a black wrinkled suit, shiny from wear at the elbows, he teetered to the grave's edge. May tensed, anxious that in his drunken state he might fall in.

"Serve the bugger right," Mam's voice said in May's head.

Dad bent and picked up a sod of earth, which he threw down onto Mam's wooden coffin. Then, turning on his heel, he departed.

The ceremony over, folk moved away, though some stopped to share condolences and May was touched at how well thought of Mam was.

When everyone was gone, the cemetery silent as the grave Mam would now spend eternity in, May looked out over greenery to the houses way beyond, where folk got on with their everyday lives. She realised life for her would never be the same, and tears spilled from her eyes.

Then a thought struck. Wiping away the tears on her cheeks with the back of a hand, she made purposefully for the cemetery gates.

She had Derek to take care of. A warm protective glow spread over May's chest.

Only eight, Derek was the baby of the family. After the last terrible raid earlier in the year when buildings were blown to smithereens and fires raged against the early morning sky, Mam had declared, "It's time Derek was safe and oot o' harm's way." So he was evacuated miles away in the country to a place called Allendale where he was billeted on a farm.

The day of his departure, May watched with Mam as the train carrying Derek, his tear-stained face pressed against a window, steamed out of South Shields station. As far as May was concerned, the bairn was too little to be sent to live with strangers—but what could she do? As a sister her opinion didn't count.

Derek hadn't been told about Mam's death yet as that responsibility lay with Dad. But the oversight preyed on May's mind. As she steered the bicycle through the damp arches and up the road towards Chichester roundabout, a car horn hooted, giving May such a fright, she nearly toppled from her bicycle. Blimey, she thought, making an apologetic face at the driver; she'd been so immersed in her thoughts she'd swerved right in front of him.

"Lass, yer not safe to be let loose on the road," she heard Mam's voice say.

Cycling up Dean Road's incline, May passed the shops—newsagent's, chemist's, butcher's—and rows of terraced houses, until she reached Whale Street. She turned left and stopped outside number twelve: Etty Milne's two-bedroom downstairs flat.

"Oh, hello, May..." said Etty, when she answered the door, "I didn't expect you tonight. Come in, but mind, ours is a madhouse tonight."

Seeing her friend, May's eyes welled. That's why she rarely went out these days; her emotions were so ragged she cried at the drop of a hat. At the overwhelming knowledge that larger-than-life Mam was gone forever and May now had no one, loneliness washed over her. She couldn't fathom how to go on because Mam had always been there to advise her.

"Eee, I won't come in, not if you're busy." May's tone was gruff. "I'll be in the way..."

Etty, as though she knew her friend's thoughts, smiled sympathetically. "Don't be daft. I could do with some grown-up company."

"Only, if you're sure."

Etty was a true friend; even though she had her hands full with a home and two bairns she was always there for May in time of need. There were times Etty went quiet and seemed withdrawn, as though uncomfortable in May's presence, but May decided to let it be. For Etty could do no wrong and she'd always be May's best mate. As Etty led the way along the dim passageway, May heard a baby's relentless shrill cry coming from the back bedroom.

She decided she wouldn't outstay her welcome, knowing that Etty had troubles of her own to contend with. In the kitchen-come-living room stood a toddler staring in wide-eyed fascination through the bars of a wooden playpen, handmade toys all around her.

"Don't let Norma's goody-two-shoes look fool you." Etty made a grim face at the toddler. "She's been a little devil today."

"How come?" May eyed the fresh-faced, blue-eyed child who appeared the picture of innocence.

"Temper tantrums." Etty held out a hand for May's coat. "Little minx is spoiled rotten by her upstairs." She raised her eyes heavenward to the flat above where her mother-in-law lived. "And seeing how I've got the two bairns to look after . . . I've neither the time nor the energy to do much about it."

Etty's beloved sister, Dorothy, had been killed in a raid earlier in the year, when the area was bombed with great loss of life. Etty's niece, Victoria, was only two weeks old at the time. Victoria's dad had been lost at sea when his ship was torpedoed and so she was orphaned. Etty and her husband had taken the bairn into their home.

"What's wrong with Victoria?"

"Teething. She's got a tooth poking through her lower gum." Etty puffed her cheeks out in exasperation. "You'd think she'd sleep. She's had me up all night."

Etty's face was bloated with tiredness, with dark swathes beneath her hazel eyes.

"I'll rock her if you like," May volunteered.

"You're very good with bairns and that's most kind, but no . . . I don't want her to get used to being picked up." Etty grimaced ruefully at Norma in the playpen. "That's what happened to this one."

Knowing she was being spoken about, the toddler threw back her head and giggled, showing off pink gums and a row of tiny white teeth.

Etty shook her head and grinned. "Come on . . . I'll make us a cuppa. Mind you, I wish it was sherry, there's a drop left in the bottle that I'm saving for Christmas. I'm sorely in need of it"—she pulled a mock face of regret—"but now is not the time when I've got the bairns to take care of."

Etty took the whistling kettle from the hob and traipsed down the two steps to the minuscule scullery. While she waited, May remembered when Derek was a baby. If he had a disturbed night, it was May who woke and rocked him in her arms while Derek stared up at her with those enormous blue knowing eyes. She was never happier than when taking care of him and making sure he was content. May recoiled from the memory. What was she doing? Like a door slamming, she closed her mind on the past. Those times when Derek was little and vulnerable were too painful to contemplate.

"How many times have I told yi' . . ." Mam's voice rebuked her, "it's unhealthy to dwell on the past."

Thing was, May thought as she sank heavily and helplessly into the couch, the voice in her head always spoke the truth.

She looked up and was surprised to see Etty standing before her, as she hadn't heard her friend return. Etty held a china cup of tea in each hand, her face etched with concern.

"Remember when Dorothy died and you never left my side?" Etty said. "You told me I could shout and scream if I wanted to, that it was what you'd do if it were your loss?"

May was taken aback, because Etty never mentioned her sister, or the time Dorothy was killed in the street by a bomb. She nodded.

"Well...since your Mam died you've done no such thing. You refuse to speak a word about her. Believe me, bottling up your feelings will do you no good and you'll make yourself ill."

"You should talk," May replied, with an honesty she could never help.

"How d'you mean?"

"Since when do you talk about Dorothy?"

Etty appeared indignant and parted her lips as if to speak. Then at a loss to know what to say, she closed them again.

"It's hard, isn't it?" May took the tea her friend offered. "I go wobbly inside if anyone mentions Mam's name. I worry I'll start bawling me eyes out and never stop."

"It's still raw with me. Even thinking of Dorothy is too painful."

"It's like you're broken inside, isn't it? And no matter how you hard you try you can't fix it."

Etty nodded. She sat down on the couch and, side by side, they sipped their tea.

May counted in her head. "It's only five months since Dorothy died...but it feels like forever since I've seen her."

Etty's chin quivered. "That's the worst. If only she could visit for a minute." She paused. "I used to hear her voice in my head."

"Eee, I'm the same with Mam. And I'm sure she's watching over us."

"How d'you mean?"

"Little things...like me bait tin keeps falling from the table for no reason. Mam was always nagging us to wash it straight away after work so I'd have more time of a morning. Then the fireguard...it topples over when I'm nowhere near it. I get this strong feeling Mam's in the room, reminding us to put the guard in front of the fire before I go to bed."

Etty's eyes held a faraway gaze. She smiled, sadly. "It's good talking about it. Mind you, anyone else would think we're barmy."

They sat in silence together and it occurred to May that the baby in the next room had settled and stopped crying.

Etty, her expression thoughtful, continued, "I mean, it could be just the imaginings of a fraught and overworked mind, but I'd like to think it's evidence of something more.... it gives me hope for our loved ones."

By, Etty was clever. That was exactly how May felt but she didn't have the skill to express her thoughts into words.

Etty smiled fondly at May. "You're such a good friend, May. You've got such a caring nature."

May was saved embarrassment when Norma started to whinge; Etty rose and picked up her daughter from the playpen, carrying her on her hip over to the couch where she sat with the bairn on her knee. Staring into space, she cuddled the toddler against her chest, curling blonde strands of her hair around a forefinger.

A thought appeared to strike her and she turned to May. "I've been meaning to ask... what about Derek? Has he been told yet?"

Anxiety rose in May's chest and she could barely breathe. They'd been over this before. Etty was critical because Derek hadn't attended Mam's funeral. But Etty wasn't aware of the complications. Of course, May yearned to see Derek but decisions had to be made first about the future. Since Mam's death she'd been so immersed in grief and misery that nothing else registered, and May was incapable of making plans.

"It might help the poor lad take his mam's death in," Etty had told her. "You don't want him criticizing your decision not to let him come to the funeral when he's older."

May knew Dad wouldn't get involved as Derek's welfare had never been any concern of his—and this lack of care had broken Mam's heart and caused many a row between the couple.

"I won't have you drivin' Derek away like you did your other sons," Mam would tell him.

The thought of Derek turning against May was too much to bear. Etty was right; Derek needed to know about Mam—and now.

She asked Etty, "What if I write to the couple he's billeted with and ask them to explain the situation?"

Derek lived with an older couple, a Mr. and Mrs. Talbot, whose two adult girls weren't interested in the farm and had flown the nest.

"Sounds like you're shying away from your responsibilities, if you ask me."

"I wouldn't...honest...not for the world. I only want what's best for Derek."

Etty, tight-lipped, didn't answer. She smoothed Norma's cotton smock over her chubby knees.

As May thought of the little lad, the heady little-boy smell of him, the desire to see him forced her to decide. May had sent Derek occasional letters ever since he was evacuated. And on his birthday, she'd included a ten-shilling note that she'd saved in the sixpenny-and-shilling jar. Derek always replied, short perfunctory replies as though it was something he'd been made to do—May smiled—which was probably the case.

"I'm going to ask for time off and go and see Derek and tell him about Mam meself."

"You're doing the right thing," Etty told May. "And if you ask me, the factory owes you leave."

*

Only two days after her mam's accident May had turned up for work, and Etty thought the supervisor callous for not sending her home.

"I don't want to be in the house on me own," May had confessed at the time.

Now, Etty agreed her friend was probably right. With her dad never in the house, May was best off in the company of the other machinists.

"If you do ask for time off, don't take no for an answer," Etty said. "With this war on, workers are just machines. Even the ample food they serve up in the canteen isn't out of the kindness of managers' hearts but to feed you so production goes up."

A look of shock passed over May's face and Etty felt ashamed of her cynical attitude. May had such a kind soul but how far would her forgiving heart extend if she knew the true extent of Etty's betrayal?

Flustered, she replied, "Sorry, May…I'm just a bit down. With Christmas around the corner and—"

"It's fine, I understand…I feel the same way after losing Mam."

Etty made up her mind she'd make sure her friend had, if not the best Christmas, an uplifting one. But how could she achieve such a thing? She decided May must never be alone over the holiday period and she must be kept busy so she couldn't dwell on her troubles—such an easy task with two kiddies around.

"You're welcome to spend Christmas with us."

May visibly cheered. "Ooo, thank you."

The arrangement suited Etty too. Trevor, her husband, would no doubt have little time off from his job at Westoe pit. What with him helping out at Newman's funerals and volunteering as a firefighter, she probably wouldn't see much of him.

Which was a shame considering how much he would have enjoyed spending time with his daughter over the festive season. *His daughter*. Even now she couldn't help but flinch at those words. Of course Trevor knew the truth of the matter because theirs was a marriage that worked on trust, but that didn't mean that Etty could let go of the past.

Recovering from her thoughts, she told May, "I'll be glad of adult company at Christmas."

Etty vowed to make this Christmas special, but how? The shortages were harder than ever: fewer cards, less paper to make decorative chains for the ceiling, scarcely any toys, more rationing and less food. Etty gave herself a mental shake; it was time to buck up and stop complaining. But sometimes, despite this year's tremendous military advances, victory and peace still seemed far away.

Deep in thought, Etty was surprised by May's next words. "Etty, I've been thinking...I've decided I want to train to become a nurse."

Etty looked at her friend, and, seeing her resolute expression, she knew the lass was deadly serious.

"What brought this on?"

May gulped air as if she'd just surfaced from drowning. "Mam died because of me."

"Pardon me?"

"I've only got me first aid certificate...but if I'd had further training, I could've saved Mam...I was there at the time and I froze 'cos I didn't know what to do. I didn't even feel her pulse and if only—"

"Whoa, May."

May's eyes, as they regarded Etty, were wild. "I heard her trip over the kerb. She fell into the path of the trolley and—"

"*She was fatally injured on impact,*" Etty quoted the coroner. "May, the end was quick. It was an accident, there was nothing you could do."

May crumpled, her eyes brimming with tears. "What if—"

"What ifs won't bring her back."

Head in hands, May sat as if unravelling some complicated mathematical problem. Then she looked up, and pulled back her shoulders, composing herself. "If I could be a nurse and help only one person to survive, then it would cancel out Mam dying, don't you see?"

Etty didn't, because May's child-like logic was beyond her. But if there was one thing she knew, it was that when May set her heart on something she always saw it through.

Etty smiled fondly at her friend. "I think wanting to become a nurse is admirable," she volunteered. "And in my opinion, with your compassionate nature, you'll make a good one."

"But will they have me?" May wailed. "I'm a dunce! Me schooling was practically non-existent."

"May, you can only try. Why don't you apply to the hospital?"

May chewed her lip. "Being a nurse would make Mam proud." She spoke as though Mam was still physically here. "She never wanted me to be a skivvy like her, and after this war is done I'm not going back to being a parlour maid." She turned a troubled gaze on Etty. "D'you know how I should apply?"

Etty's lips twitched. "I'd write a letter to the hospital, if I was you, and apply to be a probationer nurse."

May wasn't stupid, Etty knew, only uneducated.

Her expression resolute, May stood and collected her things. "I'll write to the hospital tonight and post me application in the morning, along with a letter to Derek's billet."

She left the room and made her way along the narrow passageway. Etty rose, and taking Norma's small hand in hers, followed behind.

At the door, May turned. "Thanks for the help, Etty. You're the best friend a girl could have."

A rush of guilt-ridden adrenalin surged through Etty. She couldn't meet May's gaze. She picked up the bairn and sat her on her hip. Faces level, Etty stared into her daughter's amazing blue eyes, and a stab of shame poked her.

If only she'd told May the truth long ago it would be over and done with now.

CHAPTER THREE

The next morning, as May bumped her bicycle down the front steps and steered it across the road, she felt in a positive mood. The talk yesterday with Etty had done her the power of good. Not only did May have a plan of action in respect of Derek and her own career, but she was also invited to spend Christmas at Etty's. The future looked bright indeed.

If only Mam were there to share it. In May's mind—apart from the fact that May felt guilty at not being able to save her mother—Adolf Hitler caused her death. If he hadn't started the war there'd be no need for blackouts and buses would have headlamps. May hated Hitler—for the devastation he'd wrought on her and thousands like her. Hate was a strong word, and one she'd previously never used because of her Christian upbringing, but there was no denying it was because of Hitler that Mam had died. A mild person generally, May was shocked at the strength of her rage. Etty had said there were different aspects of grief and she'd mentioned that undue anger was one of them, especially against the loved one who'd passed on. But May could never be mad with Mam over anything. And so she was glad Hitler was the one who she could vent her anger on.

It was still getting light and, although pushed for time, May was determined to post the two letters before she went to work— one to Derek's evacuation family and the other to the hospital to apply to be a nurse.

Dad hadn't come home till late last night and when he had, May was already in bed and had refrained from going downstairs because she didn't know what kind of mood he'd be in. Once upon a time, when May could do no wrong, Dad used to call her his "little treasure, sent from heaven"—but that was before her transgression... May brought the shutters of her mind down. Mam was right; it was best she lived in the present and left the past behind where it belonged.

May balanced the bicycle by its pedal against the kerb and, removing the two envelopes from her shoulder bag, posted them in the red pillar box. She'd written to inform the Talbots that she'd visit the Saturday after next as she had something important to tell Derek. She briefly explained about Mam's accident, so that they were prepared, but asked them not to say anything to Derek.

At the thought of seeing Derek again, May experienced a fleeting glimpse of happiness.

By Saturday her shift pattern would change and May would be working a night shift so there'd be no need to ask for time off. May was relieved because it would only cause a rumpus and confrontation didn't sit well with her. Visiting the farm at Allendale meant she wouldn't get any sleep but she'd gone without, plenty of times when a raid took place during the night.

Cycling along the black cobbled road, her mind drifted to the rumours that Hitler had secret weapons. Most folk didn't believe there was a serious threat and laughed the matter off and May prayed they were right. Involuntarily, she shuddered. When would this war with all its terror ever end?

She now conceded Mam was right. Derek was safe on the farm far away out in the country. For a moment, she wondered what country life was like as she'd only ever been away as far as Newcastle.

"Man, watch where you're goin'!" a male voice blasted.

May, deep in thought, had steered her bicycle perilously close to the middle of the road, narrowly missing a cyclist travelling the other way.

The cyclist's brakes screeched to a halt. "Stupid lass. What a fright yi' gave us."

May, shaky with shock, pulled over to the kerb and dismounted her bike. "I'm sorry . . . I wasn't—"

"I should think yi' are. If a motor car had been coming we'd both be goners."

"Don't say that!" Memories of Mam's accident, like a bad dream, flashed through her mind and May went cold.

The lad got off his bike and pushed it over alongside hers. May saw in the light of the awakening sky that he had a stocky build, with a wide sensuous mouth and a rather attractive rugged look. From his brown overalls, flat cap, and muffler, she thought he must work at the shipyards—or why else would he be here instead of in the army?

"You shouldn't be let loose on the—" His sparkling green eyes widened in surprise as he looked at her properly. He took in her face and then her body. "Man, where've you been hiding? I travel this road every day and I've not see yi' before." He grinned and two creases carved in his cheek.

May didn't know whether to be flattered or miffed. She decided on the former because there was something about the lad that reminded her of Billy, her former fiancé. As the lad continued to stare, with those gorgeous eyes, she decided it was his smouldering expression that reminded her of Billy. May brought herself up sharply. That same heart-stopping gaze had cost her countless troubles and heartache in the past. To be honest (which May always was) she was still suffering. Billy took up lots of her thinking time, even now. May couldn't help being attracted to this lookalike lad and, intrigued, she found herself wondering just how far the likeness went. For all his charm there was something about him, a watchfulness that gleamed in the back of his eyes, that May couldn't fathom.

"I work at..." She was going to say "the factory," but then thought of the poster on the canteen walls: "*Careless Talk Costs Lives*." May pressed her lips firmly together.

The lad rolled his eyes and laughed and, as he took off his cap, she saw a wide furrowed brow and fair hair cut in a short-back-and-sides style.

"Hawway, man, it's no big secret... I know where you work, I can see the factory gates from here." His expression changed to resolute. "I intend to pass this way at this time of day more often."

May's dander up, she forgot her earlier discomfiture at nearly knocking him over. Ignoring his latter statement, she remarked primly, "You never know who you're talking to."

"Then let me introduce myself. Alec Hudson." He held out his free hand as she met his mesmeric gaze that was the image of her former fiancé's. A picture of Billy Buckley played in her mind's eye and she couldn't resist comparing the two. There was no denying Alec was good-looking but not strikingly so, like Billy. As she thought of Billy, his magnetic blue eyes and roguish smile, May's stomach somersaulted. But she must stop this, comparing every lad she met to him. She peered at Alec from beneath long eyelashes—and decided that he was attractive in his own right.

She relented. "Pleased to meet you, Alec." She checked her watch. "I'm sorry about before... but really, I have to go or I'll be late for work."

"Aw! We're just getting to know each other."

May hesitated before mounting her bike. "Some other time."

"What's your name?" he asked as she cycled away.

She called over her shoulder, "May Robinson."

*

May sat at her bench in the stifling hot machine room, where the noise was deafening. A headache threatened from the ache in the nape of her neck. She looked around the benches, where the other machinists were intent on their work. May envied them their apparent peace of mind. The supervisor, combing the room, raised a questioning eyebrow and May put her head down hastily, getting back to the job of operating a drill press that drilled holes in aluminium disks—but still her mind jabbered on.

May used to get on well with the lasses but since Mam's death the other machinists were . . . May searched for the right word . . . edgy . . . around her, as if they didn't know what to say or how to handle the situation. May had taken to having dinner at her bench alone in the machine room where she didn't trouble anyone. To be fair, this arrangement suited her well because she wasn't ready for either small talk or frivolous chat—especially when the subject broached sexual matters which the other lasses delighted in wondering about. May avoided these conversations as she'd die of embarrassment if she let slip about her past.

As the hooter blew, May looked up from her machine and was surprised at how quickly time had flown. When the machines were switched off the silence was deafening.

She reached for her shoulder bag and brought out her bait tin. A vison of Derek popped into her mind's eye and the thought of visiting him put a smile on her face.

One of the machinists passing her bench noticed and stopped. "May . . . why don't you join us in the canteen for dinner today?"

May smiled gratefully. "Yes, I think I might."

Things are looking up, the voice in her head said.

May wanted to believe it was true.

A letter arrived from the hospital at the end of that week.

Dear Miss Robinson

Arrangements have been made for you to attend an entrance test for the post of probationer nurse. Please report to Matron's office on Monday 15th of November, at 10:30 a.m.

If you should be successful the next intake of probationary nurses is scheduled to start training on Monday 5th December.

May's hands shook as she read the letter. The moment felt surreal. There was joy too—she was amazed at having achieved the unthinkable. She didn't tell anyone, not even Etty, because how could she, May Robinson, presume to work in such an esteemed profession? She needn't worry, she told herself, as she'd never passed an exam in her life—except, of course, the Red Cross first aid certificate.

The next Monday morning, exhausted after a gruelling night shift, May arrived at the hospital entrance where the wrought-iron gates were missing—no doubt carted off when scrap metal was requisitioned to construct munitions. May, nervous for what lay ahead and how much depended on her performance, walked quickly up the drive to the main entrance and was told by a passing porter where to locate Matron's office.

Matron turned out to be a sharp-eyed woman who cut a commanding figure in her navy dress with its waistband cinched around her ample waist, her starched collar and frilled cap with tapes that fastened beneath a double chin. May doubted the woman missed anything. She told May with the voice of authority what the profession expected of nurses.

"In these days of war," Matron concluded, "it is imperative that all our probationers keep up standards of nursing etiquette."

May had no idea what she meant but gave a polite nod to show she concurred.

A porter was summoned and led May to a large classroom which had the acute smell of furniture polish and disinfectant. Four other girls stared at her as she sat at one of the desks.

"Good morning, ladies," a nurse greeted them. She seemed quite old to May, with a plump face, delightfully pink and devoid of wrinkles, and a cap covered with frills perched on silvery grey hair.

"I'm Sister Chilvers…House Sister at Preliminary Training School." She smiled an indulgent smile. "Now we are all present, we can begin."

She moved around the room handing out sheets of paper, then came to stand, fingers entwined at her waist, in front of the desks.

"Ladies, you have an hour and a half to complete the questions. Please turn your paper over."

The moment of truth. May wanted to succeed so much, it caused an ache in her belly. She viewed the first sheet, a mathematical paper filled with mental arithmetic questions— May's nightmare, as she was hopeless with anything to do with numbers. But to her joy, she understood the questions and found the arithmetic basic. Next was an English paper that May found easy enough because, as an avid reader, she was good at grammar.

The next paper asked her to write an essay about Florence Nightingale—who she was and what she did. May was overjoyed as she'd just finished a book about the famous nurse and founder of modern nursing. Picking up her pen and dipping it into the inkwell, she began writing down all the historical facts she could remember, especially about the Crimean war where Florence Nightingale put her method of nursing into practice and saved countless lives.

Before she knew it, Sister Chilvers was calling out, "Time, ladies. Put your pens down, please."

When Sister walked around the room collecting their papers, May was surprised to discover she'd filled all the blank sheets she'd been given.

As she walked back down the drive, drained but relieved, May didn't dare hope she'd done enough to qualify to one day become a State Registered Nurse. But she couldn't help the thrill of delight that ran through her when she thought of it.

She took a trolleybus home and went straight to bed where she slept soundly till it was time to get up and ready herself for the night shift. In her dreams, the machine room was aglow with the light of the lamp Nurse Robinson carried.

Next morning, as she cycled home from work, a dim glow from the masked light on her bike shedding light on the road, May passed the place where she'd met Alec Hudson and gave him a passing thought. He certainly had eye-catching features, and undoubtedly turned heads wherever he went, and she suspected he knew it, because she'd met his type before. She remembered his restrained watchful expression, as though he was trying to curb his true feelings. She shrugged—what did it matter? She wasn't gone on Alec and never could be because her heart belonged to Billy Buckley. A rush of undying love surged through May. She didn't condemn Billy for leaving her—for hers was a love that didn't ask questions and could forgive Billy anything—but May's silent prayer was that when he returned from overseas he might be ready to start over again.

She cycled through the first arch built to carry the coal trains from local pits to Tyne Dock Staithes. It was here coal poured into ships to be distributed around the country and to places abroad May had never even heard of. Beneath the second arch, May gave out a loud "Ooo" as she had when she was a child and Mam had encouraged her. As the sound echoed hollowly around the black and dripping walls, tears gathered in May's eyes as she imagined Mam's belly laugh. She sniffed. How she missed her mother. Turning the corner into Templeton Street, she pulled on the bike's brakes outside her front door.

The tall red brick terraced house had views over the ribbon of River Tyne, where cranes soared high and shipyards teemed with workers building and mending ships that voyaged the enemy-infested seas. It was eerily silent when May walked in. Parking her bike against the hallway wall, she moved past the coloured glass lobby door. As she entered the passageway, May knew someone was in by the light creeping from beneath the front room door. She knew Dad must be home because she could smell his nose-wrinkling tobacco.

In the front room Dad was sitting in the bay window, surprisingly wearing his rumpled Sunday best suit, a white handkerchief peeking from the jacket pocket and his worn shoes polished till they shone. Dad, dressing so smartly these days, amazed May and she was sad he didn't do the same when Mam was alive.

May wished, though, that the change in him would extend to Dad's sharp tongue. A roll-up hanging from his mouth, he wheezed, "I'm only here to collect the rent." Pulling a resolute face, he continued, "And if that old bloke upstairs won't pay his dues, he's out on his neck."

Mr. Herdsman, a retired seafaring gentleman who'd boarded with Mam for the last ten years, had fallen on hard times. Mam had overlooked the matter of him sometimes not paying the rent as the old gentleman worked as a handyman and did jobs around the house. The idea of Mr. Herdsman—their only lodger now—leaving, dismayed May and she wondered what would become of the only home she'd ever known if they had no boarders left. Mam had managed the boarding house alone, and left Dad to his own devices in the bay window. With no money except May's wage coming in she pondered how they'd feed the gas meter or pay—

"Have yi' thought about the future?" Dad's nasal voice interrupted May's train of thought.

"We could share the—"

"Hang on, who said anythin' about 'we'?"

"I thought we—"

"Well, you thought wrong. I've got plans."

"Plans?"

"Me and Gertie are—"

"Gertie?"

Dad looked uncommonly abashed. "The woman I'm seeing."

"I don't know how you could even look at another woman," May blurted her honest opinion. "When Mam's only been gone—"

"It's got nowt to do wi' you. But if you must know, I get lonely." Dad's gaunt face assumed a "poor me"—as Mam called it—expression. "Gertie says I need lookin' after with me war injuries an' all."

"Mam was forever looking after you."

Dad gave her a sour look. "Anyways, Gertie thinks I should rent this place out and move in with her and the bairns. A nice flat she's got in Alverthorpe Street."

May's heart beat faster. She didn't know which bit of information to tackle first. Where had Dad met this woman? And when? Heartbroken for Mam's sake, May was unsure if she wanted to hear the answers. Perhaps Dad, still grieving, was in shock and this was his way of coping. May would give him the benefit of the doubt.

Her main concern was Derek—where did he fit in all of this?

"Where's… Gertie's husband?"

"Bomb got him, poor bugger, in the last raid, when he was home on leave. He was running up the lane and…" Dad shrugged.

"Poor woman."

"Look here." Dad pinned her with a brutal stare. "Gertie's flat only has two bedrooms, one for her and the two girls share the other one."

May felt the colour drain from her cheeks. Dad would never make plans that didn't include Derek. Would he?

"What about Derek?"

Dad didn't answer and, lighting the roll-up with a match, he took a puff.

His eyes shied away from May's. "You'll have to make arrangements for him when it's safe for him to . . . you know . . . when the war's over."

May's heart pounded so fast she felt light-headed. "But . . . this is Derek's home. He won't understand. He thinks you're his—"

"I'm nowt to do wi' him." Glowering at her, he took another drag on his cigarette. "It was your mother's idea to bring Derek up as her own, I've done me best and given him a home . . . It's time you looked after him. He's *your* bastard son."

May felt her blood turn cold.

"Dad, you can't let him down. The truth will shatter him."

Dad's eyes turned to hard little stones. "The time's come for you to take responsibility for the slut you became."

May stared aghast at Dad. His eyes dismissing her, he stared blankly through the bay window. A sob escaped May and, hurrying from the room, her feet pounded up the stairs as she ran into her bedroom and flung herself on the slim bed.

CHAPTER FOUR

The next morning the wail from the air raid siren pierced the air. Etty, hurrying down the flight of stairs from her mother-in-law's upstairs flat, stopped in her tracks. As the wail increased, her guts wrenched and scenes from the past played in her mind. Acrid smells filled her nostrils, as visions of houses toppling down, craters in the road and flames leaping high in the sky flashed before her. Then, the still body of her sister as she lay on the pavement beneath a blanket.

"Etty," the voice of Nellie Milne called down the dim staircase, "is it a proper raid or a test?"

Etty slowly recovered. It had been like this since the enemy air attack in May when Dorothy was killed. As soon as she heard any high-pitched noise, her mind conjured images of her sister's death.

The "alert siren" filled the air before being replaced by the "raiders passed" signal.

Of course, she thought, it was just a test. Notice had been given in Saturday night's *Gazette*.

It had read:

> The "all clear" signal will be sounded for one minute, at 10 o'clock on Wednesday morning, then the "alert siren" for one minute, then finally the "raiders passed" again for one minute.

As the noise stopped, Etty's breathing became normal again.

"Thank Gawd for that," Nellie called from the top of the stairs. "Me nerves cannot take it."

During the last air raid, Nellie's staircase had collapsed underneath her. The staircase had been rebuilt and Nellie had fully recovered from her injuries. The two women, who'd never got along before the incident—chiefly because Etty had to deal with the consequence of Nellie spoiling Norma rotten—had now called a kind of truce. In Etty's case this was born out of necessity as her hands were full taking care of two small children and any help was welcome, even if it did come from her interfering mother-in-law.

"Go on…get on with your nappy washing," Nellie called down. "Don't worry about Norma…she'll have the time of her life wi' me. And if that other one wakens I'll call yi' to take her away for a bottle."

At first, Nellie had been adamant she wouldn't have Victoria upstairs. She told Etty, "Victoria's nowt to do wi' me. It's sad your sister got killed but her bairn is your lookout."

Etty, equally adamant Nellie either look after both kiddies or none at all, remained tight-lipped. Her mother-in-law, seeing how serious she was, was the one to give in.

Etty spoke to the black silhouette standing at the top of the stairs. "I'll only be an hour or so. Don't give the bairn any dinner."

As the door at the top of the stairs slammed shut, Etty knew Nellie's answer.

Downstairs, in the tiny scullery, Etty shrugged into an aged woollen coat and fashioned a turban-style headscarf on her head before going into the damp and perishing cold backyard, where she filled the tub with pails of hot water taken from the boiler in the wash-house. Then, back in the scullery, she pulled a pail from behind a curtain under the sink and sloshed the bucketful of rank-smelling nappies into an enamel bowl, wrinkling her nose. She'd read in one of the newspapers that working American women were using a "diaper service" that delivered fresh nappies when needed. Good for them, she thought, and hoped the idea would catch on here.

Running cold water from the tap over the nappies, she watched the foul-smelling brown water disappear down the plughole. Back in the yard, she poured Oxydol soap powder into the tub and was just about to tip the bucketful of nappies into the hot water when the backyard door opened.

May stood there, her hand on the sneck, her face ashen.

"What's up?" Etty dumped the bucket on the ground and hurried down the yard. "Why aren't you in bed? I thought this week was night shifts."

May gulped, "It is but... I couldn't sleep. I had to come and see you. I knocked at the front door but got no answer." She swallowed hard as if trying to keep tears at bay. "So I came around the back..." she ended, her voice breaking.

"Come in, sit down. I'll make us a cup of tea."

Nappies forgotten, Etty led the way into the kitchen, where a coal fire blazed yellow flames that licked up the chimney.

May stood uneasily at the scullery door. "You've got enough on your hands."

"For goodness' sake, May, just tell me what's wrong."

May moved into the room and stood in front of the fire. "I don't know what to do." Her pink and watery eyes implored Etty. "Dad's disowned Derek."

Etty was flummoxed. "How d'you mean, disowned?"

May looked for a moment like a scared rabbit that wanted to bolt, then she shuddered and the whole story poured out, about how her dad had a girlfriend and was moving in with her.

My God, Etty thought, his wife was barely cold and the man had replaced her with another woman.

"Dad says this Gertie's flat has only two bedrooms so there'll be no room for Derek." Panic evident on May's face, her eyes pleaded with Etty as if she held the magic answer.

At times like this, Etty felt her friend was like an overgrown innocent child and her heart ached for May.

"Can't they all live in your house?"

"Dad says he's putting it up for rent. Besides, he wants a break from the past."

Don't we all, Etty surprised herself by thinking.

"But he can't just...ditch his son." He could, Etty knew, because she was aware of the truth—that Mr. Robinson wasn't Derek's father—and she knew who was.

"Etty, I've something to tell you. Prepare yourself for a shock." May braced herself, as though she were about to throw herself to the lions.

"Derek belongs to me...he's my son." She waited for a reaction and when none was forthcoming, she continued, "I won't go into details. The thing is, Mam volunteered to bring him up as her own. She said it was best as my life would be ruined." May sniffed hard. "Now, I'm not so sure. It was purgatory watching him grow and him preferring Mam to hug him rather than me..." Tears slid down her cheeks. "Mam never complained about the work but Dad...he...never wanted—"

"May, please stop. I have a confession to make." It was Etty's turn to brace herself. "I knew about Derek being your son."

Her mouth went slack and May looked stunned. "You did. But how?"

"Dorothy told me."

Guilt stabbed Etty at betraying her sister but she didn't want to hide anything from May any more. *You still have the big one,* the voice of conscience spoke in her mind. Etty could never reveal the truth; not only would it kill May but their friendship would be over. The bond between them was more than friendship, she knew—it would be as traumatic as losing another sister.

Blanking her mind, she went on. "Don't think badly of Dorothy...we only had each other and always shared confidences and swore never to tell."

Brought up in an orphanage, the two sisters had relied on each other. It was a case of them against the world.

"Eee! I would never…Dorothy was a true friend. There wasn't a grain of malice in her and she'd do anything to help anybody. I'll always miss her."

May's tribute to her sister touched Etty. It was her turn to find it difficult to speak.

"So, I don't have to tell you the whole story?" May's pinched face displayed relief. "And d'you know who Derek's dad is?"

Etty nodded. She couldn't bring herself to say his name. "So, what are you going to do about Derek? And where are you going to live if your dad lets the house out?" she asked.

*

May's mind went blank like it always did when a problem needed solving. It was Mam that usually helped find a way out. At the thought of her parent, the sorrow and heartache returned.

"I honestly don't know," she told Etty. "I don't want Derek to suffer. All I want is for him to be happy."

May sat at the table while her friend made tea in the scullery. When Etty returned she handed May a cup.

"It's Horlicks. A cure-all in my book when times get hard." She sat beside May.

"You don't need to do anything yet." Her tone was practical. "Derek's in safe hands at the farm. What you do have to think on is what you'll do when it's safe for him to come home. How you'll manage."

Etty was right, of course. And it came as a relief to May to realise that she didn't have to make a decision now. The little lad would be devastated when he heard about Mam and that he didn't have a home. Best to leave him where he was until May figured out a plan. The thought was daunting but Derek's happiness was paramount, she reminded herself.

"Have you considered telling Derek the truth?"

As Etty's words sank in, panic rose in May and she had an urge to flee the house and go to the seashore to breathe some fresh sea air. Too much was happening all at once and making this kind of decision was too much.

"It's only a suggestion, May. You don't have to do anything that doesn't feel right."

Etty's voice, like a salve on a wound, calmed May and she was able to think sensibly again.

"I . . . I could never. He loved Mam. I'm frightened the truth might . . . damage him or he might end up hating me."

Etty didn't pursue the matter.

A long silence followed, with both of them lost in thought.

Then May spoke, as her nerves couldn't stand long silences. "I took your advice. I sent a letter to the Talbots to say I'm visiting on Saturday. I told them about Mam and explained I'd prefer to tell Derek myself."

"Oh, I am glad . . . it'll do you both good to see each other."

At the thought of seeing her son (May only dared to say those words—"her son"—in her head) a warm apple-pie glow spread through May's stomach and for the first time since Mam's accident she allowed herself to feel a smidgeon of happiness.

"Come on, give me a hand." Etty made for the scullery door. "Those nappies won't wash themselves." She pulled a knowing face. "If I know you, even though you're bone-tired after the night shift, you won't get a wink of sleep for worrying."

Etty knew her so well.

In the yard, May took her frustration out on the nappies as she pounded them with a poss stick. Meanwhile, Etty fed the dripping cloth through the mangle's wooden rollers.

"D'you believe what's being said about the war?" May paused to rest her aching arms. "That the tide's turned . . ."

Etty shrugged, noncommittally. "I only know what Mr. Churchill said in his speech after the victory at El Alamein: '*This is not the end. It is not even the beginning of the end. But it is, perhaps, the end of the beginning.*'"

May thought this far too clever for her to unravel.

"The papers say that this year is a turning point," May said, "and that the enemy's strength has been crushed."

Etty brushed a strand of hair from her forehead. "Trevor and I were discussing the bombing of German cities last night by—"

"Don't!" May cried. "I can't bear the thought of civilians being bombed, no matter what their nationality." She shook her head in a bemused fashion. "Who would've thought both sides would be guilty of bombing innocent people?"

Etty looked surprised. "The Germans started it," she replied, then laughed, shamefaced. "Hark at me. I sound like a bully girl in the schoolyard. *She started it.*"

She fed another nappy into the mangle and, turning the handle, watched it disappear through the rollers, niftily catching the cloth as it came out the other side.

"I can't imagine peace, can you?" She heaved a long sigh. "I'm weary of long queues and shortages...worrying if I've got enough coupons." Her expression changed to one of optimism. "D'you know what peace means to me? I mean, besides the obvious of not having the worry over bombs and the blackout."

May shook her head.

"Walking into a butcher's shop, mulling over what joint of meat to buy and what size...and boiling an egg anytime I fancy...and—"

"Smothering butter on newly baked crusty bread," May chipped in, "and the tea caddy always full. Christmas cake with nuts and raisins and warm scones made with eggs—"

"Don't!" Etty pulled a tortured face. "All this talk of food makes me starved—and like old Mother Hubbard, my cupboards are bare."

"Who was Mother Hubbard, anyway?" May wanted to know as she resumed pummelling the nappies in the tub with the poss stick.

"I haven't a clue." A gleam of fun glinted in Etty's eyes. "But I know she was old."

"And she had a little dog," May joined in.

The two girls' eyes met and they began to laugh, a belly laugh that wouldn't stop and made their stomach muscles hurt.

And May forgot her troubles for a while.

Later, as they sat at the kitchen table, a cup of tea in their hands, watching the nappies blowing in the wind on the yard line, Etty turned to May, eyes now serious.

"When is your dad moving out?"

"He says soon. But I can stay till someone rents the house."

"That's generous of him." Etty's voice was thick with sarcasm. "I wish we had a spare room here so we could put you up."

May didn't want to be a burden. She realised that now, more than anything, she wanted herself and Derek to be together and share a home. Somehow, she'd make it work. She'd find cheap rooms, she'd find work that—

A new thought struck, and she froze. She could never now become a nurse. According to Matron, if May did succeed in passing the entrance exam, she would have to live in the nursing home for the next three years—and Matron didn't make exceptions.

May made a decision. No matter at what personal cost, Derek would always come first in her life.

Relinquishing her dream, with a heavy heart, May told herself it was for the best.

CHAPTER FIVE

The bus trundled along the twisting road and May, looking out of the window at the soaring countryside, gasped in amazement. The moor, with its rugged elevations where farmsteads nestled in dark hollows and minuscule trees stood out on an undulating skyline, took her by surprise. As she pressed her brow against the cold windowpane, she smiled, thankful that Derek could thrive in such fresh and invigorating countryside.

The journey so far had been thrilling but not without anxiety—travelling so far alone was something May had never done before. From South Shields, she had taken the steam train to Newcastle where she was overwhelmed by the platforms swarming with people, porters pushing trolleys laden with suitcases, and the trains pulling into the station, blasting steam that billowed in the enclosed area. Soldiers poked their heads out of train windows, some with cigarettes dangling from their mouths, saying goodbye to stiff-upper-lipped relatives and tearful wives.

Finding the correct platform, May had boarded the train bound for Hexham. She sat comfortably in the carriage, content to stare out of the window and watch the world hurtle by. She was tired after her night shift.

At Hexham—a charming market town with impressive buildings, and narrow bustling old-world streets—she found the bus station. Boarding the number 38 bus, she sat transfixed watching the scenery go by for the eleven miles it took to her destination.

"Allendale, miss," the ruddy-faced conductor told her, giving her a curt nod. When they arrived, May found herself in a quaint village square surrounded with sedate hotels, a cute little church and a holiday atmosphere that made May wish she'd more time to take a look around. But her business here was important, and May had no time for such frivolities. She made a promise to return another day.

She approached a wiry, older gentleman in overalls, who stood beside a lorry that had milk churns on it.

"Excuse me, I wonder if you could direct me to Hillcrest Farm?"

The man crooked his arm and put a hand on his hip. "Aye. Yi' need to go back aways, miss…" He pointed to a road that left the square. "Go back to the main road and turn left, then bear right and walk a stretch up the hill till you can't go any farther. It's there you'll find the Talbots' farm."

Following the man's directions, May left the road and walked up a steep gravelled path shaded by overgrown trees. She stopped for a moment to take in the scene of Allendale below and the big sky up above and a sense of freedom enveloped her. No wonder, May thought, people spoke so highly of the Northumberland countryside.

Approaching the rim of the hill, May saw, in the distance, the stone-built, pitched-roofed farmhouse. At its side was a huge wooden haybarn. As she got closer, she saw hens strutting the courtyard, and two mean-looking geese stalking them from behind, while everywhere in the air hung the smell of hay mingled with dung.

As she walked over the cowpat-splattered cobbles, May saw movement behind the doorway of the farmhouse. A dog was yapping.

"Shush, Spot." A woman emerged from the gloom of the house, a black and white terrier jumping up at her side.

The woman had slate-grey hair done up in a bun, plump rosy cheeks, a beaming smile and twinkling eyes. She was exactly how May imagined a farmer's wife to be.

The woman came over.

"Pesky geese…" She flapped the offending creatures away with the pinny she wore over a white open-neck blouse and tweed skirt. "They're always on the scrounge and turn nasty when they're out o' luck." She gave May a friendly smile. "You must be May…Derek's sister." She held out a hand. "Maud Talbot…Maud, to you."

The terrier jumped at May, still yapping.

"Enough, Spot, or I'll lock you inside."

The dog obeyed and sat demurely on her haunches at Maud's side.

"I've come to—"

Just then, a goose waddled back and, screeching, stretched its skinny neck and alarmingly, appeared to double in height.

"His screech is worse than his bite." Maud clapped her hands and the creature, with an outraged expansive flutter of wing, waddled away.

"Thank you." May felt foolish because she didn't know how to react to farm animals. "I've never met a goose before. I didn't know they could be so…tall."

"God love us…I forgot you're a townie…same as young Derek when he first arrived." She chuckled good-naturedly.

May couldn't help feeling a little possessive.

"The lad's made up for it since." Maud looked up at one of the farmhouse windows. "I expect he's lurking there…he's been actin' strange lately. I told him you were arriving as he isn't keen on folk calling."

Folk! In a rare moment of pique, May was outraged. She wasn't folk; she was Derek's family! Then she reprimanded herself. What was wrong with her today, why was she so temperamental? She should be grateful to Maud for caring for Derek and giving him a decent home. But still she felt envious. She was tormented by the thought that Derek might love Maud more than her.

A north-easterly wind blew around May's naked legs (stockings were in short supply, though she'd drawn a line up the middle of the back of her legs to pretend she wore a pair) and May realised that her green wool jacket, matching skirt and T-bar mid-heeled shoes, wasn't suitable attire for the country.

She shivered, not from the cold but the task ahead. She dreaded telling Derek about Mam and seeing his darling little face crumple.

"I'm sorry for your loss," Maud said and May reckoned her expression must have betrayed her feelings. "It must be very hard."

May didn't trust herself to speak but nodded appreciatively.

There was a silence as Maud appeared to be making up her mind about something.

She spoke at last, but her demeanour had turned somewhat edgy. "I suppose you'll be wanting to take the lad home. I've heard things are quieter now on the coast, since the Luftwaffe were sent to the Eastern front."

That would be a dream come true.

She prattled, "Yes. There've been no major raids in the town since we sent Derek here." May hesitated. She didn't want to go into personal business. She could never admit that Derek's dad had rejected him and neither did she want to confess he was without a home.

She continued. "But if it's fine by you, the bairn's probably best off if he stays here for a while."

Maud visibly relaxed. Her round face beamed. "It's no problem. Me and me old man have grown fond of the lad." Jauntily, she made for the front door. "Come in, such a long morning you've had...I expect you could do with a cuppa." She stood aside to allow May to enter the house.

The living room, with its blazing coal fire, low ceiling and saggy couch, had a cosy feel and, looking out of the small but deep sash window, May could see for miles over open countryside. What caught her attention most was the hearty, meaty aroma permeating the room from the kitchen.

A shrill noise pierced the air.

"Kettle's boiling." Maud hurried through an open door that led to the back of house.

As the minutes ticked by, May's eyes strayed around the place and landed on the door to an adjoining room. The door open, May saw a long wooden table with places set all around it. To her amazement a large jug of milk and glass dish with creamy, yellow butter inside stood in the middle and on the sideboard was an enamel bowl filled with large, brown eggs—albeit covered with hen's business. May drooled in amazement. It paid to live in the country, she concluded.

"Do you take milk and sugar?" Maud returned into the room empty handed. She followed May's gaze. "For the land girls, God love them. Mr. Talbot and I don't know what we'd do without them." She nodded, the loose skin below her chin wobbling. "By the way, Mr. Talbot... Alf says he's sorry not to be here but there's some trouble with the tractor. He'll try and catch up later."

May nodded.

Suddenly impatient, she said, "I'll leave the tea for now. I'd like to see me brother, please."

A sombre expression crossed Maud's face. "I don't know how the lad's going to take the news of his mother. He's always on about her. Thought the world of her, he did."

A lump in her throat, May didn't trust herself to speak.

Maud disappeared through the doorway. "Derek, come down," she called. "Your sister's here."

There was a long pause. "Derek."

Maud thudded up the stairs, and then came down again. "He's nowhere to be seen... probably hiding in the barn." She removed her shoes and pulled on a pair of black Wellingtons.

May teetered behind Maud's stout figure as they crossed a field of damp grass, and wondered why Derek would want to hide.

The barn, stacked with bales of sweet-smelling hay, was cold and draughty.

"Derek…I know you're in here, son," Maud called out. "Your sister's come a long way to see you."

At first, nothing happened, then a movement came from the topmost bale of hay and a figure jumped down. Derek stood before them, dressed in a blue knitted sweater, grey short pants and Wellingtons. May was staggered by how much he'd grown. And he'd lost his cute, chubby look.

His head bent, he didn't meet May's gaze.

"I'll be in the kitchen if you want anything." Maud excused herself.

May was shocked by how awkward she felt. "Hello, Derek. How are you? Pleased to see me?"

He gave an imperceptible nod.

"D'you like it here on the farm?"

He nodded emphatically but still made no eye contact.

"Mrs. Talbot seems nice." May knew she could no longer go on with this pretence. At the prospect of what lay ahead, her stomach churned.

She went to sit on a bale of hay and patted the spiky straws, "Come and sit down besi—"

"I'm not coming home," he rounded on her, his pink watery eyes meeting hers, "and you can't make me."

CHAPTER SIX

Every fibre in May's body tensed. "Derek, I want you to listen. It's about Mam...she—"

"I know. Mammy died and I won't see her again." His high-pitched voice ended in a howl that pierced May's heart like an arrow.

May did what came naturally; she rushed over and put her arms around him. His young body shuddered and he sobbed—huge sobs that made his shoulders heave.

May felt distraught seeing him like this. She would do anything to make him feel better but she felt totally helpless. They stood like that for a while and when, finally, Derek stopped crying, he pushed her away.

"Gerroff." He wiped his nose with the arm of his sweater.

Reluctantly, she released him. "How did you know?" was all she could think to say.

There was only one person who could've told him but surely Maud Talbot wouldn't do such a thing, not without owning up?

"They thought I was in bed," Derek sniffed, "but I listened behind the door." He looked at her with big frightened eyes and she saw at heart he was still just a baby.

"Aunty Maud said she got a letter which said Mammy had been run over by a trolleybus..." A tremor in his voice, he stopped to recover before continuing. "When she showed Uncle Alf he said I should see Mammy in a cof...coffin but Aunty said I couldn't because it was too late. Then Uncle Alf said I'd be going home." Derek's big blue eyes sought hers. "But nobody came."

May's stomach twisted with guilt.

"Darling, I'm here now."

"But I don't want to go home." Derek appeared to shrink and looked the little boy he was. With a pang of realisation, May realised she must make this all about him—what Derek wanted.

"What would you like to happen?"

He looked surprised, as if he hadn't expected to be considered.

He thought awhile. "Home won't be the same without Mammy. I'd like to stay here with the animals and help with the milk." He sniffed hugely and his boyish face looked eager.

Adrenalin coursing through her, May enquired, "Won't you miss Dad?"

"No," he said, with the truthfulness of the young.

"Or…me?"

"I…don't think so…besides, if I do stay, you can come and see me like now."

For a second, it crossed May's mind to tell Derek that she was his mother and how much he meant to her, but the naïve trust in his gaze stopped her.

May steeled herself. "Y-yes, I suppose I could. But what about after the war when it's safe to come home? Would you like to come back and live with me?"

She forgot to breathe.

"I don't think so. Not now Mammy's not there. I've made friends at school here…and Uncle Alf lets me ride the horse."

Though devastated, May nodded as if she agreed with every word.

He glanced sideways at her as if unsure whether to share or not. "I like Aunty Maud, she's kind, like…Mam." His chin wobbled. "Aunty's girls are big now and gone away. She told me if she'd had a little boy she'd want him to be just like me."

May felt her heart would shatter in tiny pieces. She made sure none of this emotion showed on her face.

"May..."

"Yes."

"I miss Mammy."

"I know."

"I didn't want to see her in that coffin box." He fidgeted in agitation. "And I don't mind if I don't see Daddy any more."

She ruffled his blonde wavy hair. "Promise me something..." He sniffed and stared at her in wide-eyed expectancy. "If you're in trouble or need me, tell Aunty Maud to write to me. And before you know it I'll be here."

He didn't understand the urgency in her voice, she could tell, but he nodded anyway.

As May dragged her way back down the gravelled path, she despaired. It was as though she'd left part of her heart behind. The urge to run back to the farmhouse and cuddle Derek close and never let him go overwhelmed her.

As the bus made its return journey back to Hexham, May's blurred vision couldn't make out the scenery. Thoughts sprang up like unwanted weeds in her mind. She'd lost Derek a second time—and if her heart ached, she could only blame herself for the blunders she'd made in her life.

May sat bolt upright. She wouldn't think like that. Loving Billy Buckley was never a mistake. Though it was still painful that they had broken up, May considered herself lucky she'd experienced the all-consuming love she felt for Billy. And you never know, when Billy returned from the war, maybe this time round he might be ready to settle down.

She rubbed the window pane clear of condensation with a hand. Scenes of green fields passed by and undulating hills with skinny trees rose on the skyline. A memory played in her mind's eye of the first time she and Billy had made love, and a sweet ache stirred in May's groin. She closed her eyes and imagined herself back on that knoll on Cleadon Hills. She'd been seventeen, and remembering the thrill of that moment, of discovering that Billy Buckley, whom she'd worshipped since schooldays, loved her, made her heart pound with happiness still.

"That lad was and always will be jack the lad and only after one thing," Mam spoke in her mind.

May ignored the voice. But there was no denying May could never repay Mam for what she had done at that time. For, by the time May discovered she was pregnant, Billy had left her for pastures greener and a new lass. May didn't condemn him because she knew in her heart that like a wild animal Billy couldn't be tamed—and he had made it clear that he didn't want kids. So when Derek was born, Mam had solved the problem by bringing Derek up as her own. Something that May had agreed to, unprepared for the pain and suffering she'd have to bear. As May thought of Derek's trusting gaze, her eyes misted with renewed tears. She felt wretched about the lies he'd unknowingly endured, and that she'd had to sacrifice her own relationship with him as a result.

Although teary with emotion, May smiled as she recalled the time when Billy came back into her life. The war had just begun and impulsively he'd both joined up and asked May to get engaged. Thrilled, May thought she'd died and gone to heaven. But it wasn't to last. May began to irritate him with what he called her clingy ways. As a last-ditch plea, she'd told Billy about his son. Outraged, Billy had accused her of lying to keep him.

After he left he was posted abroad and she hadn't seen him since. She'd written letters, though, telling him of the news from home but careful never to mention personal matters. He responded in the same tone and her heart had begun to lift at the idea there was still hope for the two of them.

"Heed my words, you're better off without him," Mam's voice told her.

May shook her head. Mam, for once, was wrong. She didn't know Billy like May did. Billy was capable of change and when he did, May would be ready and waiting.

"Such is the foolery of love," came Mam's voice again.

As the bus trundled down the main street and turned into Hexham bus station, May wondered, with a leaden heart, what she was going to do with her life. With nowhere to call home and no expectation of living with Derek, the future looked bleak—except, her mind thought with a little spark of enthusiasm, at least now she could consider nursing again.

One thing was for sure; Dad's life was mapped out and his plans didn't include her or Derek. She didn't condemn Dad for what he did, because as Mam said, "till you walk in someone's shoes, you should never judge them." Smart woman that she was, Mam would have been the first to encourage her husband to drop his old self-destructive ways and begin again. But May couldn't forgive him.

As she got off the bus, May made up her mind. With these thoughts swirling in her brain, she knew she'd never be able to take the short nap she'd intended before the night shift began. She needed company. She decided that when she got home she'd head to Etty's and tell her about the visit.

It was dark by the time the train pulled into South Shields station. May opened the carriage door and stepped onto the platform, where steam billowed all around. Outside, a wall of damp, impenetrable fog met her making her feel panicky. The weather report in the newspaper had warned that conditions that night would be dry over most of England but there'd be considerable fog in the north.

May fumbled for a torch in her shoulder bag and, switching it on, shone its beam at her feet. Her heart rate beat faster whenever traffic passed in the road. She couldn't help thinking back to the night of Mam's accident. Mindful of where she walked, May hugged the wall as she plunged forward into darkness.

Then she froze.

The noise of a plane, like an enormous lone bee droning in the skies, came from the direction of the coastline, then another followed and flew low overhead. Bombers. May's heart skipped a beat and she stood transfixed, looking heavenward.

Someone bumped into her. "Man, watch where you're goin'."

"Is that a Jerry bomber?" May asked, her mouth dry.

"Nay, lass." The fellow's figure was indistinguishable in the dark foggy night. "Probably a couple of returning Lancasters ... I used me lugs and could tell by the noise from the four engines. Poor souls can't find the airfield in this bleedin' weather ... Sorry, miss, for the langua—"

The terrific engine noise directly overhead drowned out his voice.

When the bombers passed, May heard the sound of engines faltering.

"God help the brave lad ... he's out of fuel."

Time stood still as the noise of the stuttering engine diminished towards the Sunderland area. Then, far off, came a noise that made May fear the worst: the scream of a plane nose diving and a muted thud. Far away, the foggy atmosphere was lit by an orange glow.

"Smelling salts." Etty held the bottle under May's nose.

"I can't stand the smell of ammonia." May wrinkled her nose and pushed the small bottle away. "But thank you, anyway."

Etty replaced the cap on the bottle. "Poor blighters ... that crew were some mothers' sons. It must be worse knowing that they'd been successful only for the pilot to lose his way and run out of fuel so close to home."

Etty knew that May was still shaky and didn't want to talk about the disaster. But she also knew that talking about it would help her get the experience off her chest.

"The night's a blur," May told her. "I can't remember catching the trolley at the bottom of Fowler Street or making my way down Whale Street or even when you opened the front door, Etty."

Even though May was sitting in front of a blazing fire, she shivered.

"You're not supposed to be at work tonight, are you?"

"Yes, I am. To be honest I'm glad. After all today's events, I'll never sleep for thinking."

Etty let the matter drop. "Thank goodness both bairns are bathed and asleep early for once. Though, what's the betting I'll suffer for it later." She pulled a rueful face. "Trevor will be home from work by then and though I do grumble that he goes out so much he's a marvellous help with the kiddies when he's home."

She sank down in a comfy winged-back fireside chair and got out her drawstring sewing bag, one of Trevor's knitted socks and a darning needle. She pulled the sock over the round end of a mushroom bobbin and threaded the needle with some wool.

She looked up, and, attempting to coax May's mind away from the crash, asked, "Come on, tell me what happened at the farm. Was Derek thrilled to see you? Was it awful telling him about . . . his mam?"

Etty could tell that evening's drama had wiped today's events from her friend's mind, and it took a minute for May to gather her thoughts.

"He already knew about Mam." May went on to tell Etty what had taken place and finished with, "Derek's adamant he doesn't want to come home."

All the while she listened, Etty darned the hole in the sock. "What do the Talbots think?"

"It suits Mrs. Talbot if Derek chooses to live there."

"I know it's a nasty blow but...maybe that's just as well. Because, when you do find a home you'll have to work to pay the rent. And, May, you won't have time to look after Derek."

"He'd be at school most of the time." May's tone was mutinous.

"Things change, May. Don't give up hope. You never know what will happen next in life."

"I can't see Derek changing his mind. He's become too attached to Mrs. Talbot. And I can see why...she's such a lovely person. And life on the farm is so good for him."

"May Robinson. You're too accommodating for your own good." Etty pulled a mock-despairing face. "I hope you never meet Adolf...I'm sure you'd find some redeeming trait even in him."

"I'd never! How can you say such a thing?"

Etty held up her hands in defeat. "Okay, sorry. Just teasing you. But promise me you'll never give up on Derek coming home to live with you."

"I would never." May was resolute. "One day I'll make it happen and we will be together. I couldn't bear it otherwise."

Etty's face became serious. "As Derek grows up, his family will become more important to him."

"I know, but to Derek I'm only his annoying big sister."

"You're more than that, May. You're part of him." Her words hanging in the air, Etty returned to darning the grey sock.

She didn't look up when she next spoke. Heart hammering, she asked, "D'you still write to...Billy Buckley?"

"I stopped at first when he didn't answer, then I plucked up the courage and wrote him again and told him all the home news. Billy likes me to do that as long as I don't mention anything personal. His battalion has been posted abroad and I haven't heard from him in quite a while." May chewed her inner lip.

"That's normal, isn't it?" Anxiety rose in Etty's chest.

"Yes, a letter usually takes around six weeks to arrive."

"Gracious. All Billy's news will be ancient by then."

"Oh, he isn't allowed to write about important matters, where he is or what he's doing and the letters are censored for security. Servicemen are only allowed one sheet, whether for convenience or cost I don't know, and the army copies the letters and reduces the size of the print. I need a magnifying glass to read it. The letter is then printed on the thinnest paper."

"Blimey. I didn't realise."

"The silly thing is, that as time goes by, I don't get a single letter, then a glut of them arrives all at once."

There was a pensive silence.

"May."

"Yes."

Etty steeled herself. She had no ulterior motive; she was only trying to help, after all. "I don't want to intrude, but you owe it to yourself to move on from Billy. Start afresh with somebody else. Don't let life pass you by." She laughed, shamefaced. "Hark at me with all the clichés."

"I don't know what a cliché is but I know Billy."

Etty inwardly groaned. May, poor lass, was blinded by love.

May went on, "He does care…you should have seen the wreck he was when his dad died of a heart attack. He went to great lengths to look after his mam and kid sister. He cares about family and he's good at heart and…"

"Fickle," Etty exploded and then clapped her hand over her mouth.

May looked at her in a peculiar way. "Why d'you say that?"

As she tried to think of a satisfactory answer, the heat of shame rose in Etty, culminating in her neck and cheeks flushing. "All I'm saying is, don't ruin your life waiting for Billy Buckley to settle down."

May didn't answer but Etty could tell by her stubborn expression that that was exactly what she intended to do.

When she felt ready to leave, May caught a trolley home. Sitting in a window seat, she went over the day in her mind…Derek at the farm, the aeroplane crashing with probable loss of civilian life, the certain knowledge she must find somewhere to live… The future, a black hole of unpredictability May was afraid to explore, looked bleak, especially now she didn't have Mam to rely on. But the dream that one day she could become a nurse played in the recesses of her mind.

She got off the bus at her stop in front of the shops and over the road from Tyne Dock entrance. There was no point in knocking, she decided when she arrived at her front door, as she could tell by the open curtains at the bay window that Dad wasn't in. As she closed the front door and switched on the passage light, May saw two envelopes sitting on the door mat. She made her way along the passageway, wondering who had sent the envelope addressed to her. In the kitchen, she switched on the light and the room, with its air of neglect, became visible. May set the letter addressed to Dad on the table and, ripping open the one with her name on it, read its contents.

Dear Miss Robinson,
I am pleased to inform you that Edgemoor General Hospital has accepted your application to train as a probationer nurse.

The letter went on to explain that she was required to send a note of acceptance and inform Matron of her dress size for her uniform. The letter ended,

Starting date is 5th of December at half past eight. You are
required to collect your uniform from the sewing room and
change. Then make your way to report to Matron's office.

The letter described the training school and what was to be expected of her. As May's hands formed a steeple over her mouth, the letter fluttered to the mat.

She could hardly believe what she'd read. She—May Robinson—was going to train to become a nurse.

Etty was right; you never knew what was going to happen next in life. She picked up the letter and clutched it to her chest.

The next morning, leaving the factory after the night shift, May pedalled along the road. A cyclist drew alongside her.

"Hang on...where've you been hiding?"

In the half-light, she looked into the strikingly handsome and determined face of Alec Hudson.

"Pull over," he commanded.

May did as she was bid and stood holding the bike's handlebars as she waited at the kerb.

Alec came to stand next to her, straddling his bicycle. "I'm early in to work. I've kept an eye out for you all week," he greeted her.

"I've been on night shifts."

"Ahh! I never thought." His eyes locked with hers. "I wanted to ask you out."

Flummoxed, May didn't know what to say. She fumbled, "I don't even know you."

"You know me name and that I ride a Raleigh bike and you must have twigged I work at the yards." His green eyes twinkled. "What more d'you need to know?" She laughed when he pulled a hurt, boyish face. "I'm single and fancy-free and with this war on it doesn't pay to wait."

She began to mount her bicycle.

"Look, I'm not asking for your hand in marriage...just to walk out. How about the flicks, ice cream parlour...? Anywhere you like."

May made up her mind and, mounting her bike, she cycled off. Laughing, she called over her shoulder, "On your bike."

"I won't give up that easy," he shouted back.

At the end of November, excitement was building within May. For soon she would be following her dream to become a nurse—she felt like pinching herself.

But leaving the only home she'd ever known with memories of Mam in every room—her best china on the plate rack, trinkets covering every surface, the peculiar lived-in, mildew smell of the place—would be a wrench. Then there was Derek, who'd been born in the attic bedroom, spoken his first word and taken his first faltering steps in the front room. Happy and sad times, all shared in the space of the four walls of the Templeton Street house.

"Change is always frightening," Etty had said when May visited and shared both the thrilling news of her acceptance at the hospital and her misgivings about leaving home. Etty was the only person she'd confided in about becoming a nurse apart from the labour manager at work. When May had gone to his office to hand her notice in she'd asked him not to mention her leaving to anyone as she didn't want a fuss.

Etty had continued, "With this war on, change is inevitable and sometimes, as we know, for the worse. But your news is the jolliest I've heard in a long time. A change for the better! Blimey. Grab it with both hands."

"You're right"—May grinned—"and without a doubt if Mam were here, she'd be brim-full of pride."

*

With only three days to go before she left work, tired and drained from the long night shift, May arrived home hungry and desperate for a kip. In the semi-light, she bumped her bicycle up the front steps.

The door opened and a small woman with permed silvery-blonde hair stood in front of her. Her expression belligerent, she closed the door behind her to prevent the light shining out, and, folding her arms, stood outside on the front step.

"Hello." May presumed this must be Dad's lady friend, Gertie. "Pleased to meet you. I'm May."

"I know who you are. But what I'm thinkin' is, what are you still doin' here?"

"Pardon me?"

"You heard." Gertie drew herself up. "Folk have answered the advert and we've—"

"What advert?"

"In the *Gazette*, to rent this house. We've had an offer too good to miss from a dentist whose house foundations are shot after the last raid."

May couldn't believe what she was hearing.

"I told your dad to be firm but he's soft and he's left it up to me to inform you. The family interested wants to move in as quick as possible, with Christmas just around the corner."

She turned and moving into the dark hall, returned with a battered leather suitcase. "You're a grown lass with a job. It's time you fended for yersel'."

She dumped the small suitcase at May's feet. "Your stuff's in there."

"But I've nowhere—"

"That's no fault of ours . . . you've had plenty o' notice. I'd try rooms in Ocean Road, if I was you."

As May picked up the suitcase, she saw Dad's gaunt and white face staring from the bay window.

Gertie, entering the hall, slammed the door behind her.

"The bitch," Etty exploded, when May told her what had happened. "She threw you out?"

Seeing the state her friend was in, Etty ushered her into the kitchen.

"Does this Gertie have a job?" Etty asked.

They sat at the drop-leaf table over a breakfast of porridge. The baby was still asleep and Norma wriggled in her high chair as Etty tried to feed her.

"I don't know anything about her... Not even how she and Dad met."

"If you ask me, she's after his money."

May couldn't believe anyone would be that calculating and said so.

"You're priceless, May. It's a pity there aren't more folk like you... the world would be a far better place." Etty wiped milky sludge from the bairn's chin. "Let's not talk about the woman any more. I can tell you're pooped and done in. Why don't we go for a walk by the sea and blow Gertie's evil aura away?"

May rose from the chair. "I need sleep." Then as realisation hit, she slumped down again. "But I've got nowhere to go."

"Yes, you have. You're staying here, my girl, and that's final."

"But won't I be in the way?"

"Only if you make a complaint about the incessant racket in this mad house. You can kip in our double bed during the day. Luckily Trevor's on the day shift."

Forced to admit she had no other choice, May agreed. "You're too good to me, Etty."

At her words, the old suffocating cloud of guilt and doubt overwhelmed Etty. She could never make up to May for what she'd done.

"Besides," Etty said, surfacing from the emotions that plagued her, "it's only for two days, then you'll be off to pastures new. For now, go and have a kip or you'll suffer later when you're at work tonight."

In the bedroom, the curtains drawn, Etty's clothes strewn on the floor, May undressed to her underwear and lay on the unmade bed. Pulling the sheet up to her chin, she smelled the warm, comforting smell of the previous occupants. She tossed and turned for a while, thoughts nagging her brain, and then fell into a fitful sleep.

Later, when she woke up, she looked around and wondered where she was. Then it clicked. May checked her watch. She was ravenously hungry.

She dressed and went through to the kitchen-come-dining room where embers glowed in the grate. She looked at the clock on the mantle. Half one. Etty, sitting at the table, was feeding the baby from a banana-shaped bottle while Norma sat in her playpen stacking wooden building blocks.

Etty gave a rather preoccupied smile, then nodded to the bottle. "This is my life; I've become a feeding machine. Saying that, you'll be famished... there's left-over pie in the scullery."

May visited the lav down the yard and then washed her hands in the scullery under the cold water tap. She cut a slice of the corned beef pie standing on the drainer and returned to the kitchen.

"You'll scarce taste the corned beef it's spread that thin," Etty told her, "but needs must when you've to stretch two meals out of a tin."

They purposely avoided talking about Gertie, for which May, who was still in shock somewhat, was thankful. Instead, they talked about shortages and the state of housing after the raids.

"Did you hear that if you take in a conscripted miner you can earn twenty-five shillings a week?" Etty said.

"A conscripted miner?"

Etty rolled her eyes. "Don't you listen to the news?"

"I'm whacked after I've finished me shifts. And I can't hear the newsreader's voice at work because of the racket in the canteen."

"Bevin announced earlier in a speech that one in ten men between the ages of eighteen and twenty-five who've been called up will work in the coal mines," Etty said.

"How will that work?"

"By lottery."

"You're kidding me?"

"No, really. Servicemen's numbers will be put in groups of ten and to make the system fair figures from nought to nine will be put in a hat. Bevan's secretary will pull one out. The serviceman with that figure at the end of their National Registration number will find himself down a coal mine."

"Seriously?"

"So the man said." Etty's expression was one of disbelief. "You'd think they'd take a more scientific approach."

"Yes. I find it hard to believe a man's fate would be decided by lottery."

"Precisely. And can you imagine some toff from London having to live with us heathens up here?"

"The scheme's never going to be popular," May agreed.

"I feel guilty because part of me is glad about it."

"How d'you mean?"

"Because Trevor was about to enlist."

"Doesn't he like working down the pit and helping out at the funeral parlour any more?"

Newman's funeral parlour, situated over the road in Whale Street, consisted of two houses knocked into one, with the Newmans living upstairs and the funeral parlour and workshop on the ground floor. Trevor, in his time off from the pit, helped Mr. Newman out (and May thought it admirable that he did). And for his effort, Trevor learned the funeral trade. His hope was that after the war was over, he'd have a permanent position at Newman's. Providing, of course, the Newmans' son was agreeable. Danny, the Newmans' beloved only child and heir, was a pilot in the air force, and his folks expected that one day he'd take over the family business.

Etty confided in May, "Trevor wants to do his bit and be in the thick of it. He now wishes he'd acted earlier to enlist because there's no possibility he'll be allowed to leave the pit under these circumstances." She pulled a satisfied face. "And I'm glad because I don't want to see his name in the paper's Roll of Honour."

May glanced at Norma, her chubby arms outstretched, wanting to be lifted from out from the playpen.

"We don't want your daddy dead, do we?" May told the bairn. Glancing at Etty, she was baffled as to why her friend suddenly looked so flushed, and she wondered what she'd said.

CHAPTER SEVEN

May always caught Etty off guard. It was usually a simple thing like now when she mentioned Norma's daddy—when the truth of the matter was: it wasn't Trevor.

How Etty wished she'd owned up about Norma's parentage from the beginning when their friendship was casual but, in those days, Etty had never dreamed the pair of them would become so close.

May, with her truthful nature, expected everyone else to be the same and she'd never understand Etty's deceit. So, afraid of losing her friend, Etty had kept her secret. If she told the truth, Etty had convinced herself, she'd only hurt May—and what was the point of that? But, deep down, Etty knew she was only kidding herself, and that she was a despicable coward.

All it would take was for Etty to say, "Trevor isn't Norma's daddy...her real dad is Billy Buckley." To confess the act only happened once, on the night raiders bombed South Shields market place, when the pair of them, together in the air raid shelter, feared the walls were about to cave in and they were going to die.

From the first time May introduced them there was an attraction between Etty and Billy. Though, as May's fiancé, he was strictly out of bounds as far as Etty was concerned. But in times of war when you think you're about to die—things happen.

In the silence, Etty became aware of May staring at her with a mystified expression.

"Something wrong?" May asked.

A cold sensation crawled over Etty. She shivered. "Someone just walked over my grave." A stupid expression, she thought, and she saw her friend recoil.

From the look of her pallid face, May was still reeling from the events of the last few days.

"What time does Trevor get home from work?" May asked.

Etty checked her watch. "Any minute now. His shift is six till two."

May pushed back her chair and stood up from the table. "I'm going for a walk...it'll do me good and give you two time on your own."

"Don't be daft, May. That never happens...not with these two."

"I'll take Norma with me, if you like."

"Now that's an offer I can't refuse."

With Norma swamped in knitted blankets in the pram, May slung her handbag and gas mask over a shoulder, and, taking hold of the handlebars, bumped the wheels over the front step. The weather, cold but dry, would put colour in both her and the bairn's cheeks.

As she set off, she thought how thankful she was for Etty's kind heart, for without the offer of a bed May would've had to find a room and she didn't know if she'd enough money to stretch to that. She'd spent most of her savings on a pair of black sturdy shoes and pocket watch on a chain, requirements for when she started at the hospital. All the money she had, she calculated was—

"May, is that you, girl?" Ramona Newman's strident voice called from over the street.

Dressed in the green uniform of the Women's Voluntary Service, the brimmed hat a little battered, Ramona wore a thick muffler scarf and mittens and carried a leather shoulder bag and her gas mask.

"It is, isn't it?"

May pushed the pram over the cobbled road. "Hello, Mrs. Newman. How are you?"

"Don't you hello me. You know fine well you've been avoidin' me."

Mrs. Newman, normally at pains to speak so properly, forgot she was a lady when she was vexed and lapsed into Geordie twang.

"Not a sight have we seen of yi' since the funeral." Her thin lips bunched. "You'd think, after all Mr. Newman and I've done, we deserve a visit. What I'd like to know is, what's happened to me sister's possessions?"

For the life of her, May couldn't think what the Newmans (she was never allowed to call them aunt or uncle) had ever done for the family, except they'd once hired her as parlour maid—which Mam had been deeply opposed to because, in her opinion, her sister was a stuck-up cow who thought she was somebody just because she'd married into money.

"Sorry. I didn't realise you'd want a keepsake of Mam's."

"Your mam was my sister and nothing will change that fact." A tell-tale crack in Ramona's voice surprised May. But, as Mam had often told her, blood was thicker than water. Poor Ramona, she thought, to lose a sister before they'd had the chance to make up—and it was too late now.

"Me mam didn't have many possessions, only clothes and a few trinkets. You can have her wedding ring if you like."

"I want nothing to do with that man. Your dad was my sister's ruin and I'll never forgive him." Ramona's stout body quivered with vexation. "Anyways...that's not what I want to talk to you about." She regained her regal stance. "It was me who asked Mr. Newman to be lenient with Ivy's funeral bill. Your dad said he couldn't pay because he was skint...as per usual...and was in between jobs. Ha!"

May was dumbfounded. So locked in grief was she that it had never occurred to her who would have to pay for Mam's funeral. How daft can a person be?

The whites of Ramona's eyes, awash with tears, were pink. She swallowed. "No way was my sister going to be buried in a pauper's grave. So . . . here is the offer. Either you can pay the bill in weekly instalments from your salary, or," she said expansively, "you can come back and work for me as a parlour maid. Your board and lodgings will be free and the money you earn will be docked off your bill."

In other words, May would be working for nothing. She remembered Mam saying that she didn't want her daughter to be a skivvy for the rest of her life.

"No, thank you, Mrs. Newman. I'll take the first offer, if you please. You see, I'm starting training to become a nurse at Edgemoor Hospital shortly."

"A nurse! Eee." Ramona was impressed, May could tell. "You certainly don't take after *him*. It's our side of the family has the professional streak. Let's think on . . . no . . . you're the first to have a medical vocation. Wait till I tell your cousin Danny."

May, surprised at her reaction, lost her tongue. Never before had she been allowed to have anything to do with Danny. She could imagine Mam laughing in heaven.

Mam's voice played in her head. "By, I don't envy Ramona's cronies. They'll be sick and tired of hearing about her gloating about her niece . . . how she's training to be a nurse."

Norma, bored, poked her head from the hood of the pram, her little body twisting in agitation as she started to grizzle.

"Mrs. Newman, I must be off."

"Me too. There's certain matters need my attention." She gave a sniff.

May told her, "I'll see to it that the funeral bill is paid off quarterly . . . if that meets with your approval."

Ramona gave a magnanimous smile. "Certainly, dear, and do let your uncle and I know how you get on at the hospital."

*

The next morning, when she finished her shift, May made for the cloakroom, a headache throbbing in her temples. The ten-hour shift had taken its toll.

In the cloakroom she went to weigh herself on the penny scales. Like most women at the factory, though she ate stodgy canteen meals, she still lost weight, and, with her pallor, she was worried she might come down with some ghastly illness. It would be just her luck now that she was going to fulfil her dream and work at the hospital.

May noted, as she stood on the scales, that the pointer didn't move past the seven-and-a-half-stone marker.

"Aye, hinny, we're all the same," an older woman collecting her coat from the peg told May. "Skin and bones we'll all be, when this war is done." She shrugged herself into her coat, which hung off her bony shoulders. "It'll get worse if the powers that be get their way. Wantin' production stepped up, they are... and it's us mugs that have to do the work." She eyed May sagely. "You look out for yersel', lass. There's plenty more to take your place as far as management is concerned."

May, a little staggered at this unpatriotic talk, didn't reply. Everyone had to do their bit, she thought. But she shouldn't judge as it took all sorts, and the poor woman looked tired to the bone.

"Tomorrow's my last night," May told her.

"Never. Where you off?"

"Training to be a nurse."

"I'll be buggered." A broad smile split the woman's weary face. "Wish it was me. But I went and had all them bairns, didn't I? Because nobody telt us there was another kind of life." A guilty look crossed her face. "Mind you, I wouldn't be withoot one o' me bairns." She stopped to think, then winked. "I take that back. I could think of a couple of rascals I might get shot of."

May collected her coat, bag and gas mask and followed the woman to the factory exit where the pair of them walked some way together towards the factory gate.

When May went to fetch her bike from the bicycle shed, the woman called, "Don't take this wrong way, hinny, but I hope I never see you in that hospital."

"I won't." May smiled. "Ta-ra."

May thought of the woman's words, as she pushed the bike towards the gate and passed through security. She might not want another life, but things had changed since the war started; women had tasted freedom, and some wouldn't want to go back to what they considered the dull routine of housework and looking after menfolk.

Outside the gate, May mounted her bike.

The dim beam of a torch highlighted her face. For a heart-stopping moment, May thought the male voice belonged to security from the factory.

"Hi, May Robinson."

The artificial light shone beneath the speaker's chin and a rather ghoulish-looking Alec Hudson stared at her.

His audacity appalled her. "You'll get into trouble if the factory warden catches you."

The torch switched off.

Factory workers, in a dash for home and to snuggle down into a nice warm bed, swarmed past the pair of them.

"What are you doing here?" May asked.

"What d'you think?"

"I'm too tired to think. Go away."

"I told you I don't give up."

She made to pedal away but he grabbed the handlebars. "Look here, agree to a date and I'll be gone."

She thought him rather pushy but she couldn't get mad, and she laughed despite herself. "You're right. You are determined."

"I like to get my own way." She heard steel in his voice. "Hawway, confess you're over the moon to see us."

May knew a flirt when she met one. She tried not to think about Billy's expertise in this area.

But where was the harm in a bit of flattering flirtation? As Etty had said, May should live a little.

"Well, I wouldn't say that... but I'm on my way home." May caved; she could never hold out against male persuasiveness. Besides, the lad had got out of bed early before work to meet with her.

"Hawway, I'll walk some of the way home with you. I've plenty of time before work."

"As long as you behave."

Billy never could. He was always touching her or making suggestive comments.

"Are you suggestin' I'd do something smutty? I'm always a gentleman."

Now she'd upset him. May would have to stop these comparisons.

"No. It's me. It's been a while since... I've had dealings with a chap."

Chap! Since when did she call blokes that? She felt totally out of her depth.

"Aye... and this *chap* let you down, didn't he? The rotter."

"He didn't real—"

"Though I'm grateful to him. His loss is my gain."

May could hear the confident smile in his voice. She decided to let go for once and just let things happen.

They walked together side-by-side pushing their bicycles, footsteps echoing as they went under the arches. Occasional traffic—a motor car, cyclist and a clopping horse pulling a cart—passed them by on the road.

"What do you do at the shipyards?" May eventually broke the unsettling silence.

"I'm a shipwright carpenter at the Middle docks." His voice held a certain pride.

Despite her tiredness, May was interested. "What does that involve?"

"Making sure the ship's safe when it comes into the dock, then mostly repairing the vessel's timberwork. It's a freezing cold job this time of year." Something about his tone told May that the subject of work was closed.

In thoughtful silence they walked towards Chichester round-about, where in the darkness May heard a bus conductor hooking and unhooking a trolley's booms on the overhead cables. Up Dean Road, though the rubble was gone and May couldn't see them, she knew there was many a gap between buildings where terraced houses once stood and she'd swear, after all these months since the raid, the fire-damaged buildings still gave off a sickening acrid smell.

"Is it much further?" Alec asked. "I'll have to get back."

"No. Just a few more streets. Whale Street."

"Have yi' lived there long?"

May didn't want to go into the rigmarole of the past few days and simply said, "No. Just a short while. But I'm moving soon."

"Where to?"

"To nurse training school up Dunlop Road."

"When d'you go?"

"The day after tomorrow."

"For how long?"

"Three months. Then after my preliminary training I move to the nurse's home at Edgemoor Hospital." It felt surreal telling him about it, as if she was talking about someone else.

May wanted to change the subject from herself. "How about you...where d'you live?"

He hesitated. "My nana lives a few streets from here in Wawn Street. I practically spent my childhood here."

"Why? Did your mam go out to work?"

"No. She buggered off when I was little."

May, shocked, stopped in her tracks. "Oh, I am sorry. Did your dad bring you up?"

"He wasn't that interested."

Alec made off up the street. May, hurrying to catch up, thought it best not to pursue the matter, as he obviously didn't want to talk about the past.

As they pushed their bicycles in silence, May became aware of a certain intimacy between them.

"I've never told a soul about my folks before." Alec's voice was gruff, as if it cost him to speak out about his private life.

"I'm glad you told me. They say a problem shared is halved." May thought of Etty. She was always there when May wanted to get something off her chest.

"How old did you say you were?" Alec asked.

"I didn't."

"I'd reckon"—a thoughtful silence—"mid-twenties."

At twenty-five, May was positively on the shelf and though she didn't mind, she balked at letting the world know.

"Practically an old maid." Alec became his brash self. "But don't worry, I'm partial to older women."

Things were getting too personal, and May was at a loss as to how to handle the situation. She walked swiftly away and, turning into Whale Street, made for Etty's front door.

Alec caught up. "Am I rushing things if I ask for a kiss before I go?"

The man had gall. Again, his pushy ways brought rascally Billy Buckley to mind.

"Look, it's best I tell you. I sort of have a . . . beau."

Instantly, she felt daft at using such an old-fashioned word.

"I'll bet he's the cad who left you . . ."

Avoiding answering, she put the key in the lock. "Aw! Give us a chance. You don't know what you're missing."

He was incorrigible. "Don't you have a girlfriend?"

"I have now."

CHAPTER EIGHT
December 1943

In the build-up to Christmas that year, when all sorts of everyday goods were in short supply and either had to be queued for or were unobtainable, folk—Etty included—were totally drained by the war effort. But community spirit still prevailed and often showed itself in small kindnesses.

"Here, hinny, take this. Our bairn's too big for it..." A neighbour stood at Etty's door, smiling and holding out a used and undoubtedly much-loved rocking horse. "He's a bit dilapidated but he'll do for your little one from Santa Claus."

The next kindness was from an elderly gentleman neighbour. As Etty stood in the lengthy queue at the corner shop, he pressed sweetie coupons into her hand. "There you are, pet. You'll have more use than me for these. Get some sweeties for your little lassies' stocking on Christmas mornin'."

Today Trevor had come home after a six-till-two shift. Later on, he'd helped bath the kiddies, read to Norma from a story book until the bairn, finally, fell asleep. Then, collapsing on the couch, a snore rattled at the back of his throat. Etty worried that all that filth he breathed at the pit was doing him damage.

As she ironed the white collarless shirt Trevor wore when he worked at the funeral parlour, Etty planned the Christmas dinner, excited at the thought that May would be joining them—work at the hospital permitting.

It was May's last time doing the night shift at the factory before starting at the hospital tomorrow. At present she was at the early showing at the cinema of *For Whom the Bell Tolls* with Alec Hudson. Ironing the shirt sleeve and making sure she didn't press a crease up the side, Etty said a silent prayer: *Please God let the lass make a fresh start. Please let going out with Alec be just the beginning.* For despite what May hoped, there was no future with Billy—he'd told Etty so the last time they'd met.

At the time, Billy was expecting to be posted abroad and he had asked Etty if she would wait for him. By then, she'd seen through him and realised what a two-timing scoundrel he was. She told him about Trevor and that her heart belonged to him. Billy was aghast that Trevor knew she was carrying another man's child and that he still wanted to marry her.

"Trevor is the most trustworthy, upstanding man," Etty had told him proudly. She still couldn't believe her luck that despite everything Trevor still loved her. She'd promised herself that she'd make it up to him and be the best wife a man could have.

Mechanically, Etty put the flat iron on its heel. Satisfied with the shirt, she hung it over the back of a chair.

She glanced at the little artificial Christmas tree on the tea trolley, lodged in a bucket filled with coal to secure its base and surrounded with festive paper. Baubles, like everything else, were in short supply so Trevor had made little wooden toys—a snowman, Santa Claus, a teddy bear—all meticulously painted, which hung on the branches.

When Dorothy died, Trevor hadn't balked when Etty said she wanted them to raise her sister's baby as their own. And not once, even in an argument, had he reminded Etty of her past, which had already resulted in him bringing up another man's child. He had two children and neither one his own, but Etty would swear Trevor had convinced himself Norma was his flesh and blood. One day, she prayed, she'd bear him a son but so far, and it certainly wasn't for the want of trying, they'd had no luck.

As she took the ironing cloth off the table and put the folded clothes on a chair, thoughts of Dorothy filled Etty's mind and the despair of losing a beloved sister dragged at her heart. She shook her head impatiently. She wasn't the only one suffering in this war. Other women had lost loved ones, killed in action or in a bombing raid—and they'd feel their loss this Christmas too. It didn't do to be maudlin or wallow in bitterness; best to buck up and get on with the job of living.

Etty counted her blessings. She had the dearest husband, two gorgeous kiddies, and a home—and, of course, May, who was loyal to a fault and the best friend anyone could wish for. A pang of remorse stabbed Etty at the secret she carried but could never voice. Her stomach lurched at the thought of the consequences if the truth was ever revealed.

She went into the scullery and began gathering the ingredients to make a Christmas pudding. She yawned; it had been a long day and she was at her beam end. The pudding could wait. With the girls asleep, and Trevor no longer snoring, the peace was bliss. Time for a cuppa and catch up with last night's *Gazette*.

Minutes later, supine on the couch, cup of hot tea in one hand, Etty turned the pages of the newspaper with the other.

She read an article about a woman who had heard a broadcast message from her serviceman husband on the *Greetings from East Africa* programme. How thrilling for her, Etty thought. She then scoured the "articles for sale" column and then the births, deaths and marriages.

A name in the deaths column made her heart skip a beat. She stiffened; it couldn't be…

Her stomach clenched in fear, Etty checked the list again.

It was.

*

The dark enveloped May as she came out of the Westoe Picture House—known locally as the Chi because of its location in Chichester Road. Deciding to walk home as it was only a few stops, May linked arms with Alec for security, nervous walking in the blackout.

Alec, gentleman that he was, appeared to understand and made sure he walked on the outside and kept far away from the kerb.

"It's a bugger to see when there's no moon shining," he grumbled. "I'm gonna switch on me torch."

A dim light appeared on the ground.

He patted her arm. "You're safe with me."

A motor car crawled by on the road.

"Where exactly is this school of yours in Dunlop Road?" he asked.

May explained where it was.

"Will you get time off at Christmas?"

"I don't know yet. All I do know is I'll work regular hours in school and will finish at five. All that will change if I move into the hospital nurses' home when I'll work shifts."

"Why 'if'?"

"Because if I don't pass the finishing exams after three months in school, I won't be allowed to continue."

Alec was quiet as he digested this piece of information.

They walked on in silence for a while. Then she asked, "What will you do at Christmas?"

"The usual. Have dinner with Nana. I don't know after that. Christmas is for bairns."

May's thoughts turned to Derek. She worried he'd get upset at spending Christmas without Mam. Would he miss his so-called sister? she wondered. She knew she would sorely miss him. But living on the farm there was the compensation of plentiful food—eggs, butter, milk and probably juicy slices of chicken for Christmas dinner. May's mouth salivated—the lad was better off there than at home, but that wouldn't stop May pining for her son.

To distract herself, she told Alec, "Did you know, when the Blitz was on, Christmas was called Blitzmas and it stuck ever since with some folk—including my mam."

Not this year, she thought with a heavy heart.

"I wish I'd met your ma. It sounds like she had a heart o' gold." Alec had the knack of saying exactly the right thing. May squeezed his arm.

He told her, "I'll take care of you—see you through this Christmas."

She couldn't see his handsome face but she imagined the intensity of his expression.

She mustn't lead him on, May's conscience told her—but she did feel comfortable with him and even in the short time they'd spent together she felt he sometimes took over a little too much. Yet she had to admit that it was a relief to let someone else make the decisions at times.

"Like you let me," Mam said in May's head.

As they walked past the tall terraced houses, with curtains firmly drawn, May realised just how much she'd relied on Mam. Now that she was going to be working at the hospital she'd need to learn to rely on own instincts a bit more. She was beginning to feel confident she'd manage, and, with these positive thoughts swirling in her mind, she became her optimistic self again.

"Won't it be lovely when we have tree lights aglow in King Street's shop windows again?"

"That's what I'm beginning to love about you, darlin'... it's the little things that please."

May wasn't too sure about the endearment, but Alec didn't really mean it. Did he?

"I wonder what the war situation will be this time next year?"

May didn't answer. She had faith and didn't doubt that with God and good on their side, this time next year they'd be celebrating.

"It's encouraging what the bloke said tonight on the Pathé news"—Alec's voice sounded positive—"that Jerry has been pushed back on all fronts."

In May's mind's eye, she saw again all the black and white images on the screen of scrawny, tired-looking Allied soldiers, looking old beyond their years.

"All I know," she told him, "is thank God the town hasn't had a major raid since May."

There had been so much going on in her life—Mam's death, Derek's choosing not to come home, Dad throwing her out—that May hadn't followed the news reports recently. They say troubles come in threes, and May had had her share. As she thought of the future, her resolve strengthened. Life couldn't get any worse. And tomorrow, starting at the hospital, marked the start of a new phase in her life.

But fate didn't deal in numbers.

They stood outside Etty's front door. May didn't know whether to invite Alec in or not, but he made the decision for her.

"I won't keep you when you've got a big day tomorrow, starting at the hospital. And your last shift to get through before that."

May was amazed he had such a good memory for everything she told him about her life, but found it endearing.

"I couldn't get out of working at the factory tonight." May didn't admit that she hadn't told anyone she was leaving.

"I would've shirked . . . told them I was sick."

May was shocked because that was downright dishonest. She struggled to think of what to say.

"When will I see you again?" he asked.

"I don't know."

"You can write to me once you're settled."

"I don't have your address."

"Here, I've written it down." Alec reached into his jacket pocket and pressed a piece of paper into her hand.

He thought of everything.

He leaned forward and she felt his warm lips on her cheek.

"See you later," he called as he walked away.

As she entered the narrow hallway, a heaviness in the atmosphere told May something was wrong. Her instinct was confirmed as she walked into the kitchen. Etty was standing by the mantelpiece, red-eyed, her face ashen.

"Whatever's wrong?" May hurried towards her friend. She looked around. "Is it Trevor? Where is he?"

Etty drew a deep breath and appeared to collect herself. "Gone to bed. These six o'clock shifts play havoc with him, and what with Victoria's waking through the night, he's exhausted."

"It's just... you look so upset."

"I'm fine... I—"

"It's Dorothy, isn't it? You're dwelling on Christmas without her."

Etty shook her head, speech beyond her.

"I feel the same about Mam, but Etty, we'll get through it together."

May noticed the makings of a Christmas pudding on the table. She knew from experience that Etty must be upset because nervous activity, especially at this time of night, was how she dealt with difficult times in life.

"Honest... it's nothing to worry over." Etty seemed evasive. "It's... just the time of year, it's got to me."

This May understood, as there were moments when she felt jumpy and jittery at the very thought of the festive season without Mam.

She told Etty, "You wouldn't be normal if you didn't feel this way."

As thoughts of lovable and kind Dorothy came to mind, tears brimmed in May's eyes and she swallowed hard. She missed Dorothy too.

Etty looked hesitant, as though there were something important she wanted to say, then she appeared to change her mind.

"May, sometimes you're too kind for your own good. What would I do without you?"

A cry came from the back bedroom and, like a bullet out of a gun, Etty shot from the room.

When she returned, she was holding a sleepy Norma in her arms. Gorgeous in pink pyjamas, the bairn gave an enormous yawn then nestled her head into her mammy's neck.

"Little tinker." Etty sat in the easy chair in front of the fire. "She always tries it on this time of night. I don't dare leave her in case she wakes Victoria. The thing is, I could have done without it tonight. I'm whacked."

Etty still didn't seem herself and May wondered if there was more wrong than she was telling.

Norma sucked her thumb and May took in the homely little scene before her. Etty was good with bairns; she had the patience of Job and strove to keep the two kiddies healthy and happy. Gazing at the fire's hypnotic flames, May found herself thinking about mortality.

"Etty..."

"Yes."

"I've never thought of this before but what if...something happened to you? I mean we both know it can happen and sometimes, like with Mam, when you least expect it. I was thinking... who'd look after the two girls?" She quickly put in, "Because I'm in the same boat with Derek if anything should happen to me."

Etty paused, then looked up at her friend with sad eyes. "I think of it often. With this war on I could be dead at any minute. I'm not scared for me but I can't bear the thought of Norma suffering because she's lost her mammy. I know it's arrogant but nobody could love or look after her as well as me. My worst nightmare would be leaving the pair of them." At the very thought, she clapped a hand on her heart.

"It's the same for me," May agreed, "I mean, I know Derek doesn't want me now but there might come a day when he's in trouble and needs me. The Talbots are getting on; there'll be a time when they won't be capable of looking after him."

"Her upstairs"—Etty raised her eyes to the flat above where her mother-in-law lived—"would want to take over, but with her ill health and her age, she'd flag at the first hurdle. As for Trevor... he's a decent man with the best intentions but you never know how life will pan out... God forbid, he might get killed or... meet someone else." Lovingly, she stroked her fingers through Norma's fine blonde hair. "I can't see him bringing up two bairns on his own, especially when they're..." she flushed and didn't go on.

"Trevor is a good man... and Etty, he'd stand by both of them."

Etty bit her lip uncertainly. "He only took on the responsibility of Victoria because of me."

They stared at each other and the fear in their eyes spoke volumes.

May had a brainwave. "Etty, I've just thought... what if we make a pact? I promise if anything happens to you I'll make it my duty to see both Norma and Victoria are brought up in a secure and loving home." As the idea grew, she just knew it was right; it was fate they were having this conversation. "Will you agree to do the same for Derek?"

To her surprise, Etty hesitated. She wouldn't meet May's eyes. "It's not that simple."

Stunned, May asked, "Why not?"

Etty gazed into the fire and, as if she found the answer there, gave a resolute nod. With Norma's sleepy head on her shoulder, she stood and went over to the table. She picked up the *Gazette*.

"There's something you should know. I wanted to tell you but it didn't seem the time. But now I've changed my mind."

She passed over the newspaper. "Look in the deaths column…
and May, prepare yourself for a shock."

A shadow of fear passed over her, and May did as she was bid.
As she skimmed the names, suspicion grew in her. Then her eyes
locked on a surname she recognised.

*Buckley. September 1943. Billy, beloved son of Ethel and the
late Joseph. Killed in action in Salerno, Italy. He gave his life so
that we might live. Always in our hearts. Mam and sister Emily.*

The words at first didn't sink in. Then, as reality hit, May dropped
the paper and, knees buckling, she dropped onto the couch.

She stared dumbly at Etty.

"I know. I couldn't take it in either." She heaved a troubled
sigh. "I didn't want to tell you… not yet, when you were starting
at the hospital tomorrow. But you mentioning a pact forced my
hand. May… it's time you knew the truth."

Tears seeped from May's eyes. Billy was dead. How could that
be? With his blue, twinkling eyes and cheeky grin, he was always
so vitally alive.

An animal-like howl escaped from somewhere deep within her.

Norma startled awake and began to cry and Etty comforted her.

May's mind was a jumble of thoughts—each one more painful
than the last. She'd rather lose Billy another way; have him marry
someone else rather than rot in the ground in some foreign place
she'd never heard of. She needed Mam, the only person who could
reassure her to go on because without Billy Buckley in the world,
life wouldn't be worth living.

May cried and cried until, weak and spent, she sagged against
the back of the couch.

Etty held out a cup of tea.

May didn't know how much time had passed but she was aware that
Etty, standing before her, didn't have the bairn in her arms any more.

"You've been in a kind of trance," Etty told her. "I do under-stand...I haven't got over the shock either."

As she sipped the tea, a thought struck May's overwhelmed brain. "What did you mean before...it's time I knew the truth?"

An agonised expression crossed Etty's face. She had the guilty look of someone who wished they were somewhere else.

"There's something I have to tell you, and I've never told you before because"—her voice was uncharacteristically low and unsure—"it would only have been to absolve myself." Her eyes widened and pleaded for clemency. "That's not wholly true. Although the truth would have devastated you, I didn't say anything because... I was afraid it would ruin our friendship."

"Etty, you're frightening me. What didn't you tell me?"

Time stood still as they gazed at one another, and May was baffled by Etty's tortured expression. It was as though she didn't know how to phrase the words she needed to say.

"Billy and I...we were attracted to one another, but it went no further than that at first. Then the night of the bombings in October forty-one we...found ourselves in the shelter together. I'd never been so scared; it sounded like the whole of the Luft-waffe had turned up to bomb South Shields market place and the noise of those screaming planes was excruciating. Bombs rained down and we heard buildings falling around us...We thought the end had come...Truly, I thought we were going to die." Biting her lip, Etty appeared reluctant to go on. "Honest to God it...only happened once...but once was all it took." There was a moment of hesitancy when Etty's eyes implored May's. "The result was Norma."

May's mind grappled to take in what Etty was saying. As her wits collected, she grasped the full meaning of the words, and anger—no, rage—boiled in every particle of her being.

"Norma is Billy's daughter?" *Surely not*, her mind screamed. Surely this wasn't real but a nightmare.

Etty nodded. "That's why I hesitated when you wanted me to make a pact. You realise…" Etty gulped. "Derek and Norma are half brother and sister."

The nightmare got worse.

"It's time you knew"—Etty squirmed—"no matter what you think of me."

The rage simmering inside May erupted and spilled into words. "What I think of you Etty, is that you're… despicable. How could you? With Billy, of all people?" As the full implication hit her, May felt as if she'd been punched in the stomach.

"God… how you've deceived me, pretending to be interested in Billy for my sake, when it was all an act for your own benefit. Asking where he was, when he'd be home…" Her voice, hoarse and cold, didn't sound like her own. "I trusted you like a sister, when all the time you were…" Her muddled mind thought of Dad's words. "…being a slut with Billy."

"May don't do this, it isn't like you… you'll be sorry you—"

"Yes, I am sorry! Sorry I believed you were my friend. You betrayed me, Etty, and I don't know who you are any more." Tears leaked from her eyes. "I can never trust you again."

"Please don't say that."

May banished from her mind the fact that Billy had betrayed her too. "You've hurt me badly, and at this minute, Etty, I truly hate you." May raced to the bedroom where a sleeping Trevor, beneath the bed covers, didn't stir. She picked up her packed suitcase and, closing the locks, made for the front door.

Etty was behind her. "Oh! May—don't go, not like this… let's talk."

"There is nothing to say."

"May, please, I need you."

May whipped round. Saw her so-called friend's face crumple. "I'm not your friend any more."

*

As the front door slammed, Etty sagged. Her world had collapsed. Because of her, May was hurt beyond measure. Etty wished she could turn back the clock and put things right. But would she if she could? a small voice in her head asked. She wouldn't have Norma and might never have married Trevor; originally theirs had been a marriage of convenience so that the bairn would have a name and wouldn't be considered a bastard. But time passed and their marriage had grown into one of mutual love and tenderness. Deep inside, Etty felt her life was a spider's web of guilt and betrayal that she'd spun for herself—and she didn't deserve any of the happiness she now experienced.

And life could never now be complete without her dearest, irreplaceable friend May Robinson by her side.

Etty burst into tears.

Later that night, as she slipped between the cold sheets, she stared into the dense darkness.

Trevor stirred, and his breath was warm on her cheek as he said in a sleepy voice, "Night night. Love you."

"Night. Ditto," she answered automatically.

Soon she heard his steady breathing as, peacefully, he slept.

Tomorrow, for Trevor's sake, she'd put on a brave face. He knew, of course, about Billy, but a reminder would never do. She'd told Trevor her infatuation with Billy was over—and so it was, but still when she'd read the report of Billy's death, Etty had been heartbroken. For Billy, though selfish, self-centred and an egotistical cad, was loveable too.

Etty gave a trembly smile. He wouldn't be playing any harps in heaven but, knowing Billy, he'd be chasing an angel or two.

"Goodbye. Rest in peace," she sighed, then snuggled up to her beloved husband.

Etty's last thought before sleep claimed her was a prayer. *Please God one day let May find it in her heart to forgive me.*

CHAPTER NINE

May's last night at the factory was an ordeal. Everything she did was wrong. Etty's revelation consumed her and she felt ill with the upset. May didn't know which part of her so-called friend's disclosure was worse... that she and Billy had been together, that Norma was Billy's daughter or that Etty had kept the truth from her for all this time.

Then, there was the unbearable heartache that Billy was gone forever from her life. He was never really hers, a traitorous voice spoke in her head, otherwise why would he have had sex with May's best friend?

She shook her head to banish the thoughts. She told herself her love for him transcended any transgression.

Her behaviour was erratic at work and loss of concentration was a serious issue working with machinery, so May was obliged to seek out the foreman and tell him she'd had a terrible shock recently and couldn't continue at her station. She asked if she could spend the remainder of the night at her old job in the factory's canteen where she could do no harm.

Things improved in the canteen when May was instructed to dish out the food, then clear dirty dishes from tables. She kept busy but didn't eat breakfast, as the very thought of food made her feel nauseous. When the shift finally finished, there were no farewells, as no one knew May wasn't coming back to work at the factory.

*

As it was too early to report to the hospital, and with nowhere else to go, May put her small suitcase on the pannier at the back of her bike and, securing it with a spring bracket, cycled to the seafront.

There was no one around at that time of morning, so she left her bike leaning against the bandstand wall and went for a bracing walk in the sea air. And when the sun began to rise, May looked out over the sands, past the rolls of barbed wire to miniature ships that sailed on a hazy horizon.

Instead of the solace she expected, May experienced a nervous restlessness that didn't allow her any peace. She couldn't stop thinking of all the people she'd loved and lost.

Gazing into the awakening sky, she began to weep, not for herself but for Billy, for all that might have been ahead in his life.

Sniffing and wiping her eyes, May put personal problems and hurtful memories aside. For today, she reminded herself, was the beginning of something special—a new start in her life that she mustn't jeopardise.

As May walked up the path from the main gate of the hospital, she looked at the imposing red brick building ahead and, apart from a stint in nursing school, her home for the next three years. The small brown suitcase she was carrying contained all her worldly possessions: a black and white photograph of Mam and Derek, one of Billy in uniform, toiletries, trinkets of jewellery, Mam's favourite cardigan that still had a remnant of her smell. There were the essentials she needed for Preliminary Training School too: exercise books, pens, pencils and a cotton drawstring laundry bag onto which May had stitched her name.

The building looked more like a grand house than a hospital, with its peaked portico, lawns and imposing grounds. To the left along a pathway was a low building with trolleys outside carrying laundry bags. To the right was a cluster of grim-looking stone buildings and May presumed these must be part of the old workhouse.

Entering the main building, she walked along the busy corridor and, finding the sewing room, she rapped on the door. Her nerves fraught after a night of no sleep, panic seized her and she was overcome with the compulsion to run away.

May took deep calming breaths. She was not going to allow nerves or grief to spoil her life's dream.

She entered the cramped and cluttered sewing room. Two middle-aged women sitting in front of sewing machines looked up, bored expressions on their faces.

May smiled at a grey-haired lady who wore a tweed skirt and white blouse with Peter Pan collar.

"Nurse Robinson?" The woman pushed back her chair and stood.

May nodded.

"I'm Mrs. Harrison." She gave a brief smile. "You're the last to arrive. If you go into the cubicle, you'll find your uniform dress on the chair."

As May changed clothes, Mrs. Harrison talked non-stop from the other side of the curtain about absolutely nothing that May could relate to; her family, the state of her flat as she was a working wife, her good-for-nothing husband who listened to war news on the wireless for most of the day. May was too polite to interrupt.

When she emerged from behind the cubicle curtain, dressed in a purple and white striped short-sleeved dress with starched cuffs and collar and waistband that fastened with a stud, the other machinist rolled her eyes, as if to say she had to endure this perpetual talking all day.

"Now dear"—Mrs. Harrison became surprisingly officious—"this is your apron and headwear. It's tricky to make but you'll soon get the hang of it." Two starched cloths were placed in May's hand. "Have you got a watch, dear, and scissors? Good. Put them in your top pocket." May did as she was bid. "You'll find a spare uniform piled on your bed when you get to your room at Preliminary Training School. Oh, and make sure the seams of your stockings are straight. Matron is a stickler. And, before I forget, take this." She took a black, coarse woollen cape from the back of a chair. "I'd keep an eye on it if I were you; capes are like gold dust and more often than not go missing. Now, off you go, dear, to Matron's office."

"Come in," called an assured voice.

May straightened her back and entered Matron's office. Four girls, whom May recognised from the entrance exam, stood in a line before Matron's large desk, which was piled high with neatly stacked papers.

Matron's eyes travelled along the line. "Welcome, nurses. You are in the same set." Standing poker straight behind the desk, Matron clasped her hands behind her back and cut an imposing figure. Face impassive, she explained what was expected of a probationer nurse. They were never to address a Sister by name; they were always to report to Sister when both going on and off duty and they must present themselves in an exemplary fashion on all occasions, especially outdoors, where they must walk in pairs.

She finished, "The requisite is that you obey the rules. Because blunders can do Jerry's job for him and cost patients' lives." She pinned each nurse with an unnerving stare. "Are you all sworn to follow hospital rules?"

"Yes, Matron," they chorused.

"Always remember that the uniform you wear represents Edgemoor Hospital. From now on your behaviour must be beyond reproach." A hint of a smile touched her lips. "Only your best is good enough...don't let us down."

Matron told them to find the switchboard at the main hospital entrance where a head porter would see they were shown to Preliminary Training School.

Pride mingled with fear surged through May. She didn't know the first thing about tending the sick and, for all she knew, she might panic at the first sign of blood, or worse, be paralysed with fright in an emergency. What use had she been when Mam had tripped and fallen to her death? May's confidence plummeted.

But then, as she filed out of Matron's office, the thought hit her that she was starting out on a dream come true.

"Life is what you make it, our May," Mam's voice said in her head.

May made a vow. From this day on, not only would she be dedicated to her vocation but she would also provide for Derek, so that he'd never want for anything. And one day, she didn't know when, or how, they would be together.

Feeling conspicuously new and awkward in her uniform, she followed the rest of her set to the switchboard and to the start of a new life.

Edgemoor General Hospital had been built in the countryside on the southern edge of the town. It was once known as the "workhouse," and had been home to some twelve hundred paupers (men, women and children), excluding those unfortunates who were sent to the "lunatic block." May had heard tales of the harsh and cruel conditions towards inmates. The site had only become "Edgemoor Institution and General Hospital" in the early thirties.

As she followed the others along the corridor she marvelled at the bustle of the hospital, the smells—beeswax polish mingled with medical odours she couldn't define—and thought it only right and proper that the extensive site, after its detestable past, should now be a centre for the injured and infirm.

John, the head porter, a man with a perpetual frown and the look of a man who didn't take his responsibilities lightly, was in charge of porters and orderlies.

He told the probationer nurses, "I'd put yer cloaks on if I was you, it's perishing outside."

He then hailed a porter who was passing in the corridor. "Richard, escort these nurses to Parklands, if you would."

May followed Richard, who wore a brown overall over his clothes and had a no-nonsense attitude and an intelligent gleam in his brown eyes. He led the women out of the hospital gates over the road, down a street opposite, then over a main road.

One of the set, a tall girl who looked younger than May, with legs that appeared to go up to her armpits and transparent baby-blue eyes, pulled an approving face as she followed him.

"He's a smasher," she mouthed to the others.

Richard, tall and slim, with expressive eyes, was rather handsome. But May would die of embarrassment if the fellow turned and saw them all eyeing him up and down.

He came to a halt outside an impressive detached house on a corner of Dunlop Road. The red brick, three-storey house with peaked roof and attic windows that gazed out over the rooftops, stood in its own grounds.

"This is it, then." The porter nodded goodbye to them and, with long strides, he was gone.

As May went through the front porch and into the large lounge, she was glad to see a fire burning merrily in the hearth—a welcome sight on this perishing December morning. Through a window she could see a walled garden. The house, May decided, with its traditional charm and homely wood-burning smell, was much more comfortable than she'd anticipated.

The five girls who stood in the lounge looked awkwardly at one another, as if each of them were willing someone else to be the first to speak.

"I'm Valerie Purvis." Baby-blue-eyes took up the challenge. "I've joined the nursin' profession to be out of me house. It's filled chock o' block with me brothers and sisters...I'm the bloody eldest and just a dogsbody."

She laughed, and before the others had a chance to introduce themselves, Sister Chilvers, whom they'd met before at the entrance test, came into the room.

"Welcome to Parklands," Sister's soft, though no-nonsense, voice greeted them. "Follow me. I'm here to give you a guided tour."

The thing that struck May most about Parklands was the size of the place. There was a huge kitchen with sparkling pans hanging from hooks on the walls and utensils in jugs. A smaller room was, according to Sister, used for the purpose of practising cooking patient meals. Off the corridor were doors leading to a practical room, classroom and dining room, whose long table was set for six people.

May was shown to a draughty bedroom off the first-floor landing, with three beds. Her roommates were to be Valerie and a rather plump redhead with enormous freckles peppering her face.

She smiled at May. "Maureen Gardener," she said, as she looked around the sparse room. "This basic accommodation will do me nicely."

She spoke with a refined voice.

"Not me. I had in mind a bit more comfort." Valerie dumped her case on the end bed facing the window that had a spectacular view of the garden. She checked the uniform piled on the bed. "This is mine." Gazing around the room, with its large wardrobe and chest of drawers and a locker by each bed, Valerie frowned. "They haven't gone to town on furniture, have they? And wouldn't you think they'd give us a dressing table rather than just a mirror on the wall?"

"I doubt if we'll have time to dress up and go anywhere," Maureen said.

Valerie sniffed. "Speak for yersel'. There again, on thirty shillings a month, I suppose you're right. I practically earned that hairdressing."

"I think the pay's fair," May piped up. Then she wished she hadn't when she saw the derogatory stare Valerie gave her, as if she'd just crawled out of the drains. Hesitantly, May went on, "Considering we get free food and lodgings…besides our uniform."

May could have added that at this stage in life she was only too glad to have a roof over her head.

The threesome made their way down to the lounge and joined the other two student nurses, who huddled by the fire.

The thin, pasty-faced girl introduced herself as Jennifer—Jenny for short. The other nurse, with black hair and alert eyes behind round spectacles, said that her name was Eileen.

There was a rustle at the doorway and Sister Chilvers came in. "Nurses, pay attention. I'm here to inform you of hospital rules." Her expression was business-like. "The first lesson you must learn is to stand when any Sister enters the room."

Collectively, the five of them stood to attention.

"You may sit. You will gather in the classroom at eight-thirty sharp." Sister Chilvers' gaze sought each nurse in turn. "Classes are till one, then an hour for dinner and you will finish at six. During your three-month preliminary period, you will study courses in anatomy, physiology, sociology, hygiene and practical nursing. All your meals will be served in the dining room. If you are late you will miss a meal." She pinned each nurse with a stare. "To work at Edgemoor Hospital, we expect our nurses to be dedicated and of sturdy character. Your patients and your profession must come first in your life. Do I make myself clear?"

"Yes, Sister," they chanted.

"After your preliminary training period you must pass a class certificate. If you fail you will not receive a second chance."

Was May the only one to go pale at the thought of failure?

Sister's face softened. "Study hard and the exams won't be a problem. I'm here to help you pass...we're in great need of nurses." She sobered. "But I must tell you that in my experience some of you won't have the commitment or ability it takes to complete the training."

May glanced at the others and wondered if they felt the same hysteria at the enormity of what was expected that she did. For a start, she'd have to look up physiology and sociology in a medical dictionary in the library, as she hadn't a clue what the words meant.

Sister handed out a timetable and instructions that included laundry rules, a ten o'clock curfew, and lights out ten-thirty.

As May took hers, she thrust out her chin. She would do whatever it took to pass the exams.

That night as she lay in the single bed, the blackout curtains closed and the dark pressing in on her, the terrible truth loomed large in her mind. Billy was dead and she'd lost her best friend.

Suffocating with insecurities, all of a sudden she didn't feel so self-assured.

Life at Parklands was an eye-opener. On the practical side, May was taught, amongst many other things, bed-making, how to cook light patient meals and wash bedpans. On the medical side, she learned how to take a temperature and pulse, set medical trays and take patient notes. At night after supper she tackled the ever-increasing studying.

The set of five nurses was a diverse lot but May soon got to know the others well, so intensely were they living and working together. Though living in such close proximity brought its own problems. Rows started and tempers flared, but, in the main, except for Valerie (who at times seemed to be looking for an argument), everyone got along, and if things got too heated there was always Home Sister—Sister Chilvers—to rely on for impartiality.

One morning at breakfast, prayers over, Sister Chilvers declared, "Excuse me, nurses, but I've a streaming cold and won't be joining you for breakfast. I have a special treat in my quarters. An orange, would you believe? I'm hoping the vitamin C will do me good. I'll be with you later to tell you which ward you'll be allotted."

Because of food rationing—two ounces of butter, one ounce of cheese, one egg, meat, sugar, jam, and the list went on—food was never far away from May's mind. Today's breakfast of bread, margarine that came in a block and a foul concoction of dried egg mixture, didn't hit the spot, and despite her hunger she toyed with her food. She gazed out of the window where Jack Frost had been out, leaving his ice designs.

"I hope I'm not on a children's ward...not when I've just escaped our lot." Valerie sighed a sigh of the damned.

"Valerie, I can't help feeling worried about you. I'm not so sure you want to be a nurse," May replied with the honesty the others would learn to take for granted.

"Huh!" Valerie glowered at May. Knife clattering to the plate, she scraped back her chair and flounced from the room.

The others exchanged glances.

"I hope her mood improves when she reaches the ward...or else she'll be for it," Maureen remarked dryly.

Later that morning, Sister Chilvers, eyes watering and nose red, informed them which ward they'd be on. May, when she learned she was on the men's orthopaedic ward, felt panicked as she'd no idea what to expect. But that was what she was here for, she remonstrated with herself, to learn.

"Report to John, the head porter," Sister told them, her blocked nose making her voice thick. "He'll tell you how to find your ward."

The five of them, capes wrapped around their shoulders, made their way to the hospital where John stood inside the porter's lodge and peered at them through the window.

"I'll do better than that," he said putting down the telephone. He caught the eye of a passing porter. "Richard...look sharpish. Show this set of nurses to their wards."

Richard didn't show any sign that he'd met them before as he led the way. May, being the last, was taken through Outpatients outside, down a ramp and over a pathway to a tall red-brick building. Opening the door, the porter stood back and nodded in a solemn way. His gorgeous, shining brown eyes looked at her earnestly.

"Sister Jordan runs the men's orthopaedic ward." His voice was deep and mellow.

As May entered the corridor with its faded green, chipped paint, she got a blast of a meaty smell. The ward must be near the kitchens, she thought.

Richard led the way along the corridor and then inclined his head towards the double doors that led to the ward. "Sister Jordan's a stickler for discipline but she's fair with it."

"Blimey, my first day on a ward. I could do without a hard taskmaster."

Richard was tall, she noticed, and sinewy, with surprisingly broad shoulders, though sometimes his expression changed from impartial to that of guarded. He didn't answer, his lips clamped firmly shut. Giving a shrug, he left.

May pushed the doors open and made her way towards the ward. There she found a large room with slim iron-railed beds either side, each of them occupied by patients tucked neatly under green counterpanes. In the middle were a few comfy chairs, a medical cabinet on wheels, and a marble-topped desk for the nurses. A Christmas tree the same height as May stood beside the desk, colourful baubles dangling from its branches, a silver star at the top. Paper chains hung around the walls and a banner emblazoned with the message "Merry Christmas" hung across the middle of the ward.

A pallid, sober-faced young man, part of his leg missing beneath his knee, sat incongruously beneath the banner in a wheelchair. May felt a wave of deep sorrow for him; what he must have been through didn't bear thinking about.

A woman who May presumed must be Sister Jordan walked towards her. What she lacked in stature she more than made up for in feisty character. A bristling sort of woman, Sister wore a navy blue uniform dress and starched apron, her cap perched on tawny-coloured hair.

She gestured to May to come forward. "Nurse Robinson, I assume."

"Yes, Sister. Reporting for duty."

"Tell me"—Sister's tone was sharp—"what makes you think you've got what it takes to become a nurse?"

May, taken by surprise, couldn't think of an answer.

"Be quick, Nurse, I haven't got all day."

"I just want to work in a job that matters, Sister."

"What's in it for yourself?"

"Erm . . . to feel good about meself."

Sister regarded her keenly. "The word, Nurse, is *myself.*" She made to move, then hesitated. "It isn't that your dialect is wrong—indeed you should be proud of your heritage—but it's important that patients from other areas understand us in their hour of need."

"Of course, Sister."

Sister turned on her heel and strode towards the office. "Time will tell, Nurse Robinson," she called over her shoulder, "if you've chosen wisely or not."

May was set to work on menial tasks on the ward—making beds, washing locker tops, serving meals—and she felt as though she was being used as a ward maid. She soon realised, however, how essential this work was, and that the responsibilities of patient care took time to learn. Gradually, under the watchful eye of Sister Jordan, she was given more duties.

At first May suffered from lack of confidence. She was eager to learn but worried that she wasn't getting things right which made her overly self-conscious. It only took one indignant stare from Sister to turn May's insides to jelly and she was all fingers and thumbs.

One day, as May did the bottle and bedpan round, a job that no matter how many times she did the task, it still made her squirm, especially when it was an old gent like this who couldn't manage, she was so embarrassed she averted her eyes.

The old gent looked up at her with weak soulful eyes. "Hawway, hinny, you've seen it all before. And if you haven't then take no notice o' mine 'cos it's a big disappointment."

His pyjama jacket open, his body emaciated and shrunken, he was a sorry sight. May could see each one of his ribs. As she helped with the glass bottle, acutely uncomfortable, her face reddened.

He shook his head. "That was supposed to make yi' laugh and feel better, Nurse."

May was taken aback. How kind of the old gent to want to make her feel better.

"Believe me, pet…" He lowered his voice. "I'm more mortified than you. And if you don't mind me sayin', take no notice of us fellas…we're all mouth but underneath we're scared for what's in store." As he freed himself from the bottle, he nodded. "You're an angel in disguise, for doin' a job like this." His wizened face gave an abashed smile as he handed her the urine-filled bottle.

May felt ashamed; never again would she allow a patient to see her true feelings. She was a nurse now, and it was her duty to behave like one.

She placed the bottle on the locker top.

"Mr. Townsend," she told the old man, as she helped pull up his pyjamas bottoms and made him comfortable beneath his blanket again, "we nurses are too busy to notice anything but the job in hand, don't you know," she finished with a wink.

As she walked away Mr. Townsend guffawed. "That's the ticket, Nurse."

Sister Jordan made sure May was taught hospital rules, discipline, and medical procedures. May learned not to flinch when patients returned to the ward from surgery, as she knew her reaction to gruesome wounds, disfigurement and amputations was important to the patients' confidence and recovery.

May wasn't supposed to converse with patients (especially about personal matters) unless discussing their medical care or taking case notes—like their family history. But as she grew more competent and less afraid of doing the wrong thing she began to question the rules. Hadn't Mr. Townsend said that beneath their tough exterior the men were scared? These men—some servicemen—needed extra care and attention to help them on the road to recovery.

May began to have confidence in her role as a nurse. When she put on her uniform, it was almost as if she changed mentally and became the part she was playing. She left the doubtful and immature May behind and took on the role of Nurse Robinson. Patient care brought out the maternal side in her and began to feel like a welcome responsibility. She became her patients' protector and did her utmost to make their stay on the ward go smoothly.

At breakfast one morning at Parklands, Maureen appeared looking anguished.

"What's up?" May asked.

"Didn't you hear the news this morning?"

May shook her head. "I was late and had to dash to get ready."

"Apparently, last night over four hundred bombers were despatched to raid Berlin. Twenty-five planes were shot down over enemy territory and a further twenty-nine planes journeying home crashed. Some ran out of fuel as they searched for an airfield to land in." Maureen shook her head. "There was such dense fog last night. Those poor boys, their last moments don't bear thinking about, or their families' suffering."

May shied away from these thoughts. She wouldn't get maudlin—it wasn't her tragedy. If any of the survivors came to the hospital her task would be to help them recover, and to see they got reunited with loved ones.

"I wonder if any of the airmen will come here?"

She soon found out.

Jimmy, a rear gunner, was admitted to the ward with a broken ankle. He had bailed from his burning plane as it came over land. He was considered the lucky one, the only member of his crew to survive. But the poor boy's face was so badly disfigured, he didn't think so. He didn't want to see anyone. He wished he'd stayed in the plane and ended it all.

But Jimmy, a fighter, grew stronger as time went by and was eventually going to be transferred to have surgery to reconstruct his disfigured face.

"You're alive and you've kept your sight," May told him, as she looked at the gauze mask he insisted he wore to cover his face, "that's what matters to those who love you."

"I've been told, Nurse," he said with a southern accent, "I've a long haul of operations ahead of me. I know I won't end up no Prince Charming," he joked but May heard the catch in his voice. "All I want is to look... presentable." He gave a heavy sigh. "That's what counts."

Although he was doing a man's job Jimmy seemed little more than a boy, and May sensed he had a rascally spirit that reminded her of Billy. But there was no way could she have romantic feelings for him as he was likened to a young brother.

May was choked. She admired Jimmy for his courage and determination because she'd witnessed all the pain and suffering he'd been through. She stole spare moments to strike up conversation with him, getting him to talk about himself and his life before the war and his family. She saw him visibly relax as he talked about his private life.

As the days went by, the more she got to know him, the more upset she felt for him when he got so down he didn't want to speak to anyone.

"My office, Nurse Robinson," Sister commanded one day as May made beds with another nurse.

May didn't like the ominous tone in Sister Jordan's voice. As she stood worrying outside the office door, she tried to think what hospital rule she could, unwittingly, have broken.

"Enter, Nurse Robinson."

Sister Jordan was writing at her desk. She looked up, her face stern. "Nurse, I observed you fraternising with a patient." She paused, as if giving May time to comprehend the heinousness of her crime. "We must only speak to patients about their treatment. Understood, Nurse?"

"Yes, Sister."

"I'll overlook the misdemeanour this time and I won't report to Matron."

"Thank you, Sister."

"Another thing." Sister fixed May in her probing stare again. "It doesn't pay to get emotionally involved with patients."

"I understand, Sister."

"See that you do. That's all, Nurse Robinson."

"I think Sister's right," Maureen whispered that night.

The three nurses sprawled on May's bed in cotton dressing gowns over pyjamas, with blankets wrapped round them as the weather outside was beastly cold. The room, unlike downstairs where Jenny and Eileen had the luxury of a cast iron radiator, had no heating. "We shouldn't get involved."

It was nearly ten thirty, so they kept an ear out for Night Sister, making her rounds for lights out.

Maureen continued, "I know it's difficult not to get close to the patients but consider this. What if you became attached and then the patient died? You'd be heartbroken and wouldn't be able to do your job properly. It's not fair on the other patients who need you. My way of helping is to say a prayer."

May liked Maureen best. She was an only child and you could tell she was used to having nice things. Her posh voice reeked of a good education but she wasn't remotely spoilt, her feet were firmly on the ground.

"Huh!" Valerie said indignantly. "You try tellin' that to some poor lass who's just lost her bairn and needs a shoulder to cry on." Valerie was assigned to Maternity and, though she wasn't allowed in the delivery room, she reckoned the screams she'd heard from that place had put her off marriage and having children of her own for life.

"Mind you," she told the other two, "that doesn't mean I'm not goin' to have a try of...you know what."

"How can you be sure you won't get pregnant?" From Maureen's tone, May guessed she was a little appalled.

Valerie raised her eyes. "This isn't the dark ages. Lads know how to take care of that side of things."

May was transported back to that day on Cleadon Hills with Billy Buckley when she'd thought the same thing—and the result was Derek.

"Me mam's had six bairns," Valerie told them, "and she telt us childbirth is like shellin' peas." She looked disbelieving. "That's not what I hear. It sounds like a horror picture." She shuddered. "Anyway, has anyone here gone all the way?"

May hoped she wasn't blushing, giving the game away. She was torn. On the one hand she was nervous about letting slip how she knew about such matters but on the other, she felt a responsibility to warn Valerie not to be so naïve.

"Girls shouldn't rely on lads to be accountable...I mean..." She felt she was in the spotlight as all eyes turned on her. "...it's us who would suffer in the end."

"As for praying," Valerie went on, ignoring her, a hint of scorn in her expression, "that doesn't help."

"How can you say that?" Maureen cried.

"Because it's never helped me." Valerie, for once, letting her defences down, looked vulnerable.

Surprisingly, Maureen didn't try to persuade her to say more and only gave a sympathetic nod. She exuded tranquillity, which May envied. She knew if ever she needed a listening ear she would be able to rely on Maureen.

As the wind whistled through the sash window and the blackout curtains billowed, Maureen gave a heavy sigh. "This isn't my first choice of vocation. I wanted to be a nun."

"Crikey!" Valerie looked horrified. "Why aren't you, then?"

"Mum. She was devastated when I told her. She objected to her only daughter being married to Christ. She said I'll do more good if I'm a nurse. So here I am."

"She has a point," May said.

"We made a pact. I'm to be a nurse till the end of the war and if I still feel the same about being a nun, then Mum will give her blessing."

"Blimey. Don't let Matron find out or there'll be ructions on. *A nurse*"—Valerie mimicked Matron's voice—"*doesn't think of monetary gain or do this work for any other reason than because it's her life's vocation.*"

May regarded Maureen. "What kind of job did you do before now?"

"That's the trouble—I didn't. We live in Cleadon village and Dad owns a clothes factory in the town which mostly manufactures uniforms. I was sent to learn shorthand and typing and when Dad's secretary left to enlist in the Women's Royal Army Corps, I was volunteered to do the job. I'm an only child, you see, and though my parents are good and loving they don't like to let me out of their sight. But they don't understand that working in a factory isn't what I'm meant to do with my life."

It must be nice to have someone who cared, May thought, even if it was overprotective parents. All she'd wanted was for Dad to take an interest in her.

After the others retired to their beds, May, crawling between cold sheets, thought of Jimmy, who was to be transferred to the plastic surgery burns unit at East Grinstead tomorrow. Though she was sad, because she'd become attached to the lad and knew she would probably never see him again, the move would be best for all concerned. Jimmy would start his facial reconstruction and May wouldn't be emotionally involved. She vowed never to be so close to a patient again as they became like family and it was far too painful.

Her spirits low, May found herself thinking about the manner in which soldiers died. She prayed to God Billy hadn't suffered and that the end was quick.

Tossing and turning in bed, May's thoughts turned to Alec Hudson and she found herself smiling. Though he could be impudent, he was also capable of being gentlemanly and considerate—and he got full marks for being persistent.

As her lids drooped, May remembered she'd promised to write to him when she'd settled in at the hospital. Her last thought before sleep claimed her was that she would like to get to know him better.

CHAPTER TEN

The first weeks at Parklands became a round of long, tiring days. What with work on the ward, lessons and studying by torch light till the early hours, May suffered from lack of sleep. She was prone to heavy colds in winter and worried she might be stricken with one now. And with a shortage of nurses—many had left to serve in the Queen Alexandra's Imperial Military Nursing Service (QAIMNS)—May felt she couldn't ask for time off.

One evening before Christmas, when unusually both roommates were out, May planned an early night with a stone hot water bottle. As she drew back the covers to collect the cold bottle to fill, someone rapped at her door. May was surprised to see Eileen from downstairs, dressed in mufti, standing there, polishing her spectacles with a handkerchief. Eileen was rather aloof but a clever lass too; her hand was always the first to shoot up in class whenever a consultant asked a question in a lecture.

She squinted at May. "I've just arrived back and I don't want trouble, but there's a lad outside called Alec who says he wants a word with you."

Without further ado, Eileen put her spectacles on, then turning on her heel, she rushed for the stairs.

At a loss to know what Alec was doing here, May grabbed her cloak and made her way downstairs. She opened the door and went out into the street. The night was jewelled with stars, and she saw, in the dusky light, a figure standing beneath a tree.

She hissed, "What are you doing here, Alec?"

He strode towards her. "I thought I'd surprise yi'."

"You did that. Only, lads aren't allowed anywhere near the school. You'll get me into trouble."

"Sounds like you're in prison."

She saw a scrape on his chin where he'd cut himself shaving. May was touched he'd felt the need to impress her.

"You didn't write." He sounded peeved. "I went to the flat in Whale Street because I thought that's where you lived."

"I don't."

"That friend of yours answered the door. She said you hadn't been in touch since you started here. Did you tell her to say that to put me off?"

At the mention of her former friend, May experienced a pang of sorrow which she quickly dismissed.

"I would never," she told him. If Alec only knew—he'd been the last person on her mind at that distressing time. "Look, I'm sorry I didn't get in touch but so much has been going on recently, what with settling in and learning the ropes at the hospital. I have thought of you, Alec, but to be honest I simply forgot I'd promised to get in touch."

"I forgive yi'." He put a possessive arm around her shoulders. "We're together now. That's all that counts."

She asked, "Was there a special reason you wanted to see me?"

"I wanted to carry on where we left off." He turned her chin up with a finger and gave a playful grin. "Did you miss me?"

Although May was enjoying the cuddle, she began to grow increasingly uncomfortable.

"Alec, you can't stay. I've told you, lads aren't allowed to hang around here."

"Blimey." He removed his arm. "It's like you live in a monastery. Tell us when your next day off is, then I'll go."

"I've just had one."

"We'll meet up after work one night."

"Alec, I can't. I've got a mountain of work to catch up with."

"Saturday's Christmas Day," he told her. "I'm off work. How about we meet up then?"

Christmas was her next day off, and May had no one to spend it with. Her intention was to do some studying. But, on second thoughts, all she'd do was spend the day thinking what ifs, about Dad, Derek, Etty and the bairns—Norma in particular, as she'd grown fond of the little girl. At the realisation that all ties with her were now cut, a pang of sadness overcame May. She'd known the bairn since the day she was born.

Over these last few days May had explored how she felt about Norma being Billy's. But she'd discovered that it hadn't changed how she felt about her. May smiled as an image of Norma played in her mind's eye. She couldn't help her parentage.

May shivered.

"Are you all right?" Alec's features creased in concern.

"Tired, that's all."

"Get yourself in the warm," he commanded. "We'll meet at half one on Christmas Day. I'll have had a kip by then and dinner with Nana."

Alec was companionable and it was nice to have someone to go places with but May had to be honest. "Alec…I have to tell you. I really like your company but that's as far as I want to go because—"

"For now," he said, then backtracked. "It's just a date, not a proposal. I'll settle for enjoying each other's company and see how things go."

She nodded.

"We'll meet at the Chi roundabout." He hesitated, then, with a brief nod, he strode away, and the night swallowed him up.

May was in school for the following two days. On the third day, back on the ward, wary of Sister Jordan and her pernickety ways, May thought it best to keep busy in the treatment room.

The consultant surgeon, Mr. Leonard, was doing his round on the ward, his entourage following him and Sister Jordan hovering at his heels. The great man wasn't interested in mere mortals like May, and so it was best she kept out of the way.

As Mr. Leonard deigned to stand at the patient's bedside, even the most outspoken of them were struck dumb. May was dumbfounded how Mr. Leonard could conduct his consultations without ever once speaking to a patient or meeting their eye.

As she hid in the treatment room, Sister's words played in May's mind. "A nurse is never seen to be idle." Even if she couldn't see May, Sister would check up on her later.

May opened cupboard doors, checking glass treatment bottles ranged from the smallest to tallest at the back. She swabbed trays with cotton wool dipped in surgical spirit, the strong vapours up her nostrils making her cough. As she worked, her mind drifted to the letter she'd received in the post yesterday from Mrs. Talbot.

She'd reported that while Derek was, of course, grieving his mam, she made sure he had plenty to keep him occupied. And May could be assured that if he cried at night, which was a rarity now, she was at hand to comfort him. Mrs. Talbot suggested that perhaps the time wasn't yet right for May to visit as it might be a reminder of his mam and only upset him. She then went on to report details of Derek's days—he was doing well at school and helped around the farm—and his life, May decided, sounded idyllic.

A picture of Derek being comforted in Maud Talbot's arms played in May's mind and, like the sharp blade of a knife, jealousy sliced through her. But she couldn't compete with what the Talbots had to offer. Ashamed of her jealousy, May reminded herself that with all the death and destruction in today's world, she should be grateful that Derek was safe and happy.

"Nurse Robinson."

May started as Sister Jordan appeared in the treatment room doorway. "You're not paid to daydream."

"Sorry, Sister."

"The consultant has finished his round. Mr. Oliver in bed five didn't have his bed bath this morning...Mr. Leonard arrived early and there wasn't time. Help Nurse Reeves do it now."

"Very well, Sister."

May liked doing bed baths, when the patients visually relaxed and became talkative. She found washing the patients' skin with cloth and soapy water therapeutic, especially the old men who, once they were washed, teeth cleaned and hair combed, looked clean and well cared for.

May made to hurry off.

Sister bristled. "Which reminds me, Nurse. Was that you I saw from the office window running across hospital grounds this morning?"

Blast! May had dawdled over breakfast and had had to run the last few yards to make it to the ward on time.

"Yes, Sister. I—"

"No excuses, Nurse. You know the rules. A nurse is never seen to run except in the case of fire or haemorrhage."

"Yes, Sister."

"Report to my office when you've done." She turned and marched off along the corridor.

After the bustle of the morning and with dinner over, the ward had a somnolent atmosphere. Patients lounged on their beds, snoozing or smoking. One soldier, bound around the chest with bandages, held a cigarette to another's mouth as both his arms were in plaster casts. The fitter men played cards, dominos or a game of chess in the dayroom.

Casualties of all nationalities were admitted to Edgemoor Hospital as the town was a reception centre for wounded servicemen. Soldiers were respectful towards nurses but were wont to have a joke amongst themselves to help keep up spirits. No harm was meant.

As May washed Mr. Oliver's chest, she heard a witty remark to his emaciated-looking and subdued neighbour in the next bed who had a cage over his stump. "Aye, Tommy, both of us are short of a limb but if we stick together, there's hope for us riding a bicycle yet."

May was about to shush the man in question, but refrained as she saw the reaction of the soldier he addressed. The man hadn't uttered a word since his operation, but now his gaunt, white face twisted in a wry grin. Progress indeed.

Having finished the bed bath, the basin of warm water emptied in the sluice, towels, soap, methylated spirit and talcum powder put away, May made her way to Sister's office. Nervously, she smoothed the skirt of her uniform dress before she knocked on the door.

"Enter."

Sister sat behind her desk, spectacles perched on the end of her nose. She folded a sheet of paper and slipped it into a brown manila envelope. As May waited in the spartan, meticulously clean room, she wondered what punishment she'd receive for running in hospital grounds.

Sister Jordan, as the porter had said, was indeed a hard task-master, but asked nothing of her nurses she wouldn't do herself, and beneath the stern exterior beat a compassionate heart. As far as Sister was concerned, in terms of fraternising with the patients, it was a case of do as I say and not what I do. May, on more than one occasion, had noticed Sister having a private, encouraging word with a patient. Neither did Sister shirk her role as educator, teaching her nurses—May included—all she knew.

Sister's lips drew into a thin line. "I've sent for you, Nurse, as I've noticed there are times when you appear distant and deep in thought. Home Sister tells me that she finds the same. No doubt there is a reason"—she held up her hand—"but I do not wish to hear it." Sister sat back in her chair. "We all have problems, Nurse

Robinson, but we must learn to leave them at the ward entrance door. Our patients must always come first. Is that clear, Nurse?"

"It is, Sister."

"It takes time and money to train a nurse and it does the profession no good for them to give up halfway through training."

"I would never, Sister."

"Good. You may go, Nurse."

As May made for the door, Sister returned to the papers on the desk.

"And, Nurse…"

May turned.

"Yes, Sister?"

Sister Jordan looked up and took off her spectacles. "I say this because you have the makings of an excellent nurse. Make sure you don't jeopardise your future. I've seen it happen before."

"Very well, Sister."

May left the room.

She vowed to study every spare minute God gave and pass those dratted class exams.

The next day, May worked the morning shift. After dinner and a few hours studying in her room, she returned to Nightingale Ward at five o'clock ready to learn, as she'd never worked the evening shift.

But the shift proved the same routine. Supper over, dirty dishes and cutlery collected, the trolley gone, lockers wiped, bottle round done, bedridden patients turned, the ward held an expectant atmosphere as patients waited for visiting time to begin.

As a vague smell of minced beef lingered on the ward after the meal, May made for the laundry cupboard where she tidied the few clean pillowslips and counterpanes on the slatted shelves.

Strange, she thought, there were hardly any clean sheets and it would appear no laundry had been delivered today.

Blast! She hoped she wouldn't be sent to borrow laundry from another ward—the staff were never keen.

"So, this is where you're hiding." Staff Nurse, a young woman with an affable smile appeared in the laundry doorway. "I need notes collecting for one of the patients from Casualty."

"I'll go at once, Staff Nurse."

The night was chilly, so May fetched her cape from the staff room and, as she headed for the door, the coarse material made her skin itch.

Outside, a pale moon sailed across a landscape of cloudless sky and as she set off for the hospital's main building, a dark structure in the distance, a pang of loneliness washed over May. Life wasn't the same without Etty. In her mind's eye, she saw the letter she'd received yesterday, lying on the bedside locker top. She knew the letter was from Etty as she recognised her large swirling handwriting—the same as on the couple of others she'd received since she came to Parklands. She'd opened none of them because in truth, May was afraid she'd weaken. The hurt she felt was still raw. She couldn't bring herself to forgive Etty. In May's book friends were like family and there could be no deception or secrets between them.

She reached Outpatients' doorway that led to Casualty and she was just about to open the door when someone inside did it for her.

"Watch out," she cried, as she collided with someone wheeling a trolley.

Subdued torchlight shone on the ground. A face peered at her. "Oh, it's you," a deep male voice said.

She recognised the voice as that of Richard, the porter she'd met before.

"Man! Don't you know there's a war on!" came a vexed shout, making May jump. "Put that light out."

The porter switched the torch off.

Archie, the Air Raid Precautions Warden, doing his rounds, huffed up to them.

"Sorry," they said simultaneously.

May reprimanded herself. She shouldn't apologise for something she hadn't done.

"You should have more sense." A musty smell of damp wool emanated from the ARP warden. "I know we haven't had a raid for some time but that's no excuse. Man, you can't be too careful. What if Jerry has his eye out for South Shields hospital the night?"

Then he was gone into the black night, for the moon had found a cloud to hide behind.

"Who'd have thought the man had a sense of humour." The porter's voice was measured.

"Don't you like him?"

"It's not a case of me liking him." The finality of his tone suggested the subject was closed.

May imagined his lovely brown eyes staring into the darkness. She'd met him a few times throughout the hospital, wheeling a trolley with a stretcher on it, or a patient in a wheelchair. His eyes forever watchful, a glint of recognition shone in them as the two of them passed one another in a corridor. But any conversation between staff was discouraged by Matron.

But here they were now, in the dark and alone.

"How are you getting on in the ward?" he surprised her by asking. Though his voice was hesitant, as if he expected a rebuff.

"As you said, Sister Jordan is a stickler for discipline. But everything she does is for patients' benefit, which is fair enough by me."

"The woman has always treated me right," was his cryptic reply.

"I was terrified that first day."

"I could tell." She heard a smile in his voice. "You've got an expressive face and it showed. I knew nothing I could say would help."

May could listen forever to his soft, well-spoken voice. "Thanks. Mr...."

"Bentley... Richard Bentley. Pleased to make your acquaintance." His voice sounded sincere.

"And you. I'm Nurse Robinson." Immediately she felt daft at being so formal. "May Robinson," she corrected.

May knew she should get back but Richard's laidback, yet intent, manner encouraged her to stay. She liked talking to him.

"On that first day I was convinced I'd get chucked out...that I'd be useless as a nurse."

"Never say that." Sternness crept into his tone. "You're as good as the next. All nurses are angels for the hours they put in and the work they do."

A rather embarrassed silence followed when neither of them knew what to say next.

As the moon came out from behind the clouds again, she saw his outline, his chiselled features and the strength of his jaw.

May wondered about him, why he worked as a hospital porter when most men served in the forces. She shouldn't judge, she remonstrated. Maybe he had bad eyesight or had suffered psychological problems and was unfit to be sent back to duty. She knew from experience that this kind of thing happened in battle as the same had happened to soldiers on the ward. To ask, though, would be too intrusive.

Richard made to push the trolley away but May, curious about the large bag she could make out on the trolley, asked, "Is that bag of laundry I can see for men's orthopaedic? Because I don't believe we've had a delivery today."

"Yep, it's for Nightingale. It got overlooked this morning."

"Good. We need sheets for bed-making tomorrow."

She'd become her formal nurse self again. May was amazed how easily she'd acquired this new side to her personality. "I must get on, Mr. Bentley."

She pushed Outpatients' door open and went inside.

"It's Richard," he called after her.

May collected the patient's notes from Casualty. Returning to the ward, she pushed the inner doors open. Nightingale Ward was filled with visitors (the rule was no more than two to each bed) and had a heightened busyness about it. "A commotion of jabbering noise," as Sister was apt to call it. Prone to a mother-hen attitude at visiting time, Sister's eyes scrutinised each patient in turn through the nurses' station that overlooked the ward. She checked if any patient looked discomfited. Especially soldiers who'd fought on the front and, though physically healing, were still suffering after what they'd witnessed. Many of them were waiting to be transferred to a mental hospital for voluntary treatment. Distraught and exhausted relatives thought jollying their loved ones along was all the poor boys needed.

Sister gestured to May.

May joined her in the station and Sister checked her watch. "Five minutes to go, Nurse, then you can ring the bell. Best to collect the eggs now...make sure they've got names on them."

Lots of relatives brought a precious egg for their loved ones and at breakfast many a dispute was caused if an egg wasn't identified by a pencilled name written on its shell.

Just about to reply, May noticed Sister's eyes sharpen. May followed her gaze.

Richard Bentley was walking onto the ward, and, making his way down towards the second bed where a wheelchair stood, he grasped the handles. He said something to Corporal Jennings, lying in the bed against pillows positioned in an armchair fashion. The Corporal, who was due to go to the plaster room, looked up at Richard and nodded. A visitor, a large fellow with ruddy face sitting in a wooden chair next to the Corporal's bed, stood up suddenly, pushed his belligerent-looking face up to Richard's, and made a remark.

Sister Jordan shot like a bullet out of the station. May, paces behind, was in time to hear the man say, "Fella. I won't tell yi' again. Get yer cowardly self away from me son's bed...else yer for it. Bloody conchie."

May, not sure whether to be more shocked that Richard was a conscientious objector or outraged at Corporal Jennings's dad's behaviour, stopped in her tracks—but not Sister Jordan. Twin spots of red on her cheeks, she stood between the two men.

"Mr. Jennings, isn't it?" Her voice was conciliatory. "I would thank you to consider where you are. This is a hospital ward filled with the sick."

As the visitors looked on, silence encompassed the ward.

The man bristled. "And I'd like you to consider"—he glared at Sister Jordan—"me son 'ere nigh lost a limb fightin' for his country, while this filthy, no-good conchie—"

"Da, don't. You're showing yourself up." Corporal Jennings, too ill to cope, appeared pale and distressed.

Murmurings circled the ward, the tone suggesting many were in agreement with what Mr. Jennings had said.

Sister turned to Richard and gave a surreptitious nod for him to leave. He hesitated, and then with a shrug pushed the wheelchair and walked stiffly up the ward.

"Aye...go on, run away—that's all yer good for...Cowardly sod."

"Mr. Jennings, I'll thank you to leave or else I'll—"

Whatever Sister would do remained a mystery as, at that moment, the chilling wail of the air raid siren sounded.

CHAPTER ELEVEN

At the sound of the siren, adrenalin pumped through May's veins, making her edgy. She remembered the pamphlet about air raid procedure explaining that some patients, for medical reasons, couldn't be moved to the shelter in hospital grounds. Steel helmets and gas masks were to be provided and bedridden patients were to be covered with blankets to protect them from falling debris.

"Nurse Robinson," Sister Jordan's calm but firm voice spoke, "help the men capable of walking into the top shelter. I'll stay here with staff nurse and deal with the situation here."

There was no arguing. "Yes, Sister."

At that moment, the ward doors opened and Richard returned with a wheelchair.

Sister didn't hesitate. "Porter. Take Mr. Hardy in bed five to the top shelter then return to the ward. Meanwhile"—she turned to Mr. Jennings—"there's a job of work to be done. You can either leave the premises or help us here."

Mr. Jennings's bolshie mood subsiding, he gave Richard a sour look.

"I'm stoppin' with me laddie."

In the distance came the drone of enemy planes and the faraway bark of guns on the ground.

Visitors and staff alike began evacuating the ward. Richard lifted an infirm serviceman from his bed and placed him gently down in the seat of the wheelchair, then wheeled him from the ward.

May knew assistance would arrive shortly as the procedure was that off-duty staff in the nurses' home helped out in the event of an air raid emergency.

May put a blanket around a patient's shoulders. Noticing he was wearing slippers and so could walk, she and Nurse Jones, a second-year nurse, helped the unsteady soldier from the ward.

"Take as many blankets and pillows as you can," she heard Sister Jordan call to relatives.

Outside, as enemy aircraft—like enraged bees—swarmed closer, a smiling moon sailed blissfully unaware in the heavens. May looked up and saw, by the moonlight, the threatening sight of aircraft flying high in the sky—and they drew closer. Nurse Jones, on the other side of the soldier, pulled a terrified face. May's stomach clenched as she understood how she felt.

Two semi-sunken shelters had been dug in the hospital grounds. One was to the east, beside the old workhouse buildings, the other to the south, on land behind the nurses' home. May and Nurse Jones led the man to the top shelter, to the south, and joined the throng—porters wheeling trolleys, patients dressed in their nightwear, nurses in mufti pushing wheelchairs—all hurrying into the relative safety of the air raid shelter.

The two nurses assisted the exhausted man down the steep ramp and around the blast wall, where they found him a space in a vacant bed.

"Best we get back," Nurse Jones, her eyes as big as saucers, told May.

May had the shakes because she didn't want to go to outside to be exposed to countless enemy bomber aeroplanes.

The night reminded her of the raid when her good friend Dorothy was killed. She thought of Etty and wondered how she would cope now when the memories of that terrible night would surely come flooding back. May had a fleeting desire to comfort the lass.

She and Nurse Jones ran back to Nightingale Ward, passing folk running the other way towards the shelter. Breathlessly, May reached the door to the corridor. A dark figure loomed behind and she recognised Richard's silhouette.

May was unsure how to behave around him since the events of this evening, which already seemed a lifetime ago. Nothing had changed—he was still the pleasant man she'd talked to before—but she still felt uneasy knowing that he was a conscientious objector, and she didn't honestly know what she thought. She knew some folks branded conchies as cowards. In this war people held all kinds of beliefs and reasons for their actions and that was their right—but why would a man not want to fight for his country?

"You're as good as the next," he'd said to her, and she told herself that's what she'd think about him until she found out otherwise. She wouldn't be swayed by other peoples' views. But she couldn't help feeling unconvinced, even by her own reasoning.

The siren still sounding, May heard the rumble of bomber planes. Transfixed, she looked up into the star-studded sky. Enemy aircraft, like enormous black prehistoric birds, throbbed overhead, then hurtled into the distance. A whistling noise pierced the night sky, and for a heart-stopping moment time stood still. Then May heard the sound of a faraway explosion. Above the distant built-up area a crimson glow spread across the sky. May prayed the occupants were safely out of the buildings and protected in some underground shelter.

The thought spurred her on. Back on the ward, she made way for a porter and orderly who carried a patient recovering from an operation to remove shrapnel embedded in his face and legs onto a stretcher. May looked around the ward at those patients who couldn't be moved. If it hadn't been for their eyes following the activity around them they could be mistaken for dead.

The third time May passed around the shelter blast wall, assisting an old man who walked with a stick, distant whistles and explosions could be heard from outside.

"Yi' look done in," said an elderly gentleman who wore striped pyjamas and sat in a wheelchair. Every breath he took was an effort. "Sit down…have a cup of tea. A kind nurse…had the foresight to bring me this." He held out a flask.

"Thank you, but I must get back."

"Surely…everybody's…in the shelter by now."

"I'll be needed on the ward." She gave a weary smile then hurried away.

All now was quiet except for the faraway drone of enemy bombers. Now that the rush of adrenalin had ebbed away, May was tired— the kind of weariness that left her heavy-eyed and exhausted.

As she went past the Outpatients' entrance a plane droning nearer from the vicinity of the coast made May freeze in her tracks. A burst of gunfire erupted from the docks area and twin circles of lights criss-crossing in the sky highlighted the lone enemy bomber. The plane must have been hit because as it came closer it lost height until it seemed to be skimming over the rooftops. Then came the sound May most dreaded: a stick of bombs jettisoned from the plane whistled to the ground. There were terrific explosions as, one by one, they hit the earth. As the plane thundered over the hospital, the last bomb fell and May, falling to her knees, put her hands over her head. A single shriek above made May prepare to meet her maker. Then out of nowhere a figure grabbed her around the waist and hauled her to her feet, manhandling her through Outpatients' doorway.

There was a blinding flash and, breaking free, May fell to the ground. A warm body flung itself over her. Cocooned beneath, she felt safe and sound.

There was a nerve-racking silence, followed by a deafening explosion. As the earth shook, the building creaked, dust clogged the air and plaster fell from the ceiling. In the eerie quiet May realised that if it hadn't been for her saviour she mightn't have made it.

The person shielding her moved away, but she found that she was incapable of moving herself. She knew she wasn't hurt, just stunned, and she wondered how she could be trusted to look after patients if she couldn't keep her nerve in an emergency. She analysed how she felt. Her body numb, her mind whirling out of control, she was in temporary shock, she realised, and the fact she'd lost control confused and panicked her.

Strong arms took her under the armpits and heaved her to a standing position.

"You're safe in here," a male voice told her. May looked up into Richard's concerned eyes.

"Listen." He cocked his head. They could hear the sound of an aeroplane, engine faltering. "Jerry's turned tail and is limping home. He probably got hit and that's why he jettisoned the bombs, to lighten the plane's load. He'll probably go down in the drink."

May didn't like Jerry being referred to as a person—the thought that he was a human being with loved ones waiting at home. She couldn't bear the thought of their grief. She realised then, that she was doing it again, losing her grip, allowing her mind to wander. She despaired; even though Sister had said that one day she'd make a good nurse, May now knew differently—she didn't have what it took.

Richard held her arm to steady her.

After what she'd discovered about herself, May couldn't face him, or anyone and just wanted to be alone. She cried, "Don't touch me."

Richard stiffened and, as if he'd been burned, he let go of her arm.

"It's me...I..."

"You don't have to explain." He strode off and left her.

"It's not what you think," she called, but it was too late as he'd rounded the corner.

May worried that Richard must think she thought badly of him, when in fact she was indebted to him for saving her.

Remembering the servicemen packed together like sardines in the shelter made her come to her senses. She had a job to do. The patients, who'd been through worse ordeals than this, trusted and needed her. On shaky legs, she made her way to Nightingale Ward where a frazzled-looking but commanding Sister Jordan fussed around her patients. The blast from the bomb had caused damage to the ward. Two of the windows had been blown out, shattered glass and debris littered the floor and a radiator hung off the wall, but incredibly none of the men were injured.

"Salvage and clean all you can," Sister Jordan instructed nurses. She caught sight of May. "Nurse Robinson, see that Mr. Atkins gets a cup of sweet tea, he's trembling with shock, then after the mess is cleared up report to Casualty. They'll need everyone on hand to assist with the injured."

As if on cue, the "all clear" sounded, and the clang of fire engines and ambulance bells rang out in the night air.

"Blimey, did you see the crater in the road outside the hospital?" Valerie wanted to know the next night when they'd finally got off duty and were back in Parklands. There had been no classes during the day as everyone was required to be on duty to help with the clean-up at the hospital, to assist with casualties and make sure wards ran smoothly again.

Valerie continued. "I took a minute to look at the damage this morning when I was takin' notes to records." She raised her eyes heavenward. "You wouldn't believe the crowd of folk standing like statues around the rim ogling down the hole. I half expected to see a German spy come crawlin' out." She shrugged. "I wonder what makes folk act strange like that."

"Probably delayed shock," Maureen told her. "Thank God Outpatients wasn't hit and it was just the ground outside."

It was Christmas Eve, and the three of them, sprawled on Maureen's bed, were still in the throes of disbelief after the previous night's events. Hardly anyone at the hospital had gone to bed till the early hours and in May's case she hadn't slept a wink. The three probationer nurses, wearing pyjamas and huddled in blankets for warmth, were drinking tea and tucking into shortbread that Maureen's mam had baked the last time her daughter visited home. They were made, according to Maureen, with margarine, flour and sugar, and a splash of milk to knead the biscuits. Crumbs littered the top of the counterpane.

"There's talk the bombers were headed for the airfields and that the lone raider must have been a straggler." Maureen brushed crumbs from her pyjamas. "The hospital had a close shave." She gave May a sympathetic gaze. "Thank God nobody was killed."

May was still jittery and trying to come to terms with all that had happened during the bombing—especially being saved by Richard. She sought to change the subject. "Who's going home for Christmas?"

"Me." Maureen turned to Valerie. "How about you?"

Valerie popped the last of her biscuit into her mouth and licked her fingertips. "I'm not on duty, more's the pity, so I'll have to show me face at home." She heaved a tortured sigh. "I'll have to suffer Mam going on about how I should meet a nice fella and settle down. According to her, at twenty I'm positively on the shelf." She rolled her eyes. "No fear. I don't want to end up like her with six kids and a fella that scarpered." Her eyes flashed. "Seriously, though . . . this war has helped lasses like me to escape the kitchen sink. Who'd have thought I'd be working as a nurse?" A grin spread across her face. "And though I'm happy to do me bit, I'm going to have meself a bit of fun before I settle down. And blow me mam."

Surely Valerie didn't mean she'd become a...floozy? May smiled, thinking of the word Mam called a certain type of lass. But hark at her, she thought, with her dubious past. Mentally she apologised to Valerie.

Valerie stretched and yawned. "If nobody minds, I'm calling it a night. After last night I'm beat." She stood and made to move, then turned towards them. "And I can't risk bein' late and hauled up in front of Matron again."

"Why? What did you do?" Maureen's face creased in concern.

"Apparently, Matron doesn't like the way I talk. She insists I speak proper, like."

When she'd left, Maureen laughed. "I reckon that girl is a more dedicated nurse than she lets on."

She moved to her bedside locker and, opening the drawer, brought out a package "I'm off home tomorrow," she told May, "and so I'll give you this now."

She handed over the small parcel wrapped in thin, second-hand Christmas paper.

"Oh! I haven't got you a present."

"Don't worry. It's not new. It's something I've got two of."

"I'll open it now."

Unwrapping the gift, May saw a small blue-bound book and flicking through the pages she realised it was a dictionary.

Maureen appeared uncommonly embarrassed. "I hope you don't think me presumptuous. But you're always saying you want to look words up."

"Truly, it's just what I need. Why didn't I think of having one? I am stupid!"

"Don't let me hear you say that again." Maureen's tone was firm. "You're incredibly bright and perceptive and don't let anyone tell you differently."

Maureen was an understanding soul, and it was such a thoughtful gift; May was touched. Her emotions got the better of her and her chin trembled. She suddenly found she missed Mam.

"Whatever's wrong?" Maureen asked.

May crumpled and, like a waterfall, words spilled from her mouth.

Seeing each event as it had occurred in her mind's eye as she talked, she told Maureen about how Mam died and the gap it had left in May's life, and about Derek being her son preferring to stay at the farm, her best friend betraying her and Dad throwing her out. She didn't mention Billy, as his death was still too raw even to think about.

"Such terrible times," Maureen said. "I admire your courage to withstand it all. I'll pray to God for his guidance...he won't let you down."

May didn't squirm as she usually did when anyone spoke openly about God. For, with Maureen, speaking about such things came as naturally as talking about the weather.

"Who do you have in your life?"

"I've made a friend called Alec but he...crowds me a little." May was surprised to hear herself voice her doubts. "And a porter thinks I've been beastly towards him." May was mixed up about how she felt about Richard, especially now he'd saved her from what could have been a serious injury, or worse. But why wasn't he prepared to do his bit for his country?

May had one more thing to share. "But worst of all is...I can't manage the responsibility of being a nurse." The words came out in squeaky unnatural voice.

"You're tired and you've had a shock. And you're doubting yourself. It happens to us all."

May wasn't convinced. "You were in the raid, you were pooped too, yet you coped."

"The difference is I was nowhere near the bomb...Anyway, tell me your definition of coping."

The surprise request caught May off guard. "I haven't a clue."

"It's staying put."

"Pardon me?"

"You've had more than your fair share of terrible things happen to you but you're still carrying on. More to the point, you choose to care for others when you could do with a bit of love and attention yourself."

May frowned. She was just doing what came naturally.

"You've stayed to face your lot when you could've run away and started a new life."

"I could never give up on Derek." May was appalled at the thought.

"Exactly. Your strength of character will see you through. You'll deal with each situation as it arises."

May wasn't so sure about that but it was good to have someone who had faith in her.

Maureen raised an inquisitive eyebrow. "The friend you've fallen out with. I won't ask what she did but, in my experience"—her eyes clouded with hurt—"bearing a grudge only hurts yourself."

Before May had time to question her words, Maureen went on, "What about the porter you think you've been beastly to?"

"He's called Richard and he's a conchie. I just don't understand how he can face all those brave boys on the ward…He seems a nice man, but I can't help feeling resentment towards him for it." There, she'd confessed how she felt out loud. A thought struck her. "He isn't coping, is he? He's running away from something."

"I think you're wrong. Imagine what he has to go through with people. Wouldn't it be easier just to join up and go to war?"

"Dad says conchies are cowards and it's an excuse to save their own skin."

May searched her soul. Did she really believe that? She'd never bothered about such matters before but these days life had got complicated. May had never met a conchie and that made life easier. You could lump people of certain types together and, like Dad, think the worst. But when you got to know someone, someone seemingly considerate and caring, that complicated matters. She couldn't figure Richard out. Was it possible that he'd rather save his own skin than fight for his country while others (the heartache of Billy's death returned) made the ultimate sacrifice? She thought of Richard: the concern shining in his eyes, his genuine smile. No. She wouldn't judge him until she knew the truth of the matter.

"It takes a strong person to stand up for their principles. It's…" Maureen faltered, "sometimes easier to give in."

"I would dearly like to know why he would refuse to go to war."

"Then ask him." Maureen's freckled face held a tranquillity May could only dream of possessing.

Sound advice, May thought, but on this occasion, she doubted if she'd take it. The man did rattle her—the way she couldn't stop thinking about him. But she was grateful to Maureen all the same for being a friend and trying to help.

CHAPTER TWELVE

December 1943

Christmas Day wasn't the picture postcard of snow that some folk hoped for but cold and grey with a touch of fog. May stood outside the pub at Chi roundabout, dressed for the cold in a brimmed hat, ancient black ankle-length coat, and what had been Mam's favourite fox fur stole.

Her heart rose when she saw Alec swagger down Dean Road, dressed in a dark suit whose jacket strained at the seams, collar and tie. His face, clean-shaven, held a robust radiance, and his green eyes sparkled.

"Merry Christmas," she called.

"And to you too." He took her arm in a masterful way and linked it with his. "How did you get on with the raid the other night? I worried about yi'."

May was touched that he cared. "The ward took a bit of bashing but otherwise it's business as usual."

She didn't want to think about the terrors that night as the sorrow of spending Christmas Day without Mam was enough to cope with.

"Where are we going?"

"You'll see." He gave her hand an affectionate pat.

Alec had big hands that matched his chunky body and she could see when the wind blew his trousers against his legs that they were pleasingly muscled. She gave him a sideways glance, noticing his tilted and jutting jaw.

"Did you have a nice dinner at your Nana's?" she asked.

"Aye, it was a piece of mutton."

"Was there any other family there?"

"No, why d'you ask?"

"I'm just interested. I just wondered about your dad."

"Me dad's a miserable sod and best left alone."

May thought it best not to pursue the conversation. "I opted to help serve Christmas dinner on the ward."

May didn't admit she'd gone without a festive meal because she wanted to keep busy so she wouldn't think about Mam or Derek or the fact she was supposed to spend Christmas with Etty. Besides, she didn't have anyone to sit with in the canteen.

They walked for a bit then May felt compelled to break the silence.

"It's me birthday next week," she blurted, then wondered why. She hoped he wouldn't think she was angling for a present.

"What day?"

"New Year's Eve."

"I'll have to think of something special," he told her.

May began to babble, telling him about the Christmas card she'd received from one of the patients' relatives.

"It's got a picture of a jolly Santa who's giving a V for victory sign with his fingers."

When he didn't comment, May told herself to stop talking or else she'd drive the lad mad with constant nervous chatter.

They walked down the hill towards the gas works and Alec guided her through a cut into King Street, which was quiet as all the shops were closed. He disentangled his arm and, taking her by the waist, steered her into a shop doorway.

The thing was, May knew what he intended and was surprised she didn't mind. It was lovely to engage in physical contact which she sorely missed sometimes. Even Mam, who was never the demonstrative kind, gave May the occasional hug.

As Alec bent his head to kiss her, glistening lips meeting hers, professionalism took over and Nurse Robinson became aware of hospital etiquette. She pulled away. She couldn't be seen in a clinch like this, not in public; she'd get a formal reprimand off Matron.

"Hawway, May, what's up?"

"Alec, I can't, not here, like this. I'll get into trouble at work if I'm seen."

"They don't own you." He sounded peeved. "Anyway, it's your day off."

She wanted to tell him she'd enjoy intimacy with him in the right place, at the right time but the words wouldn't roll off her tongue—May wasn't certain this *was* the right time just yet.

Frustrated, he huffed from the doorway.

In nerve-racking silence, they walked on, Alec leading the way. They passed the ferry landing and as they reached the top of a blustery Ballast Hill, he stopped.

He looked out over the murky River Tyne. "I've brought you to see the view I see every day."

As she breathed the salt sea air, May had a sense of wanting to unshackle her problems. She longed for a peace of mind she hadn't experienced in a long while.

Below were the docks where grey painted warships of all sizes were tied up to the quayside—an unbelievable number with scarcely space between them. She marvelled at the skill of the harbour pilot who boarded ships and directed their passage from the Tyne, through the twin arms of the piers and to the sea beyond.

Cranes soared high in the sky; so too did large silver barrage balloons, their job being to make it difficult for raiders to approach and to prevent low-level air attacks.

Alec followed her gaze. "Aye, it's a right bugger if one of those balloons breaks loose... it'll wreak havoc if it hits a building, worse still if folk get in the way... like that poor sod in Sunderland... killed outright, he was."

In May's mind's eye she saw the tragic scene. At the same time she wished Alec wouldn't swear.

"See that beauty?" Alec pointed to a spanking clean ship below. "She's the *Empire Crown*. She was built at Readhead's shipyard. She's a cargo ship and propelled by a triple expansion steam engine."

May didn't have a clue what he was talking about but smiled to humour him.

"Aye, she's off on her maiden voyage at the beginning of January." His chest expanded as if he had personally built the ship. May decided one day she'd bring Derek to see the yards, and who knew? He might fancy the shipbuilding trade—a reliable job that would last a lifetime.

His hands resting on the wall in front, Alec, like a ship's captain, gazed out over the water as he talked of the different ships in the war and, in some cases, the fate of those unlucky enough to cross paths with an enemy torpedo. All the while, May watched a little ferry as it busily chugged across the ribbon of River Tyne.

Alec struck a match and lit a cigarette. "D'you still 'sort of' have a boyfriend?" he asked.

May started. She didn't want to discuss Billy, not today, not any day. He was gone, but the fact still hadn't sunk into her brain.

"He died," she said with finality, "fighting for his country."

A vein started to tick in Alec's temple. May wondered if she'd hit a raw nerve.

"Me job's a reserved occupation." His tone was defensive. "I couldn't join the forces even if I begged and pleaded. Besides, I do me bit in the Home Guard."

Appalled that she might have offended him, May answered, "I've got enormous respect for shipyard workers. Without ships we'd never win the war."

Alec appeared placated and, gazing towards the sea, a smile spread across his face.

"You know what they say," he said cheerily, "anything goes in love and war." He turned towards May and gave her a smouldering look. "Despite what I said about seeing how things go between us, I've fallen in love with you."

May was flabbergasted; she'd only known the lad a few weeks and she was positive she'd done everything she could to indicate that they weren't going steady. But despite herself, when she looked into those imploring green eyes she felt a warm glow spreading over her skin.

Flummoxed and unsure what to say, she answered, "Oh, Alec, I need time... it's too early for me to—"

"Just leave it." A flash of irritation crossed his face.

As Alec escorted her home it started to rain, only drops at first and then a downpour. They made a dash and huddled in Binns shop doorway. May squeezed bedside him and snuggled against the warmth of his body. He placed his hand at the side of her head and laid it against his chest.

"I'm here now, to look out for you." His voice was husky, but he didn't attempt a kiss.

Meeting his protective gaze, May felt safe and comforted for the first time since Mam had died.

The next week passed in a flash. There were no lectures in school but Sister Chilvers made sure the probationers were kept busy. They learnt, amongst other things, how to sterilise needles and glass syringes on the ward and set trays for a bed bath. Cookery lessons were taken in the kitchen and dietary needs were observed.

"Some patients are incapable of eating large portions of food," Home Sister told them, "and so we must tempt them with smaller attractive meals. If one does go into the kitchen to make a light meal, abide by the rule that there's always a nurse left on the ward."

The next time May was on the ward, after the report was given by night staff, the food trolley arrived with breakfast for patients. The trolley was wheeled into position in the middle of the ward and the nurses, holding trays, formed a queue as Sister Jordan removed lids from aluminium food containers.

"Nurse." A ladle in her hand, Sister eyed May, the first in the queue. "A patient is to be admitted from Casualty to the ward."

"Yes, Sister."

"See to it at once. And don't forget the patient notes."

"No, Sister."

"Now, Nurse."

Collecting her cape from the staff room, May made for the outdoors. As she hurried over the grounds, she saw a porter striding across a path in the distance. Her heart quickened but it wasn't Richard's tall, broad-shouldered figure, she realised. Why did the man intrigue her so? He was a conchie. May knew that even by being friendly towards him she would be playing with fire because, if she was seen fraternising with him, people would shun her too. Why then did she catch herself looking twice at every porter she passed? Huh! She didn't care a fig about Richard Bentley, she told her pig-headed mind.

Opening the double doors, May entered Casualty department. Sister in charge, a lean woman who looked impatient with the doctor she spoke to, excused herself and approached her.

"Men's orthopaedic ward?" she asked before May uttered a word.

"Yes, Sister."

"Good. We need the cubicle. The patient to be admitted has multiple injuries. He was on a training flight and because of poor visibility his plane crashed as it made for the runway." Sister raised an eyebrow. "He was the only one of the crew to survive."

She moved to a desk and handed May notes in a brown folder. "I've buzzed for a porter. The patient is in bed three. Nurse Briars will assist if you need any help."

"Yes, Sister."

Sister went back to speak with the waiting doctor.

Casualty's double doors opened and Richard walked onto the department. His sober chocolate-coloured eyes met May's without a sign of recognition as he wheeled the trolley along the ward's linoleum floor to bed three.

May, too, moved towards the bed. Lifting back the screen, she regarded the young man. Dried blood smeared his ashen face and his eyes were bloodshot. His head, May noticed, was swathed in sterile towels at the back. Amazingly, the flight gear he wore looked intact.

"Hello, Nurse." His voice was barely audible. "I've broken my hip, so they say. But I can't feel anything."

Richard pulled back the screen. "Hello, airman." He wheeled the trolley alongside the bed. "We're taking you to the ward," he said in his gentle but firm voice, "where you'll be looked after by trained and expert staff."

Why didn't May think to say that? She had been told to talk to patients about their care, to reassure them and explain what was happening.

But still she glowered at Richard. It wasn't his place to take over.

She spoke to the airman, who looked too young to be part of a bomber crew—in fact too young to be in the services at all. "We'll put you on a trolley and then wheel you outside because the ward you're going to isn't part of the main hospital."

Nurse Briars came to stand beside May. "Are we all ready?" she asked. Richard and May nodded simultaneously. "Then cross your arms over your chest," she instructed the airman. When he didn't move she did it for him. "One...two...three," she counted.

Between them they lifted the airman onto the trolley.

May picked up the notes from the locker top and started towards the exit. Richard, wheeling the trolley, followed.

Outside, the sky was a white mask, and snowflakes fell from the heavens. May took the side of the trolley to guide it down the ramp. As she did so the airman mumbled.

"Poor lad's talking rubbish," Richard said under his breath. "He's probably in acute clinical shock."

"I didn't know you were a medical expert." May tried desperately to regain the upper hand.

"I'm not. But I know better than to let this airman get soaked in the wet." He pulled the blanket up under the lad's chin.

May felt a surge of annoyance at his cheek. She retaliated by holding the notes over the top of the airman's head.

Richard's lips twitched in amusement. "It's not a competition."

"Who said it was?" May retorted, berating herself for letting the man get under her skin.

They hurried on in uneasy silence. Richard gave her a sidelong glance.

"You didn't suffer any lasting injuries, then . . . in the bombings."

May still hadn't thanked him and though her conscience said she should, she didn't want to be reminded about the night she lost control, especially by a know-it-all like him.

"Could happen to anyone," he surprised her by saying, "losing their grip for a while."

About to retort that she hadn't *lost her grip*, May hesitated because it would be a lie. And the truth was, he sounded as if he really did care.

The wind whipped the corner of the blanket from the lad's chest. Richard let go of the trolley with one hand and gently tucked the blanket back around the airman's upper torso. May saw that the young airman was dozing and she was suddenly struck by the thought that he had been injured while keeping folk like Richard safe in their homes.

May stiffened. Richard was a conscientious objector. But then, she reminded herself, she had decided not to judge. She felt totally mixed up: one minute she took Richard at face value and thought him a pleasant bloke whom she really liked, the next (especially when she thought of Billy and the other boys who had made the ultimate sacrifice) she felt cross and resentful.

This confusion made her snap. "You should know." As soon as she spoke the words she regretted them.

He gave her a look of hopeless disappointment. "Be my guest and join the others. Have a go at me."

May remembered what Mam always said about walking in another man's shoes.

"Richard, I don't know anything about you. Except you refuse to fight for king and country and—"

"I'd appreciate it if you didn't sound so pompous." The man gave a mocking grin. "It doesn't become you."

Huh! Who did he think he was? She blurted, "What your family must think, I don't know."

"They think," he said flatly, as he approached the building's door, "the same as you. That I'm a spineless coward."

May was speechless at his answer. She didn't know what to say. She filled the uncomfortable silence by letting go of the trolley, moving forward and opening the door.

If he wanted sympathy, May thought, the man had come to the wrong place. A mean streak May hadn't known she possessed seized her.

She faced him. "I'll be honest with you. I find it hard to think you'll sail through this war and survive when others…" She grappled to control her grief. This wasn't about Richard, she realised, but Billy dying. She finished lamely, "…might not."

Richard, as he wheeled the trolley into the corridor, told her coolly, "My affairs are none of your damn business. But, for your information, I've recently served a sentence in his majesty's prison for my beliefs."

"Then you must have deserved it," she told him.

She closed the door and removed the damp woollen blanket from the patient's body. She was relieved the young lad was asleep and hadn't witnessed her unprofessionalism.

May's cheeks were burning. She was appalled at herself for allowing her emotions to rule her judgement. She shouldn't get involved. What Richard did with his life was not her affair.

A third-year nurse met them on the ward and gestured to a bed with its top sheet rolled aside in readiness for the patient.

Patients who'd recently had surgery or needed special care were kept in beds near the ward entrance where Sister could keep an eye on them through the nurses' station window. As a patient's condition improved, they were shifted further up the ward until they were recovered enough to be discharged.

The airman now safely in bed, Richard folded the damp blanket and, taking hold of the end of the trolley, wheeled it towards the ward's exit without another word.

"Best we lift the screen around the bed," the third-year nurse told May.

She looked over May's shoulder and visibly stiffened.

May, following her astonished gaze, saw the porter's departing figure. Pinned to the back of his overall, for all to see, was a white feather.

Serves him right, was May's first reaction, but then a wave of shame overtook her and her lenient heart bled for Richard.

CHAPTER THIRTEEN
New Year's Eve 1943

"You have my permission, Nurse Robinson," Sister Chilvers told May. "Put your request in the late book."

"I will, Sister, thank you."

With breakfast finished at Parklands, May had waited until Valerie and the two other nurses from downstairs had vacated the dining room. Maureen had a day off and had spent the night at her parents' home. She'd told May she wouldn't be back until later that night.

Alec had written to tell her to put her glad rags on as he was taking her somewhere special. So May had asked Sister Chilvers' permission to stay out late as tonight was New Year's Eve and her birthday.

"Not a minute later than eleven o'clock, Nurse, as I have to stay up and lock the front door."

"Yes, Sister."

May put the spoon in the empty porridge bowl and, scraping back the chair, moved towards the door.

"And, Nurse..."

"Yes, Sister."

Sister's faded eyes twinkled. "Happy birthday."

Applying lipstick, May looked into the wall mirror and rubbed her lips together. Though lipstick wasn't rationed, it was expensive and so she used it only for special occasions and never at work as make-up wasn't allowed.

"You don't need it," Maureen had told her, "not with your snow-white skin and those ridiculously long and thick black eyelashes."

Not knowing where she was going tonight made it difficult to know what to wear—not that May had much to choose from. She decided on a dark green frock with exaggerated shoulder pads, nipped in at the waist with a flared, panelled skirt that reached to her knees. She didn't wear a suspender belt or stockings because she had only one pair and, afraid she'd get a ladder in them, she kept them for work. She wore black high heels—a little worn down—with an ankle strap and she drew the obligatory eyebrow pencil down the back of her legs to give the impression that she was wearing stockings.

It was good to be in mufti for a change, she thought, as she shrugged into her mothball-smelling outdoor coat (which reminded her of home and Mam). Her uniform had become like another skin.

Alec was waiting for her as arranged outside Parklands at quarter to seven.

May slammed the door to keep the light in and hurried along the path to meet him. He was standing beneath a tree shrouded in the shadows of a moonlit evening.

"Happy birthday, May." His lips brushed her cheek.

He smelled of Old Spice aftershave and wore a two-piece suit, collar and tie. May was gratified he'd dressed up for the occasion.

"By, it's cold, the night." He rubbed his hands together. "I wished I'd worn me overcoat but with the shortages I've lost that much weight it's massive on us now." His cold hand took hers and he led her to the bus stop in Dunlop Road.

"I've had a bath at Nana's and even though she ignored regulations and give us double the amount of water I still froze and I've never been warm since."

Reaching the bus stop, May followed his example and talked small talk, as, annoyingly, he wouldn't tell her where they were headed.

She told him, "I read an article that the king sets an example by only having the regulation five inches of bath water."

"More fool him," Alec shocked her by saying, "I'm sure if I was him, me bath would be full up to the brim. And no one would be any the wiser, would they?"

May thought His Majesty should be applauded but didn't say that as she feared upsetting Alec. He didn't like his opinion challenged.

A tingle of excitement ran through her. "I hope I'm dressed properly for what you've got planned."

"You look smashin' whatever you wear."

She returned the compliment by telling him, "You look a real gent."

The trolley came and they stepped up on the platform.

As they sat on the seat, May's heartstrings pulled as she thought of Billy and the many nights they had done the very same thing. Pictures of him passed through her mind, how handsome he looked in his khaki uniform, his rascally smile, and a sweet, physical ache radiated in her groin. Billy had convinced her that as an engaged—practically married—couple it was acceptable for them to have intercourse. Not, to be fair, that May had needed much persuading.

"May, man…leave work behind." Alec's voice broke into her thoughts. "Tonight, you're gonna have some fun." He squeezed her arm. "Remember tomorrow might never come and it won't if Jerry doesn't behave tonight."

May shivered. Like a kid, she felt the need to protect herself by spitting on her hand and crossing her heart for reassurance.

She stared out of the window into the blackness. She couldn't see the destruction, but she knew it was there, the unkempt and torn look of the town. But South Shields folk, weary and worn down with the struggle to survive the war, held the dream that the Allies would defeat the enemy soon.

"Our stop." Alec stood and made his way down the aisle.

May climbed the steps to the Hedworth Hall doorway and a shiver of anticipation ran through her.

As the pair of them walked into the foyer and closed the door, May read the notice pinned to the wall.

Grand Charity Dance.
Tonight 7-11 p.m.
Music by Albert Sutton and his three-piece band.
Spot Prizes
Tickets 3/- Forces 1/-
Money in aid of South Shields shoeless children's fund.
The Hall was lent rent-free for the occasion.

Alec's face split into a grin. "Surprise, birthday girl!"

May clutched her heart. "Ooo...thank you, Alec. I can't remember the last time I came to a dance hall."

She handed her outdoor coat to the cloakroom girl, who gave her a ticket in return.

Alec led the way into the dance hall and the scene that met May's eyes was better than eating a box of chocolates—a rare treat in wartime.

Couples, most of them in uniform, swirled around the polished dance floor, quickstepping to the tune of Glenn Miller's "Chattanooga Choo Choo."

Alec led the way to a table in the corner of the room, then left her to buy their drinks. As she waited, May watched as the spot prize took place on the dance floor.

The music stopped and a compere on the stage stood with his back to the dancing couples.

He called to a member of staff, "Take two paces to the right . . . four in front, and the couple on your left are the lucky winners."

The man did as he was bid and then handed over the spot prize to the lucky couple, and May longed to see what was inside.

A St. Bernard's Waltz came next.

Alec came over and, putting the drinks on the table, took her hand and led her to the dance floor.

Encircling her waist with his arm, he led as they circled the room. What with the spotlight, a huge ball scattering silver beams around the hall, and the music—especially the trombone, her favourite musical instrument—May was transported to heavenly bliss.

She danced the night away but when things heated up and the band played jazz music, May made her excuses and retired to her seat. The jitterbug was a dance she'd never got the hang of. The lively music filled the hall. Servicemen tossed their partners over their shoulders, then skilfully thrust them through parted legs and twirled them around. May was sure the girls must have felt dizzy.

She smiled at the scene, at those brave boys having so much well-deserved fun. They deserved to forget duty for a while.

Unexpectedly, Richard appeared in her mind's eye, his disillusioned look as he told her to "be his guest and to have a go at him like the others."

Imperceptibly, she shook her head. Why think of him when there were more deserving candidates she could feel sorry for?

The exhilarating music ceased, and May watched as the servicemen and their partners left the dance floor.

Alec, his expression intent, followed her gaze. "I could join the forces if I want."

"How come?" May wondered what had brought this up, especially at a dance.

"That politician, Sir Smedley something or other, has been asked to consider us blokes in the Home Guard."

May never had time to keep up with all the news. "Why?"

"Because…we want the right to be on the assault on the continent. The lads agree; we've got the training, we should have the opportunity to fight."

His gaze swept the room, eyeing the servicemen, and May thought she saw a hint of envy gleam in Alec's eyes.

"Would you go?"

"Course." He gave a cheeky grin. "If only to impress you. I bet I'd look a charmer in uniform." His brow creased. "The thing is… I want to stay here and look after you."

May was both confused and touched. Didn't Alec know she was capable of looking after herself?

People made a circle on the dance floor, preparing to do the hokey-cokey.

Alec stood up. "I'll get us another drink." He went to join the refreshments queue.

May took the opportunity to go to the cloakroom, where she went to the lav and freshened up.

As she came back into the dance hall, she bumped into a fellow in a Royal Navy uniform, who was waving at one of the dancers instead of watching where he was going.

"Watch out, mate," he said. Turning, his eyes appraised her. "Beg your pardon, miss. Are you all right?"

May smiled. "Yes. I saw you on the dance floor with your girlfriend. You look good together doing the jitterbug."

"She's my sister and we've practised all week," he laughed.

They exchanged pleasantries about dancing, and then May returned to the table.

Alec, a pint glass in front of him, leant over the table. "Who was that?"

May noticed a vein in his temple was ticking.

"Just a nice bloke I bumped into."

"Pull the other one."

"How d'you mean?"

"I saw how he looked at yi'. How long have yi' known him?"

Confused, May replied, "I've never seen him before in my life."

"Tell us the truth."

Alec reached over and grabbed her arm, his fingers digging into her flesh.

"Ouch! That hurts."

He released his grip and looked nervously around.

"Alec... what's got into you? Honestly, that's the first time I've clapped eyes on the bloke."

He didn't answer.

The evening spoiled; she wanted to go home. She checked her watch and couldn't believe it was half past ten.

"Eee, I have to go."

"Who's taking yi' home... yer fancy fella?"

If May hadn't known better she would've sworn Alec was drunk.

She ignored the remark. "I'll be for it if I'm not back on time."

May rose to fetch her coat. Alec didn't do likewise.

She told him, "You can stay if you want."

"That would suit, wouldn't it?"

He looked over the room towards the Royal Navy serviceman, who threw back his head and laughed at something the girl at his side said.

"Mebbes it's too late. Yer fancy fella seems to have met somebody else."

May didn't know what to think. She wanted safe and reliable Alec back.

"Don't be daft," she quipped. "Come on, let's go."

Alec followed her to the cloakroom, where he waited like a sentinel outside the door.

*

Outside, the clouds had disappeared and the heavens had changed to a twinkly starry night.

"Don't fret, I'll make sure you get back on time." Alec seemed to have reverted to the friendly lad May preferred.

She decided to put aside his earlier behaviour and concentrate on returning to Parklands.

As they stood at the bus stop at the top of Dean Road, she looked across to Whale Street and Etty came to mind. May, recalling the happy birthdays she'd spent with her friend, felt infinitely sad.

The trolley came then and the couple climbed aboard and sat on the wooden seat for a few stops. Then, alighting from the platform to the pavement, they hurried along the street towards Parklands.

May told him, "Thank you, I've had a lovely evening."

And she had, apart from the last hour.

She felt awkward as she didn't know what was now expected of her.

"The night's not over, yet." Alec, making his motive plain, moved her some yards away and they stood beneath an enormous gnarled tree.

In the hazy moonlight, teasingly, he brushed her bottom lip with his index finger and then he bent forward to kiss her. May wasn't too sure at first but it was only a kiss, she reasoned. He embraced her tightly in his arms and, as the kiss lingered, a needy ache, strong in her groin, made May forget all sense of time and place.

She registered a movement, as Alec's hand reached beneath her coat and fondled a breast. Startled, she came to her senses and pulled away. She didn't mean for this to happen—but how to explain? Since Derek had been born, she'd considered her breasts for feeding and not sexual entertainment—her mother had instilled that into her.

"Ah! Hawway, May, you can't stop now." His rasping breaths sounded as if he'd been for a run.

"I must go. I'll be late." And it was true, she would be in deep trouble if she overstepped the time limit.

She buttoned up her coat.

"When's your next day off?" he wanted to know.

"I don't know... the off-duty book hasn't been done for next week yet."

"Write and let me know when you do."

"I will."

She started to make her way towards Parklands.

"Promise."

"I said I would, Alec."

A pause. "You know that fella you told me about... the one you said was yer beau."

"Yes."

"You're over him, right?"

May didn't think she could ever let go of Billy.

Alec must have taken her answer as confirmation of what he'd said. She imagined the dimples in his cheek as he grinned.

"Look here." His voice was contrite. "About before. That Navy fella at the dance. I do believe yi'... the thing is... it's because I care so much and I couldn't help but get jealous."

May stole up the path leading to Parklands. Trying the handle on the front door, she found it locked. In the darkness she couldn't see her watch but she was sure she was past her deadline. Where was Sister Chilvers? Surely she hadn't forgotten to leave the door unlocked. May tried the knocker and heard it echo in the house.

Then, thankfully, the door opened and May hurried in. As she closed the door, the electric light came on.

Maureen stood there, wrapped in a blanket.

"When did you get back?" May wanted to know.

"Dad brought me in the car a couple of hours ago."

May still couldn't get over the fact that Maureen's parents owned a car. She didn't know anyone else that did. Or how he got petrol with all the shortages?

"When I couldn't find either you or Valerie I looked in the late book."

"Where is Valerie?"

"In bed." Maureen raised her eyebrows as if there was more to the story. "Then I met Eileen from downstairs in the kitchen making a Horlicks. She hadn't a clue where you were but said Sister Chilvers had gone to bed early. When I saw your name in the late book and saw Sister's signed approval next to it I realised she must have forgotten about you." Maureen wore a worried frown. "I've waited for you here in front of the fire just in case." She shook her head. "I don't think Sister's been right since that nasty cold she had."

"I agree. It's time Sister retired. She's very forgetful and, poor soul, she sleeps half of the time."

"But what else would she do?" Maureen's expression was a picture of concern. "By all accounts her profession is her life."

May had a sudden thought that this was how her life could turn out too.

Maureen brightened. "I didn't realise you were going out. Did you have a good time on your birthday?"

"Yes, thank you. It was a last minute thing. A surprise from Alec."

"Where did you go?" Maureen asked.

"He took me to a dance. It was fun."

"So why did you look so glum when you came in?"

Maureen was very observant.

May decided to voice her concerns, as she trusted Maureen's opinion.

She told Maureen about the scene at the dance hall and Alec's accusations. Unconsciously, she rubbed her arm where he had grabbed her.

"He apologised and said he was jealous," she confided. "I'm worried it's my fault...that I led him on."

"You're not responsible for Alec's actions." Maureen glanced down at May's arm. "Are those finger marks?"

"Yes. But he couldn't help himself. You see, it's because he cares so much that he acts the way he does."

"No, May, I don't see." Maureen's voice was firm. "What I do know is that caring for someone means trusting and never hurting them."

Maureen's expression had changed and now she was the one who looked unsure.

There was a thoughtful silence, then Maureen spoke up. "By the way, I should warn you...Valerie's on the war path."

Glad to have the subject changed, May replied, "Is that why she went to bed so early? Is she in a huff?"

"I'm afraid so...poor girl, she expected we were all going to celebrate the New Year together. She thought I'd be back earlier and she was miffed you didn't tell her you were going out."

May felt bad. "To be honest I didn't think Valerie would want to spend New Year with us. We don't get along all that well."

"Valerie's easily upset. She has troubles of her own."

"Am I allowed to know?"

"I don't see why not. She didn't tell me in confidence." Maureen's expression was full of sympathy. "You know Valerie's the eldest and her mum wants her to stay home to look after her brothers and sisters while she goes out to work. She's been offered a job in a munitions factory."

"But Valerie has a job."

"I know."

"I thought Valerie's mam wanted her to settle down."

"She does."

"But...none of it makes sense."

"Life often doesn't." Maureen heaved a sigh as if she should know. "Her mam isn't the stay-at-home type. I suspect Valerie suffers because deep down she wants the best for the bairns but neither does she think it fair that she should be the one to look after them. Poor girl's in a predicament."

Maureen had this knack of making you feel special, May thought, and she was a good listener—no wonder Valerie had chosen Maureen to share her problems with.

May made a mental note to be friendlier with Valerie, even if she didn't respond—because everyone needed a friend. Her mind fleetingly thought of Etty and May wondered who she shared confidences with now. She gave a longing sigh.

Maureen put the fireguard up at the fire. "Best we go upstairs. Sister might decide to do the rounds."

The vision of Sister Chilvers half asleep, stealing along the landing in her nightdress, suddenly amused May and she had the urge to giggle. It must have been nerves because she was exhausted and the night with Alec hadn't been the success she'd anticipated.

She got a grip of herself.

"Before we go, can I ask you something?"

Maureen nodded.

"When you mentioned that caring for someone meant you should never hurt them, I got the impression you were upset."

"Didn't I say you were clever and insightful?" Maureen smiled. She let out a wistful sigh. "The thing is...Mum doesn't want me to become a nun...she's afraid she'll lose me. And she will, if she carries on the way she does. What Mum doesn't realise is that her actions are driving me away." She massaged her temples with her fingertips as though she wanted to rub away the problem from her mind. "I'm starting to resent her . . . and, May, it's killing me."

May was shocked that even with all that belief in God, Maureen still had complications in her life.

"I think you should tell your mam what you've told me." May nodded with conviction. "If I was her I'd want to know."

"D'you think so?"

"I know so. Mams just want the best for their bairns . . . no matter what age."

Maureen put her arm around May's shoulders. "One day that son of yours you've told me about will realise what a treasure he's got as a mum."

Touched, May didn't know what to say.

"Come on." Maureen led the way. "Let's go upstairs. I've got a present for you."

As they tiptoed into the room, they could hear Valerie's even breaths while she slept.

"Don't put the light on, it might disturb her." May was nervous of the ramifications if Valerie did wake up.

A torchlight switched on and May, sitting on the bed, saw Maureen fishing in her locker drawer. She made her way back to the bed and placed something in May's palm. And by the torch's beam May saw what it was.

"Rosary beads."

"They're mine but I want you to have them. They'll keep you safe. Come a day when you're desperate and need to pray, use them and ask for guidance."

"I couldn't . . . they're—"

"I insist."

At that moment, Valerie stirred and turned over.

In the silence that followed, May felt torn; though she appreciated the gift, she doubted she would use the rosary beads because since Mam had died she found herself questioning her faith.

Maureen pointed the torch beam at her wristwatch.

"My goodness! It's a minute past midnight. It's nineteen forty-four. Happy new year, May. I pray all your dreams come true."

"Happy new year to you, Maureen, and I wish the same for you."

May hoped that her friend hadn't heard the catch in her voice. She'd managed to stay busy all day, and keep her upset at bay—until now.

There could be all kinds of reasons why Derek hadn't sent a birthday card, not least being that neither he, nor anyone else at the farm, knew when May's birthday was. But the fact remained, the lack of contact hurt like blazes.

As tears seeped from her eyes, May was glad of the dark.

CHAPTER FOURTEEN
January 1944

The next morning was May's half day on the ward, and she stood with the rest of the nurses at the centre table and waited for Sister Jordan to lead prayers.

"We'll begin with the Lord's prayer," Sister told the patients as she did every morning. She smiled at the patients, encouraging them to join in.

After prayers, when the staff returned to the office, Sister gave out duties.

"Nurse Robinson, help Nurse Bell to prepare the side ward for a new admission."

Side wards were used for special care nursing. When a patient's health had improved satisfactorily, they were transferred back into the main ward.

As she hurried along the corridor, May searched her still sleepy brain to think who had vacated the side room.

Nurse Bell, a second-year nurse, petite and pretty with a heart-shaped face, greeted her with a pleasant smile.

"Morning, happy new year, Nurse Robinson." First names weren't allowed on the ward. Nurse Bell carried a basin and put it on the locker top. The room reeked of a strong, antiseptic smell.

Together they stripped the bed and put the dirty linen in a laundry bag.

"Whose bed was this?" May asked, as she began washing the mattress and bed. "I recall it was empty when I went off duty yesterday."

Nurse Bell stood up from washing her side of the bed, and her eyes clouded in sorrow. "The airman's...he was moved in here early yesterday evening. Poor boy didn't make it."

As they made the bed, an atmosphere of deep sorrow descended upon the room.

"Bloody war," Nurse Bell surprised May by saying. "Taking ordinary lads in their prime. You can't stop to think about it, though, can you?" She checked her side of the counterpane matched the length of that on the other side of the bed, and then her troubled gaze met May's eyes. "What concerns me is, I'm starting to get immune to it all."

May told her, "I don't think so. The very fact you're concerned means you care. But we can't get involved or else we wouldn't be able to do our job." May repeated Sister Jordan's words. "But that doesn't mean we aren't without compassion."

Nurse Bell looked at May with renewed respect. Then her eyes grew round with scandal. "The airman had company during his final hours."

"How d'you mean?"

"According to what I've heard, one of the porters sat with him. He was delivering an oxygen tank to the ward and saw the lad in the side ward. He took it upon himself to sit with him when he wasn't on duty."

"Didn't Night Sister tell him to scarper?"

"Night staff were rushed off their feet and I think she turned a blind eye."

May was glad for the airman's sake Night Sister wasn't one of the old school nurses and didn't keep to the rule book.

Uncannily, May experienced a sense of déjà vu. She just knew what Nurse Bell would say next.

"The porter was that conchie bloke nobody's got time for. Cheeky blighter. Night staff were appalled and questioned Sister's judgement—but only between themselves. But I agree with them...For heaven's sake, who'd trust a conchie?" Her face sharpened in judgement. "The nerve of the man. If I had my way I'd throw him to the lions, so to speak."

With a snort, the nurse smoothed the top of the counterpane, and began to wash the bedside locker inside and out.

May, astonished at the outburst, found herself wanting to defend Richard. After all, he had comforted the young airman in his final hours and so he must have a compassionate heart. But she didn't say anything because Nurse Bell had made her judgement and wouldn't change her mind. It only went to show that where conscientious objectors were concerned, it brought the worst out in people.

May thought of the mean way she had herself treated Richard. She blushed. A certain admiration had grown within her for him—for all he put himself through.

The door opened and Sister Jordan stood there, bristling with impatience.

"Nurses. You've taken your time." May stood to attention. She knew Sister Jordan meant business.

"There's been another crash landing, a Halifax bomber this time...another landing practice that didn't go well. The co-pilot is to be admitted to this ward." She turned to May. "You, Nurse, will go to the Casualty department and escort the patient to the ward." She looked at Nurse Bell. "While you will set up an enema tray for those patients about to have surgery." She pulled herself up to her full height. "Before either of you go to dinner see that the beds are tidy with pillow flaps facing away from the door, counterpanes straight and the ward orderly."

"Yes, Sister."

"Might I add, all of this should have been done long before now?" Sister Jordan gave each nurse a glacial glare, and then stalked away.

Nurse Bell wanted to know, "And when have we had time?"

"Sometimes," May sighed, "there's no pleasing Sister Jordan."

In Casualty the cubicles were full of nervous-looking people who wished they were somewhere else.

Then May saw Richard talking to a patient lying on a trolley. Did the man ever sleep?

Then, without glancing round, Richard wheeled the trolley away and left through the double doorway.

May was confused and didn't know if she was glad or disappointed that he hadn't acknowledged her. Then she wondered why she cared. Why did the man intrigue her so and draw her like a magnet? Common sense told her to back away but the empathetic part of May that saw the good side in folk, especially in someone who took it upon themselves to spend time with the dying, didn't want him to suffer and felt bad for how she had treated him before.

Her duties done, May made for the large and echoey dining room with round tables dotted around the room and a multitude of nurses both in uniform and mufti. Maids served dinner: lentil soup, then shepherd's pie. May sat at a table with five nurses whom she knew by their appearance only but none of them acknowledged her. Each of them was recounting what they'd got up to on New Years' Eve—two bemoaning the fact they'd had to work the night shift.

"Use your loaf..." a nurse told them, "at least you got Christmas off, jammy bugger. You can't have it all ways."

"I've never had Christmas off for three years," another nurse complained.

"Were you busy?" someone asked.

"Yes. We'd two deaths on the ward. Two old dears who'd been hanging on for days."

"Bad luck."

"Not really. We had a bet with ward eight—the other geriatric ward—on who'd have the most deaths during the night and we won."

Everyone laughed and May smiled good-naturedly. Finishing her shepherd's pie, she rose and left the table. She knew those nurses would give their patients the best possible medical care and without doubt they weren't cold-hearted or uncaring. Having a macabre sense of humour was sometimes the only way to cope. May knew those nurses had the choice but didn't run away from their responsibility.

It struck May that this was the kind of wise thing Etty Milne would say. As she walked over the hospital grounds towards Parklands, she stopped in her tracks. Etty wasn't her friend any more. Pain squeezed in her chest and she could barely breathe. So much had happened recently she'd almost forgotten what the row was about. It had only been a few weeks since she'd last seen Etty, but it felt like a lifetime.

Suddenly, it was as though her mind cleared, allowing the simple facts to present themselves. How could she—May rebuked herself—take a moral stand when she too had borne Billy a child out of wedlock? But May was confused, she admitted, as she didn't know how she felt about her friendship with Etty any more.

Billy had never promised her anything. Being Billy, he'd wanted the excitement of getting engaged because he'd joined up and was going to be sent abroad to an uncertain future. But he would never have settled down, May knew that now. She'd believed she could change him, but would she want him to change? In her heart, May would always love him but now was the time to let him go.

With that thought, May realised that though the time had come to forgive and make up with Etty, she wasn't quite ready yet. She had to get used first to the idea Billy was no longer part of her life.

Tears welling in her eyes, May set off to walk the relatively short distance to Parklands.

Lectures that afternoon were given by a plastic surgeon: a tall, well-dressed man with a fine bone structure and a polished look about him.

After tea, the nurses made their way up to their rooms.

"Guess what?" Maureen's expression held fervour.

The three student nurses, wrapped in blankets—for the weather outside, grey skies and rain, was depressing—lounged on their beds.

Valerie pretended to be studying because she was still in a huff with the others.

"I'm going to visit my parents and do what you suggested," Maureen told May. "They are stifling me and it's time I did what's right for me. I'm not a little girl any more."

"Oh my god." Valerie's tone was sarcastic. "Mummy won't be at all pleased about that."

May was horrified. Valerie had no reason to speak to Maureen in such a way.

"No, I expect she won't"—Maureen spoke civilly—"but she'll have to get used to the idea."

"So, what will you do?" May suspected she knew the answer.

"I'm going to follow my heart and become a nun." She looked intently at May. "Being a nurse is all very well but it upsets me when I have to leave a patient when they need me most and I'm forbidden to talk with them. I'm not cut out to treat them medically." She looked bashful as if she didn't know how to go on. "It's... their souls that concern me. Sometimes, all patients want is someone to listen to them."

"Jolly good show," Valerie's voice broke in. Her tone was outlandishly posh. "You can help absolve all their sins."

Appalled, in an instant May knew what this was all about. Valerie was jealous of her and Maureen's friendship and she felt left out.

Weary of Valerie's outbursts, May retorted, "Grow up, Valerie. You're not the only one with problems."

"I never said I was." Valerie pouted. "Anyway, I wasn't talking to you."

May got mad now. "Stop acting like a schoolkid."

Valerie stood up and looked as if she was going to throw the medical book she had in her hand at May.

"Don't..." Maureen's voice was calm.

Valerie hesitated, then, turning, she slammed the door as she left the room.

The bang still ringing in her ears, May collapsed back on the bed.

Maureen rolled her eyes in mock horror. "I'm the redhead. I'm the one who's supposed to have the temper. Seriously, though, the poor girl feels left out," Maureen confirmed.

"There's no need to take it out on others, though." May was cross for Maureen's sake.

"Promise me something. Valerie might live to regret her outburst in future, and if she does and I've left by then, tell her I forgive her and wish her well."

"Why, when are you goin'?"

"I'll tell Mum and Dad first, before handing my notice in to Matron."

Alec had written to May asking her when her next day off was. His nana apparently was dying to meet her and had invited May to tea. Alec concluded, *she says she'll bake scones—Nana's speciality.*

May felt bad that she hadn't contacted Alec as promised, but she'd had reservations about meeting him after their last date. She was still disturbed by the memory of him grabbing her arm and making a fuss about that nice Navy serviceman who was, after all, only being friendly. May could understand his jealousy in a way as she'd often felt the same way herself when Billy had flirted with other women—but May had suffered in silence. She reminded herself that it was because Alec cared so much he acted the way he had.

But Maureen's words rang in her ears: *what I do know is caring for someone means trusting and never hurting them.*

May came to a decision. She would meet up with Alec, explain she wasn't ready yet for any kind of romantic involvement and say that with work commitments and studying it would be best if they didn't see each other for a while. That would be the kindest thing to do. She would be gentle as she knew Alec would be upset because he cared for her.

May wrote to Alec telling him that her next day off was the following Sunday. She had intended to study all day but decided to set her alarm an hour earlier each morning before she went to work so she could make up studying time.

Sunday arrived, and May spent the morning revising but kept out of Valerie's way because the rift between them hadn't been mended.

News broke that British forces had captured Maungdaw in Burma—an essential port for Allied supplies. The update brought further hope and spirits ran high that the New Year might bring peace at last.

Late that afternoon, May made her way down Dunlop Road to meet with Alec at the corner of Chi.

Halfway down the street a male voice called out, "Wait, Nurse Robinson."

May turned and saw the son of one of the patients on the ward. Mr. Harrison was recovering from an operation on his back and May had seen his son visiting at the hospital.

Mr. Harrison junior caught up with May. A pleasant, good-looking bloke, he wore a khaki uniform. May knew that he had a wife and bairn because Mr. Harrison senior kept a photo of them all on his locker top.

He beamed a friendly smile. "I've just been in to visit with Da this afternoon. He's doing grand. When d'you think he'll come home, Nurse?"

Embarrassed, May was at a loss how to answer. She'd get into trouble discussing patients on the street.

"Better talk to Sister," she answered diplomatically.

"Sorry, Nurse." He cocked an eyebrow. "I'm speaking out of turn. But I just want yi' to know the family's appreciative, like, for all you've done for Da. Because we all know he can be a right bugger—sorry, Nurse—at times."

"Your dad is a model patient," she told him, tongue in cheek.

They chatted some more as they walked, mostly about recent war news. Then, as they approached the roundabout at Chi, May saw Alec waiting on the opposite side of the road.

She waved but he didn't respond.

Mr. Harrison hesitated. "I'll leave you then. I'm goin' the other way down Laygate. Bye, Nurse. Thanks again."

With a smile that showed a row of lovely white teeth, he turned left and, whistling, continued down the road.

"Who was that, then?" Alec asked when she approached.

"Oh, just a fella whose dad's on the ward." Purposefully, she moved on from the subject of Mr. Harrison. "It's kind of your nana to invite us for tea."

"She can't wait to meet yi'." Alec took her hand and started up the street.

They walked down Whale Street to the bottom block, passing Etty's house on the way. May imagined the two little girls indoors, felt the warm atmosphere that swept over her every time she walked into Etty's kitchen. A pang of sadness enveloped May as cosy thoughts from the past filled her mind but she banished them away as this was not the time to deliberate what to do about Etty.

Alec stopped outside a green door with peeling paint but a gleaming brass knocker.

A wiry, grey-haired, elderly lady answered the door. She wore a pinny on top of a high-necked grey dress and cosy-looking furry slippers.

"Come in ... make yourself at home ..." She was rather bent as she led them along the dark passageway, which had that peculiar stale smell that invaded old folks' homes sometimes. The kitchen reminded May of Etty's the way the range's fire seemed to belch smoke into the room.

"May, this is Nana."

"Pleased to meet you, Mrs. ..."

"Call me Nana, everyone does."

"I've told you, Nana, to have that chimney seen to."

"Eee! You did, our Alec, I promise I will."

May couldn't call the next two hours pleasant exactly, but she did survive and for Nana's sake she tried to appear as though she was having a good time. The trouble was, Nana was too anxious to please and it put May on edge.

"Mmm, scones." May was genuinely delighted when Nana took scones out of the oven and put them, risen and golden, on the table. "They look delicious. How d'you get them to rise like that?"

"I don't use that dried stuff, I use—"

"An egg," Alec interrupted. "Nana saves her ration egg for me 'cos she knows scones are me favourite."

Nana fussed over everything and nothing was a trouble. Were the scones warm enough? Was their tea the right colour? No, May should sit down, she'd get the milk. Had they had enough scones, because they could share hers if they'd like? They should just say if they were cold, because it was no trouble to put more coal on the fire ...

"I've just borrowed a bucket of coal from me neighbour next door," she told Alec, who sat stiffly in the chair looking morose, probably because he couldn't get a word in.

Nana's eyes darted about the room as she spoke and the poor old soul reminded May of a nervous bird.

May was thankful when Alec stood up from his chair and said it was time for them to go.

"So soon? You've just arrived..." Nana looked as if someone had caught her pinching from the gas meter money pot. "Is everything all right, son? You're not upset, are you?"

Alec peered at the mahogany clock that ticked on the range mantelpiece. "Nana...we've been here over two hours."

Nana vigorously nodded. "All right, son. You know best."

With a fretful expression, she scurried away to bring their coats.

When she returned, she looked at her grandson. "You're not mad with me again, are you, Alec?"

Without saying a word, he shrugged into his coat and left, May trailing behind.

CHAPTER FIFTEEN

"Let's stay out a bit longer and go to the pub," Alec said.

They stood at the top end of Nana's street and the bigger than usual moon hanging in the sky held a ponderous expression as though it was trying to tell May something.

"If you don't mind, Alec, I'm bushed. I want an early night." May intended to tell him about the break-up when they reached Parklands.

The vein ticked in his temple.

"I want…" Alec spat. "I know what you're up to. You're meeting with that fella, aren't you?"

"What!"

"Him—I saw you talking to earlier."

"You mean Mr. Harrison? I told you who he—"

"I saw the idolising way you looked at him…and his smile was all knowin'."

"Alec, he's a patient's son and he's married with a kid."

"When did that ever stop anybody?"

In the moon's eerie white light, Alec's livid face was unsettling.

May put on her professional head and thought of him as an angry and overwhelmed relative.

"You're upset. When you calm down we'll talk this over but for now let's—"

"You conniving bitch…all the time carrying on behind me back. How many are there? Besides the one I saw at the dance and him this afternoon?"

His face was now vicious. May, stunned and frightened at such abominable behaviour, knew arguing wouldn't solve the matter.

Alec had turned into a jealous lunatic.

"I'm off home," she said, with authority, though she felt at a loss and vulnerable.

As she turned to go, he grabbed her arm. May wriggled but couldn't get free.

A man passing by in the street, cigarette in his mouth, looked at them from beneath the rim of his trilby hat.

"Please help me," May pleaded but the man ducked his head and hurried off along the street. Probably he thought it was just a lover's tiff and didn't want to get involved.

"Let go of me." She struggled.

Out of the corner of her eyes she saw a trolley coming from the left towards the bus stop the other side of Dean Road.

It came to a halt.

"I never want to see you again," she told Alec.

"We'll see about that," he sneered. "You're not goin' anywhere unless I say so. Or else I'll beat the living daylight out of yi'. That'll teach you to double-time me."

He let go of her arm and raised his own as if to strike her. Terrified, but with her wits about her, quick as a flash, May darted across the road. As the trolley pulled away from the kerb she jumped onto the platform and clung onto the centre pole for dear life.

The conductor, a middle-aged man, tipped the peak of his uniform cap in agitation.

"Miss, d'you want to get yerself killed?"

Like Mam, May thought. And her chin wobbled—at this moment she desperately needed comfort from her mother.

Her breath coming in short gasps, she found a window seat in the first row after she left the platform. Pulse racing, May was terrified. She gave an incredulous shake of the head. This was Alec, someone she'd grown fond of—but now a person who scared her witless. May would never trust her judgement about a man again.

His poor nana, she thought, no wonder she acted so nervous.

May paid her fare and the conductor gave her a ticket. The trolleybus, moving along Dean Road, turned at the roundabout and stopped while the conductor alighted from the platform. The passengers waited as he changed the trolley's poles to another set of overhead wires. The deed done, the conductor came aboard again and rang the bell. The trolley continued up the road to the next stop.

"Hawway, fella," the bus conductor shouted, his hand on the bell, "I'll wait for you."

May gathered that someone was running to catch the bus. The hairs on her neck stood up. She knew before she turned who the "fella" would be. She twisted around in her seat and, in the moon's revealing light, she stared into the taunting eyes of the man she now most feared.

He gave a nonchalant nod and then swaggered to the front of the bus behind the driver.

She sat rigid, wondering what to do. She could explain to the conductor, but what could he do? He was just doing his job. The best course of action was to be first to alight from the platform then run hell for leather to Parklands.

As the bus neared the stop, May rose and made for the platform. The bus conductor pressed the bell to alert the driver to stop.

Alec stood up and started to make his way up the aisle.

She said in an undertone to the conductor, "I'm a nurse at the hospital and the man behind is pestering me... Can you think of a way to give me a few minutes' start when I get off the bus?"

"Leave it to me, pet."

As the bus pulled up to the kerb, the conductor walked away to the front and blocked the aisle.

"Fella," May heard him say. "Ticket please. I don't recall you buying one."

May didn't wait to hear more. Leaping from the platform, she raced across the road, all the while expecting Alec's hand to grab her by the shoulder. She heard a bell ting and presumed it was the signal to start the trolley. On she ran until she tripped over the far side kerb, and landed painfully on a knee on the pavement.

"Are you all right, hinny?" A woman from the hospital kitchen peered down at her. There was a short queue of folk behind her. May realised that it must be past eight o'clock and the hospital had changed to the night shift. This queue was the staff making their homeward journey. Alec wouldn't dare harm her here in front of everyone. She hesitated.

Alec's figure loomed in the darkness of the road.

Without stopping to think, May, knee throbbing, hobbled towards the sanctuary of Parklands. She was only a few yards away when she heard the sound of breathing as someone ran up from behind. A hand gripped her by the hair.

"Turn around," he demanded.

The roots of her hair felt as if they were being pulled out and May, in agony, had no choice but to obey.

"I told you it would be the worse for yi' if you tried to get away. You belong to me and that's how things are going to stay."

Despite the pain, defiance zipped through May. "I'll never belong to you and you can't make me."

Alec raised his free arm ready to strike and May closed her eyes, waiting for the painful blow.

It never came.

She heard gurgling noises. Opening her eyes, she saw an arm tight around Alec's neck.

"Let her go or I swear I will throttle you," a calm and composed voice said.

May recognised the voice. Mercifully, her hair was released but her scalp still stung.

The arm released from around Alec's neck and he looked up at his adversary.

Richard Bentley.

"You'd better watch out." Alec, massaging his throat, spoke thickly.

"Why? What are you going to do?"

"Give yi' a hammerin'."

"Choose a time," Richard goaded.

Alec looked for a moment as if he'd go for Richard, then, as if he thought better of it, he sloped away.

"I'm warning yi'. Watch your back."

"And I'm warning you," Richard shot back, "if you ever touch a hair of this nurse's head, then I'll come after you. Believe me, you will be sorry."

They sat in a dim corner of the smoky pub with a beer in front of them. May didn't like beer but she'd heard it was an acquired taste and besides, she didn't know what else to ask for. She knew Richard was uncomfortable, worrying that someone might see them, and he kept checking around. May was touched.

After Alec skulked away, she hadn't been able to stop shaking. She hoped Richard wouldn't notice.

He did. In his deep and casual tone he asked, "How about I take you to the pub? You've had a scare. It'll give you time to get over what happened."

It was the second time that day May had been invited to the pub, but although she had vowed she'd never trust another man again she knew with a certainty that comes from following her gut feeling that she was safe with him.

May took another sip from the half pint of beer and tried in vain not to wrinkle her nose. "Where did you spring from?" she asked.

Richard had this habit of pausing before he spoke, as if he liked to think over what he wanted to say.

"I'd just finished the late shift and was queuing at the bus stop when I saw a figure running from behind the trolleybus as if Satan himself was chasing her." His smile was brief. "I didn't recognise it was you. Then a bull of a man raged after you and I knew that whoever you were, he spelt trouble."

"You came to the rescue."

"I just wanted to make sure you were all right."

May thought of all those other upstanding men in the queue who had looked the other way. She knew she was being unfair as some folk didn't want to get involved, but she would be forever grateful that Richard wasn't one of those people.

"You're supposed to be a pacifist," she reminded him.

"When I saw it was you," he began, and then he paused and pursed his lips as he thought, "something snapped and I just wanted to stop that man whichever way I could. I've never felt that kind of hostility towards another man in my life."

"Good job you were bigger than him," May joked, as she tried to process what he'd just said.

"It was clear the man was a coward at first sight."

May shifted uncomfortably but Richard didn't seem concerned that he was using the description he was so often labelled with. "He chooses his opponent's strength... that's why he preys on defenceless women."

"That's not me, any more," May vehemently replied, for she'd had enough of being manipulated by men. Dad—yes, if she were honest. Then Billy, too. Now Alec. But not any more.

She said to Richard, "You were ready to brawl."

"The man only needed a scare. He's probably afraid of his own shadow. He's a bully."

"So is Hitler"—she didn't like the disapproval in her voice—"but you won't do anything about him." There! She had told him what she thought.

Richard took a swig of his pint, and then put the glass down on the table. His gaze held hers for a moment. "People should have the right to follow their innermost conscience. Mine tells me war and killing is wrong. I won't be forced into helping in any way with war-making."

May pressed further. "Is it to do with your faith?"

"I'm a Catholic, yes, but I'm not practicing. Though it has to be said that Christ preached love and not bloodshed." His lips pursed in that mutinous way May was beginning to recognise. "It's a belief inside you can't deny whatever your religion."

"Surely there was alternative work you could do."

"At the tribunal I was registered to join the army for non-combatant duties but I refused to go. It was still helping their war."

"What happened?"

Richard paused as two men in uniform came into the pub. As a gust of cold air whipped around the tables, the servicemen closed the door. Richard watched as they passed the table and found a seat by the bar.

"I was sentenced and taken away by military escort."

He shook his head. Though his eyes roamed the room, May realised he was someone who, though high-principled to a fault, cared not a jot what folk thought about him or the outcome of his actions.

"The upshot was I was sent to Wormwood Scrubs prison for six months." A haunted look came into his eyes. "Something I wouldn't wish on my worst enemy."

May wondered how bad things had got but didn't like to ask because Richard, a seemingly private and proud man, wouldn't want to invoke anyone's sympathy.

"And after?"

"Finally, I was exempted by the authorities and I was sent to work in the hospital."

May knew by his tight-lipped expression this wasn't the whole story but she didn't press for more information. She didn't know what she really thought about him. On one hand, she admired him for having the courage to stand up for what he believed in. On the other she agreed with folk, especially those who'd lost loved ones. Why should he be exempt while others were being killed keeping the country safe for the likes of him?

Her dander up, May asked him, "What if everybody thought like you? Hitler would win."

Richard thought awhile, and then nodded. "I could say if all those that fought did think like me there'd be no war to win, but that's too simplistic. The only fair answer I can give is that every man must do what is right by him and let God be his judge."

He stuck out his chin in an obstinate fashion and May couldn't help but notice his chiselled features.

She needed to take a step back, May thought, she was getting too involved. "I have to go." She jumped up and took her coat from the back of the chair.

"I'd like to see you safely home to Parklands...if that's all right by you."

How different he was to Alec, for whom everything was a demand.

Richard drained his glass, then stood up, tall and fine with his black shiny hair and rather intense handsome face. Lordy Moses, she thought, why were the off-limits men so attractive? She'd always thought most married men were handsome brutes.

"I'm fine, thanks. I can take care of myself."

She saw the twinkle in his eyes and had the grace to blush.

"All right," she said, "I give in." The thought of Alec lurking in the shadows was not a pleasant one. "Just this once."

She wanted to make things clear.

*

After he left Nurse Robinson at Parklands, Richard decided to walk home. He needed to absorb all that had happened and besides, there was no rush to get back.

It was as he passed the magnificent town hall's sweep of steps that he began to recognise the uneasiness burning within him. Remembering what he said about how "men must do what is right for them and let God be their judge," he knew he'd upset the nurse in some way. She was the kind of person who couldn't hide their feelings. He was surprised that it mattered to him what she thought. But he couldn't share his self-doubt—not with her or anyone. He alone must live with it.

He thought of the horror he felt every time a soldier was admitted to hospital with injuries so terrible the sight made Richard wonder at the human race. That men would sacrifice morality to do such terrible acts of violence to one another. God-fearing people, who under normal circumstances wouldn't hurt a fly. He felt guilty that young lads were fighting for peace while he was living in relative comfort on the home front. But he couldn't change his standpoint on war. It went so deep that nothing—not even the isolation, humiliation and contempt he had to suffer—would alter his mind.

His leanings towards pacifism had started when he was in his teens and had joined, with his Quaker girlfriend, the Peace Pledge Union that had campaigned since the early thirties for a warless world.

Then his Uncle Jeffrey, who had served in the Great War, had confided in him about his experiences and reinforced Richard's conviction.

"Lad," he'd said one Christmas Day when the rest of the family were out for a walk after lunch and the pair of them were huddled by an open fire, "think twice before you join up if there's another war. There surely will be, since that is man's way."

His eyes had glazed over as he watched the leaping flames, as if he was looking down the years at the horror of it all.

Uncle Jeffrey lit his pipe. "I tell you this for your own good but also to keep my mates' memories alive. I've never told their families the truth about their boys, how they died, because the lads wouldn't want their relatives to suffer on their behalf."

As he rambled on, the young Richard, intolerant of the old, wished he'd gone out in the freezing cold with the others for a walk.

"Three of us, there were," Uncle Jeffrey went on, "joined up together. We were excited because we'd been no further than the town we lived in before then. Known each other since we were young lads...went to school together." He puffed on his pipe and clouds of smoke billowed to the ceiling.

"Such excitement to be at sea...to land in France...but that's where the fascination at being in a foreign land ended. We were stationed at a place called Ypres in Belgium which must have once been a lovely town but not any more, not when Johnnie, Simon and I were there, late summer of nineteen-seventeen.

"The battles were fought in bloodied trenches around Ypres. There was torrential rain every day, a wilderness of stinking mud that could swallow a fellow, never to be seen again. That's what happened to Johnnie after a grenade got him. They say thousands of bodies were never recovered, and my mate Johnnie was one of them."

He sucked at his pipe. "Poison gas got Simon in the trenches. Poor sod. Nineteen, he was. Good men that could have done something with their lives. Instead, they're barely a memory now."

Uncle Jeffrey came out of his reverie, and when he turned and faced Richard, it was the first time Richard had seen a grown man cry.

"It was hell on earth, lad. Don't you be going, not if you want to keep your sanity."

The effects of poison gas stayed with Uncle Jeffrey until his untimely death in his late forties.

Later, when Richard thought of his uncle's tale, the thought of his friends' deaths affirmed his pacifist principles.

His little brother came to mind, who had paid the ultimate sacrifice. As Richard remembered the dreams Jeff harboured as a little lad—the desire in those far-off days to be a train driver—his throat tightened as grief overcame him.

Richard never wanted to be a part of the madness of war. Not because he was afraid, but because of Simon and Johnnie. Had they made a difference? Richard thought not, because here the world was in the grip of another war.

But the repercussions in his family over his position were something Richard could never come to terms with. The Bentleys never expressed emotion, were never the kind of close-knit family Richard craved as a youngster. His pa, a stiff upper-lip army type, was Richard's hero and he would have done anything to make him proud. Then war was declared and Richard, a committed pacifist by then, summoned the courage to tell his father that he refused to enlist in the army. Furious with his son, Pa labelled Richard both a coward and a disgrace and virtually disowned him.

Richard, now near the bottom end of Fowler Street, willed his mind from the past to thoughts of pretty Nurse Robinson, who reminded him of an actress but he couldn't think of her name. Under normal circumstances he would have made advances but since the war had begun he was wary of approaching a girl. For one thing they were more interested in men in uniform, but more importantly, it would go against them if they were seen with him—a conchie—and he understood their dilemma. An alliance with a conchie was considered as bad as consorting with the enemy. Richard shrugged. He would have to admire Nurse Robinson from afar.

He had an instinct that she looked at life from a different perspective than other people. Ever since that first day when he had escorted the latest set of probationer nurses to Parklands, Richard had been attracted to Nurse Robinson. Her candid eyes possessed an innocence that was appealing, and like a child, she was curious about all things and people. She was an open book, every emotion she experienced showed on her face and she had a blistering honesty which left you in no doubt what she thought of you. Richard smiled. Didn't he know it; she had told him in no uncertain terms what she thought of his unwillingness to fight for his country. He sobered. Would he have fought for her? He remembered the anger he had felt at the numbskull who was going to strike her. The passion Richard had felt shook him, though he had been able to stay in control and avoid a brawl. But the residue of anger still inside was anathema to him.

Richard made his way along Ocean Road to the place he called home these days. He passed a young soldier and his girlfriend linking arms as they came out of the Scala Cinema and an unaccustomed ache—of loneliness? Self-pity?—overcame him. His thoughts again turned to Nurse Robinson. The woman was no fool. She was quick and intelligent, but the unique thing about her, and what Richard found so appealing, was that she seemed unaware of these qualities. Yes, he thought, as he turned the corner into Salmon Street, once upon a time he'd have made a play for her but not under these circumstances—there was no way he'd want to undermine her integrity. Besides, he didn't think she was interested. She'd made that plain with her cool and aloof attitude towards him when he'd left her at Parklands earlier.

"Thanks, Mr. Bentley," she'd said, "for getting me out of a fix tonight. I don't know what I'd have done if you hadn't been there." She hesitated, a frown wrinkling the smooth skin of her brow. "And I have to say, I do admire your inner strength to stand up for your beliefs."

Her tone implied that she didn't agree with them, though.

He paused and tried to think of a suitable answer but failed.

He replied, lamely, "Any time you're in need of help, I'm at your service."

She gave him a bold stare; an *I don't think so* kind of stare.

*

When May entered the lounge, Maureen was sitting alone by the fire, looking pensive.

She looked up. "Oh! Hello... had a good time?"

May hesitated. She wondered if she should tell Maureen about Alec, as the lass had become not only a friend but also a confidante. In the past, May realised with a twinge of sadness, Etty had been the one she'd shared her troubles with. She found herself thinking about the letters Etty had sent to Parklands that now lay unopened on the bottom shelf of May's locker. At the time, she'd refused to read them but found neither could she throw them away. After a while the letters stopped. A sign that Etty must have given up on the friendship. A pang of remorse gripped May's stomach—she didn't want that. She vowed that when the time was right she'd swallow her stupid pride and—

"Everything all right?" Maureen's voice penetrated her thoughts.

Maureen's expression concerned, May made up her mind to tell her about this evening. When she came to the part about the near assault, Maureen's face not only expressed shock but sorrow too.

"Oh! Goodness. What a brute." She shook her head. "I've come across his controlling type before. I expect he suffers from some form of desperate insecurity."

Trust Maureen to empathise with the aggressor, but that was her way and May's too, usually, but not now when she was the innocent victim.

"That doesn't excuse his actions," she replied.

"No, but it helps understand them. I'll pray for him."

May moved on to the scene with Richard.

"Thank goodness he was there to intervene," Maureen said with relief. "Please tell me that's the last you'll see of Alec... he needs some kind of help."

"I never want to see him again. Though I feel sorry for his nana. I realise now she was scared of him."

"I'll pray God works his wonders and helps them both."

Maureen's serene face shone with hopefulness and May envied her her faith.

"I know the chap you mean, who came to your rescue," Maureen continued from the earlier conversation, "the porter who works at the hospital." Her face creased in concern. "Do be careful, associating with him. People tend to be biased when anyone befriends a conscientious objector."

"Maureen Gardener! You of all people saying such a thing! I mean, I thought you'd be the first to defend the underdog."

"I'm thinking of you, May. With all your troubles you don't need to take on another one."

May plonked herself down on the couch and turned towards her friend. "As far as Richard Bentley is concerned I'm thankful to him for what he did, but that's as far as my gratitude goes."

Maureen put an arm around her shoulders. She said, "If only your eyes told the same story."

May blushed. She knew she was confused about how she felt about Richard. The man's arrogance infuriated her and yet she was intrigued by his forthrightness.

"That's enough said about the porter."

But May found herself wishing she'd been a little nicer to him—after all, he'd had the decency to escort her home.

She concentrated on Maureen. "What was up with you before? You looked preoccupied."

"I telephoned Mum and told her my decision... I was a coward and couldn't face her in person."

"What did she say?"

"To say she was disappointed would be an understatement." Regretfully, Maureen shook her head. "She tried to talk me out of it."

May laid a hand on her friend's arm. "Did you stay firm?"

"I told Mum it was too late and that I'd already handed in my resignation."

May gasped. "Gracious...what did she have to say?"

"I think she was resigned to the fact that she couldn't say anything. Mum can make me feel guilty with silence. Anyway"— determination glinted in Maureen's eyes—"I talked for some time with the priest at the church. The outcome is, I'm travelling to a convent in London."

"A convent..." May repeated stupidly.

Maureen wore the happiest smile. "Yes, a nursing convent. It will be rather like here. I will be with twenty others as a novice in training."

"W-when will you go?"

"Matron was rather disappointed that I was leaving but she expressed relief that my nursing training wouldn't be wasted. She agrees I can leave on my next day off, so I'm travelling down to London on Wednesday."

"So soon."

May was happy for her friend but the little insecure voice in her mind wouldn't be silenced. *Someone else to say goodbye to.*

CHAPTER SIXTEEN

May missed Maureen sorely when she left, and, as if she were in mourning, she felt as though she were under water and had slowed down. With no one to spend her evenings with, May was at a loss to know what to do.

One evening after work, as she lay on the bed staring into space, Etty's letters came to mind and May had a never before, irresistible urge to see what they said. Turning on her side, she opened the squeaky locker door and, slipping her hand beneath a heap of underwear, she brought out a pile of white envelopes. May slid from the bed and, making her way downstairs, she sat in an armchair by a comforting open fire that spat and crackled. She tore open the first letter. As she read, Etty's world unfolded in May's mind: the two kiddies, what antics Norma got up to, general gossip about the neighbourhood, moans about rationing, news about the war. At the end of each letter—and there must have been a dozen or so—was the plea, *please forgive me. I miss you.*

As the letters lay in a heap on her knee, May gazed into the dancing flames.

"Oh! And how I miss you too," she whispered. "I don't know when or how but when things quieten down I'll have to get in touch."

Valerie had moved out to the downstairs bedroom before Maureen left, taking Jenny's old bed. A rather nervous and meticulous type,

Jenny had decided she'd had enough of nursing when a patient on Women's Medical vomited down her spotlessly clean uniform apron. After finishing her shift, Jenny was never to be seen again.

"No strength of character, I've seen it many times before." Home Sister gave a knowing nod.

The atmosphere since New Year's Eve, when Valerie had been spiteful to Maureen, was dire, and even though the kindly nurse had tried to patch things up between the three of them, the situation hadn't improved. May, now alone in the bedroom, felt this was her destiny—to lose those she dearly loved and cared for.

Maureen had said when she left, "I might not physically be with you but spiritually I'll be by your side wherever you go. I'll pray every day that your path in life will be smooth and one day, God willing, you'll be reunited with your son. Believe me, there will come a time when I'll be but a fleeting memory; your life will be so happy and full."

May didn't think so but she smiled anyway to humour Maureen.

As she said goodbye, dressed in mufti, tears brimming her eyes, Maureen had told her, "I will miss you terribly."

Then she was gone.

May received a letter at the end of January, its contents glowing, saying how happy Maureen was and how she'd made exactly the right decision.

I'm to be a "postulant" for some months and I live in a cell-like room. I don't go out unless it's to tend the sick but it all seems like home to me and I've never been happier. And, May, if I gain Mother Superior's approval I'll be given another name... and so the letter went on, ending... *You mightn't hear from me but know I am contented to be here serving God in an atmosphere of peace, tranquillity*

*and prayer. And just as it's your heart's dream to become a
registered nurse so it is mine to become a nun.*

May realised then she was being selfish. Maureen was following
her dream and building a life around it. May, instead of moping,
should be thrilled and doing the same thing. From then on, she
bucked up, and whenever she thought of Maureen, it was with
a fond smile.

A month passed and by the end of February, May was mentally
and physically exhausted from long shifts on the ward, training at
Parklands, lectures and constant studying. After one long day spent
in the classroom, she felt a beastly cold threatening. She thought
that having an early night and refraining from putting the alarm on
to study before work early next morning might stop the wretched
thing from developing, but remembered she was supposed to meet
up with the two nurses from downstairs to do a spot of studying.

As they were down to three probationers now, Eileen had
suggested they team up at night and work together. This, May
thought, might be due to the fact that Eileen was wary of Valerie's
temperamental behaviour which could, and often did, cause
disruption. With class certificate tests next month, Eileen would be
nervous and jittery about getting some serious studying done—not
that the lass would need it, clever soul that she was. May, ever the
optimist, thought working together might help the relationship
between her and Valerie. After all, they were grown women and
wasn't there enough confrontation in the world without them
adding to it with juvenile clashes? Still, she was wary as she knew
Valerie could be unpredictable.

One day not long after Maureen had left, Sister Chilvers,
standing at the front of the class in lessons, had drawn herself
up as if to prepare herself for something taxing.

"Nurse Purvis."

"Yes, Sister."

"This morning, I was advised to let a maintenance man in to change the light bulb you reported wasn't working."

"Yes, Sister." Valerie's voice had sounded cautious.

"Nurse, your bed wasn't made. Worse, you'd left your nightdress thrown on top of it for everyone to see. The rules are explicit. Your nightdress should be neatly folded and placed beneath your pillow, your dressing gown hung behind the door. I was highly embarrassed, Nurse. What the young man thought of such indecent behaviour, I dread to think. Let this be a warning. I don't wish to witness such improper behaviour again or I shall be forced to report you to Matron."

Valerie's face had flushed pink with anger, and May could tell the lass was going to erupt. She'd willed Valerie to control her temper. Fortunately, Sister had left the room then to fetch a glass of water before class began.

Valerie, slowly and deliberately, had picked up the inkwell and slung it at the door. Sailing through the air, the inkwell had hit the side of the front desk and to this day there was an ink stain on the floor.

"Stupid cow," Valerie had seethed.

May did understand because the rules had got her down too. Student nurses weren't supposed to think for themselves but follow orders even if they did seem antiquated or unfair. But if Valerie wanted to continue in the nursing profession, she would have to learn to abide by the rules. At that precise moment, seething with indignation, May had imagined Valerie might be considering leaving. To her credit, the lass had got over the incident and carried on.

But the other nurses were fearful of her temper. At times like that, May dearly missed her friend, Maureen, the keeper of peace amongst them.

As they now congregated in the luxuriously warm downstairs bedroom to study, there was a distinct atmosphere of unease. It was plain by the indignant look on her face that Valerie objected to May being there.

The night started reasonably well, as the student nurses fired medical questions at each other. The two beds were littered with medical textbooks, papers and pencils, while "Bones" the skeleton they'd pinched from the classroom hung from a hook behind the door, with his empty eye sockets and ghoulish smile.

"How would you prepare an intravenous injection for—" Eileen began.

May interrupted, "Don't ask me first, me mind's gone blank."

"Nobody's asking you." Valerie's tone was sharp.

"Before an injection," Eileen hastily intervened, "a nurse must approach the patient, draw the screen around his bed, tell him he is going to have an injection…" She did her best and the tricky moment passed.

The atmosphere tense, May was aware of Eileen giving the other two nurses a nervous glance, so she kept her counsel and went to great lengths to avoid an argument, as she could tell Valerie wanted any excuse to quarrel.

"I'm off upstairs," she finally declared, deciding it was obvious she wasn't going to learn anything that night. Besides, despite the heat, she felt shivery cold and wanted to be beneath the bedclothes with a stone hot water bottle.

"Why? Aren't we good enough?" Valerie was gunning for an argument.

May, now frustrated beyond reason, retorted, "Valerie, it's useless talking to you when you're in this kind of mood."

Valerie glared at her but before she could reply, May shot off the bed and made for the door. At this moment she loathed Valerie, but paradoxically she felt a kind of sympathy too as the lass could no more help the way she reacted than May, who once upon a time couldn't help loving Billy to distraction—which had proved self-destructive too.

"Night!" She opened the door and made for the bedroom upstairs, the sight of Valerie's spiteful expression lingering in her mind's eye.

The only redeeming thing about the situation was that she'd have the early night she'd promised herself.

Sometime during the night, May, hot and sticky with a temperature, awoke to the sound that brought fear and trepidation into the sturdiest heart—the air raid siren. Before she had time to turn back the bedclothes, enemy raiders droned overhead—the noise so thunderous, it sounded as though the raiders skimmed over rooftops.

May, jumping out of bed, peeked from behind the thick blackout curtain and gazed up at the sky. As wave after wave of bombers travelled across the heavens, May was thankful no black blobs fell from any of the planes' bellies. The raiders, seemingly not interested in the coast, were probably making for airfields further inland. May's heart was heavy; she felt for the poor souls who'd cop Jerry's wrath this night.

In the early hours she finally got to sleep and the next morning, as she looked into the mirror, May saw dark swathes beneath her eyes. She sighed. So much for a peaceful and restorative night. But her cold did feel better.

She thought of those folks who'd borne the brunt of the enemy in the night and who wouldn't know this morning's light. She couldn't dwell on it because she'd be eternally depressed. She took a deep and steadying breath. She had a job of work to do.

She dressed in her uniform and went down to a breakfast of oatmeal, a slice of bread, margarine and homemade jam.

Valerie, sitting opposite, avoided any eye contact.

As May arrived on the ward, she put her cloak in the cloakroom and reported to the office.

"Nurse Robinson reporting for duty, Sister."

Sister Jordan, sitting in a captain's chair behind her office desk, looked surprisingly as weary as May felt.

Night Sister came to give the report and when she left, Sister Jordan addressed the nurses on day duty.

"Breakfast has arrived," she told them briskly. "I'll be ready to serve as soon as I've finished reading this report on the new patient. You, Nurse Robinson, can feed the patients who aren't able to feed themselves."

"Yes, Sister."

"We have a busy day ahead." Sister's eyes travelled the staff. "There is a long list of operations." She faltered. "The pilot admitted yesterday in bed one has had his leg amputated below the knee. The surgeon says there's hope yet to save the other one. Keep a close eye on him, nurses."

"Yes, Sister," they chorused.

May moved onto the ward and began the task of giving the infirm patients a drink from a china cup with a spout.

Making her way to the kitchen, May passed bed one, noticing the metal cage in the bed that protected the pilot's leg. His thin, wan face watching, he looked older than his years. May smiled and glanced at his chart that hung over the end bed rail. His name caught her eye.

Phillip Jordan.

Sister, May thought, had given out breakfast and done her duty around the ward without a hint of the suffering she must surely be feeling inside.

"Nil by mouth for Mr. Foster, Nurse, he's first on the list for surgery. He was prepped earlier." Sister Jordan was relentless with tasks this morning.

"Yes, Sister."

The morning wore on and then it was time for the drinks round. May wheeled the trolley onto the ward.

Sister walked over from the medicine cabinet. "Nurse. You are to report to Matron's office."

Crikey! What had May done now?

"Shall I finish the drinks first, Sister?"

"No, Nurse... I suggest you hurry. Run along now."

May knocked and waited outside Matron's door. Her mind went through all the misdemeanours she could possibly be accused of. She hadn't run anywhere and all her night attire was out of view in the bedroom and she was never late...

Footsteps tapped from behind and when she turned, Valerie Purvis stood glowering at her.

Then the office door opened and Matron appeared. "Enter, Nurse Robinson. You too, Nurse Purvis."

As she entered, the heat belching from the cast iron radiator made the room both stuffy and claustrophobic. Standing alongside Valerie in front of the desk, May was struck by the thought that maybe Matron was aware that the two of them were at loggerheads, for nothing escaped her; she had eyes and ears everywhere.

"Nurses." There was gravity in both Matron's voice and expression, and May prepared herself for a reprimand. "Mr. Gardener has been in touch."

At first, May didn't grasp who that was.

"Maureen's dad?" Valerie's voice held surprise.

"Prepare yourself for a shock," Matron told them. "I'm sorry to inform you both but your friend and colleague was killed during an air raid."

May heard the words but they didn't register.

Matron went on, "Mr. Gardener telephoned to inform me there was a raid during the night and Nurse Gardener made with the others for the convent shelter in the cellar. She realised one of the convalescing patients staying at the convent was missing and went back to search for them. By the time the fire brigade arrived, the convent was a raging inferno and..." Matron swallowed and looked noticeably sad. "Nurse Gardener didn't emerge."

A silence followed as the two of them digested the news.

"Mr. Gardener," Matron continued, "asks that I tell you he is grateful as he knows how close you girls were and thanks you for the friendship you showed to his daughter. It means a lot to both him and Mrs. Gardener." Matron drew herself up. "You may go to Parklands and make yourself a sweet cup of tea. Stay only until breaktime—it will give you time to digest the news, then return to your ward. Work is a great healer. First, you must inform your ward Sister that I've advised leave of duties till then."

"Yes, Matron."

As they filed out of the room, Matron handed May an envelope.

"For you," she said.

Valerie hurried off along the corridor and May found herself alone outside Matron's office.

She didn't know what to do or what she wanted, but the urge to scream at a God so lapse he didn't take care of his own made May beside herself with anger.

Maureen was dead. May wanted to run and not stop until she was so physically exhausted, she'd fall into a comatose sleep where it would be impossible to think.

No way could she do as Matron suggested and go to Parklands, where memories of Maureen abounded.

When May returned to the ward, Sister was wheeling the medicine cabinet back into place.

She beckoned to May to join her in the kitchen.

Sister closed the door and faced May. "Matron told me about Nurse Gardener. You have my condolences." Her eyes clouded. "We...live in difficult times."

Maureen was dead. May couldn't take it in.

"Matron says I'm allowed to go back to Parklands till break-time." May's voice sounded muffled.

"Is that what you want, Nurse?"

"I...not really."

She would never see Maureen again.

Sister took a deep steadying breath. "In times of trouble a nurse hides her personal feelings and gets on with the job in hand."

"Yes, Sister."

"Keep busy, Nurse, till you drop."

The door opened and Richard Bentley came in. He looked startled, as if he knew something was up. "I've brought the dinner trolley," he told Sister.

"Thank you, porter."

As he left, Richard gave May a concerned glance.

The morning was busy, getting patients to and from surgery, and then attending to aftercare. As Sister advised, May got on with the job but she felt numb. Nothing she did seemed real as she went through the motions.

But that was better by far than feeling the pain of Maureen's death. May feared she'd dissolve into tears and never stop crying.

At dinner time, instead of going to the canteen, May opted to go to the ward's visitors' room, where she sank into one of the red-cushioned high-backed chairs. In the solitude, where posters on the walls blared war-time messages, it seemed the atmosphere was charged with relatives' grief.

May took the letter Matron had given her out of her pocket.

My dear May,

Forgive me that this is an impersonal letter but I can't venture out of the house, as I don't trust my emotional state, because the pain of my daughter's death is too raw.

I want you to know Maureen told me about you and how she was lucky to find such a good friend.

She told me of your discussion about how she felt suffocated and how you suggested she speak to us, her parents, and told her that we only want what is best for her.

I won't lie. At first, I resented your interfering and thought you a busybody who should mind their own business. I realised later that was the fear of losing Maureen that was talking.

I'm so grateful to you. I could never forgive myself if my only child had gone to the grave and we hadn't made up. We had, and I gave her my blessing to follow her vocation in life. I realise our children are only on loan and we must learn to let go when the time is right.

I asked Maureen's forgiveness and now I have peace of mind.

Thank you, my dear child.

Maureen is with her maker now. Remember her not with sadness but with the happy memories you shared together. God willing, one day I too will be able to do so.

Elizabeth Gardener

Tears streamed down May's cheeks, dripping onto her uniform. Brushing them away with the back of her hand, she folded the letter and put it back into her uniform dress pocket.

She sniffed hard and stood up. She had patients to attend to. The ache of sadness afflicting her wouldn't go away and nor would May want it to. It showed how much Maureen meant to her. She would live on forever in May's memory.

I'll be at your side wherever you go.

As she opened the door and stepped into the corridor, May smiled through her tears.

The first person May saw on the ward was Richard, wheeling a patient back from surgery. Did the man have no work to do other than on this orthopaedic ward? She reported to Sister that she was back on duty.

"That's the last of the patients back from surgery, Nurse." Sister looked at her keenly and May was aware of her red blotchy eyes. "I suggest your first job is to see to the laundry bags... then tidy the ward in readiness for visiting. Bed tables cleared and screens around those patients who have had operations."

"Yes, Sister."

"Only two visitors to each bed. No exceptions. I want an orderly and quiet ward this afternoon."

May made for the laundry room, passing Richard in the corridor, pushing an empty trolley. He gave her an intense look.

She ignored him.

The afternoon passed swiftly and May dreaded the return to Parklands, particularly facing Valerie, for she didn't know how the lass would react. May just wanted peace and quiet to grieve and reminisce.

"Nurse Robinson, off duty," she told Sister Jordan at the end of her shift.

Sister was speaking to the pilot in the first bed. May's fragile mind wondered how he was related to her—but Sister Jordan, in charge of the ward, would keep her personal life private.

May left the building and was surprised at the relatively mild February air. She didn't need to huddle beneath the cape she wore as she made her way to Parklands. The night still pleasurably light, there was a hint in the breeze that spring was just around the corner. Walking down the hospital path, she emerged from the gateway.

"That fellow hasn't been bothering you again, has he?"

May started. She turned to see the outline of Richard Bentley leaning up against the hospital's entrance wall.

"What a fright you gave us. What are you doing here?"

His easy-going smile made her hackles rise and May couldn't explain why.

"Waiting for you."

"Why?"

He stood up and towered above her.

"I was concerned about you."

His wide sensuous mouth had full lips and he had a dimple in his right cheek when he smiled. Richard, she realised, had the knack of making May feel that every word she uttered was important.

She told him, "I've been informed that a good friend of mine…" She heard the wobble in her voice and it took all her willpower not to cry. "…died in a London raid."

"The probationer. It's all around the hospital." His rich deep voice was soothing to her. "She was special."

Reality hit like a hammer and May couldn't help the tears that spilled from her eyes, trickling down her cheeks.

She began to walk away.

"Wait." With long strides, he caught up with her. Fumbling in his jacket pocket, he brought out a handkerchief and handed it to her. "You're in no fit state to be on your own tonight. Is there someone you can be with?"

At that moment, a thin woman with a coarse face and disgruntled expression walked towards the gate. May recognised her as a hospital ward maid. The woman, looking from Richard to May, shook her head in disgust.

"Shame on yi', consorting with a conchie." She hurried off as if she might be tainted.

"You'd best go. You don't want to be seen associating with me." Richard gave what appeared to be a shrug of regret.

May, unable to control her emotions, felt a spark of anger towards the woman ignite within her.

"Why must people be hateful towards one another? That woman doesn't know you, yet she condemns you."

You can talk, the voice of honesty spoke in her head.

Richard shrugged. "It's human nature. You don't know what that woman might be going through; I might just be bearing the brunt of her suffering."

As she looked at him, how calm and collected he appeared, May realised she felt a little out of control. In a bolt of clarity, she understood that the cause was fear—fear that death could creep upon you any minute like it had with Maureen.

In her distress, she thought of all the innocents, Maureen's parents, Richard's . . .

"Your mam and dad, how they must suffer."

Richard didn't reply at first but his jaw worked.

"Having me as a son, you mean?"

"No. I didn't—"

"As I've told you before, Ma and Pa disapprove. They have the same views as that woman."

"And the rest of your family . . . brothers, sisters, what do they think?"

Richard paused; as always he seemed to weigh up his words before he spoke. "I had a brother, but he died fighting for his country."

May was shocked and didn't know how to respond. What her empathetic heart did know was that Richard had suffered and the cause of his convictions went far deeper than she'd imagined. Drained by the mixed emotions of the day, she couldn't summon up the energy to think of a suitable answer. What was certain was that with folk ostracising him, it was Richard who needed company.

"Would you like to go for a drink?" she asked. "I don't want to be alone tonight to think."

CHAPTER SEVENTEEN

The trolleybus came to a halt at the bottom of Fowler Street and Richard helped May alight from the platform. They crossed the road and he halted outside the door of the Criterion public house.

"No one should know us in here"—his brow ridged into an anxious frown—"but you never know and gossip soon gets around the hospital. Maybe we should find somewhere safer. I don't want you getting a bad reputation on account of me." He paused and looked thoughtful.

May braced herself. "I'm not afraid of malicious wagging tongues. But neither do I want to be the latest hospital gossip."

"I don't want that for you either."

"Tell me, Richard, where d'you live?"

"Not far from here in Salmon Street."

"Alone?"

"Yes. Apart from the owner of the house downstairs."

"Can we go back to your place?"

"D'you think that's wise?"

"Not if you're going to tell anyone."

"You know what I mean."

"Richard, I'm guessing you won't take advantage of me." She gave a playful grin. "Besides, apparently, I've got a chaperone downstairs if needs be. Seriously though, there's nowhere else to go and I don't want to be on my own." She didn't add that he intrigued her and she couldn't help being interested in him, in seeing where he lived, and finding out what made him tick.

"If you're sure."

They passed the tobacconist's on Marrs Corner then as they went on past the Scala Cinema, May noticed *The Song of Bernadette* was showing. She stopped and an aching lump hurt her throat. Jennifer Jones, the actress, dressed in a nun's garb, wore the very same serene expression Maureen had done when she'd told May she was leaving the hospital to become a nun.

What if—May had the unbearable thought—in her last moments Maureen had regretted the decision? But, May reasoned, this would never be true; Maureen's faith transcended doubt, she believed life was ordained and she'd be ready to meet her maker. For the first time since she'd learned that Maureen had died, May was comforted.

A hand grasped hers and, looking up, tears blurring her vision, she met Richard's understanding gaze.

"Maureen gave me her rosary beads..." Her voice cracked and she couldn't go on.

He squeezed her hand and they continued walking.

They turned the corner into Salmon Street where May saw a row of terraced houses that shouldered up the hill. The evening sun broke through the clouds, yellow sunlight chasing the dark shadows away. May felt heartened, as if she'd emerged from the long black tunnel of winter into spring.

Richard stopped at a tall house with a blue wooden front door whose paint flaked off in places. He brought out a key.

"Does this belong to you?" she asked incredulously.

"Don't be daft, I could only buy a shoebox on my pittance." Richard laughed. "I rent the two upstairs rooms."

Inside, it was gloomy and smelt of damp. A door further along the passage squeaked open.

"Is that you, Richard?"

"Who else, Ernie?"

A light switched on and an older man emerged from a doorway. His hair was grey and he stooped slightly—probably because he was so tall.

"Ernie, this is May Robinson."

"Ahh! Pleased to meet you, hinny." He held out his hand and May noticed that his other shirt sleeve was empty and pinned at the elbow.

She smiled and shook his hand.

"I'm makin' a cuppa," Richard told him. "D'you want one?"

"Don't bother yourself about me." Ernie gave May a wink. "He's the best lodger I've ever had. Heart of gold. Nothin's too much for the fella. Looks after me proper, he does."

He withdrew into the room and closed the door. She wondered if Ernie knew Richard was a conscientious objector.

"I know what you're thinking and yes, he does," Richard told her as he led the way upstairs.

"He seems nice. Does he have a wife?"

"No, she died in childbirth. Ernie never remarried. He rents out the two rooms as much for the company as the money."

"How did he lose his arm?"

"In the Great War."

Richard led her to the landing where he opened a squeaky door and May entered a spacious room with a high ceiling.

Richard bent and picked up newspapers, a book with a lending library date on the open page and a tea cup from the floor, placing them on the table. May surveyed the room. There was clutter on most surfaces—the mantelpiece, table beneath the window and bureau—and she deduced that Richard wasn't the tidiest of people.

"The rooms are just a base," he justified. "I'm hardly ever in."

The furniture, though old, was tasteful. Two worn leather winged-back chairs with Queen Anne legs (the same as Sister Jordan's desk) stood in front of a tiled fireplace. The room must have come furnished, she thought, as she couldn't imagine Richard owning anything. She could see him leading a nomadic kind of life.

"Make yourself at home." Richard made for the door. "Tea?"

"Yes, please."

Once alone, May took off her woollen jacket and placed it over the chair. She went over to the table where a wireless stood and switched it on. Tommy Handley's voice came through the grille. May, not a fan, turned the knob to another station and Vera Lynn's yearning voice singing "We'll Meet Again" came into the room.

May then caught sight of the black and white photographs assembled on a mahogany bureau top. She moved closer and studied them. The larger one was of a man and woman and it looked as though they were attending a wedding, as they had buttonholes in their coats. The man, distinguished-looking, wore a bowler hat over his dark hair and a moustache brushed his upper lip. The woman had a carefree smile showing perfect teeth and wore the most gorgeous wide-brimmed tilted hat with an enormous bow at the front. The two smaller matching-sized photographs were of the same middle-aged man, only this time he wore a uniform, as did the young man in the other picture frame who looked remarkably like Richard.

"My younger brother, Jeffrey," Richard's voice spoke from the doorway. In his hands he held two cups of tea.

As Vera Lynn's heartrending voice continued to sing in the background, May noticed Richard's eyes had a faraway look.

"Were you close to your brother?" she asked.

Richard appeared to give himself a mental shake and, crossing the room, handed her a cup of tea. May sat on a wing-backed leather chair, while Richard sat opposite.

"Jeff was my younger brother by four years," he eventually said. "He lied about his age and joined the army when he was seventeen."

"Goodness me, what a shock for your parents."

Richard took a sip of tea. "On the contrary, Pa was proud… he already had one son a coward."

Uncomfortable, she decided not to comment on his statement. "It must have been terrible for the family when your brother was killed."

"Pa felt that Jeff upheld the Bentley name and died a hero."

May heard the bitterness in Richard's tone and didn't know how to reply. Her nurse training came to the fore and she decided to let him do the talking.

"Jeff died at Dunkirk. He was dodging bullets as he ran towards an enemy machine gun post. He managed to throw his grenade but was killed in the resultant blast."

Pride gleamed in Richard's eye.

"That was brave."

During the silence, as they drank their tea, May imagined the scene—the terrible injuries Richard's brother would have endured if he'd lived.

She asked, "Is that your dad in the other photo, in uniform?"

"Yes, that's Pa."

"Did you live on an army base?"

"Yes, while Pa was at Aldershot. Then when he was posted abroad Ma went with him. They left Jeff and me behind."

It seemed a strange arrangement but May thought it best not to say so.

"Who brought you up?"

"My maternal grandparents. They saw to it I got a university education."

"What did you study?"

"Originally, I was going to study theology."

"What's that?" May hadn't come across the word.

Richard hesitated before choosing his words.

"Let me answer this way. As a committed Christian I wanted to study to help me understand Christianity more deeply. I spent a lot of time with my grandfather. A man I hugely admired. He was a vicar but not the Victorian kind…he had a huge sense of humour. I grew up wanting to spend more time in his company than I did with Pa."

"Is your grandfather still alive?"

"He died of a heart attack the year war started."

"Did you speak with him about…"

"Me being a conchie? Yes…and before you ask"—his eyes twinkled—"he told me I should do what's right for me…to be guided by my conscience."

"But you would naturally be influenced by him," May put in. "Because you admired him so much and you knew that's what your grandfather would do if the situation arose for him."

Richard's eyes gleamed in admiration.

"You confess to having not had much schooling…but you have real insight. That, in my book, counts far more than university qualifications."

May, embarrassed, changed the subject. "So, what did you end up studying at this university?"

"I wanted to become an architect and build houses. So that people wouldn't have to live in slums."

The more she got to know Richard the better she liked him.

He gave a mock long-suffering sigh. "Are we done with the interrogation? Anyway, how about you telling me something about yourself."

What could May say? Every part of her life was a minefield to talk about and she didn't want him to know. It mattered that he kept his respect for her. She evaded the question by telling him about her lack of schooling, how ignorant she was and how becoming a nurse was a dream come true.

In the silence that followed he looked intensely at her.

A burning curiosity made May ask, "What did . . . Jeff think—"

"About me being a conchie?" he finished for her. He stood up and placed his cup and saucer on the table.

"Jeff looked up to me when we were growing up," he told her. "We were very different. I was the lanky awkward one while he was outgoing and sporty—the son every father wants." His tender smile showed no resentment. "But Jeff couldn't understand my view on war." A dark shadow crossed Richard's face. "We had lengthy discussions that turned into heated arguments. When Jeff couldn't make me understand that it was every man's duty to join up, he grew angrier than I'd ever seen him and he called me a bloody coward."

"What did you say?"

"I told him to go to hell." Richard, staring into space, relived the scene and looked visibly upset. He continued, "Jeff had a volatile temper, and I figured if I left him alone, he'd come around and we could talk sensibly. Jeff was fair-minded and I knew that given time he wouldn't hold my views against me."

"So, did you make up?"

Richard shook his head. "The next day he joined up." He swallowed hard. "I never saw him again after that."

In the silence that followed, May's pity for Richard knew no bounds. How many more lives would be ruined by this war? Richard walked over and, reaching out, he took the empty cup from her hand and paused to stare wonderingly at her.

"I've never told anyone that before. Or that I'll carry the guilt of not making up to Jeff till my dying day."

His imploring brown eyes met hers and the air between them electrified. He leaned forward and their lips met.

*

Richard was startled. He hadn't meant the kiss to happen but it had just seemed the right thing to do in the moment. But had he taken advantage of her?

To be fair, he mused, May was party to the kiss too. But it nagged Richard that he'd kissed her when her defences were down. What about later, when she came to her senses and realised what she'd done?

He hadn't known her long and originally wondered if this was just an infatuation. But when he'd seen her tonight by the cinema billboard, her face blotchy with crying but still beautiful, he knew then he'd fallen in love with her.

Vera Lynn now singing "I'll Be Seeing You" blared from the wireless, and Richard knew the song would always remind him of that special moment.

Of course, May might never want to see him again—and he wouldn't blame her. Neither did he want her to suffer because of his beliefs as she surely would if they became a couple. It was best he kept his distance from now on.

But was he that selfless?

"I have to go." She appeared uneasy as if she'd done wrong. The kiss would never be mentioned, he knew. "I need time to meself."

"Look, at least let me see you back to Parklands."

"No." She stood and made for the door. "I'll catch a trolley at the bottom of the street."

When she'd gone, the room held a lingering sense of her captivating presence, Richard picked up the photo frame and regarded Ma and Pa. Had they ever been in love? he wondered. They'd been aloof with each other for as long as he could remember.

Pa was a shadow of the man he used to be, while Ma blamed him for their youngest son going to war.

When they were notified of Jeff's death, she'd raged at Pa, "My son wanted to live up to your expectation of him. He was afraid of you. You ran this family army-fashion. All Jeff ever knew was regulations and confrontation."

For all that Ma despised war, she seemed resentful towards Richard because he refused to go. Her disappointed gaze made it plain she wished it were he who had died and not her favourite son. Richard had had no alternative but to leave the family home.

Pa couldn't abide pacifists. His mantra was that every man's duty was to fight for his country as he had done in the Great War without question. Richard ran his fingertips through his hair. Though he respected Pa's views, he also knew if he ever had kids, they'd be allowed to have their own opinions, and if Richard didn't agree with their choices he'd never disown them.

As he laid the photograph face down, overwhelming weariness swamped Richard. Poor Pa, bitter and resentful, had suffered a nervous breakdown, while Ma had turned out the stronger of the two.

Richard thought long and hard about his relationship with his parents but as always came to the same conclusion. He couldn't have done anything differently.

He'd done what was right for him and that was all a man could do. Why, then, did he feel so bloody bad about his decision?

CHAPTER EIGHTEEN

May, making her way in the darkness along the cobbled street to Parklands, was confused by what had taken place at Richard's place but strangely exhilarated too. His kiss was tender but was it a spur of the moment kind of thing and, if not, what did it mean? She chewed her bottom lip. Whatever the kiss meant, it had made her pulse race.

Like turning a knob on the wireless, she switched the subject of Richard Bentley off in her mind. She knew she was a muggins where men were concerned, and she refused to get involved again, especially with a conscientious objector.

As May opened the door and came into the downstairs room, she saw Valerie sitting in front of the fire, textbooks at her feet on the floor.

Valerie looked unsure. "I've been waitin' for yi'." She spoke in a small voice. May could tell by her puffy eyes that Valerie had been crying.

"I don't want to argue," May told her.

"Neither do I... not tonight... not any more. Maureen would want us to be friends."

"Valerie, I'm whacked, can we talk about this some other time? I'd like to go to bed."

Valerie mightn't keep to her word and May had had more than enough emotion for one day.

She made for the stairs.

"Wait," Valerie pleaded. When May turned, Valerie said, "I'll never forgive meself for being so mean to Maureen." Her chin trembled. "She was the nicest person and I..." She let out a sob and her face crumpled. "I was mean to her when she told me she was leaving. I...ridiculed her and I hate meself for it." Tears leaked from her eyes. "But even then she was kind to me. I'm such a fool but now she's dead...and I can't ask for forgiveness."

It was the second time that day that someone had talked about losing someone they cared for without having the opportunity to make up—and May hadn't had an answer for either of them. But her heart ached for Valerie who she could see was truly broken-hearted.

May remembered her promise to Maureen. She moved over to the couch and sat beside Valerie.

"After you left that day"—she put an arm around Valerie's shoulders—"Maureen said if ever you were to feel guilty about how you acted I was to say she understood and forgave you."

Valerie's watery eyes searched May's face. "You're kidding me?"

"It's true."

"And you're not making this up just to make us feel better?"

"Cross me heart. You were mean to Maureen that day but, lovely soul that she was, she knew you were going through a rough time."

"I was jealous of the way you two got on and I felt left out." Valerie confirmed May's suspicions. "I...always blamed myself for Dad leavin' us. Me Mam once said it was us kids that drove him away and I got it in me head I was a nuisance and nobody would like us. Maureen was always caring towards me." She sat up and faced May. "I do believe if Maureen were here now, she'd tell us she forgave me. I reckon she was a saint and she's in heaven now with her maker." Fresh tears rolled down her cheeks.

The pair of them sat in silence for a time thinking about their friend.

May broke the silence. "At the time I thought Maureen meant she would be away at the convent but now I'm not so sure." She turned to Valerie, "I think she had a premonition she was going to die."

"Don't say that... you're givin' us goose bumps." Valerie shivered. "I'm not religious but I do feel Maureen's presence around us and it's comforting, like she's still somewhere in the universe."

May inwardly smiled. Valerie's sensitive side was emerging.

"Don't you see?" May continued. "It was as if she did have forewarning... Maureen wasn't afraid." She shook her head.

"You never know, though, do you, what's gonna happen in life? One thing's for sure, I've learnt me lesson." Valerie looked bashfully at May. "I'm gonna grow up and be a nicer person from now on... For Maureen's sake."

"Till the next time," May laughed and it eased the awkward moment.

They sat in comfortable silence.

"Maureen was special, wasn't she?" Valerie mused and then shook her head. "But I couldn't be a nun though, could you? Not with all that silence and prayin'."

"We won't be anything if we don't study for the class certificate," May told her.

Later, as the pair of them sat in front of the fire and shot medical questions at each other, May said a silent prayer to Maureen. *Every cloud has a silver lining and on this tragic day mine is that me and Valerie have made up and become friends.*

Later still, when May retired to bed, she tossed and turned. In her mind's eye, she saw Richard's smouldering eyes as he kissed her.

Sitting up, she punched the pillow into a comfortable shape. The question was, could she give her heart to anyone again?

*

On the day of class exams, the third of March, the three remaining nurses were nervous and exhausted, because none of them had slept. They stood in front of Home Sister.

"As you know, nurses," she told them, "you will have two days of exams, oral and written, and a half day in the kitchen."

"Who will be the examiners?" Eileen asked.

"Three Sisters from the wards." Her kindly but serious eyes penetrated each of theirs in turn. "I won't wish you luck, as luck has nothing to do with passing exams. Hard work and study will see you through. I trust each of you has been enthusiastically dedicated to both."

"Yes, Sister," they chanted.

Shortly after that, three Sisters entered the room, each of them in blue uniform, a cape around their shoulders. May was surprised to see Sister Jordan was one of them. Their eyes met but the Sister kept the detached look of a stranger.

The written tests came first. They took up most of the day as they had to be answered in essay form. May was thankful that the first question focused on sterilising equipment on the ward, a subject she was competent at.

The oral exam came next and May surprised herself by knowing the answers to the questions about the different sorts of bandages. In the practical, she was delighted she had to apply a many-tail bandage.

Next morning, she breathed a sigh of relief when she was asked to make a meal for a patient on a light diet, setting to work on a thin consommé made from chicken bones.

Later in the afternoon, Home Sister Chilvers summoned each probationer in turn into the classroom to give the results of the exams. When it was her turn to be seen, May's hands shook as Sister handed her a sheet of paper with the results. May was thrilled when she read she had achieved average scores in all subjects and excelled at the circulatory system. Well I never! she thought. She was over the moon she'd passed, but the reality wouldn't sink in that she, May Robinson, was going to carry on at Edgemoor General Hospital.

Her joy was complete when Sister Chilvers shook hands and said, "Well done, Nurse Robinson. Both your dedication and sense of vocation will see you through."

"Thank you, Sister."

"And, Nurse, it hasn't escaped me that your manner of speech has improved."

"I try, Sister."

Sister gave a brief smile.

"Did yi' pass?" Valerie stood at the front door, suitcase at her feet.

May grinned. Nothing would induce Valerie to change her Geordie twang, not now—not even the wrath of Matron.

"I did," she told her friend proudly.

"Me too." Valerie beamed from ear to ear. "And, of course, Eileen, the clever clogs, was top of the class."

The thought that Eileen might fail had never entered May's mind. "Which ward did sister say you were allocated to?"

"Outpatients department."

"Casualty for me."

A sudden thought nagged at May and she felt a little down. Mam wasn't here to celebrate and in fact there was no one to tell her good news to.

"I'm rather sad," she told Valerie, "to be leaving men's surgery."

"Which reminds me. I can't believe Sister Jordan." Valerie's voice broke into her thoughts.

"Why? What has she done?" It had been four days since May had been on the orthopaedic ward.

"Haven't you heard? That son of hers… the pilot on your ward, developed septicaemia and died after his second amputation." Valerie shook her head in a bemused fashion. "Poor lad was scarcely cold when Sister took the exams. She's the talk of the hospital."

May gave a heartfelt sigh; Sister Jordan didn't deserve this kind of treatment.

She defended Sister. "The woman has a heart of gold and will be coping the only way she knows how...by submerging herself in work."

Valerie looked shamefaced. "I suppose so. I only hope one day I'll have the same kind of dedication."

So say us all, May thought.

The three nurses made their way to the Nurses' Home, accessed by a paved walkway from the back of the main hospital. Home Sister Bertram met them in the day room, which smelled of stale cigarette smoke. A large room, it had a polished parquet floor, and tables and chairs dotted around.

"Welcome, nurses." Her tone was authoritative. "This will be your home for the next three years. You are expected to live in, apart from days off—and there will be no exception." Her eyes travelled the three of them. "Requests for holidays will sent by letter to Matron and a thank you note will be expected at the time of your return. The house rules are as follows: the front door is locked at ten and lights out is at ten-thirty when everyone should be in their own rooms...which, might I add, should be kept tidy at all times." May could have sworn Sister glowered at Valerie.

"You may request a late night as you did in Preliminary school and if it is granted you must put the request in the late book which is kept here in the nurses' day room." She nodded towards a wooden schoolroom desk behind the three of them.

Sister continued, "Men are not allowed in any part of the building and the windows leading to the fire escape must be kept locked at all times with the key kept in the lock." She raised her eyebrows. May just knew there was a story to be told behind that rule.

"Dirty linen will be disposed of in a laundry bag and left at the end of the corridor to be collected on Tuesdays. Each floor has its own kitchen and bathroom where you will use the water sparingly in line with wartime regulations. Is that all clear?"

"Yes, Sister."

"I will now give you the keys to your rooms and Nurse Bradley will show you the way."

A nurse sitting on a chair drained a cup of tea, stood up and smiled witheringly at them, as if she'd seen it all before and first-year nurses were such a bore.

May was delighted to find the three of them were on the second floor. They poked around in each other's compact rooms and when they came to Valerie's they discovered their quarters were all identical. A slim bed, radiator (hurray!), desk with chair, wardrobe with drawers at the bottom and—

"A full-length mirror behind the door." Valerie beamed at herself in the glass.

"When you've unpacked," Nurse Bradley told them from the doorway, making it obvious by her restless manner she couldn't wait to leave, "put your suitcases in the day room, where a porter will collect them and take them to the cellar." That said, she hurried away.

"Blimey. What a cow." Valerie heaved a sigh. "But I suppose she sees us as a chore."

May went back to her room and unpacked, then picking up the empty case, she took it down the flight of stairs to the day room. Opening the door, she saw a porter standing with his back to her.

Anticipation surged through her as she hoped it was Richard. She was surprised she hadn't heard from him at all but perhaps he was trying to protect her because he feared he would damage her reputation.

The porter turned. "I'll take that, Nurse." A mature man, he limped towards her.

May hoped the disappointment she felt didn't show.

*

That night after supper in the canteen, May opened the door of the day room and the hubbub of noise that blasted from inside took her by surprise. Nurses, some in mufti, others in uniform without their caps or starched aprons and with the studs of their collars open, lounged on chairs, chatting to one another. In the background came the strains of Jo Loss's Orchestra playing on the wireless.

"Have you got a ciggie spare?" a second-year nurse, sitting on the arm of a chair, asked May. She had a wan face with dark smudges beneath her eyes.

"Sorry. I don't smoke."

The girl, losing interest in May, spoke to the nurse who sat in the armchair. "I'm gasping. Go on, Mavis. Be a pal, halve your last ciggie with me. It's pay day tomorrow."

"Oh, all right," Mavis huffed.

"Shh! Listen to the news," someone called from the throng.

A hush descended on the room.

"...is the BBC." May heard a male newscaster's vigorous voice resound into the room.

The newscaster went on to tell them that Hitler's bombers continued with deadly raids on London and how the city bristled with guns and searchlights criss-crossed in the night skies.

"They say it's a revenge attack by Hitler. Here, Betty." Mavis cut the cigarette with scissors and handed it to the nurse sitting on the arm of the chair. "They say attacks only last an hour or two but the cost to lives and buildings is devastating. Apparently, hospitals are filled to capacity."

Betty lit the half cigarette. "The papers are dubbing it the Baby Blitz."

"How long have the raids being going on now?" Mavis asked.

"Since January. Two months." Betty let out smoke with a long, beleaguered sigh. "I thought we were supposed to be winning this war."

A sudden burst of disbelief overcame May. Here she was at Edgemoor Hospital conversing in the nurses' day room with bona fide nurses, one of which she now had become.

The downside was the bad news from the war had them all nervous and jittery.

CHAPTER NINETEEN
March 1944

When May reported to Casualty at half past seven that first morning, Sister sent her into a cubicle to take an elderly man's pulse and temperature.

Sister Grieves, a slender woman with thin blonde hair through which her pink scalp showed, had a perpetual sneer and nothing pleased her. That first morning, Sister found fault with everything May did.

Haven't you got eyes, Nurse? Can't you see the laundry bag is full and needs changing? That sheet on the bed in cubicle three won't change itself...

"She's not so bad once you've settled in. She's testing your mettle," Doreen, a second-year nurse, told her when they met up in the canteen at dinner time. "Sister does that with all the nurses straight out of school." Doreen, a redhead, gave her a look of sympathy. "I'll show you the ropes. Just shout if you are in doubt."

With a pang of sadness, May was reminded of Maureen. She too, had red hair and was always there for anyone in need.

Late one afternoon, May was in a cubicle with a patient who was waiting to see the doctor. The young man had been in a collision with a car while riding his bicycle. He didn't show signs of concussion but May knew he needed checking over. The young man, called Reuben, was emaciated with a sickly pallor.

As she took his pulse he surprised her by saying, "I'm an atheist, Nurse. I don't believe in no God."

May suspected that the accident had caused him to think about his mortality.

She didn't answer but nodded.

He took this as encouragement to talk. "I was shot down at the beginning of '42. Spent the time since in a prisoner of war camp."

"In Germany?" May knew she should get on with her duties but something told her the man needed to talk.

He nodded. "I got a kidney disease and I was repatriated a few months ago. They say I'm lucky…" He gulped and his eyes went pink and watery.

May had seen this reaction before. Men, weakened and fragile, who couldn't handle strong emotions or upset. She waited, knowing he would go on.

He turned towards her, agonised eyes meeting hers. "All I ever wanted, Nurse, was to come home and see the wife. You see, wi' just got married beforehand and Lilly got pregnant straight away." May could see the emotional state the poor lad was in and so left him to do the talking. "I never saw me kid and when I came home…well…he's two now and doesn't know me from Adam. It's the same with Lilly, we're like strangers…awkward with each other. Even Mam isn't the same. She used to be bolshie but now she's frail and wouldn't say boo to a goose. The war's changed everybody. I'm like a guest in me own house."

He tried his hardest not to let his emotions get the better of him.

May thought of Maureen and how she'd handle the situation.

"Give it time. It's just as difficult for your wife. You're a stranger and she's had a tough time bringing up your son on her own. See if you can talk to her about it. If I was you—"

"Nurse." Sister Grieves appeared around the screen. "Finish up here and take these notes to records." She looked at Reuben, then May. "Now, Nurse."

She handed over the notes and marched away.

Reluctantly, May stood up. "I'm sorry but I must—"

"Nee bother, Nurse...You've got a job of work to do." May made to hurry away. "Nurse..."

May turned to see an appreciative smile spreading on Rueben's gaunt face. "I want to say thank you for helping us out. I never thought to look at things from Lilly's point of view. You've made us see things differently. When I go home I'm goin' to have a chat with the wife."

He welled up and couldn't go on.

"I'm glad I could be of help." May smiled.

Aware she had no choice, she hurried away.

As she made for the exit, the door opened and she almost collided with a man entering Casualty.

"Oops, sorry," she apologised.

It was Richard. As if in a quandary as to what to do he just stood there and gaped at her.

"Oh, it's you," she said. Maddeningly, her face flushed and her pulse raced.

She felt his bemused eyes on her as she hurried from Casualty into the corridor.

After delivering the notes, May came back to Casualty and saw that Reuben's cubicle was empty. She assumed he'd been seen by the doctor and taken to X-ray.

Mercifully, Richard Bentley wasn't to be seen either because May couldn't afford the distraction.

She took her watch from her uniform dress pocket and saw that her shift had finished two minutes ago. She checked all was tidy in Casualty and then made for Sister's office.

She rapped on the office door and entered. "Nurse Robinson reporting off duty, Sister."

Sister looked up from her desk. "Keep it up, Nurse. You did well today."

"Thank you, Sister." May's face turned pink with pleasure. She had received not a reprimand, but praise. She might enjoy her time on Casualty, after all.

In a happier frame of mind, she opened the door leading outside and headed over to the Nurses' Home.

A cold northerly wind was blowing and she wished she'd thought to wear her cloak.

Richard stood beside the wall halfway up the path.

She told him, "It seems wherever I go you're following me!"

He looked amused. "I've just finished duty and I'm enjoying a cigarette." He held up his hand to verify that indeed, he was smoking.

Though May felt a fool, she was glad she'd made an excuse to stop and speak to him.

"But now that you're here"—his eyes studied her—"I'd like to apologise for the other day when—"

"Don't bother. I haven't given it another thought."

Of course May had.

The trouble was, instead of being shocked by the kiss, May had enjoyed the experience immensely—and that was why she'd fled from the house. She was flustered because she couldn't trust herself. She hardly knew the man and yet, she discovered, she had strong feelings towards him. And when he turned those stunning brown eyes on her, her insides were reduced to jelly.

"The kiss was spontaneous. I didn't want you to think—"

"Shush!"

A nurse walked by and stared at both of them.

After she'd passed he told May, "It's best you're not seen with me here."

May felt a sliver of guilt at the cool way she often behaved towards him, because Richard clearly had her welfare at heart, after all.

He drew on his cigarette and studied her, choosing his words before he spoke.

"Why are you so nervous around me?"

His direct question left May lost for words. But wasn't she the same? They both liked to be honest. Only in this case it was awkward because she didn't want him to know the truth, which she was only just beginning to realise herself.

Richard studied her with a stillness that calmed her jangling nerves.

"I'd rather not answer that question."

He dropped his cigarette onto the path and ground it out with his foot. Folding his arms, he gazed good-humouredly at her with twinkling brown eyes.

"What I think is . . . you look frozen. How about we wrap up and take a wander together and talk this through?"

May nodded. She could think of nothing she would like better.

Even though it was dark, they agreed to meet far away from the hospital grounds and prying eyes. She changed into outdoor clothes—her old wool coat, the red beret she'd been thrilled to find in a second-hand shop, knitted scarf and mittens. Flurries of snow were beginning to fall.

As she saw Richard approach from along the street, wearing a long trench coat with the collar turned up and a trilby hat, her heart beat faster. She knew then what her problem was . . . this intensity of feeling for him . . . She'd fallen for Richard Bentley— and the rational side of May told her that this couldn't happen.

"Where to?" he asked when they met at the bus stop.

"Let's just walk." She shrugged. "I need to clear me head."

"How about we get a blast of sea air?"

"Yes, let's."

Inside, her stomach felt like it had been pummelled by a poss stick.

They took the trolleybus to the coast. May looked out of the window, lost in thought. Scenes passed by: terraced houses boarded up after the bombings, Westoe bridges, a shop advertising whale meat in the window. For though fish wasn't rationed, it was hard to come by. May was reminded of the Ministry of Food's advertisement to try and encourage folk to eat whale meat. *When fisher-folk are brave enough to face mines and the foe for you, You surely can be bold enough to try a kind of fish that's new.* But the Ministry hadn't reckoned on obstinate Geordie folk, though.

She was procrastinating, she knew, thinking these thoughts, as the present situation was difficult to contemplate. May didn't trust herself to speak as she needed to acclimatise to what was happening—the thrill of discovery she felt within her. She was in love with Richard Bentley. She'd known he was special since they first met, she realised now. There, she'd clarified how she felt. But then reality hit; there was no joy in knowing as it only complicated matters.

The trolley came to a halt along Ocean Road beside South Marine Park. As she got down from the platform, Richard took her arm and guided her over to the promenade in the dark. It was eerie to hear the waves swishing back and forth on the shore and not to be able to see them. They strolled along the coastal road, easy in each other's company, not saying a word, just breathing in the bracing sea air. As she walked, May imagined the twin arms of the piers sheltering the harbour, and the ruins of Tynemouth Priory that dominated the headland by daylight.

Though her face and nose were cold in the chilly evening air, she was snug and warm beneath her coat. Aware of Richard beside her, she wondered what he was thinking.

"I was just wondering," he said, "if it's true that there's a gun battery built underground beneath the priory."

War. They couldn't forget it for a moment.

She laughed. "Typical man. Thinking of war," she answered glibly. "While I was—" She covered her mouth with her free hand. What was she thinking?

"What?"

"Oh, it's nothing." She removed her arm from his.

She heard a match strike and then saw the glow of a cigarette.

After a while, as they walked side by side shrouded by dreamy darkness, May imagined life without war, and her and Richard openly seeing each other without a care.

"I know a little seaside café that might still be open." His voice startled her. "How about we warm ourselves with a cup of tea?"

The café was just about to close but the woman behind the counter was a cheerful soul who agreed they could sit in the warmth and have a cup of tea.

"Though I do have Horlicks," she told them.

They sat at a table for two beside the small paraffin heater placed by the window where blackout curtains were drawn to prevent light shining out from the cosy room. A red and white tablecloth covered the table.

The cheery woman brought two steaming cups of Horlicks over and set them down on the table.

She appeared glad of their company and wanted to chat. "My Joseph's away in the war and there's nobody to go home to. The bugger used to drive us mad when he was at home with his daft carry on, but what I wouldn't give for one of his silly jokes now." After a while she left them alone.

"My feet have just thawed and I can feel them again," Richard laughed. "And your cheeks have turned a delightfully rosy pink."

As they sipped the hot malty drink, they chatted about the hospital and the people they knew.

Listening to Richard's velvety voice, an unrestrained need stirred in May. *Live for today, tomorrow might never come.*

She should stop this now, her rational mind said, before it was too late. She had no future with Richard—a conscientious objector who folk despised—as she would be reviled too. But May's heart told her otherwise.

Richard, as if guessing her reckless thoughts, gazed longingly at her.

"It's pleasant in here," she said for something to say. They both looked around as if noticing the place for the first time.

Then Richard, clearing his throat, turned towards her. "I wanted to get in touch you know after..." He trailed off.

"I wished you had. I thought you didn't..."

"You did?" His adoring gaze met hers and something sparked in their eyes—something affirmed.

She gave an almost imperceptible nod. "I'm a late shift tomorrow."

He smiled tenderly in understanding. "Shall we go?"

"Yes."

"You're sure?"

Again, she nodded.

Richard paid the bill and left the woman a generous tip.

Outside, May took his hand. He led her past the park and a few streets along Ocean Road from the coast to the two rooms he rented in Salmon Street.

Upstairs, he took her to the sparse bedroom that smelled of aftershave, where his striped pyjama bottoms, the creases still in the shape of his body, were flung on top of a thick and cosy-looking bedspread. Removing his coat, Richard dropped it on the floor; his shirt and vest followed.

He hesitated. "I want you to know this is not just a fling. I've loved you from the first but this—"

She smiled in agreement and put her fingertips over his lips. A forgotten longing bubbled up within her until she couldn't bear the exquisite sensations any longer.

Richard removed her skirt and knickers, then peeled off her stockings (that she'd left on after work) and suspender belt.

He lay down on the bedspread and reaching out, pulled her naked body beside him. When their skin touched, little shocks of anticipation surged through her nerve endings. He cuddled her head close into his chest and brushed his fingertips down her spine to the cleft in her buttocks, which made her shudder. She turned her face up and when their lips met, the kiss was long and tender.

"I don't want this moment to pass." His voice, when he broke free, was husky. He gazed at her and his expression changed to that of wonder. "Why, it's right here." He spoke as if to himself.

"What's here?"

"My dream." He sat up, placing an elbow on the bed and rested his head on a hand. He smiled down at her. "Everyone has one. What's yours?"

She thought for a time. The house was silent and it was as though the outside world, the horror of war, rationing, the routine of work life, had stopped and they could live purely in this moment.

She felt shy. "This moment is rather dreamy."

"You feel it too." His eyes shone with happiness. "My darling girl…I feel the same way. If this is as good as it gets then I'm one happy fellow."

Tears of joy prickled her eyes.

"Have I told you lately I love you?" He nuzzled down beside her.

She laughed, a pleasant tinkling sound. "Not in the last five minutes, you haven't."

He pouted. "It would be rather nice if the sentiment were reciprocated."

Ridiculously, May made a mental note to look the unfamiliar word up in Maureen's dictionary. At the thought of her friend now cold in the ground, she shivered.

"What is it?" Wrapping his arms around her, he cuddled her again into his bare and delightful curly-haired chest.

"My friend who died...she never got to have a life." In the warm glow of the lamp, she turned her face to look up at him. "The war, working at the hospital and seeing its effect, has changed the rules I used to live by. You have to grab the chance to be happy because you don't know how long it will last."

His gaze, as he looked down at her, was troubled. "May, I want you to be sure about this. I don't want ours to be a back-street affair. I want to protect you but I can't change my—"

"I love you, Richard...for all that you are."

His eyes widened in wonder. He bent to kiss her and then froze and smacked his forehead with the heel of his hand.

"I haven't got—"

May had been caught out before, she reminded herself. But as she gazed into his tender eyes, she slammed the door on caution. *Live for the moment.*

"I've never been surer of anything in my life."

He stroked her hair from her brow and kissed her forehead. "Darling girl, we shouldn't—"

Again, she put her fingertips over his lips.

"Yes, we should."

As memories of the sweet release of climax shivered through her, May, overcome with sleepiness, drowsed in Richard's arms and then fell deeply asleep.

When she woke, she reached across the bed for him but he was gone.

"Richard," she cried, and then noticed the bedspread had been tucked in around her.

"Here I am. Tea is served." He walked into the room, now dressed and carrying a tray.

On it, she discovered two cups of tea, a plate of cream crackers with a smidgeon of margarine and a jar of jam. "Ernie downstairs has a lady friend who makes jam." Richard smiled. He lounged beside her. "You okay?"

"I'm starved."

She placed the tray between their legs. Cream crackers and tea, she discovered, had never tasted so delicious.

Then, all of a sudden the happiness left Richard's face and it clouded with uncertainty. "What are we going to do?"

May thought of her love life so far. Two men—Billy and Alec—had professed to love her and both in their own way had hurt her. But she knew instinctively she was safe with Richard. He was her future.

"Nothing. Let's just wait and see. For me, it's enough to have found you."

His expression altered, became contented. "Me too."

He put the tray on the floor and, taking her in his arms, kissed her—not with passion, but a tender kiss of love and reassurance.

As they lay back on the bed, Richard's long fingers stroked her hair. "By the way," he said, "that young man, Reuben, spoke highly of you."

"You spoke to Reuben?"

"Yes, I met him outside as he left Casualty department. I'd finished for the day and was going to find John to tell him I was away home."

May nodded. "How did he know we were acquainted?"

"He saw us collide in the doorway and asked if I'd give you a message."

"Which is?"

"To thank you for your help but he needed to get back home. He looked rather dazed and I asked if there was anything I could do to help."

May smiled affectionately. Richard was sensitive towards others in need and would notice the lad was in an emotional state.

"Yes," she told him, "I was worried when I left him in Casualty, he was in turmoil."

Richard continued. "He said there was nothing wrong, indeed, he admitted he felt better and it was all due to the nurse he'd spoken to on Casualty... which, of course, was you. He said he couldn't wait to see a doctor because he wanted to go home and be with his wife and start on their new lives."

"He told you that?"

"That was the gist of what he said."

Richard might be a coward to others, but not to May. Once you got to know him, you realised he had a kind and caring heart and he'd go out of his way to help folk.

She turned on her side and, resting a hand beneath her cheek, she faced him.

She teased him. "Another thing, you didn't admit to it before but how come every time I turn around there you are, no matter which department I'm on? Are you following me?"

"Of course. I'm always first to take the jobs on the department you work on. Because, my love..." He sat up and kissed the tip of her nose. "I could stare at your beautiful face forever."

May had never been called beautiful before and, amazingly, in that moment, seeing the rapture in his gaze, she felt it.

May and Richard began to meet regularly, usually after May finished the day shift and always in the seclusion of Richard's rooms. They both knew that their affair had to be a secret, and that if Matron found out May was seeing a man alone in his room she could lose her job.

Though exhausted with shift work, May kept up with her studies, sometimes working through the night.

May didn't tell anyone, even Valerie, about the relationship. For, although they'd made up and were now friends, she didn't know how the other girl would react if she knew May was involved with a conchie.

She found out soon enough.

Late one night, as May lay on her bed studying, a knock came at her door.

Valerie entered. She threw an envelope onto the bed. "This letter came this morning when I collected me post. I forgot to give it to you. Sorry."

May recognising the handwriting, her heart did a somersault. Etty was in touch. She shoved the envelope under her pillow, promising herself to read it later.

Valerie raised her eyebrows but didn't pursue the matter.

An air of unease came into the room when neither of them seemed capable of speaking.

Valerie knows, May thought.

She broke the silence. "How's everything at home... your mam and the bairns?" "Same as usual." Valerie didn't elaborate.

"D'you see them often?"

"All the time when I can. Me mam's been sick. Besides"—she gave May a disapproving look—"there's nee one here to talk to."

When Valerie was upset, she lapsed into Geordie twang.

May felt bad. She hadn't been there when Valerie needed her. "You should have said about your mam."

"Huh! You're never here to tell."

May wondered if she should broach the subject of Richard.

Valerie's cheeks were the colour of a plum; the lass was clearly struggling to keep control of her temper.

May did what she should have done some weeks before. "Valerie, I'm... seeing—"

"I know, the conchie porter." Valerie glared at her. "You didn't think you could keep somethin' like that a secret, did yi'? It's whispered all around the hospital. It does your reputation no good."

The two of them stared at each other.

"Sorry, I should have told you before."

"You should never have started the affair. What if Matron finds out? You know fine well if we even look at a fella when we're in uniform—"

"Matron can't dictate who I see in my time off."

Valerie raised her eyebrows in disbelief. "What on earth possessed yi'?"

"He's not what you think. He's caring and—"

"A coward, according to most folk."

"What about you?"

Unable to check her annoyance any longer, Valerie exploded, "Just look around the hospital! Those brave lads, without limbs, faces burned beyond recognition, bodies…minds broken. What do I think? I think you're crackers, May. The man doesn't give a damn about anyone but himself."

She barged from the room and slammed the door with such force May feared it would come away from its hinges.

May sat for a long while staring into space, hearing everyday noises outside her door: the thuds of the nurses' feet as they tramped along the corridor floor, laughter from the kitchen, muffled chatter through the thin wall from next door.

She felt alone and wished with all her heart Maureen was here. The lass always knew what to say to reassure May. She also realised she hadn't heard Mam's comforting voice in her head for a long while. She wished she could hear it now because her mother always knew the right thing to do.

She remembered the letter under the pillow. This was the first correspondence she'd received from Etty since Parklands. She berated herself. Why hadn't she made time to visit her friend and make up before now?

"Because, lass, you've had your troubles to contend with."

May smiled; she didn't know where this voice came from—it might even be her own—but all she knew was it sounded like Mam and her voice always comforted.

But why was Etty in touch now?

CHAPTER TWENTY

Dearest May

I'm glad you've opened this letter. If you don't get in touch, I'm going to go to the telephone box and ring the hospital because I've got something important to tell you.

Your cousin Danny is dead. The Halifax bomber he was flying was hit by anti-aircraft fire. Danny ordered the crew to bail out but he stayed with the plane as he tried to reach his airfield. However, his plane was seen to fly into a hill.

Mr. and Mrs. Newman are broken. I know Ramona Newman is your mam's sister and they weren't close but I thought you'd want to know this. Ramona is a pain and thinks she's a cut above the rest but, poor soul, she didn't deserve this.

Trevor says the Newmans can't think straight but there's talk of a memorial service at St. Michael's Church. I'll let you know if I hear when.

I don't know when, or even if, you'll ever forgive me, but for the record, I miss you—loads.

Etty xx

As she placed the letter on her locker top, a wave of sadness overwhelmed May. Another life cut short. She didn't know Danny personally but he was the Newmans' pride and joy. He was the reason they'd built up the funeral business and kept it going— Danny was supposed to take over one day. It was unbearable to think of all the hurt the Newmans would be going through.

She'd write and send her condolences, but words, May knew, wouldn't ease their pain. At times like this, it was important folk pulled together and, by doing a kindness or simply by being there, helped those who mourned a loved one if only by showing that they cared. May realised with a shock that with all that had been going on in her life recently she'd overlooked paying Ramona the money she owed for her mother's funeral. It was an oversight she'd put right immediately, not that the poor woman would be thinking of such matters. She made a mental note that every time she got paid she'd post a sum of money to the funeral parlour.

"Pay your debts and sleep peacefully at night." May was delighted to hear Mam's voice in her head.

May still struggled over what to do about Etty, though. Life these days was a jumble of intense and mixed emotions, so making the simple decision to visit Etty and make it up should be an easy one. May was acutely aware that in wartime you couldn't hesitate as you could be here one minute and gone the next. So, what was stopping her? Surely, she didn't still harbour bitterness towards her friend—if so, she was only hurting herself. It was time to forgive and, if not to forget, then to lay the past to rest.

It was while she thought these thoughts, May had an epiphany— of course, the wounds she carried still hurt and though she'd made the decision to forgive Etty in her head she knew it would take a while longer to filter into her heart. She wasn't ready to meet with Etty just yet, especially not with all she had to deal with already. She worried that if Richard found out about the hospital gossip, the dear man, wanting to protect her, would insist they stay apart for now. To end the affair was something May couldn't endure.

"It was on a training exercise, Nurse," the young lieutenant in the first cubicle on Casualty told May. "I got this bullet in the leg."

A blonde-haired, good-looking bloke, the lieutenant's expression was affronted. "It hurts like hell."

"The doctor will see you shortly," May assured him, "he'll give you something for the pain."

May hadn't been feeling too well recently, she'd been ill with a tummy upset. She hadn't asked for sick leave, as there was no pain, but neither did she want to pass anything on to patients as the spread of infection was something all the staff at Edgemoor Hospital went to great lengths to avoid. That included the eagle-eyed maid who, with the help of subordinates, ensured that floors were polished, curtains and windows washed, and every nook and cranny dusted, till Casualty positively gleamed.

Leaving the lieutenant in the cubicle, May went to check on the woman in cubicle four who she'd left on a bedpan.

The pale and emaciated woman lying back against the pillow looked exhausted, as if she hadn't the strength to lift her head.

"Nurse," she asked in a weak voice, "how long d'you think I'll be in here?"

No doubt once pretty, life had taken its toll. Her mousey-coloured hair hung lank and worry lines were carved into her careworn face.

"I'm worried sick about who's looking after me bairns."

May glanced at the name on the notes on the locker top.

"How many have you got, Mrs. Pearson?"

"Three. Tommy, Joseph and Pamela. The eldest's only eight." Her eyes brimmed with tears. "I've left them to God and good neighbours."

The woman tried to struggle up. May helped by taking her beneath the armpits and hauling her up. The poor soul was all skin and bone.

"Bert, me husband," the woman continued, taking huge gasps of breath, "went down...with HMS *Kelly* in forty-one...in the battle for Crete." This was said with a certain look of pride on her face. "You know what, Nurse? I haven't got the foggiest idea where that place is."

May knew about the destroyer and its fate. Built at Hawthorn Leslie shipyard at Hebburn on the River Tyne for the Royal Navy, the ship was lost in action with the loss of a hundred and thirty men. This poor woman's husband was one of them.

Though May knew she shouldn't get involved with patients, the plight of this woman touched her heart. All the poor soul wanted was to know her bairns were safe. When the patient finished her business, May slid the bedpan from beneath her bottom and, holding the warm rim in her hands, made to move away.

"I'm so sorry for your loss," she told Mrs. Pearson, who slumped back against the pillow.

"Poor souls...me bairns have been through enough. We were bombed oot of our house months ago and we live in temporary accommodation. After I collapsed it was the husband from upstairs that went to the phone box and called for an ambulance." She turned tragic eyes on May.

May made up her mind. She bent down next to the woman's ear, and said under her breath, "Tell me the address and I'll go and check on the little ones for you."

May then lifted back the screen and took the bedpan to the sluice. On her way back to Casualty she felt the sickly feeling rise from her stomach into her throat. Hand clasped to her mouth, she raced to the ward lavatory where she was violently sick in the pan. As she crouched, the sour taste of vomit in her mouth, a thought struck May.

She couldn't be.

She totted the weeks up, and realised she'd missed two periods. May knew, in all probability, she was pregnant.

She panicked. She needed someone to talk to—someone to tell her what to do. But, with Maureen and Mam dead and her not speaking to either Etty or Valerie (since they'd fallen out over her relationship with Richard) there was no one.

May thought of all she'd achieved recently. Becoming a nurse, the responsibility that entailed. Making decisions about her love life; Billy, Alec then darling Richard. She took a deep breath. She must draw upon her newly acquired confidence and rely on herself.

CHAPTER TWENTY-ONE

"Sorry, mate, it's nowt to do with me," John the head porter told Richard one sunny but blustery morning in early May. "Orders from above. You'd still have a job, lad, if it was up to me."

The man couldn't meet his eyes—and Richard knew the reason why. Matron was short-staffed, but the gossips had found out and spread the news that Richard, a conchie, was going out with one of the nurses on the staff.

He took a minute to mull things over before he replied. "Don't worry, John, I was thinking it was time I moved on." He put the fellow out of his misery. "I'll empty my locker and then I'll be gone."

"There's no rush, man. There's only an hour to go before you finish the late shift."

Richard bit the inside of his cheek and, giving John a nod, walked away.

He knew the turmoil that was gnawing inside didn't show. He was good at hiding his feelings.

Questions buzzed like agitated wasps in his brain. Who the hell would employ him—a conchie? How would he pay the rent with no job? His main concern, however, was for May. If this had happened to him, it was likely she'd get the sack as well.

Making his way down the corridor towards the hospital exit, he passed the switchboard where the woman behind the pane of glass gave a twisted smile, as if to say "you've got your comeuppance at last."

In that moment, Richard made a decision. He had no other choice.

For May's sake he'd end the affair and make it publicly known.

Richard walked home, needing some air. Gazing up at the cloudless sky where the sun dazzled his eyes, he tried to work out how he could tell May. He decided the best way was to lie and say he'd made a mistake and the affair was over, because if he told her the truth she would stick by him no matter what. It would break her heart but May was stronger than she imagined and she'd get over it in time.

He berated himself. He should've known the situation would come to this, but love had blinded him and he'd kidded himself that as long as they took care not to be seen, no one at the hospital would be any the wiser. But some ruddy busybody had noticed and reported them.

In turmoil, he searched for alternatives. Even if she did leave and go with him, what kind of life could he offer? No. It was best to be cruel to be kind. His reward one day would be that May would fulfil her dream and become a State Registered Nurse. And maybe she'd find some—

Christ! His mind slammed shut. He wasn't that benevolent. The thought hurt like hell.

Ernie wasn't in when he arrived home and that suited Richard because he was too distressed to chat. He pulled a small suitcase from beneath the bed and, opening the wardrobe, took out items of clothing and threw them on the bed. He could just leave, but that would be cowardly and cruel, and besides, he wanted to see her one last time. He hoped when he told her, May would hate him enough to let him go. And rightly so, because Richard would never forgive himself if she suffered on his account. He loved her and knew there'd never be anyone as precious in his life. May, with that open-book, beautiful face, was the only girl for him. He closed his mind to her loveliness, because that only made what he had to do all the harder.

His possessions packed, Richard snapped the lid of the suitcase shut. He waited for May to arrive.

He didn't think about his new life, where he would go—all that concerned Richard was May. Her happiness was paramount.

She was late. Surprised, if not a little worried, because May prided herself on always being punctual, Richard wondered what could have happened to her.

Then footsteps thudded up the stairs and before she reached his door, he grabbed the handle and opened it. May stood there, breathless, smiling, her eyes sparkling—but something lurked in the back of them he'd never seen before.

She wore a sailor-style blue top with a white collar, and a pleated skirt beneath an overcoat that had seen better days and white sandals and socks. She looked like an adorable adolescent going on a first date.

As he gazed at her, she did a twirl. "It's amazing what you can find in the second-hand shop." She bent over and kissed him. "Sorry I'm late, but there was something I promised to do for a patient."

She began to come into his room but Richard blocked the way.

"I thought we'd go for a walk, for a change." He closed the door.

She looked baffled. "What if someone—"

"It's almost dusk... no one will see us. But just in case, I thought we'd be safe taking a ride on the ferry."

Her eyes widened in surprise. "Ooo! I haven't done that since I was a bairn." Then her face clouded. "Maybe it's best if we go inside first; there's something I need to tell you."

He took her arm and guided her to the stairs. "You can tell me on the ferry. Besides... there's something I want to say to you too."

She gave him an anxious, doubtful look that made him wonder if the gossips from the hospital had told her about his dismissal.

As they walked along King Street towards the market place, May told him why she was late.

"Those poor bairns, Richard." She went on to tell him about Mrs. Pearson in the hospital and how her husband was lost at sea. "The conditions in the flat were terrible. Damp and mould everywhere. You can't blame Mrs. Pearson, she's doing all she can on her own. The cupboards were bare, the sink full of dirty dishes and there was a bucket of wee under the sink. Oh Richard," she despaired, "I think the poor woman has given up."

"What did you do?"

"I tidied up a bit. The elderly couple upstairs are looking after the bairns. The folk next door gave them some clothes their kids had grown out of. Folk in the street were rallying around. When I told a neighbour how Mrs. Pearson fretted about her bairns, she said she'd pay a visit to the hospital. She's going to put Mrs. Pearson's mind at rest about it and tell her they'll be taken care of till she's better."

"People are good at heart," Richard remarked, then added in his head, *those who are not gossips who get innocent folk sacked, that is.*

"It's true," May agreed. "Everybody's tired to the bone and fed up with shortages but they're united when it comes to looking out for each other. With that kind of survival spirit, we're bound to win this war—we can go on for as long as it takes."

At the fierce expression on her face, Richard couldn't help but smile.

Thick clouds were now in the sky which meant the evening had turned dark early and, as they wandered through the market place—where a terrible air raid in forty-one had destroyed buildings although the old town hall thankfully stayed intact—they arrived at the ferry landing. Richard saw the outline of the little boat as it chugged over the waters.

They stood together and watched in the growing twilight as the *Northumbrian* came alongside the landing and felt the bump as it docked. The gangplank, a huge wooden door lowered by clanking chains, came down and foot passengers, some pushing bicycles, swarmed from the ferry, followed by a few motor cars.

As they stood on the deck, Richard debated where to sit.

"Not in the covered area." May wrinkled her nose. "As I recall, it's rather smoky and smelly."

"We'll go up top." Richard's voice was decisive.

He guided them to a secluded spot on a wooden seat. He watched as a slight breeze lifted May's hair and, like a child about to ride on a merry-go-round, her face lit up with excitement.

As the little steamboat chugged away from the landing, the odour of oil wafted up into his nostrils. Richard longed to put his arm around May's shoulders and cuddle her in to keep warm but, his heart heavy, he realised that it would be inappropriate, given what he was about to tell her.

The ferry continued across the Tyne, zigzagging its way through the gaps between ships.

"Blimey! I can't see the riverbank." May sat transfixed, looking at all the ships waiting for a mooring.

Richard told her, "That's why Jerry planes concentrate on the area. You'll have heard about the ferry moored by Middle Docks which was sunk in the air raid in the autumn of forty-one?"

"No. Was anyone killed?"

"Four of the crew, I heard."

As they contemplated this disturbing news, Richard reflected on the futility of war. He wondered if, in a couple of hundred years' time, people would know, or care, about the suffering of these brave men—and more to the point, whether the powers that be would learn from history. He doubted so.

May sat up and ran her fingers through her hair. "You said you had something to tell me."

Richard tensed. He didn't want to spoil the moment, not yet. "So did you."

Her black irises, as she stared at him, seemed eerily large.

"You go first," he told her.

There was a moment of silence as the little ferry forged its way over the murky waters.

"I'm going to have our baby, Richard," she blurted.

At that moment, a hospital ship, lit up with a big red cross, loomed out of the now misty twilight. His eyes followed the huge vessel as it sailed up the still waters, and a calm settled over his mind.

May told him, "I went to sick bay and saw the doctor. It's okay," she quickly put in, "it would be unethical for him to tell anybody. He has to abide by the code of confidentiality."

Richard remained silent as he let the news sink in. Then, the wonder of knowing he was going to be a dad dawned on him. Excitement rippled through him.

"Have you known for long?"

"I've suspected for a bit but it became a reality when I realised I'd missed another . . . you know . . . the curse."

Richard laughed. He'd have to get used to women's talk from now on.

He beamed. "This is . . . the best thing that's ever happened to me, apart from meeting you, that is."

Then, like a strike of lightning, he remembered the suitcase waiting in his bedroom and reality hit Richard hard.

To divert the conversation and give him time to think about what he was going to do, he asked, "What will your family think?"

Although Richard had opened up about his personal life, May had always been guarded about hers. He respected that because May had her reasons and he knew she would tell him when she was ready.

The moment, it seemed, had arrived.

The words came tumbling out; about the drunken father who had disowned her, a loving mother who was killed. How she had met a man called Billy Buckley who went to war and that she had become pregnant by him.

"I was madly in love," she told him in a small voice. "Billy was a...free spirit and didn't want to settle down. I made the mistake of thinking I could change him."

In other words, Richard thought, this Billy was a two-timing cad who liked to have other women in tow. He'd met the type before.

May heaved a great sigh. "Billy was killed in action. Though I mourned him, Richard, I don't love him any more." He saw the outline of her perfect shaped face as she looked out over the waters.

She turned towards him. "It's you I love, a different kind of love...all I want is to be near you. But Richard"—her voice became firm—"after you've heard about my past, I won't blame you if you walk away." She hesitated. "What I want you to know is...I gave up one bairn but whatever happens this time round, that's not going to happen again."

There was that fierce determination in her voice again.

"The baby? What happened?" he asked.

"Billy didn't want kids. I was young...and didn't know what to do. I couldn't have tolerated it if he—Derek—had been branded a bastard. When Mam suggested she bring him up as her own, I agreed."

From the hurt Richard saw etched on her lovely face, he knew she had regretted the decision ever since.

May went on to tell him how Derek had been evacuated out in the country and how he wanted to stay there after his "mother" had died. Again, Richard could see that this had hurt May dreadfully.

"And you've never told him that you are his mother?"

It beggared belief that lovable May, honest to a fault, hadn't wanted to put the record straight.

"I didn't want to hurt him...he loved Mam."

"But you were hurting."

"I didn't count."

"Derek deserves to know the truth of his parentage, no matter how messy it is. It's his right."

May looked conscience-stricken. "I've never thought of it like that. Mam, you see, doted on him and wanted him known as her son."

"May, he's your son...and it's time you told him so."

The ferry approached the landing on the other side of the river. The pair of them, there for the ride, stayed on for the return journey home.

As the ferry bumped against the landing, Richard's mind buzzed. May's story was a lot to take in, and his mind reeled as he tried to digest all of the information. But nothing had changed, he discovered in wonder. May had a past—so what! She was still the girl Richard loved and as far as he was concerned, nothing would change his high opinion of her and all she'd accomplished.

But there was still the problem of him being an outcast—and now his unborn child would be tainted too.

I won't blame you if you walk away, she'd said. But how could that be the right thing to do now there was a baby to consider? Richard asked himself.

The other passengers had now left the top deck and they were alone. May looked small and defenceless as she sat waiting for an answer. His instinct was to protect her—even though she was doing a fine job of looking out for herself.

"May, I love you. I always will. Nothing you do would ever change that fact."

"And you can live with what I've told you about Bi—"

He took her in his arms and kissed her hard until he worried that her lips might be bruised. He never wanted to let her go but he had to. For, he thought, as he released his grip, he had no job, nowhere to live and no prospects.

I'm going to be a dad. The words reverberated in his brain.

He thought of his own father, remote from him all of his life, never showing any love or affection.

How could he make things different for his child?

In that moment, the need to protect his unborn child grew so strong, it astounded Richard. He realised the power of parental love. And he knew something else; if anyone should harm the child May carried, he would surely kill them with his bare hands.

Richard now knew what he must do.

CHAPTER TWENTY-TWO

On the return journey, the ferry crossed the smooth and murky waters of the River Tyne.

May, sitting in the darkness, inhaling the rejuvenating sea air, was overcome with happiness and joy. She couldn't have asked for a better reaction. She'd feared Richard might reject her after she told him about the baby. But this was Richard. Honourable and trustworthy. The man she truly loved.

The relief that she'd confessed about her past was enormous. She'd learned a lot from the time she'd spent with Billy and she didn't want to make the same mistakes again. This time round things would be different. Never again would May be as needy as she had been with Billy. If she and Richard were to have a future, it would be on level footing.

"When we get off the ferry let's go to your rooms." She stroked his cheek and felt his prickly stubble.

He hesitated. "I...it's late, sweetheart and you always study when you go back home to the hospital. I don't want you overdoing things, especially now..." He snuggled his head into her neck. "...when you're carrying our child." He patted her abdomen.

He tilted her face towards him and kissed her, such a long sensual and hungry kiss that May was surprised he didn't want to go back to his rooms to satisfy it. Briefly, she wondered why, but then a couple came up the ferry's steps and sat on the wooden seat opposite them.

Richard pulled away and she sat up. They lapsed into a comfortable silence for a while.

When they arrived back at Shields and the ferry bumped the landing, Richard held her tight. Chains rattled as the huge wooden gangplank went down and folk started to hurry off the gangway to their destination; Richard guided May off the boat, and held her tight around the waist as though she might disappear before his very eyes.

As they waited at the bus stop for the trolley to take her back to the hospital, May remembered something.

"You never told me what it was you wanted to say."

The atmosphere filled with hesitation and...apprehension? Richard gazed at her as though heavy thoughts plagued his mind. In the dimming light, she saw clarification shine in his eyes, as if he'd finally made up his mind about something.

"It'll keep. You'll know soon enough."

The trolleybus arrived and May didn't get the chance to pursue the matter. They boarded the trolley and talked of inconsequential things.

When they arrived at their stop, Richard hesitated.

"This is as far as I go."

Suddenly she felt uncertain. "I wish we could kiss goodnight."

"May, promise me you'll never tell anyone about you and me."

"Richard, is something wrong?"

Intuition told her there was. Maybe tonight's revelation was just sinking in and his mind was reeling.

"Everything's fine. I feel so right about...what's happening, kiddo."

May went cold at hearing the name Billy had always called her coming from Richard's mouth.

She needed to feel secure. She sank against Richard's chest and inhaled the masculine smell of him. But the niggle of uncertainty wouldn't go away.

Richard pulled away and began to leave.

"Goodnight, darling May. Always remember I love you."

Then he was gone.

At breakfast next morning, May stood with the other nurses on duty around the table waiting for Matron and Home Sister to enter.

"We will say the Lord's prayer," Matron said as she did every morning, taking her place at the top end of the table.

Afterwards Matron gave out notices and told those unfortunate nurses who she was required to reprimand to wait outside her office door after breakfast. Fortunately, May was not one of them.

"You may sit," Matron told them as she took her seat. May, acutely aware of Matron and Home Sister eyeing her as they spoke, was suspicious that they knew about her pregnancy. Maybe when she had vomited in the lavatory someone had heard and reported her—but surely not. May was just being overly anxious.

Her intention was to work as long as she possibly could but that would depend on how long she could hide her bump. The reality that a baby was physically growing inside her shocked her momentarily. But it was Richard's baby. And Richard would propose, of that May was certain. They'd have to speak seriously soon about the practicalities of the future. May acknowledged how she felt; she was more than a little afraid. She didn't know how they'd manage and, if she were truthful, she was devastated at giving up her dream of qualifying as a State Registered Nurse. But maybe, like Maureen when she had left to become a nun, May was starting out on another dream. The dream of a home, husband and babies. A home filled with the love she had been deprived of because of Dad and Billy. The thought of Maureen lingered on, and May was grateful she had a life to plan for. When the war was over, she and Richard could move away and he could find a job and build houses like he wanted to. No one need know about his background. But in her heart she knew this would never be an option. For Richard was principled and would never run away from a tricky situation. That wasn't his way.

A maid placed a dish of porridge in front of May and she attempted to eat a few mouthfuls but refused the stodgy national bread and margarine.

Shortages were cutting in more than ever; May's allowance of butter was only two ounces a week and though she was allowed one egg she hadn't seen one for the past fortnight. May thought of the farm in Allendale, the plentiful eggs on the table. She was glad for Derek's sake. At the thought of her son May felt suddenly teary. How she wished she could tell him he was about to become a big brother. In her mind's eye May's new dream now was for her family to include Derek and for them to be a foursome.

She came back to reality and looked around the table.

Despite the war and shortages, folk got on with their lives, she thought as she watched nurses munch into their bread and margarine. The usual British good humour prevailed around the table and that was what made the difference—there was always someone to give you a laugh if you got down. Death was part of life in this war-torn world and everyone had—or knew someone who had—lost a loved one. And at this sobering thought, May's problems seemed small in comparison.

As she thought of the future, May's optimism grew. If what folk were saying was true, the long-awaited Allied invasion of Europe could soon become a reality.

That day, May worked a busy shift in Casualty. She wasn't planning to see Richard that night as they both worked a late shift. She wished she could though, especially after her revelation last night and his wonderful reaction. She wanted to discuss his thoughts about the future.

May worked till two p.m., had the afternoon off and then went back at five to Casualty for the evening shift. She should, by rights, have had a kip that afternoon as she'd been kept awake for a large part of the night listening to the drone of Allied aeroplanes roaring overhead as they returned home. At one point May had been alarmed because one of the aeroplanes' engines didn't sound right and she was concerned for the pilot and crew. Her thoughts automatically went to the possible injuries the crew might be afflicted with if there was a crash landing. Her mind fully awake, May started to wonder how many engines bombers had and resolved to look it up in the morning.

The next day, her morning off, she decided to walk to Richard's flat as it was such amazingly hot weather for the time of year. She'd compared rotas earlier in the week with Richard and knew that today was his day off.

Walking beneath Westoe Bridges, May passed a young girl pushing a pram with a fringed canopy protecting the baby from the sun. A surge of wellbeing mingled with apprehension overwhelmed May and, as she thought of motherhood, her own mother came to mind. She counted her blessings that she had had the greatest role model to follow.

She walked on and, coming to the top of Fowler Street, she passed a mother and small laddie who was eating a carrot on a stick like a lollipop. Ice cream was practically non-existent these days, so it was the next best thing and far healthier than a lollipop, though given the choice she knew what the child would prefer.

Carrying on into Ocean Road, she turned into Salmon Street, and her heart rose at the idea of seeing Richard and the thought that they could start making plans for the future. A tingle of excitement rippling through her was replaced immediately by a stab of anxiety as nurse training again surfaced in her mind. May knew she was kidding herself. Would she really get over the heartbreak of giving up on her dream?

But there was nothing else she could do. Or was there? A forgotten thought returned to the forefront of her mind. She'd heard somewhere that there was a hospital that provided a nursery where you could leave your baby while you worked. This was something May was determined to look into, but for the time being, she'd concentrate on the present.

Arriving at the flat, she opened the front door with the key Ernie had kindly made for her. She couldn't wait to see Richard.

As sunlight shone along the passage from the fanlight in the front door, May made her way to the stairs.

The downstairs door opened and Ernie stood there.

"A word, lass." May tried to analyse the look on his face—pity, sorrow. Dread, like a heavy rock, weighed in her stomach. "I've something to tell you."

May refused Ernie's offer to go into his living room.

"Please, just tell me what's happened. Is it Richard?"

"Aye lass, he's gone." His sorrowful gaze met hers. "He left a note pushed under the door. It said he wouldn't be back and there was a couple of pound notes for the rent he owed."

No! May's mind screamed.

Ernie shook his head. "I thought I knew the bloke. The least he could do was to tell us to me face he was goin'."

"I'm pregnant," she heard herself saying.

Ernie appeared to reel. "The bastard. Mebbes he is the rotten coward everyone says."

May turned and started back along the passage.

"Lass, don't go. Not like this. You're in shock. Stay for—"

May hurried along the passageway and banged the front door behind her.

*

She couldn't remember how she got there but May found herself at Pier Parade.

She walked along the pavement and, looking along the sweeping arm of the mile-long pier towards the lighthouse, she saw silhouetted, minuscule figures looking over the rail into the calm waters of the harbour.

Nostalgia washed over May as she remembered Dad taking her along the pier when she was a little girl to see the little dolly—reported to have been stuck in the wet cement when the pier was built in the last century. May could see in her mind's eye Dad picking her up and the smell of pipe smoke emanating from him as she sat high in his arms. She pined for those family times, when Mam, Dad and her brothers were the mainstay of her life.

Now she had no one.

Tears trickled down her cheeks. She licked the salty water taste on her lips.

She didn't know whether she was crying about Dad, Mam or because Richard had left her.

She brushed away the tears with the sleeve of her knitted cardigan. May had believed in Richard, loved him, and he in turn, like the others—Billy, Alec—had fooled her.

From far away came the drone of planes, then the sky blackened with Allied bombers that thundered overhead and flew up the coast.

As the bombers became tiny blobs in the sky, May wondered about the crew's wives, their families, the daily worry they had to endure. The knowledge that maybe their loved ones wouldn't have a tomorrow.

May drew herself up to her full height and started to walk back to the hospital. She'd a lot of planning for the future to do.

*

Back in the Nurses' Home, May unlocked the door to her room. She'd have to hurry to be on the ward after dinner when her shift began. She noticed an envelope had been shoved under her door.

A flash of hope seized her as she imagined the letter to be from Richard. She picked the envelope up and tore it open but, seeing the writing, disappointment engulfed her.

> *Dear Miss Robinson,*
>
> *I'm writing to advise you that Mrs. Talbot was involved in an accident some weeks ago and I can't look after Derek myself.*
>
> *I'm busy with the farm and visiting my wife in hospital and so I would appreciate it if you could come and collect the lad as soon as you can. The bombing is not so fierce I have read and so the young chap should be safe back in his hometown.*
>
> *I hope this doesn't cause too much inconvenience.*
> *Your faithful servant,*
> *Alfred Talbot*

As she folded the letter, May's hands shook. What was she going to do?

The next day, her day off, May set off to visit the farm in Allendale. She hoped to convince Mr. Talbot to allow Derek to stay until she'd made alternative arrangements. She hadn't sent a letter because, in all probability, she'd be there before it arrived.

The journey was uneventful except that she missed the bus at Hexham and had to wait an hour before the next Allendale bus arrived.

It was a warm day in May with a blank grey sky. May trekked up the familiar steep gravelled hill. The scene was devoid of magic now as May tried to foresee what difficulty she'd have to deal with at the farm. Did Mr. Talbot expect her to take Derek home immediately? If so, what would she do? With little money left from her pay to rent a room, even if she were granted permission to leave the hospital, there was nowhere to go.

She decided she must talk to Matron and explain the situation—maybe she could think of a solution. But the very idea of discussing her problem made May shudder.

But first she'd ask Mr. Talbot if he could give her a few days to work something out.

As she walked up the dusty path the scene that met her eyes was the same: the stone farmhouse on the rise of the hill, the strutting hens, the geese in the courtyard, which May bravely shooed away, the same dreadful dungy stench that seemed worse in the heat of the afternoon. At least May was wearing sensible lace-up brogues this time.

She knocked on the door and an elderly gentleman opened it. From the bowels of the house she heard the terrier yapping.

Mr. Talbot was a small, thin man with an impatient air, probably because he was anxious about his wife. His weather-beaten face had white crow's feet from years of wrinkling his eyes in the sun.

"Mr. Talbot?"

"Who wants to know?"

"I'm May Robinson."

His face visibly relaxed. Holding out a gnarled hand, he said, "Come in. Thanks for comin' so prompt. I'm glad to see you."

The unkempt living room didn't look the same. In the gloomy, dusty room there was paraphernalia on most of the chairs—newspapers and clean clothes that looked as if they'd been taken off the clothes line, and the table was littered with unwashed dishes and condiments. The air, however, still held a heady country smell of grass and freshness.

"Quiet, Spot," Mr. Talbot yelled and firmly shut the room door. The yapping stopped.

Mr. Talbot surveyed the room and shook his head in despair. "The place didn't look like this when the wife was here."

"I'm sorry to hear Mrs. Talbot is ill," May told him.

The old man's eyes shimmered with tears. "She's gone," he said. "Passed away yesterday."

May didn't know what to say but then her heart went out to Mr. Talbot and Derek; the poor lad had lost two mother figures in close successions and May worried about his state of mind.

"I'm so sorry for your loss."

The man sank onto a high-backed wooden chair.

He looked at her, his face slack. "I cannot take it in..." He choked back the tears.

"Are you up to telling me what happened?"

"I mean"—he looked stunned, as though he wasn't listening— "folk send their bairns out here in the country to keep them safe...and now look what's happened." His face crumpled. He looked up at May, disbelief in his eyes. "Nice night it was... when Maud decided to take Spot for a walk up to the moors. A bomber limping home from a mission crash landed in the top field." His voice cracked and he gulped. "Maud, being who she was, rushed to help...just as the plane exploded into flames." He wiped a tear away with the back of his hand. "Silly bugger... Maud didn't realise the crew had bailed out."

"Oh! How dreadful."

"She and the injured pilot were taken to hospital." Mr. Talbot shook his head. "I knew by the state of her she wouldn't survive." His voice wobbled. "In the end I didn't get the chance to say goodbye."

"That must be so hard. Your wife was a lovely woman, Mr. Talbot, and so brave."

He drew a laboured breath and nodded.

He wiped his eyes with a hand. "You've come about Derek?"

"Yes." May realised now that the poor man was in no fit state to look after a young boy.

"Look here...I've come to think a lot of the lad and, if this hadn't happened, he would've been welcome to stay. But not now Maud isn't here. I don't know what I'll do. Whatever it is I think the lad's best off with his own family."

"Does he know about Mrs. Talbot?"

"Aye, I've told him...blunt, like, because I don't know any other way. He's cut up but I don't know how to comfort him... I'm not meself any more."

"Of course not. Leave Derek to me."

"I'm sorry to land this on you...but to be honest, I cannot manage."

"Where is he?"

"Upstairs. He won't come out of his room."

Mr. Talbot's red-rimmed eyes pleaded with May.

She found Derek in the small musty-smelling front room, beneath the bedcovers.

"Derek. I've come to take you home." Her mind grappled with the question of where she could take Derek tonight. The only idea that presented itself was to take him to Salmon Street to Richard's old lodgings and ask Ernie if he had a bed for tonight. Not ideal, but what alternative did she have? It was then that May realised how alone she was in the world and the thought in her present condition frightened her.

"I don't want to," a firm muffled voice said. "This is me home."

"Mr. Talbot can't look after you any more."

"I can stay and help him around the farm."

"He mightn't be staying."

"Aunt Maud would want me to be with him."

"Derek...your Uncle Alf is very sad and can only look after himself just now. You've to come home with me."

A blonde head appeared from beneath the covers and Derek sat up. May's heart plummeted as she noticed the first flush of round-cheeked boyhood had left him.

Derek's ashen face appeared rebellious.

Her only hope was to be firm. "Derek, this isn't your home. You only came here to be safe from the bombing, remember? Mam thought it best until the time—"

"You can't make me do anything. You're not me mam."

May didn't know what to say. She decided the time had come to be honest and tell the truth.

"Yes I am, Derek."

They sat on a stone seat by the squeaky wooden gate that opened out onto a stretch of boggy land covered with thin reeds. Far below, black and brown cattle grazed in the fields and further still, folk in the diminutive town of Allendale went about their business.

As silence grew between mother and son, May wished she was one of the townsfolk without a care except what to have for tea.

Derek gave her a sidelong glance. Beside him on the grass stood the little brown case that Mam had packed all those months ago. Thoughts of her mother swirled in her mind, and May knew she would approve of what she was about to do.

"I am your mammy, Derek." How could she put the story in words he could understand? "You see...when you were born you were my son but you had a different daddy then and he had to go away to war. I couldn't marry him and that's what's supposed to happen. So, our mam made you her son...because she loved you so very much and she was married."

She hoped he could follow and understand.

"Where is this other daddy, now?"

"Your dad was a very brave man, Derek…he died fighting for his country."

Dear God, she prayed, *don't let all this talk about death warp the poor bairn's mind.*

Derek perked up a bit. "Did this other daddy fly aeroplanes?"

"He was a soldier."

"And carried a gun?"

"I suppose so."

Derek's eyes glazed as he imagined and his boyish expression looked pleased.

"Derek, we have to go now and catch the bus."

He turned and looked at her. "You don't act like a mammy."

May laughed. "How do I act?"

"Like a sister."

"It's okay by me if you want to think of me in that way. But one day I'd like to be your mammy."

His little face crumpled.

Derek had heard enough to cope with for one day.

She stood and picked up his small suitcase. As they walked down the hill, she felt a small hand creep into hers.

His tear-stained face looked up at her. "I'm glad I had another daddy. I didn't like the one I lived with."

It was while May sat on the homeward-bound bus—watching the countryside pass by the window, pointing out to Derek the tall and pink rosebay willowherb in hedgerows—that the idea came to her. She knew what she could do now to give Derek a home until she'd formed an alternative plan.

"Did you ever meet Mam's sister?"

May saw confusion cloud Derek's expression.

"You mean my real mammy, who died?"

A twinge of sadness pulled at May's heartstrings. If that was how her son could cope then she would accept it.

"Yes," she answered. "Mam's sister is called Ramona and she and her husband are very sad and I wondered if you could help make them be happy again."

"How?"

"They had a son like you. He flew aeroplanes but his got shot down. I'm sure they'd like a boy like you to live with them until I can—"

"Was he brave like my other daddy?" Eyes shining, Derek interrupted.

"I'm sure he was."

"Did he fly the plane?"

"You could ask Aunt Ramona."

"When will I see her?"

"We'll ask if you can stay for a while."

Derek looked a little tearful again. "What if she dies like Mam and Aunt Maud?"

May knew then her son had inherited her own sensitive and anxious nature.

"Their deaths, Derek, had nothing to do with you."

"Cross your heart."

May did.

"And Derek…maybe we'd better not tell Aunt Ramona about your other dad. We'll tell her I'm your sister. It's our secret."

Derek gave a delighted smile. He liked secrets.

CHAPTER TWENTY-THREE

May stepped off the train onto the platform at South Shields station. Derek followed, his small body appearing to droop.

He looked around and his chin wobbled. "This is where Mammy waved when I lef—"

A train came steaming into the station and his voice got drowned.

May took his hand and led him outside into the damp late afternoon air. She noticed the ground was wet and was surprised because she hadn't seen rain all day.

She removed Derek's cap and ruffled his blonde hair. "Mam thought you were such a big boy, Derek, how you settled at the farm. She said she was proud of you but she missed you so much. D'you know what I think?"

He squinted as he looked up at her. "What?"

"Mam's in heaven with Aunty Maud and they're talking about you."

"Really?" His pinched little face flushed with pleasure. "What d'you think they're saying?"

"Let's see, Aunty Maud will be boasting how you were such a big help at the farm. And Mam...she'll show off and say how you made a cup of tea and brought it to her one Sunday morning while she was still in bed."

"She was pleased," Derek joined in, his voice eager, "but she said I hadn't to use a kettle full of hot water again till I'm older."

"So, you see, if you get lonely for Mam, just imagine her talking in heaven about you."

A satisfied little smile split Derek's face. Neither of them had eaten anything since breakfast and so May treated them to a cup of tea and sandwich at Binns department store café.

"Where are we going now?" Derek wanted to know as later they stood at the trolleybus stop in King Street.

"To Mam's sister I told you about. She lives in Whale Street."

May rang the bell on the funeral parlour door and it was Mr. Newman who answered it.

"Come in, May." He looked bemused as he led the way through to the upstairs living quarters.

Both the Newmans looked shadows of their former selves as they sat on their sumptuously cushioned couch—or "settee" as Ramona preferred to call it.

May, perched on a wooden chair with Derek standing at her side, explained the situation.

"Mr. Talbot's in a right state and can't look after Derek any more. And so I had to bring him home... only there's no home to come back to, seeing as how I live in the Nurses' Home."

"Another tragedy." Ramona's voice was weak, as if her suffering had affected her throat.

Gone was her irritating air of grandeur, replaced by a sense of hopeless listlessness. Her shoulders drooped, her hair hadn't had its usual immaculate coiffure and the frilly white high-necked blouse she was wearing had tea stains down the front. Since her son had died Ramona had lost all interest in life and let herself go. But then, thought May, wouldn't she be the same if anything happened to Derek? The light of her world would have gone out and she couldn't imagine how she could go on.

A rush of compassion surged through May and she wanted to help somehow.

"Now, now, dear, this isn't our tragedy," Roland Newman told his wife.

He leapt from the couch and, removing his round spectacles, began to pace the floor as he polished them, as he always did when cornered by a tricky situation. Sensitive to all the Newmans' nuances and moods since she'd worked for them as a parlour maid, May would give him time to respond in his own way.

"Let's hear what May has to say." He looked expectantly at her.

May gathered her thoughts. "As you know, I'm training at the hospital and I have to live in. So there is nowhere for Derek to stay."

"What has this to do with us?" Ramona spoke sharply. Her pinched expression made it plain she wanted to be left alone so she could continue to wallow in grief.

"Now dear, I think May has a valid reason to be here"—Mr. Newman perceptively eyed the small suitcase at Derek's feet—"and I think it has something to do with this young chap."

May smiled, appreciatively. "I am here because of Derek. The thing is, he's . . . this has all come as a surprise and he's got nowhere to sleep tonight and I've nobody else to turn to. I thought, being relatives, you might be kind enough to help. I wondered . . . could Derek stay here for a while until I make alternative arrangements?"

She sensed Derek shifting uncomfortably at her side and she laid a hand on his back to help him stay calm.

"What about that man . . . me sister's layabout husband?" Ramona's voice was disapproving.

"Dad's . . . made a new life for himself."

"Typical, his wife not long gone and he waltzes off from all responsibility."

A gleam of hope dawned in Mr. Newman's otherwise desolate eyes. "It's true, families do stick together in times of trouble, especially during times of war. The young lad will perhaps bring a breath of fresh air into the house." Though his expression was tentative his voice, as he spoke, was determined. "Since our boy passed on we've been…reclusive."

May suspected he meant Ramona as she knew Mr. Newman had kept himself busy with work.

"What we need is a new direction in our lives," he continued.

"Roland! What are yi' sayin'? We could never replace our Danny…"

"No, dearest. I wouldn't think to try. But think on…what would Danny want? Our lives to stop because of him? No. He'd want us to find a way forward out of our grief and in doing so we will also be helping someone out. Just imagine if Danny was here. He'd be delighted to assist and he'd treat this young chap like a kid brother. Who knows," he beseeched his wife, "the lad may even be interested in the business one day. Ramona, this is your sister's boy. He's family."

This was all a bit much for May but, she reprimanded herself, beggars can't be choosers and the Newmans would be doing her a great service.

Ramona sagged. "Danny was the most giving person…and you are right, Roland, he would be the first to lend a hand to anyone in need." She laughed through the tears shining in her faded blue eyes. "Can you remember when he was a little lad, all the creatures he brought home? A little bird with a broken wing, the smelly mouse that kept escaping out of the cage…" She choked and couldn't go on.

Mr. Newman moved to put a hand on her shoulder. "I remember, dearest."

Ramona wiped away the tears with a handkerchief. She sniffed and addressed Derek. "Would you like to live with us for a while?"

"Would I have me own room?"

"My own room," Mr. Newman corrected. "You'd have Danny's."

"He flew aeroplanes, didn't he? May, me... *my* sister"—he gave May a look of acknowledgement that he'd kept their secret—"told me he was brave and flew aeroplanes for the war."

"Danny was a fine pilot." Ramona stood up from the couch. "Would you like to see his room? There are games and a Meccano set in it."

"Oo, yes please."

Hysteria rose in May. She felt left out as if this was family business—a family she wasn't part of. But Derek was her prime concern and she'd move heaven and earth for his happiness.

Ramona stood and looked at May. "We all have regrets..." Surprisingly, it seemed as though she understood May's pain. "What I regret is that I never made it up with me only sister... and it's too late now."

She took Derek by the hand and led him from the room.

Feeling the pain of parting with her son again stabbing in her ribcage, May could hardly breathe. She looked around the room that she'd kept spotlessly clean as a parlour maid for so many years. Dust lay thick on ledges, there were crumbs on the carpet and the linoleum surrounds needed a mop.

Mr. Newman interrupted her thoughts, telling May, "We'll take good care of the lad. He'll want for nothing."

May wanted to protest that the arrangement was only for a short period but she couldn't deny the hope she saw in Mr. Newman's eyes. Besides, she had no hope of providing Derek with a home in the foreseeable future and what more could she ask than to have him taken care of by two responsible people in such comfortable circumstances?

But as she followed Mr. Newman downstairs, the sense of making the wrong decision overwhelmed May. The impulse to race up the stairs, grab Derek and flee from the household took hold.

But instead, common sense prevailed, and she smiled gratefully at her old boss. "Thank you for helping me out. I appreciate this so much." And she did. "I'll be in touch as soon as I can."

Mr. Newman opened the parlour door.

Sincerity shining from his eyes, he said, "Thanks to you, May, that was the first time I've dared mention my ... Danny's name in front of the wife since he was taken from us." He stood tall and smiled. "Derek could be the making of Mrs. Newman."

As the door closed behind her, May was anguished. She didn't want Derek to be the making of anyone. She wanted him all to herself. Automatically, she laid a hand on her abdomen, over the new life inside her. She didn't know what to expect or how she'd manage but the need to protect both Derek and the baby she carried grew strong.

As she set off up the street, profound loneliness overcame her. She felt as though everyone had someone in their lives to love but her. She'd thought she had a future with Richard but he'd scarpered once he knew about the baby. Blast! Hadn't the affair with Billy taught her anything? How could she have been so wrong about Richard? Because he had seemed genuine, her mind cried. May had to face facts; when it came to men she was easily duped. And just like Billy, she had something to remember Richard by.

Gone was the sense of achievement she'd previously experienced and the pride in what she was now doing with her life. Instead she was racked with feelings of inadequacy and the fact that she'd lost all respect for herself.

"I love you unconditionally, lass," Mam's voice spoke in her head. She missed her mother so much and the voice comforted her. If only Mam were here.

But she was gone, May reminded herself, and it was time she took command and sorted her own life out.

A door opened on the other side of the street and Trevor Milne, Etty's husband, came into view. He didn't turn, and shutting the door, he hurried down the street.

What should she do about Etty? May remembered her thoughts from a while ago about how by harbouring bitterness she was only hurting herself. May hadn't been ready then to make up with Etty but she knew in her heart that she was now. Life was unpredictable, especially in wartime, and who knew what side of the moral compass you'd find yourself on. May forgave Etty and she needed her back in her life. Not just for selfish reasons, as someone to confide her troubles in. No. May wanted to share her life again with Etty, the good and the bad times like they used to, and to see those two gorgeous little girls again.

Etty had made a mistake but May couldn't condemn her, not with her own messed-up history. She'd heeded what Ramona had said about not making it up with her sister before it was too late.

It was time for May to stop feeling sorry for herself and face the future and it would be marvellous to have her best friend to share it with once more.

Purposefully, she set off over the road and rapped the heavy black knocker on Etty's front door.

May only hoped she hadn't left making up with her friend for too long.

As the door opened, May heard Etty's voice say, "Trevor, not again. You're always forgetting—"

Etty, in full view now, Norma in her arms, stopped mid-sentence, her face changing from mild annoyance to an expression that looked positively unsure.

"May, what are you doing here?"

"I came to see you. Can I come in?"

For a split second Etty's face showed incredulous disbelief. May, taking it as a sign of displeasure, expected the door to slam in her face.

Then Etty broke into a wide grin. "Course you can. It's taken you long enough." She spoke with her usual candour. "But seeing how much I wronged you, I'm not surprised."

She swallowed hard and, eyes glistening with tears, led the way along the passageway and into the kitchen.

She set Norma on the floor and the bairn, looking adorable in pink pyjamas, looked at May with wide-eyed curiosity.

Etty said, "It's nearly bedtime, pet. Here's your picture book." She handed Norma a large book off the table. "Find Mammy an elephant."

The bairn crouched on the floor and began turning the book's pages.

May looked around. The place looked comfortingly the same as it always had. She was thrilled there was no animosity in the atmosphere. Etty, as open as the picture book Norma looked at, would tell her straight if there was.

"Where's Victoria?" May asked. "I bet she's grown since I last saw her."

"In her cot. Unlike this little monkey." Etty nodded to her daughter. "Victoria likes her sleep."

Etty plonked on a fireside chair. "I can't tell you how good it is to see you. I've missed you so much, May."

"I feel the same way."

"I don't blame you. I do understand how devast—"

"Don't. It's over and done with now. I don't want anything to come between us any more. Besides, you wouldn't believe the mess I've made of things recently."

"Try me."

May flopped into the opposite fireside chair. She gazed into the meagre fire that had a large mesh fireguard surrounding it.

"May, you've always worn your heart on your sleeve. Is it to do with work?"

"It's...everything."

Etty looked directly at her friend. "I know what you're thinking. Come on, you can tell me. I want to share your troubles."

"That not why I've come. I'm here to say I'm sorry for not answering your letters."

"You were mad at me...and you had every right to be."

"And for calling you a slut."

"Yes. That was a bit much." Etty gave a mischievous grin.

May asked. "Does Trevor know about...Billy?"

Etty opened her mouth to answer but Norma stood up and came over to show her the book.

"Elfant," she said.

"Clever girl." Etty clapped her hands. "Now find Mammy a pussy cat."

The bairn crouched on all fours.

"Yes," Etty answered, "I told him before we married."

"Blimey. And he still went through with it. He's a man in a million."

Etty gave a fond smile. "I know. I don't know where I'd be without him. Probably in the workhouse. That's what can happen to unmarried mothers."

May felt the blood drain from her face.

"May, you're scaring me. What's wrong?"

"Oh, Etty I don't know where to start."

"From the beginning."

Like a dam overflowing, the words spilled from May's mouth. All the while Etty listened, open-mouthed.

"So, how can I condemn you, me best friend," May finished her story, "when I've behaved much worse? Me da's right; I've become a slut."

"May, don't say that. In your case you fell in love and both men turned out to be bastards."

A part of May wanted to rebuke Etty, tell her Richard was anything but; then she considered the facts and had to admit that was how things appeared.

"How awful for your friend Maureen." Etty shook her head sorrowfully. "She sounds special."

"Oh, Etty, you've no idea. I don't think I'll ever meet anyone so pure of thought and deed in me life."

Etty went silent and May knew her friend needed time to digest all she'd told her.

"It sounds like a story from the flicks," Etty finally said, "but then I never worry because I know the story is contrived and will have a happy ending." She regarded May and gave a helpless shrug. "All this is too much to take in, let alone for you to live through. May, how strong you've been to endure these troubles."

Norma toddled over with the picture book. "Gog." Her fat little finger pointed to the page.

"Dog," Etty corrected.

She hauled Norma onto her knee and nuzzled into her neck. The bairn broke free and whinged to be set down, where she picked up a dolly and put her in a rather battered little pram.

May, watching the toddler's antics, voiced her thoughts. "I can't imagine loving another bairn as much as I do Derek."

"Love is like elastic and can be stretched," Etty told her. "I found that out when Dorothy died and I took in Victoria. Even though she's my niece I love her just as much as Norma."

They lapsed into a contemplative silence.

Then Etty spoke, her voice gentle. "You've big decisions to make. I'm here to help . . . if you'll let me."

May thought of how vulnerable and alone she'd felt earlier, and how different things were now she was reunited with her good friend.

"Thank you...it's good to have you back in my life again."

"First we must tackle what you're going to do when the baby starts to show."

"I haven't a clue. I avoid thinking about the future. I pretend none of this is happening." She met Etty's anxious gaze. "I do know it's time I faced reality."

"Have you any thoughts about what you're going to do when the baby arrives?"

"I'm not giving this bairn away."

In the heavy silence that followed May knew her friend's thoughts.

"I know. I might have no other alternative."

She burst into tears.

CHAPTER TWENTY-FOUR

"Nurse!" Night Sister's voice brought May out of her trance. "Are you dozing?"

Startled, May jumped. "Of course not, Sister."

Weeks had passed and May, sent to do a stint of night shifts by Matron, found herself assigned to the Maternity ward.

She was sitting in the nursery feeding a baby from a banana-shaped bottle.

Night Sister Turnbull glared at May. "Baby will be sucking air and getting wind if you don't take care."

"There's still milk left in the bottle, Sister."

Sister didn't hear as she'd already left the nursery and closed the door.

"Dozing indeed," May told the little one in her arms. His pink cheeks sucking, he looked up with all-knowing blue eyes.

"I am taking care of you, cutie, aren't I?" May smiled.

The bottle now drained, she moved to the changing table and, placing the baby on it, she removed the sodden cloth nappy and replaced it with a clean one from the basket. Securing the nappy with a safety pin, she placed the baby, wrapped tightly in a blanket, in the cot.

May washed out the bottle and then proceeded to stack the side bench with fresh cotton nightdresses from the airing cupboard.

The nursery door opened and Staff Nurse walked in.

"Your turn for supper." She eyed all the silent cots. "Gracious, Robinson . . . you seem to know the trick of having a quiet nursery. I'll do nights with you any time."

"I like being in the nursery," May replied. "Especially when I'm bottle-feeding. It passes the time."

It was true, she thought, as she made for Sister's office. She enjoyed seeing the little ones' faces seemingly bloat when they were satisfied. She snapped her mind shut as her thoughts turned to the scrap of life she carried; she couldn't allow herself to fall in love with it or think of it as a person.

Sister sat with the door open, notes before her on the desk.

"Nurse Robinson reporting off duty to supper, Sister."

"Very well, Nurse." Sister didn't look up. "Leave the door open. I want to hear if I'm needed in the labour room."

As May hurried over to the dining hall she looked up into the bright starry sky—the kind of night to expect an air raid.

There were only two women in the delivery room. One had delivered half an hour ago and the other was in the last stages of labour. If Jerry did show up, it was May's job to get those able patients with babies into the shelter. But those in the delivery room unable to be moved stayed with their babies as no mother was to be parted from their little one. Night Sister stayed with them on the ward.

May entered the bright and noisy canteen where nursing staff sat at large round tables. She went over to the counter and decided she'd have sausage and mash followed by semolina pudding.

As she ate someone came and sat beside her and when she looked up she saw Valerie, elbow on the table, head resting on her hand, gazing intently at her.

"I hear the conchie's gone."

"I hear you've got a fella in tow."

"Ooo, May. That was sharp. You've got good at answering back." When May didn't reply, Valerie continued, "I thought I'd find you here. I didn't want to go without tellin' you I was leavin'."

Fork in hand, May gaped. "Why? Where are you going?"

"To work at the factory. It's regular work with good money and no bums to wash." Valerie pulled a jokey face.

May's fork clattered on the plate.

"But why?"

Valerie sobered. "Lots of reasons but the main one is I get to live at home with Mam and the bairns and I don't have to study."

"I thought you wanted to get away from all that."

"So I did, but when Maureen died, a lot changed in me mind."

"Like what?"

"Who I am…" Valerie looked young and carefree, without that belligerent look on her face. "I can't run away from meself. It killed me to see how Mam couldn't cope when I went home on me days off and the bairns suffering. Here was me looking out for other folks when…" Her chin wobbled and she couldn't answer. "I mean if anything happened to any of them…" She collected herself. "Hark at me getting maudlin. Anyways, I'm not cut out to be a nurse. I knew straight away but I was fighting it. You have to do what your conscience thinks is right…Maureen taught me that."

They avoided each other's eyes; the hurt was still too raw for both of them.

"Matron can't have been pleased."

"That's putting it mildly. She was convinced there was a fella." The defiant smirk was back. "Course, I denied it."

"Who is he?" May wanted to know.

"His name's Norman. He works at the pit and lives just a few doors up from Mam."

May could swear she saw a dreamy look in her friend's eyes.

"Anyway." Valerie appeared uncommonly serious. "I came to tell you I was sorry the way I acted about that Richard fella. To be honest, if he wasn't a conchie, he seemed a decent sort."

For one split second May was going to confide in Valerie but the moment passed as she noticed her friend's eyes glaze over.

Valerie stood. "I won't miss this place. But I'm glad I got to say goodbye to you."

May smiled. "Same here."

"See you." Valerie gave a little wave and walked away.

They both knew they'd probably never meet again. That was life, May believed. Sometimes you encountered someone for a purpose and when that reason was met, you might never see them again.

Maybe Valerie had been sent with her contrary moods to toughen May up—and to remind her of what Maureen had said.

You must do what your conscience thinks is right.

May pushed the plate of food away.

When May did the night shift she found that by six o'clock in the morning her brain had turned to mush and she was so tired she was unable to think. But it was also the time when babies were handed out from the nursery for an early morning feed. May had to concentrate or else she might get muddled and give a baby to the wrong mother.

A baby in May's arms, she read with special care the name written on a band around its wrist. When all the babies were safely in their mothers' arms, May made a beeline for the kitchen and revived her dead brain with a cup of tea.

As soon as her shift finished and the day shift nurses arrived and were given the report, May hurried from the ward. Instead of making for the Nurses' Home and sleep, she went to the little chapel in the hospital. Here she sat in one of the seats staring at the Virgin Mary, whose head was embellished with a golden halo and who held little baby Jesus in her arms.

The chapel had only three rows of seats and May imagined all those folks who'd sat, heads bent in prayer, making bargains with Christ as she was about to do now.

She put her hand in her pocket and brought out the rosary beads Maureen had given her.

> *Dear Lord, my conscience is telling me not to give up the baby on any account. But I don't know how to manage, without a home, and no job and nobody that really cares except Etty and she has her hands full.*
>
> *I know there's a way around this but I can't think of anything. You can work miracles; please work one for me now and I promise this bairn will be christened and brought up in the faith.*
>
> *Amen*

May crossed herself, something she'd never done before and she felt rather foolish but she wanted Him to know how sincere she was.

He can see in your heart, a voice whispered in her head. May's overtired and overwrought mind thought it might be Mam. May found the idea of her still being around comforting. She stood and made her way out of the hospital and over the grounds to the Nurses' Home where she passed the open door of the day room. The voice of a newscaster blared from the wireless and through the open door.

"Hey, Robinson, is that you?"

May entered the room where a few nurses were lounging on chairs. A second-year nurse who May had worked with told her, "You missed a letter yesterday so I popped it under your door."

"Thanks."

May hurried up the stairs and, unlocking the door, picked the white envelope off the floor.

She didn't recognise the handwriting at first but then her muddled brain remembered.

Pulse racing, she tore the letter open.

Darling May (Please read this!)

Forgive me. I do love you and I never intended to hurt you as you must think.

When you told me the wonderful news of our baby I meant every word I said. But what you didn't know was that my news was that I'd been given the sack. I suspect because of us! John told me. He's a decent sort and he was upset on my behalf.

Darling girl, I despaired because I didn't know what to do but when I heard about our baby my world rocked and, in that instant, I knew I couldn't carry on as my conscience had changed and my duty belonged to you and the baby.

If I'd told you my intention, I mightn't have found the courage to leave you. My love, I applied to the tribunal to overturn my plea as a conscientious objector. It has now been done. I went to the labour exchange and joined up. With my previous record I was posted to—the next words were censored—*to become a medical orderly. As well as basic training—first aid, stretcher-bearing, bandaging and so forth—I have to learn military discipline which includes drill. And though the Royal Army Medical Corps is a non-combatant unit I do have to learn about weapons but for self-defence purposes only—which as you can imagine, suits me fine. I'll be posted to a unit after training and then I'll be sent who knows where.*

This letter is a lot to take in, I know, but my heart belongs to you wherever I go.

My main worry is for you and the baby, how you will manage about money as I know your days at the hospital are numbered.

I have arranged for the large portion of my pay allowance to be sent to you so you won't have to worry immediately about finances.

My other news is that I went to see my parents but with no joy. Ma and Pa still display resentment towards me which I can live with. I could see by their expressions that being a medical orderly didn't fit the bill. But I wanted them to know about you and their expected grandchild and so I told them where they could find you and it's up to them now as I've done my bit.

Darling, please find it in your heart to forgive me for leaving. The reason for all I've done recently is for one thing only—so I can look my child in the eye, tell them I did my bit to help keep you and them in a country safe to live in.

I promise when I return home I'll prove my love and hopefully you will agree to wedding bells and all that entails. Darling, this isn't much of a proposal but I will do the deed properly on my return.

Meanwhile, send me a photo so I can see your lovely face for real.

Love you, my darling. Keep safe.

Your Richard XX

Tears glistened in May's eyes. Her prayer had been answered.

CHAPTER TWENTY-FIVE

June 1944

Rain came down in torrents from a grey sky and pattered on the leaves of tall trees. The soaked earth beneath Richard's boots had, in some places, churned to mud.

"Mate, I don't know about you but I'll go crazy if I don't get to know what's happening soon." Charlie Oakley lit a cigarette. Charlie had moved down south in the same truck as Richard from Boyce barracks. They were in a transit camp somewhere on the outskirts of Southampton where tall trees provided camouflage, and they shared a tent. The food was surprisingly good in the camp and they had access to showers close by.

Charlie continued. "We've been kept like prisoners in this godforsaken wood for days."

Richard nodded. He regarded Charlie's khaki uniform, battle-dress, gaiters, boots and beret with its own distinctive RAMC (Royal Army Medical Corps) badge and felt surprised at the pride he felt. He'd never expected to belong to an army unit—but life was rich in surprises, and meeting his sweetheart, May, had been the best surprise of all.

They'd corresponded in the month or so he'd been at the RAMC Depot and Richard had been both overjoyed and surprised at May's response to his first letter—because he had feared her reaction and she must have thought him a scoundrel for deserting her in such a way. She'd forgiven him the unforgivable, trusting soul that she was, and they'd continued their blossoming court-ship by letter. His love for her had deepened. After his decision to overturn his stance on being a conscientious objector his life had changed out of all recognition. So, here he was in this wood with the troops. A rumour had spread that something big was afoot and the whisper was it was the second front but no one knew for sure as top brass were keeping it secret.

Richard would have liked to divulge all this news to May but letters home were now forbidden—which clinched the idea that something important was about to happen.

He told Charlie, "I've heard tell some infantry have been taken out to the Channel to practise landing."

"What the hell...? And we're stuck here with only an early morning march outside for any sort of exercise." He threw his Woodbine down on the wet earth. "What I want to know is, are the rumours right? Is this the big one?"

Charlie's wish was granted four days later.

Their commanding officer, Major Parkins, told them early in the morning as the unit stood at attention. "Soon we will all be involved in the gravest undertaking...the liberation of Europe."

Richard's mind reeled at the enormity of the first operation he was to be involved in, and he couldn't take in the reality of it all. But the brown sealed envelope that was handed to him, that held instructions and photographs of where they were going, helped convince him.

Major Parkins and some nursing orderlies along with the Field Ambulance were the first to go the next day, on the sixth of June.

To a man, he knew, they felt lucky to be part of the operation that would lead to the liberation of Europe.

*

A collective "hurrah" went up in the nurses' sitting room. May, sitting in a saggy but comfortable armchair, wondered what all the fuss was about. Cup of tea in her hand, she made her way over to the group of tired-looking nurses, just finished from the night shift, gathered around the wireless listening to the news.

"What's up?" she asked a brunette wearing a dressing gown.

The lass grinned. "The Allies have landed in Normandy."

"Oh my goodness!" May clasped her hands to her heart.

As they listened to the newscaster's voice, the buzz of excitement in the day room was palpable.

After the news had finished, the nurses looked at one another in wide-eyed wonderment.

"So, the rumours were true." A nurse, cigarette in hand, grinned at the others. "There is a second front. But no one expected the landings to be in Normandy."

The brunette chipped in, "I've heard the hospitals down south are clearing wards in readiness for casualties."

The nurse with the ciggie frowned. "I've just thought, I've not heard from my Tony in a while. He's in the Durham Light Infantry and I bet that's why. The powers that be will have wanted it kept hush hush and stopped letters home."

"Same with my fiancé, Jack," someone called from the day room kitchen. "I haven't heard from him in an age, either. Poor lad, I've been calling him something rotten."

May went cold. She hadn't heard from Richard in a long while either. Although tired, she couldn't sleep and sat with the rest of the nurses glued to the wireless for most of the day, listening for any more news.

The next night on Maternity, as May helped one of the mothers breastfeed her baby, the young woman asked, "Nurse…have you heard the latest news?"

"No. I haven't seen any papers yet." May, in fact, had spent an agitated day trying to get some sleep but too much was happening and her wound-up brain refused to relax.

"The landings were a massive operation, Nurse. Mr. Churchill said there were over four thousand ships and thousands of smaller craft crossed the Channel. Now, I've never seen the size of the Channel meself but it seems amazing how none of them ships bumped into one another."

She looked down at the sleeping child at her breast and smiled tenderly. "Have you got a sweetheart in the army, Nurse? D'you think he's in the thick of it like I do my George?"

"Yes, I do think my Richard is there."

"I'll remember him in me prayers when I say a word for George before I go to sleep."

A lump came into May's throat. Folk were kind in times of war and looked out for each other.

Next morning, after May had breakfasted in the canteen, she couldn't settle, and reclining on her bed in her pyjamas, she brought out Richard's letters from her locker drawer.

My darling, dearest sweetheart... As she read the endearments, she felt cherished and the words were like music to her ears. The letter ended, *Out of sight doesn't mean out of mind as you are with me always.*

Tears brimming her eyes, she re-read another letter:

> *I've been thinking things over about Derek and somehow, someday he must become part of our family. I will love him because he is a part of you.*

That Richard was prepared to take on another man's son reminded her of Trevor, Etty's husband, who had taken on two kiddies and neither of them were his. May's admiration for both men went up a thousandfold.

It was then she felt a flutter like the touch of a butterfly's wing in her abdomen. The baby was moving—Richard's child. A smile of delight spread across May's face to be replaced, as she thought of the future, with a wrinkled frown of worry.

It occurred to her that the insomnia she was experiencing had nothing to do with recent news, as momentous as it was, but more the thought that soon she would no longer be able to hide her pregnancy. She'd managed to hide the growing mound of her stomach so far because she worked nights and her bump wasn't that obvious yet but May couldn't hide her pregnancy for much longer.

If only Richard were here to talk to. She could imagine his studious expression as he mulled things over, the hesitation before he spoke his views, which she had now come to value.

The realisation that Richard might be in the thick of the fighting at the front reduced May to helpless anxiety. She wondered if it was having a baby that had made her so teary recently.

May sat up and pulled herself together. She'd encountered worse things before, Mam's untimely death for instance, and had coped on her own.

Sleep eluding her, she stretched and pondered Richard's allowance, which she was saving. Though it was a wonderful help, it wouldn't be enough to manage rent and all her needs once she'd stopped working. Her head ached trying to think of a way she could manage once she left the hospital, which would be soon, she thought, as she stretched her cotton nightdress over her bump.

As May looked out of the window, she noticed the bright sunny weather. At this precise moment, she decided, her worries could wait. There were two things she now craved—to be outdoors in the sunshine and to spend time with her son.

She dressed in a summer blouse, skirt and sandals and, taking some money out of her savings biscuit tin, made for the outdoors.

*

May stood on the shaded side of Whale Street and pressed the bell on the funeral parlour door. She waited, rehearsing what she was going to say.

Mr. Newman, round spectacles down his nose, a frown of concentration on his face and wearing an apron down to his ankles over his clothes, opened the door.

"May, what a lovely surprise... come in, come in. Only I'm busy so you'll have to come through to the workshop." He hesitated. "But maybe it's Mrs. Newman you want to see."

"No, it's fine... I only want to ask something and I can speak to you just as well."

The front parlour hadn't changed and, though dusty, the familiarity of Mr. Newman's heavy desk, shelves around the walls that featured glass globes with angels within them, comforted May.

She followed Mr. Newman through into the workshop at the back of the house whose windows looked over a redbrick back yard. Even though it was summer the fire was lit in the grate as it heated the pitch Mr. Newman used to seal coffins. A kettle sang on the hob. May took a seat on a stool next to the bench that lined a wall and gazed around. The floor was full of wood shavings and dirty cups littered the bench—something that never would have happened when she worked here. Mr. Newman, standing next to a coffin, picked up a hammer.

"So, exceptional news, yesterday, eh? Only Mrs. Newman finds any war news hard to take at the minute. She buries her head in the sand... if you get my meaning. Victory at the moment means nothing to her." He gave a sad little smile. "That brother of yours has done her the power of good though, she never stops talking about him." He gave May an appreciative nod.

"It's Derek I've come about." At his look of concern, she hurried on, "It's such a lovely afternoon and as I work nights I thought I'd take him to Readhead Park to ride on the swings."

Mr. Newman looked dumbfounded. "May, it's a school day."

The night shift had taken its toll and she felt confused, as the thought of school had never entered her mind. Her spirits sank.

"Lass. Is something wrong? Or are you overtired? You look done in."

May couldn't take words of kindness at the minute. The enormity of all that had happened recently, the baby she carried, the Normandy landings, the idea that Richard might be in danger... Everything hit her and, feeling panicky, she could barely breathe.

Dissolving into tears, she blurted, "I've got nowhere to live."

Mr. Newman dropped the hammer onto the bench and came to stand at her side. He patted her shoulder. "Tell me all about it."

Even though she was so upset May recognised he was assuming his professional demeanour. She faltered. Then made up her mind. From now on her life was going to be an open book, she wasn't going to be ashamed. If Richard could start anew then so could she. She sniffed hugely and then words came tumbling out of her mouth, about Dad, Billy, Derek's true parentage, her fears for Richard, and her pregnancy. The liberating feeling was wonderful. May didn't care what anyone thought any more, Richard loved her for what she was and that was enough.

She finished her story and in the silence that followed, Mr. Newman handed her a handkerchief from his apron pocket.

His smile was gentle. "I remember Ramona being like this when she carried our Danny. She could dissolve into tears at the drop of a hat."

The thought of Ramona pregnant and vulnerable was strange to contemplate but May knew she shouldn't judge; you never knew people's motives or what went on in the privacy of their homes.

"I didn't mean to—"

Mr. Newman put his hand up to stop her. "May... in my line of work I'm many things to people and father confessor is one of them. I pride myself that people's confidences are safe with me.

You wouldn't believe what folk tell me. And I am honoured that it is me they choose to confide in."

He gave her a quizzical look. "So, let me get this straight. Derek is my great nephew. Does he know?"

"Yes, and it's unfair I made him keep it a secret."

"I agree. And this fellow, Richard, you say has renounced being a conscientious objector and is now, you believe, at the second front."

"Yes."

"May I ask, are you two...hrmph...do you intend—"

"Richard proposed in one of his letters." A spark of defiance flashed within her, "But even if he hadn't, I'm determined to keep this baby."

Mr. Newman didn't react as May expected. He liked things right and proper and didn't hold with anyone flouting the rules of society and, like most folk around here, he considered it a mortal sin for babies to be born out of wedlock.

But here he was, with tears swimming in his eyes.

May was startled.

"I've seen enough of death," he told her, "in these past few years of war to know that life...born in any circumstance...is precious and a miracle to behold." He shook his head regretfully. "I only wish there was some way Mrs. Newman and I could help."

May was so touched she felt teary but, determined to stay strong, she blinked hard.

She gazed again around the messy workshop as the idea grew in her mind. There was no harm in trying.

"There is, Mr. Newman." As his eyebrows raised, she went on. "You haven't got help these days and the place is in a mess." Her truthful self came to the fore.

"That's true." Mr. Newman might be officious but he was a practical man. "Mrs. Newman...isn't ready to engage in conversation with strangers."

May understood.

"I've got an offer to make you." She took a deep breath. So much depended on his answer. "If I could live here for a while after I leave the hospital, till I get myself sorted, I could do my old job as parlour maid instead of paying rent. Don't worry, I'll keep out of Mrs. Newman's way. I guarantee you wouldn't know I was here."

She could tell by the startled expression on Mr. Newman's face he was taken aback.

"Gracious. I'll have to think this over."

"There's no need to rush." May crossed her fingers; there was every need for haste, this baby was growing bigger by the minute. "Have a word with Mrs. Newman and see what she thinks."

May couldn't believe how manipulative she was being. Mr. Newman, like many men, liked to think he was the man of the house and made all the decisions.

"On second thoughts... I can make a decision now." His demeanour changed and he appeared master of the household. "What you're suggesting is splendid. We have plenty of room and besides, as I maintained before, families should stick together."

"What about Mrs.—"

"I'll explain that it's our duty to help out. But between you and me I'm hoping the company might do Ramona good. This arrangement could be a blessing for everyone."

May was doubtful his wife would take her presence in the house as a blessing. But May was relieved at least she had somewhere to go when she was forced to leave the hospital.

CHAPTER TWENTY-SIX

In the early hours of the morning, Richard lay on the camp bed and, by the light of a candle, he looked at the black and white photograph May had sent him of her in uniform. She was squinting in the sunlight but the loveliness of her face was unmistakeable, those gorgeous eyes (Richard wished he could see their colour), luscious cupid bow lips and cute snub nose. He could go on looking forever but a noise at his side alerted him and he put the picture away beneath the blanket.

"Your girl?" Charlie whispered. Bare-chested and wearing only underpants, he gazed down at Richard.

"Fiancée," Richard whispered back and was amazed how the word rolled off his tongue so easily. A glow, like sitting contentedly in front of a warm fire, washed over him and it felt good to belong to someone.

"You got a girl?"

Up until now they hadn't discussed private matters; they'd never had the time.

"I got married by special licence before I came away." Charlie grinned. "Can't wait to get back to her."

Richard nodded. "What's her name?"

"Margaret."

"Nice. Anyway, what are you doing up at this time of night?"

"Same as you. I couldn't sleep. I've been moon gazing." Charlie made to move away then paused. "Could be us departing soon."

"Yes."

Presumably, thinking about the landings was what kept Charlie awake as well. It was amazing how anything so daunting could be exhilarating too.

Richard held up the candle and looked at Charlie's hairy chest. "Where are your dog tags?"

"Bloody identification... they got in the way when I assisted with a bloke who 'accidentally'"—he raised his eyebrows—"shot himself in the foot. When I'm hot I open the top button of my shirt and the damn tags dangle in the way when I'm tending to a casualty. D'you not find the same?"

"Yep. But I wouldn't take them off. Knowing me, I'd lose them."

"I always pop them in my battle dress pocket. I'd have been for it if I was caught today as I forgot to put them on because..."

"For God's sake..." a man in the next bed to Richard hissed, "I'll make casualties of the both of you if you don't shurrup and let me get some kip."

Charlie raised his eyebrows and walked off, while Richard blew out the candle.

Next morning after breakfast, a male voice of authority spoke over the loudspeaker, instructing those units departing in the next twenty-four hours to get ready for embarkation. Richard's unit was one of them.

This was it.

He gathered his equipment: tin hat covered with net, rucksack, gas mask and water carrier.

Early the next day, before the camp's breakfast, Richard's unit was transported to the nearest port, where he had the boyish pleasure of smelling the bracing salt sea air which reminded him of home and holidays. When he saw the port, however, crammed with grey and camouflaged ships lined up against the quayside, the reality hit hard—this was no holiday trip, by God, this was for real.

Richard boarded a Landing Craft Tank at midday and as they sailed out of Southampton docks he wondered when, and if, his feet would touch British soil again. Soldiers, packed like sardines, smoked and joked with one another. But Richard saw behind their eyes the same fear and apprehension that he felt about what they'd find on the other side of the Channel.

As a strong wind blew, the hours crawled by but then, as Richard looked out over the side, the first sighting came of a brown French coastline, littered with a surprising amount of ships of all sizes.

The LCT found a gap between ships, coming closer to shore, and Richard saw figures in the water, and running across the sands. The occasional ear-splitting explosion of a shell came from the beach.

His brother Jeff came to mind. A swell of pride for the kid gripped Richard.

The LCT pulled alongside a large grey ship, then, pitching in the choppy waves towards the shore, it skirted a wrecked landing craft.

As he waited to disembark by way of the gangway, Richard noticed figures floating in the water and was shocked to realise they were the bodies of dead soldiers.

He peered towards the shore and the scene that met his eyes matched photographs he'd scrutinised in the information envelope: villas and houses along the sea front.

His stomach beset with nervous anticipation, he put on his tin hat, checked his white armband with the red cross on it and disembarked from the LCT into the relatively warm waters of Sword Beach, the code name given to one of the five beaches for the Normandy landing areas.

With his medical kit weighing him down, Richard waded through the waves with the others and made for the shore.

All along the beach were long lines of soldiers and equipment snaking from ships.

A lone shell screamed over and exploded on the beach, and everyone dived to the sand. A soldier running farther along dropped to his knees and then fell. Richard, running towards him, crouched and shrugged off his haversack to tend to the soldier's wounds. But on closer inspection, he realised the soldier was beyond help—his war was over. He looked down at the young lad, the staring shocked eyes that had no life in them. This could be his brother, Jeff, he thought, a deep sadness overwhelming him.

Following the others, Richard saw mangled tanks and bicycles. A line of German prisoners marched by. Christ, he thought, if this is a day after the Allied invasion when the beach head was taken, it must've been hell on earth yesterday.

Reaching the top of the beach, he saw a white flag with a red cross sticking out of a trench dug out of sand and soil.

It was here he found his commanding officer, Major Parkins, and the unit regrouped.

Someone clapped him on the back and when Richard turned he was delighted to see Charlie Oakley.

Sweat ran from Major Parkins' brow into his eyes, and his uniform was caked in mud and sand.

He told the unit, "The plan to take Caen from Sword Beach yesterday by nightfall didn't happen but the Allies have been successful and established four sizable beachheads." He turned to survey the wounded behind him in the trench and the dead, covered in blankets. "Not without considerable cost."

A shell screamed overhead and he waited until it had exploded further down the beach. "We'll do what we can here and then move further inland."

It was crucial, Richard knew, that the wounded were treated as quickly as possible. A soldier's life depended on it. The success rate, when hordes of casualties needed vital treatment at one time, depended on the speed with which the wounded were moved along a complex chain of medical units. He got to work at the Regimental Aid Post, the first stage where casualties were assessed and either patched up and sent back to the fighting or shuttled by stretcher to the next medical team.

Later that afternoon, his unit moved inland towards the front line.

CHAPTER TWENTY-SEVEN

June 1944

May intended to tell Matron about the baby as soon as her stint on the Maternity night shift finished. Her bump would be noticed soon and she'd rather leave of her own volition than be dismissed by Matron.

Collecting the jugs of water from locker tops and placing them on a trolley, May thought about how her life had taken a turn for the better recently. What with Mr. Newman agreeing she could live in with them till she found a place of her own and knowing Richard was, after all, the honest and morally decent man she'd given her heart to, she could find the courage to resign from the hospital.

Richard had once told her, "With all the destruction I want to build houses for the future."

And so, when Richard came home from the war, he could go back to being an architect and they could start a home together.

She thought, wryly, that with all the bombing that had left folk with nowhere to live, Richard would never be out of a job.

She wheeled the trolley into the kitchen and put the jugs on the bench to fill, and a smile played on her lips as she recalled his last letter.

> *My darling May,*
> *I have arrived safely and I'm somewhere* The next paragraph was missing as it had been censored. *This letter*

*is difficult to write as there is so much I can't say because
of censorship, and so I shall be brief.*

*I don't know how much longer I can stay in contact but I
want you to know I don't regret my decision to join in with
the war one bit—except for the fact of leaving you behind.*

*I'm so glad I met you and that we will have the rest of
our lives together—it's what keeps me going, kiddo.*

You are with me always.

Take care of yourself and that baby of ours.

Your Richard XX

Back in the ward, she wheeled the trolley to the first bed
and replaced the filled water jug on the locker top. She pictured
Richard's face as he concentrated on writing the letter. She couldn't
believe her luck that she'd met him and that he wanted to grow
old with her.

"Eee, Nurse, I'm sorry to ask but can I have a bedpan please?
I'm dying for a wee."

The young lass in the bed, newly delivered, had just come
from the labour room onto the ward and was to be kept in bed
because she'd confessed she felt rather faint.

"Of course."

May hurried to the sluice.

Later, as May stood outside Matron's office door nervously
awaiting the conversation ahead, John, the head porter, passed.

"What you been up to?" He quipped, "I hope you've not been
causin' trouble."

If only he knew.

She always made time to speak to John as she felt sorry for the
man. Richard had told her that he had lost his son earlier in the
war. John didn't hold a grudge against Richard being a conchie

but he did against the warmongers that caused his only child to die on the beaches of Dunkirk.

She told him, "I suspect Richard might be over in Normandy."

"That'll be a worry for yi', all reet." John's face flushed in annoyance. "That lad's got guts and I hope the gossips are ashamed of themselves."

Before May could answer, the office door opened and Matron stood there.

"You may enter, Nurse Robinson."

John winked and moved away.

May stood in front of Matron's desk wondering how to broach the subject, then she decided simply to dive in.

"I've come to hand in my resignation, Matron."

Matron leaned back in the swivelling captain's chair. Lips a thin line, her sharp eyes considered May from beneath her grey hair and frilled cap.

"I wondered when you'd decide to tell me."

"You know?"

"A Sister on Maternity is no fool, Nurse Robinson. It is her job to recognise a new mother-to-be when she sees one." She sat upright. "Normally I would ask a nurse who makes this request to consider the money and the time her superiors have put into her training. But in this particular instance I can see no other option than to agree. You must resign. You may continue to work until the end of the month."

The meeting was over.

May couldn't help but feel a failure and that she'd let people down.

"I understand, Matron."

She made to leave.

"Nurse Robinson…"

"Yes, Matron."

Matron's expression stayed grim and May felt her knees wobble.

"You have made, so far, an exemplary nurse. My wish is that someday you will find a way to return to us and finish your training."

May was speechless. It meant so much that Matron had found it in her heart not only to forgive her but to recommend she return to the profession.

"It is my wish too, Matron."

Matron nodded. "And, Nurse, before you go"—her eyes sparkled—"let us hope you make as good a mother as you do a nurse."

As May made her way to the Nurses' Home for some precious sleep before night shift, she marvelled. She would never have guessed Matron capable of that level of warmth and kindness.

*

The unit made their way along a track situated halfway between Caen and the landing beaches. Ahead was a village and beyond an airstrip held by the enemy. On either side of the track there was white tape marking an area cleared of mines. In the distance the sound of gunfire and screaming shells came from the front line but after Sword Beach it was a sight for sore eyes to see green fields and trample over sweet-smelling grass.

As soon as the RAMC unit arrived at the site, they pitched tents and spent time familiarising themselves with their surroundings and readying the makeshift hospital for the wounded—for the front line was only a stretch up the road and close to a village.

Starved, Richard brought out his ration pack of food and, sitting on his hunkers, devoured every morsel. All the while the distant artillery sounded from the front line.

"How you doing, mate? Orders are to bring in the wounded." Charlie Oakley towered above him.

Richard rose and clapped Charlie on the back. "Let's get started."

Stretcher-bearers evacuating the wounded were always at risk because they were continually in the line of fire. And the job was made difficult when it was imperative they didn't jolt the casualties.

Richard, as a non-combatant, didn't stop to think about his own safety—that he was at risk. All that registered were the fatigued, frightened eyes of wounded soldiers as they lay helpless after a bitter battle—some alongside the mortally wounded. After ferrying stretchers for hours, and especially soldiers that weighed a ton, Richard's hands were bloodied and blistered. His arms ached like blazes and he couldn't stand straight from his aching back. But as far as his tired mind could reason, this was his way of making amends for not doing his bit for all those years.

That night as Richard lay on the ground, scenes of the wounded disturbed his mind and he couldn't sleep. He felt in the pocket of the battledress that covered him for the photograph of May that was folded in a letter she'd sent. As he touched the photograph he imagined her gorgeous, smiling face.

"Night, my darling." Richard touched his fingertips to his lips and then pressed them against the photograph.

As sleep finally overtook him, in his dreams he felt her snuggle up to him.

He was awoken by Charlie tugging at his arm, "Come on, fella, bail out of bed. The battle for that bloody airfield starts at 0200 hours."

The enemy wanted to hang onto the airfield as the Allies would use it as a strategic position to refuel and repair aeroplanes and for emergency landings.

To get to the airfield the troops had to go through the village, which was still occupied by the Allies.

By the light of a star-studded sky, a squad of four stretcher-bearers marched with the infantry behind Churchill tanks towards the front line.

Richard, teamed with Charlie, brought up the rear. Boots clatter-ing, they approached the village, all shuttered up, its people in bed.

Charlie whispered, "Wish it was me in—" He stopped at the sound of gunfire.

A sniper in one of the nearby trees, Richard thought. He fell to the ground to take cover.

There were more shots, this time from the infantry and a body fell out of a poplar tree that lined the road.

As the troops marched on behind the tanks, one soldier stayed on the ground. Richard hurried and crouched beside him, opening his haversack.

The soldier reached up to his shoulder, then gazed up at Richard with surprised eyes. "The bloody thing whizzed past and I just dropped. Me shoulder hurts like hell."

Richard assessed for an entry wound but there wasn't one, nor any blood. The soldier's breathing, consciousness and pulse were stable and he didn't appear in shock.

After further investigation, he told the lad, "I'd say it's a clavicle fracture."

"What's that?"

"Collarbone."

Richard made a sling to support the arm. "That's you out of this skirmish."

"Aw, I'll never live it down with the fellas."

"Back to camp, soldier. You'll fight another day."

The soldier stood and, picking up his rifle, moved back along the road.

All alone on the road, Richard reckoned Charlie must have gone on ahead.

Shrugging the haversack onto his back, Richard was just about to move when he heard a sudden noise—a moan—that made the hairs on his neck stand on end.

Another noise, grunting this time.

Then a voice, "Anybody...out there..."

Moving towards the sound, Richard made for the poplar trees at the side of the road.

Another shell screamed and exploded down the road and the blast lit up the area.

Richard noticed a gap in an overgrown hedge. Pushing through, he saw a silhouetted figure sitting on the ground, his back leaning against a tree. Beyond was a narrow track and in the distance was a farm, with black metal gates and shuttered windows.

The figure was Charlie.

"Bugger . . . they got me."

CHAPTER TWENTY-EIGHT

Charlie had removed his battledress and in the stark moonlight Richard saw a dark wet stain spreading across the front of his friend's shirt.

Charlie told him, "Took a bullet in the chest."

Richard evaluated the situation. Charlie was able to talk so his airways were clear. He did a quick examination of his chest and looked for other wounds. He took a dressing out of his haversack.

"Charlie... apply pressure with this." Richard put the dressing in Charlie's hand and placed it over the wound.

Charlie was in a bad way and his wound needed urgent attention.

"I've got to get us out of here." Richard spoke to himself as much as to his friend. "There's a farm not far from here but I'm worried it's in occupied territory. I'll have to take a chance."

"So cold. Took battledress off to check injury..."

Hypovolaemic shock, Richard thought. Charlie probably needed a blood transfusion.

Richard shrugged out of his battledress and covered Charlie with it. Another shell burst not far away and Richard was sure the earth shook. There was no time to lose. Richard fumbled in his haversack for the morphine.

"Charlie I'm going to give you a—"

Charlie's hand slid to the ground and his head slumped to one side.

Richard stared into his friend's glazed, unseeing eyes.

A shell screamed through the air and there was an almighty explosion, as a frisson of fear gripped Richard. The blast was the last thing he knew before his world went black.

Richard opened his eyes to a cold and dark world. Birds twittered above and a cow dung smell drifted on a soft breeze. He rubbed his eyes and opened them but in the pitch black, he couldn't see. Where was he? He couldn't remember. He wished the moon would shine. He tried to stand on shaky legs but the pain in his right thigh took his breath away and his right arm hung by his side and no matter how he tried, it wouldn't work. He felt his chest and the flesh felt strangely loose. Pain throughout his body tortured him. He lay back on the ground in the foetal position and let blessed sleep claim him.

When he awoke, a hot sun burned his exposed skin. Hellish pain still racked his body. To make matters worse, he couldn't recall who he was. He opened his eyes but was unable to see the sun. He rubbed his eyes but still no sight came. He was blind, the voice of alarm cried in his head.

He sensed he was in danger. It pained him to stand but instinct drove him to get away. He fell. Hauling his painful leg, he crawled over rough terrain. If only he could remember where he was. He felt, now and then, around the immediate area but his hand only touched the bark of trees. Still, he crawled on. The track he travelled didn't seem to end and he had no way of telling the time of day. Unable to bear the pain, he rested for a while.

He must have slept, for when he awoke it was raining. His mouth parched, he cupped his hands and slurped droplets from his palm. He couldn't resist the urge to move, only this time his body refused. He lay on his back and felt rain patter on his cheeks.

Voices came to him then... or was he dreaming? There they were again—and they spoke in a foreign tongue.

His gut instinct was to hide, but the pain exhausted him and he couldn't move. His breath came in shallow gasps and even that cost too much effort. All he wanted was sleep. As sounds and smells receded, his sightless world slipped into oblivion.

*

"See what I mean, Nurse," the woman told May. Her face hot and flushed, the mother was at her wit's end and looked exhausted. "Little monkey...he does this every time he feeds. Sucks for a few minutes then falls asleep."

As May sat beside the mother on the bed helping her to breastfeed, her tired mind only half listened. She sorely missed getting letters from Richard but then, hadn't he told her not to worry as he didn't know when he'd next be in touch? She smiled fondly at his afterthought in a recent letter. "Out of sight doesn't mean out of mind as you are with me always."

"It's no laughin' matter, Nurse."

"Oh, I'm sorry. My mind tends to wander at this time so early in the morning."

"Don't apologise, lass. It's me. This bairn's turned me into a grump. This is me fourth and I've never had this trouble feeding before."

The blackout curtains were drawn back and early morning sunlight streamed through the tall window behind the patient's bed.

The mother turned a distressed face to May. "I don't know what I'm ganna do when I'm home the morra if it takes him this long to feed. I won't get anythin' done."

The little tinker, May saw, had gone into a rosy-cheeked sleep and nothing would wake him.

"He thinks I've got all day."

Sister Turnbull, doing her early morning round came to stand at the side of the bed.

"I'll show you how it's done."

She flicked the pink sole of the baby's right foot with her forefinger. Startled, the baby opened his eyes, his contented little face crumpled and he started to howl.

"That did the trick." Sister went on her way.

The mother, with a look of distress, clutched the baby to her chest.

When May's shift finished, she didn't want breakfast—she only wanted bed and sleep.

Collecting her letters, she sifted through them as she made for her room. There was one from Maureen's mam—who still kept in touch—and a postcard from Mr. Talbot informing her of his new address as his son-in-law had taken over the farm and he'd moved into the village.

As she saw the handwriting on the last letter, she gave a sharp intake of breath.

A letter from Richard.

She raced to her room, removed the cumbersome uniform hat, undid the press studs on her collar and reclined on the bed.

She tore open the envelope. A cry escaped her as she scanned the first line.

My darling, I hoped you would never receive this letter because it means I have gone from you. As if all the blood had drained from her body, May went limp with shock. She didn't want to read any more. She wanted to pretend this letter had never arrived.

Yet, she knew she had to read on.

I'm sorry, sweetheart. After all you've been through I didn't want to put you through this. I've written your name and address on this letter so whoever finds it will post it to you. I've carried the letter in my battledress pocket to make sure you had something of me on the day I died because my last thought will be of you, sweetheart. Know that I have no regrets because some people go a lifetime without finding a love like ours. There again, I do have one regret: that I won't see our child. I love whoever it is already and know that you will be the most wonderful mother. I'm so thrilled we made the child together, it has made my life complete.

May, I love you with all my heart and I'll be watching over you. You are stronger than you think and will survive this. Please, please get on with your life. I want you and our child to have the very best, even if that does mean you find someone else.

You deserve to be happy, kiddo.

What more can I say, except you have shown me how to live life to the full and the last few months were the happiest I've known. Thank you with all of my heart.

God bless my darling.

Your Richard xxx

Tears streamed down May's cheek, dripped off her chin and wet the hand that held the letter. A spot in her throat hurt like hell.

She sat up and bunched her hands, her nails digging into her palms till they hurt. She couldn't do this. The heartache was unbearable. She wanted to scream, break something, run until she was exhausted.

She collapsed back on the bed. As she lay there, a thought came and she knew exactly what she had to do. Etty was the only person who would understand.

They sat either side of the kitchen table. Trevor had taken both of the children out for a walk and so they had the place to themselves.

In the silence, Etty turned to face May. "Don't you want it verified that Richard is—"

"Dead. No. Richard put that letter on his person as he would want me to be one of the first to know if he...didn't make it."

"Don't you want to know the details of his death?" Etty persisted.

"That would mean getting in touch with his parents. And all they will ever know is that Richard was killed in action."

The pair of them lapsed into silence.

Then Etty spoke. "It'll take a long while but you must do as Richard says and get on with your life. That's what you'd want if it was the other way around."

May sniffed.

"What a man! To express how much he loved you so eloquently."

May sniffed harder. "How...can I go on?"

"People say take one day at a time but it's not that easy."

"What then?"

"I'd say take one minute at a time and if you survive without crying then try for two."

"Etty, it kills me to think what he went through when folk thought him a coward."

"You changed his life, remember?"

"And he changed mine. But I thought we would be together forever."

"He'll be forever in your memory."

"I want more. I want him here. I'm never going to love again. It hurts too much."

"You know that's not true. You'll love Richard's child growing inside you. Believe me, there will be a lot of joy and happiness in the future. Only...it takes time."

The tears came again and Etty, rising from her chair, moved around the table and hugged her tight. May cried and cried, great shuddering gasps that made her shoulders heave up and down and her stomach muscles hurt.

When, finally, the tears had finished, May sat bolt upright and held her face in her hands.

In her mind, she heard Richard's deep and rich voice, his measured words. He would ask what she wanted to do.

May blew her nose on a handkerchief.

"I'm going to make Richard proud. I don't know how...but only I can sort me life out. I'll think of a way to bring up this bairn and give Derek a home too. Other mothers that have lost their loved ones do it...so why not me?"

A knock came at the door. Etty went to answer it.

A voice came from the doorway, a voice May couldn't distinguish. She went into the passageway to investigate.

Ramona Newman stood there, dressed head to toe in black. Her face drained of colour, she looked pityingly at May.

"Trevor met Mrs. Newman in the street," Etty explained, her expression uncertain. "He told her about your loss."

Ramona gave a nod. "And if you're going through half the pain I am, lass, then I'm sorry for yi'."

May didn't know how to respond. She wasn't ready to face folk yet. She couldn't handle sympathy.

"I haven't come to dole out sympathy." Ramona must be a mind reader, May thought. "You'll get plenty of that and I know from experience it does nee good." She moved along the passage towards May. "What I've come about is practical matters. Mr. Newman's explained about your offer to have your old job back in exchange for lodgings. Well...I accept. He also told us about the bairn you're carrying. I've been thinking. After it's born you can stay on if you want."

There was an imploring note in her tone.

She went on, "I've come to like having Derek around and I don't want to go back to livin' like before. Just Mr. Newman and me."

"Mrs. Newman, I—"

"That's another thing. From now I want yi' to call us Aunt Ramona."

CHAPTER TWENTY-NINE

He was on a hospital ship, the nurse told him.

A babble of male voices sounded and the smell of disinfectant wafted in the air.

"How bad are my injuries?" he wanted to know.

The nurse hesitated.

"You came around for a time in France and the doctor assessed that you were blinded and had lost your memory. Your chest needs an operation as does your right leg."

"Do you know how I was injured?"

He heard rustlings and then felt the nurse's warm fingers on his wrist as she took his pulse. "Probably a shell blast. That would cause loss of sight and memory."

"How did I get here?"

"A Frenchman, a Monsieur Dubois, it says here in a letter in your notes."

From her voice, he imagined her to be young and from the southern counties.

"Monsieur Dubois is a farmer. He took you to a doctor in the nearest town who had you transferred to a hospital at base area where you were assessed before boarding this ship for the journey home."

Home. What a wonderful word—but where was home?

The nurse continued. "The doctor left a letter to put in your notes so you'd know the history of when you were found."

"This letter . . . does it say if anyone else was around when I was found?"

"According to what it says here, there was just you. Monsieur Dubois's son found you on a track at the side of their land. You were in a bad way and the son took you for dead but when he realised differently, he carried you back to the farmhouse."

"Where was this?"

"On the outskirts of a village in Normandy. According to the doctor's letter, Monsieur didn't want to take any chances of a soldier being found on his property by the Germans. Mr. Dubois destroyed your dog tags and uniform and dressed you in his son's clothes. So, soldier, we don't know your identity."

"We know I was in the army?"

"It would seem so."

"I'll write and thank both Monsieur and the good doctor."

Then he remembered he was sightless.

"Where am I now?"

"On a ward below deck with double tiers of bunks. You're on a lower but don't attempt to get up."

Knowing how weak he felt, the warning was unnecessary. His mind was blank. He couldn't recall who he was or where he came from.

"Nurse." His mind sharpened. He must ask the question. "Will I be able to see again?"

"I honestly don't know."

"Where will they send—"

"I have to go." Her voice travelled from a distance.

"Thanks. I appreciate your time," he called.

Unable to take it all in, he fell back against a pillow listening to life below deck. Nurses, orderlies, doctors, bustling about, calling to each other, and the strange thing was, it all sounded familiar.

*

As May helped Nurse Smythe get a bed ready for a patient from the labour ward, the level of noise from the mothers in the day room increased.

"Good grief," Henrietta Smythe, a second-year nurse scoffed. "You'd think they were here for a holiday."

The new batch of mothers had hit it off and tended to gather in the day room at every opportunity. They sat in dressing gowns and slippers, needles clicking, cups of tea on the arms of their chairs.

"A word." Sister Turnbull beckoned to them from the office doorway.

When they were inside the office, Sister closed the door.

"I won't have you discussing patients." She glowered at Nurse Smythe. "You should take care what you say, Nurse. Indeed, this might be the nearest those women ever get to having a holiday."

May was surprised, as Sister Turnbull, usually a stickler for rules, ran a peaceful ward and strictly no jollity was allowed.

"Yes, Sister, sorry, Sister."

Sister bristled. "Have you not seen the appalling conditions some of these women live in? Back-to-back houses with an outside toilet between goodness knows how many properties. Filthy, damp, dismal places with a coal fire they can't afford to run."

Sister Turnbull was certainly in a pickle and May wondered what had caused this unusual outburst. But she knew what Sister said to be true. She remembered Richard saying he wanted to help change things by building better homes for people. At the thought of Richard a tearfulness that seemed to hover permanently beneath the surface of late, overcame her. May blinked hard and concentrated on Sister Turnbull.

Etty had warned her this might happen but May had insisted she return to work. She'd told her friend, "I want to work my notice. I need to keep busy."

Henrietta replied to Sister, "No, Sister, I've never been to that kind of area."

"Then it might pay, Nurse, for you to do a stint on the district. Perhaps then you'd learn not to be so flippant."

Henrietta flushed from the neck and pouted as if she'd like to retort, but knew she couldn't.

"Yes, Sister."

Sister Turnbull appeared to take a minute to collect herself.

"Is the bed ready for the new admission?"

"Yes, Sister," both nurses replied.

Mrs. Watson was nineteen and this was her second baby.

"I lost me other one, Nurse, from scarlet fever," she said, as May pulled screens around her bed. "Can I please have Pamela next to me bed? I don't want to let her out of me sight."

"What a lovely name." May smiled. "Baby is in the nursery just now getting weighed but I'll have a word with Sister..."

A noise from outside made May look out of the tall window behind Mrs. Watson's bed.

The drone of aeroplanes.

The Maternity ward had been built as an afterthought on the edge of the hospital grounds and all the windows had a scenic view of the moors in front and a golf course behind.

It was still light and, with no blackout curtains drawn, May could see two aeroplanes flying low in the blue sky and heading in this direction. Small for bombers, she recognised them as Spitfires.

"Something wrong, Nurse?" Mrs. Watson's voice sounded distant.

May tensed. She knew what a plane in trouble sounded like.

Galvanised into action, she tucked a blanket around Mrs. Watson. As the scream of planes came closer, the faltering engine sounded terrifyingly low, as if it wouldn't make it.

He's making for the golf course, May thought.

There came an almighty thud that seemed to shake the very foundations of the building; for a split second the world stood still. May, fearing what could happen and with no time to think, threw herself down and covered Mrs. Watson's slight frame with her own.

A terrific explosion followed, then a sickening crescendo of breaking glass. As May looked up at the window, a large piece of glass, like a sharp knife, sliced the side of her face.

She passed out.

CHAPTER THIRTY

He awoke to a black world feeling woozy, some kind of block each side of his head preventing movement. He was in bed and didn't know the time of day or where he was. It was terrifying.

"All right, mate," a cockney voice above him said. "You're safe 'n' sound back on the ward. It's important you don't move yer 'ead."

He croaked, "Water..."

"Lord above, you can't just now, mate."

A wet cloth touched his lips.

He must have slept because when he swam back through the blackness into reality again the wooziness was gone.

"How are we today?" a voice, female this time, asked.

Today?

"How long have I been here?"

"You were transferred to Moorfields hospital in London, remember." Her kindly, mature voice soothed him. "You've been down for an eye operation and you've bandages on your eyes that must stay on for six days. You'll be groggy for a while, but you've slept through most of the effects of the anaesthetic."

Some sort of funnel was inserted into his mouth and Richard sucked gloriously cold water. The dribble at the side of his mouth was brushed away with something soft.

As he shuffled his backside for a better position, he found he couldn't move his leg and a sharp pain pierced his side.

He winced.

"That'll be your broken ribs, and your right leg is in a plaster cast in a hoist."

It all started to come back. The treatment on the ship.

He heard a pen scribbling over paper.

Surprised, he remembered why he was here. "When will I know if I have sight?"

"It can vary. We won't know till the bandages are removed."

More scribbling.

He tried to think of his name. Something—anything. He remembered the nurse who had read him the doctor's letter on the ship but alarmingly nothing before that.

Noises drifted into his disturbingly unseeing world. The clatter of dishes, voices, the rattle of wheels, smells—the aroma of fish, mingled with antiseptic.

"I can't remember who I am," he confided.

There was a pause in the writing. "Give it time."

*

"You're a local hero." Etty held out the *Gazette*. "Here, the facts are all there."

Days had passed and May was in sick bay in the Nurses' Home. It consisted of a small ward, kitchen and a day room where visitors were allowed.

The two friends were sitting in deep comfortable chairs in the day room while Sister, with a disapproving eye, kept checking to see if her patient was overdoing things.

May declined to look at the newspaper her friend had brought and so Etty read out:

> *A Spitfire on a training flight from Lancashire is believed to have had engine failure and crashed in the grounds of the town's Edgemoor Hospital. The pilot was killed. No*

damage was done apart from windows broken in two
wards and Maternity unit. The only injured was brave
nurse May Robinson who endangered herself in order to
save her patient.

Etty folded the newspaper and looked unsure. "It goes on to explain what you did." She tilted her head to one side. "Aren't you proud? You should be."

"I didn't think at the time . . . It's what any nurse would do."

"All the same, it was you that saved that mother from serious injury," Etty protested, "and look where it got you. Talk about hitting a person when they're down." She made a fist to the heavens.

May couldn't smile because it hurt her wound and she was afraid the stitches might burst.

"I admit seeing the plane flying towards us was terrifying. I swear I saw the pilot's face. Poor lad . . ."

She turned her mind away from the tragedy. She hadn't slept. She'd thought about Richard all night long—how if that plane hadn't crashed where it had she might have joined him.

May met her friend's gaze. "My face is disfigured."

"You've seen it?"

"When they changed the dressing."

"How bad is it?"

May took a deep breath and tried to stay brave. "A three-inch gash from the edge of my eye to my cheek."

Etty leaned back and surveyed the bandage around May's face and head as if she was viewing a painting. May knew she'd get the absolute truth from her friend.

Etty shook her head. "I imagine the wound looks grim what with the stitches and all, but won't it fade in time?"

"It's a deep slash, raised on both sides and a row of black ugly stitches."

She could feel the tightness in her throat but she refused to cry. She braced herself. May had seen many burnt and disfigured faces and she was ashamed at how she'd comforted soldiers by telling them what mattered to their loved ones was that they were alive and that it was the person inside that counted. She realised now these platitudes didn't help. Nothing helped. She knew that injuries could change a person's life. Even Etty couldn't disguise the pity on her face as she listened to May's description of her injury.

"To be fair, you could have lost an eye, or the baby. Just count yourself lucky you've escaped with only a facial injury," Etty remarked helpfully. "Won't it look loads better once the scar's healed and the stitches are gone?"

May thought of those boys with half their faces blown away.

"I suppose I could grow me hair long and have it hang over the—"

At that moment the door opened and Sister walked in.

"A Mr. and Mrs. Bentley have arrived and wish to visit."

May's mouth dropped open.

"Is that—?" Etty began.

"Yes. Richard's mam and dad."

"Do you wish to see them, Nurse?"

May didn't know. "I suppose so."

"Patients are only allowed two visitors," Sister told Etty pointedly.

Etty stood. "I'll go. You'll want to see them alone." She collected her things and made for the door.

Following Sister from the room, she turned and made big eyes at May. "Let me know what happens."

When they came into the room, Mr. and Mrs. Bentley were nothing like May expected. She remembered them from the photograph she'd seen at Richard's place. Distinguished-looking, they'd seemed to have the look of superiority of those who never listen to another person's point of view and who consider themselves always right. Yet, here Richard's parents were, an ordinary, grey-haired, ageing couple.

Mr. Bentley, who in the photo had been tall with a ramrod-straight back, was now bent at the shoulders and walked with a stick. His wife was painfully thin with what May could only describe as a panicky, uncertain look.

"It's good of you to see us." Mrs. Bentley moved towards May and handed over a bunch of flowers wrapped in newspaper. "From the garden," she said.

The atmosphere was awkward. May nodded to two chairs. "Please, sit down. Sorry I'm not dressed but—"

"Please don't apologise," Mrs. Bentley told her. "You look perfectly decent in your dressing gown."

Mrs. Bentley sat in the nearest chair while her husband stood next to her.

Mr. Bentley gazed in fascination at the bandage around May's head. His wife stared in horror.

If this was the reaction May was to expect, how much worse would things get when folk could see her scar? She thought of those brave boys who had lost limbs. She drew herself up and stared at Richard's parents with determined eyes.

"We came because we felt it important you should know. We've received a telegram." Mrs. Bentley's face had a ghastly pallor and tears were swimming in her eyes. "Prepare yourself for a shock, my dear."

How many times had May heard those very same words spoken on the ward?

"I know. Richard is dead," May told her woodenly.

"How did you know?"

May told her about the letter in Richard's battledress pocket.

Mrs. Bentley nodded. "Whoever found Richard must have taken that letter and posted it." Tears brimming in her eyes, she continued, "Richard's superior officer sent us a letter describing the nature of our son's death and how brave he'd been. The officer said a photo and letter from a sweetheart were found in Richard's battledress pocket. And I presumed the photograph was of you. He loved you so very much."

May's emotions were all over the place. She didn't trust herself to answer and quickly changed the subject.

"How did you know where to find me?"

"We saw the article about you in the *Gazette*..." Mrs. Bentley began, then looked at her husband. When he didn't respond, she went on, "Before he left, Richard came to see us and told us all about you, where you worked...and about the baby."

"He wrote and told me he had," May replied.

She remembered how Richard had described them being resentful and making it clear that him being a medical orderly didn't fit the bill. Her lenient heart hardened.

Mrs. Bentley went on, "Unfortunately, we didn't arrange..."

"There's nothing unfortunate about it. Your son came to see you to make up before he went to war. To tell you his future plans. He wanted to be a family and you—"

"Now, now, young lady." Mr. Bentley's cultured voice held an air of authority. "You don't know the circumstances of—"

"Oh, but I do. Richard explained about him and his brother. He didn't say but I could tell he felt he wasn't good enough for you." She saw Mrs. Bentley's face crumple. She didn't wish to cause any further heartache. She told them, "Your son was the kindest, most considerate man I've ever met. He stood by his convictions, no matter what cost to himself."

She drew a quivering breath. "Now he's dead and he'll never see his baby or watch it grow and...and..." Her voice squeaky, she finished, "I loved him so." She burst into tears.

Mr. Bentley looked astonished, as if he didn't know what to say. He reached into his jacket pocket and brought out an immaculately folded white handkerchief.

May wiped her eyes and blew her nose. "I think it best if you go."

Mrs. Bentley's hand flew to her mouth. "Oh no...please hear me out."

"Sarah...we can do no good here," her husband said. His bushy eyebrows were raised as if he'd had a fright.

"Terence, for once let me say my piece. Our son is dead and I for one am ashamed of how we behaved towards him..." Overcome, Mrs. Bentley took a minute to collect herself, then faced May. "Both our sons were brought up to compete, to be the best in every venture they undertook. I'm guilty of allowing this to happen."

She gave her husband a hard look. "Jeffrey felt it was his duty to sign up, to prove he was a man when he was still just a boy. He didn't question, but did as he was taught and paid the ultimate price."

She heaved a long sigh. "Richard was the sensitive one, the thinker, though he wanted to please like most children do. But in a household where duty rules and you have to obey without question, it was difficult for him. I see that now. Against all our wishes, he followed his beliefs." She looked up at her husband. "And I for one am proud of him and only wish I could turn back the clock and tell him so."

Though May felt for this woman who hadn't had the courage to stand up to her husband for her children's sake, she didn't react. Her loyalty was to Richard—because he'd suffered so. But she also knew he'd have the grace to forgive his parents and would be eager to start anew.

Sarah Bentley gave her husband, who stood apparently unmoved, a stony stare.

"I'm so glad Richard met you, and you made his last months so special and wonderful...which were—"

"His words," her husband finished for her. His chin wobbled. "And for the record, he would have made a much better father than me."

His face softened, losing its granite expression, as he searched for words. And May saw Richard in his father.

"You remind me of him," May told him.

As if this was too much to bear, Mr. Bentley appeared to sag. "I was more soldier than a father," he admitted, his voice hoarse. "Ahem! But no excuses. I loved both my sons...in my own way." He visibly gathered himself. "Look here, this helps no one." He turned to May. "What my wife and I would like, if you would be willing, is to be part of our future grandchild's life."

"We wouldn't interfere," Sarah Bentley put in quickly. "Just to see the child would be enough..."

Later, when the Bentleys had left, May laid her head back against the chair, her emotions in turmoil.

Richard's parents had ruined his life. But had they? He was happy despite them and because of his circumstance he'd left home and found his way to her. How could she stay mad at them when all he'd wanted was to make up? Besides, Richard's bairn deserved to know its grandparents. Her mind made up, May could picture Richard's smile of joy and contentment.

As she daydreamed about him, grief returned to overwhelm her—but May took solace from the fact that she'd made the right decision.

CHAPTER THIRTY-ONE

Screens were pulled around his bed.

"Today's the day," he heard Mr. Percy, the eye specialist, say in his booming voice.

After days lying on his back with his head seemingly in a vice, he felt woozy sitting up.

"Scissors, please, Nurse." Mr. Percy sounded as though he was concentrating hard. "Don't be disappointed, Mr.... erm... if you don't see anything straight away... that can happen sometimes."

The last of the bandages were taken off and Richard's stomach turned as if he were on a ship on a choppy sea.

"I can see light," he exclaimed.

He soon realised that that was all he could see. Everything was blurry, as though gauze was over his eyes.

"I did explain that you'd need further surgery." Mr. Percy's voice had a placating tone.

The screens were taken away and, left alone, he sank back against the pillow. He was glad he wasn't allowed to get up yet as his ribs still hurt like blazes and his whole body felt as though it had been run over by a bus.

He searched his brain as the thought triggered something in his mind, a vague memory... He was sure he'd heard the phrase "run over by a bus" before. But where refused to surface in his mind.

"Damn it," he cried as he strived to remember.

"Aye, mate, sorry it didn't go your way," the fellow in the next bed called.

Richard gave a wave of the hand.

Footsteps came to his bed and then he heard a tray being set down on his bed top table.

"Milky drink," a nurse with a mature voice told him. There was a rattle of cup on saucer.

"I thought I had a memory then I lost it."

There was a pause. "You're still recovering...give yourself time."

"How long d'you think it will take?"

"Recovery or memory?"

"Both."

"You'll be here for a time then sent to convalesce." Her tone was professional. "Ships are delivering large numbers of casualties and beds throughout hospitals are stowed out."

A new thought came to disturb him. "Where will I go after I've convalesced?"

"Don't worry about that now. Think positively. You may have regained your memory by then."

"What if I haven't?" He wanted to take his frustration out on someone. But he calmed himself, as he knew none of this was the nurse's fault. She was doing her job to the best of her ability. "Wherever I belong they'll probably think I'm dead by now."

"Remember what the specialist told you?" He heard a hint of sympathy in her voice. "Your memory could return at any time, today, next month..."

"In a few years' time," he finished cynically. "Why didn't that shell just finish me off?"

"Mr. Shell Blast...that's no way to talk. The good Lord spared you for a reason and feeling sorry for yourself won't help you get better. You should be ashamed."

Her footsteps stomped off.

He felt mortified; the nurse was right. And he vowed he would never give in to self-pity again.

"That's you told, Mr. Shell Blast." A male voice, with a laugh in it, came from across the ward.

He saw the funny side. "That must be the nickname the staff have given me. I bet the nurse doesn't realise she's spoken it aloud."

"The nurses have gorra have a sense of humour after all they've got to deal with."

Something stirred in his memory but wouldn't emerge as proper thought. "Where d'you come from?"

"Why, man, I'm a Geordie from Newcastle...can yi' not tell?"

He wanted to know why the accent was so familiar...perhaps it was a clue to where he came from.

There was a kerfuffle from the other side of the ward.

"Ger-off," the Geordie man shouted.

"What's all this?" The nurse with the mature voice was back, her tone stern.

"I'm not havin' nee conchie shavin' us, and that's final."

For some reason the comment riled him. "Give the man a chance," he cried.

In the resentful silence, he wondered why he cared so much.

*

Late July 1944

The bell rang as May entered the funeral parlour. Mechanically, she pulled her long chestnut-brown curls over her cheekbone to hide the healed and unsightly scar, a habit she'd acquired to avoid the pitying glances she received.

It was still early morning, and Mr. Newman (she hadn't been invited to call him uncle) looked up from his desk where he was doing accounts. He frowned at the bag she carried.

A month had passed since May had left the hospital. She sorely missed the structure and routine, and especially the patients, but her bump had grown and she knew it would be too embarrassing to be on the ward, even if she had been allowed.

She'd moved in with the Newmans in an upstairs bedroom that overlooked the red brick backyard. Derek was in the small bedroom at the front of the house and it was like old times seeing him every day. May was delighted that Derek wanted more of her attention, particularly when he came home from school when he was eager to share what he'd been doing all day—especially sport, which was his favourite activity. For though the Newmans were kind, they liked him to be academically inclined and this put pressure on the laddie. He could relax when he was with May.

He accepted the scar with the curiosity of the young and asked her a barrage of questions. How had they taken the stitches out? Did they really use a needle? And what a shame she hadn't kept any of them.

Only once did he mention the bump. "Is your baby going to live with us?"

"Why? Do you want it to?"

"Albert at school, his mam's just had a baby and he's a big brother now."

"Would you like that?"

He nodded. "Only if it's a boy, though."

May laughed and ruffled his blonde hair. "That I cannot guarantee, laddie."

Now, as she passed Mr. Newman's desk, he turned a page in the account book.

Then, sitting back, he took off his spectacles and rubbed the bridge of his nose.

He eyed the bag she carried. "Should you be carrying such a load in your condition?"

May had been out to the corner shop to fetch the rations. "There's not many heavy things in the bag, just potatoes."

May couldn't wait till Derek arrived home from school this afternoon, as she'd brought him her ration of sweets—two ounces of sherbet lemons, his favourite sweeties. The ration for sweets used to be sixteen ounces a month but now, with the shortages, the allowance was reduced to eight ounces.

"Very well." Mr. Newman replaced his spectacles and resumed bookkeeping.

May climbed the stairs.

"Have you seen this?" Ramona stood on the landing, an open newspaper in her hand. Dressed in a light blue summer frock with a white collar and buttons all the way up the front, Ramona had finished with wearing black.

"The man's mad."

May glanced at the article in question. She saw a picture of a V-I flying bomb that the Luftwaffe were terrifying Londoners with.

"Apparently, Hitler," Ramona went on, "sees this as a vengeance weapon. Stupid fella. Does he not know he's on a losin' battle? Churchill himself said we'll defend our island whatever the cost." Her voice wobbled.

Poor soul, May thought, and Ramona's cost was losing her only son.

May had read all about the bomb that looked like a small aeroplane and the strange rasping noise it made when it was in flight.

She told Ramona, "I've heard that when the noise stops, that's when folk have to worry. Sometimes it glides for a bit or it can simply drop with its explosive load."

"Eee, those poor Londoners. As if they haven't had enough to put up with."

Ramona gave May's grocery bag a cursory glance. "I hope you're not overdoing it. You shouldn't be carrying heavy loads."

For the second time that morning, May insisted she was perfectly fine.

This war had changed people and some, like Ramona, for the better. Folk were more tolerant of each other and "a trouble shared was a trouble halved" was, for most, the motto of the day.

Ramona folded the newspaper. "I'd like a word." An uncertain look crossed her face. "It's about Derek. I thought it best if we have a talk while he's at school."

The atmosphere tensed, and May felt the hairs on the back of her neck bristle.

She suspected this talk was not good news.

It wasn't.

"It isn't just me who feels this way," Ramona said as they sat either side of the kitchen table a hot cup of tea in their hands, "Mr. Newman thinks the same too. We've discussed the matter at great length." Her gaze dropped to the table. "As we've said you can stop with us after this bairn you're carrying is born. But it stands to reason at some point you'll meet another fella and you'll have another bairn with—"

"Aunt Ramona. What is this about?"

Ramona looked her boldly in the eye.

"Derek. Me and Mr. Newman want to adopt him."

*

August 1944

Richard had been on the ward for five weeks now and the specialist's morning round was part of his day.

Fully dressed, he sat by his bedside on a chair.

"The hospital can do no more for now," Mr. Percy told him in his hearty manner. "You're to be discharged to a convalescent home where you will continue to gain strength."

After the latest eye operation, he was still sightless and had reconciled himself to the fact that he was going to stay blind. Mr. Percy planned to do another operation but he wanted Richard to recuperate for a time first.

The skin grafts on his chest had healed and now his plaster cast had been cut off, he could walk with the aid of a stick.

Later, when the big man and his team had left the ward, the nurse with the mature voice told him, "Your bed will hardly get the chance to get cold before somebody else is in it."

Though it was said in jest, he understood they were desperate for beds. But this place had become his home, the only home he could remember and the idea of leaving was ... bloody alarming.

"Where will I be going?"

"Sister hasn't divulged that piece of information yet. But wherever it is, keep out of trouble."

"Chance would be a fine thing, Nurse."

She laughed. "He's got opinions, this chap, and once he's made up his mind there's no changing it."

The nurse had turned her head away and seemed to be talking to someone else. "Hold the fort while I go and ask Sister if she's finished with his notes."

As she walked away, he became conscious that someone was standing at his side.

"Tell me," he said, "how do I look? They've dressed me but nobody told me what I'm wearing..."

"It's a very nice navy suit."

He cocked his head and listened. Her voice was young and keen but slightly nervous.

"I haven't heard your voice before. Are you new?"

"I've just started training."

"What made you want to become a nurse?"

She smelt of fresh fragrant soap.

"I've always dreamed of becoming a nurse but I never thought I'd be good enough."

An excited tingle went up his spine. He'd heard those words before—and by gosh, he knew who'd spoken them. Her beautiful face swam up from his subconscious.

Richard beamed. He knew exactly where he'd go.

Home, to see May.

CHAPTER THIRTY-TWO

Breakfast that Thursday morning was bread and homemade jam and a cup of tea in the kitchen-come-living room. Then came the best part of May's day, when she walked Derek down to Chichester roundabout and over the busy main road to his school in Laygate Lane.

When she arrived back home, Ramona was waiting for her at the kitchen table by the window, two cups of tea in front of her.

"I'm off to help in the WVS canteen," Ramona told May as she joined her at the table.

Servicemen who came into the area didn't have many places to go during the times they were off duty. The Women's Voluntary Service had requisitioned a local hall where men could congregate to have tea and food at minimal prices and join in with a game of cards or dominoes.

"My stint is half ten till three." Ramona slurped her tea. "I was wondering, would you mind making a pan of vegetable soup for dinner as there's nowt much else in the pantry? Mr. Newman's away at the docks to try and get wood. He'll be starved when he gets back."

"Of course. And it'll do for Derek's tea."

"Why don't you put your feet up this afternoon? You make us nervous the way you're always gaddin' about. When I carried my Danny…" she began.

May only half listened to the drawn-out tale of when Ramona's waters broke. Poor woman, her face lit up every time she described the memory of when she first glimpsed her newborn son.

A life wasted. Like those of thousands of other young men who'd died. And her beloved Richard was one of them.

With him gone, despite what Mrs. Newman thought, there'd never be another man in May's life. Love like theirs came only once in a lifetime.

She spared a moment to think of the Bentleys, who'd lost their sons. Life must be unbearable for them.

May had written and told them where she was now living and, as promised, Mrs. Bentley kept regularly in touch.

As for Ramona, May held no malice towards the woman. Grief-stricken, she'd reached out for a bit of happiness and thought Derek could replace her son. The day she'd asked if she could adopt him, May had told her straight:

"Over my dead body. It's time you knew. Derek is my son and in his short life he's been hawked from one home to another. But not any more. From now on he's stopping with me."

May expected an angry outburst and to end up being shown the door. But neither happened. On the contrary, once Ramona had got over the shock of May's disclosure, she reverted back to being this new and tolerant person whom May had come to admire.

She told May, "Eee, I don't blame you, hinny, I would say the same if somebody had suggested taking my Danny away from me. The truth is, lass, I'm terrified you'll up and leave with Derek. Then we'll have no one."

May's heart ached for the woman. "Aunt Ramona, whatever happens in the future, Derek and me and this baby will always need you and Mr. Newman. You're part of our family."

Ramona's round happy face smiled.

Finishing her tea, Ramona stood and started for the door.

"Oh, by the way," she turned and told May, "a letter came for yi' this mornin'. I propped it by the tea caddy."

With that she was gone.

May wandered over to the caddy on the bench. Picking up the letter, she recognised the neat handwriting as Mrs. Bentley's. May slit open the envelope.

> *Dearest May,*
> *I wish I could tell you this in person. Sit down dear, as you're in for the biggest shock.*

May didn't want any more shocks. Nervous for a split second, she felt like throwing the letter in the fire. But curiosity got the better of her.

> *I'm writing this from Moorfields Hospital in London. We received notice from the hospital.*
> *May, it's Richard. He is alive!*

As her legs buckled May nearly fell down, but gripped the table. Her mind reeled as she read the words again. This time she did sit down.

Yes. She'd read the words correctly. The letter did say Richard was alive.

The rush of adrenalin she experienced made her giddy.

> She read on, *I find it difficult to describe the wonder Terence and I feel at this miracle and so I won't try and will keep to practicalities for now.*
> *Immediately we heard, Terence went to the phone box and phoned the hospital. He was told Richard was to be discharged into a convalescent home as the hospital is desperate for beds. The reason we hadn't heard anything of him till now was because Richard had lost his memory but has regained it now. And he can't wait another minute to come home.*

The hospital specialist agreed that we could collect him. So here we are at the hospital where we are staying overnight in a relatives' room. We're hoping to return home with Richard tomorrow but that will depend on how packed the trains are with servicemen. Though Richard still needs to recuperate, he is strong enough to travel but not on his own.

If we are successful, I think it wise, because of Richard's weakened condition, that he rests after such a journey. Perhaps you could leave seeing him till Thursday. You have our address. May quickly calculated. Today was now Thursday and her heart raced . . . She read on, *May, another shock. Richard is blind. I don't know all the ins and outs of how Richard was blinded and lost his memory but for now, all that matters is that our son is alive.*

I must go, dear. I will pop this letter in the hospital post box as I leave. I thought it right you should know so you can prepare yourself.

Oh, May, Terence and I have been given a second chance. Our boy is coming home.

With very best wishes.

Sarah Xx

May stared into space in a stunned daze. From downstairs, she heard the front door slam as Ramona left the house.

May found herself tidying up in the living room. The nervous energy she felt wouldn't allow her to stay still. She looked at herself in the mirror above the mantlepiece. How could she prepare herself? The news wouldn't sink in.

Richard. Alive. And blind.

My poor darling, was her first thought, closely followed by, *thank God he won't see my disfigured face.* Then she felt bad that the thought had popped so quickly in her head as it hadn't mattered unduly before. May could cope with stares of pity from strangers, and her loved ones took her for who she was. But she couldn't have borne it if instead of seeing love in Richard's eyes, she'd seen pity.

But what was she saying? Her love for Richard transcended her needs. He was alive and surely that was all that mattered.

She checked her wristwatch. Ten o'clock. At the thought of seeing him again she felt a kind of schoolgirl nervousness. Then her spirits dipped. The Bentleys mightn't be able to get a train until today. But the longing to see Richard was so strong that May decided to go to his parents' house anyway.

She moved to the kitchen and, picking up the letter from the table by the window, she checked the Bentleys' address.

A car door slammed outside in the street below and May automatically looked through the window. A taxi cab stood at the kerb and a man was climbing out of the passenger side.

May recognised the person as Mr. Bentley.

Mr. Bentley helped someone out of the back of the taxi cab. When the taxi drove off, a man with a white walking stick in his hand took Mr. Bentley's arm.

Her nerves jittery and shaky, May undid the bow of her pinny and took it off, then adjusted her hair over the sides of her face.

A bell tinkled. Voices came from the parlour below.

In a dream-like state, May descended the stairs and moved through to the parlour.

A tall man, rake thin, wearing a navy suit that hung from him, tapped a white stick in front of him as he limped towards Mr. Newman's chair.

He turned.

May's knees went weak and she almost collapsed.

"It's May," Mr. Bentley told him.

He gave a broad smile. "Hello, my darling."

May clasped her hand on her heart.

Her voice was barely a whisper, "Richard, how can it be you?"

His eyes didn't focus but stared past her towards the staircase door.

"May, you've had a shock...the baby..."

As if he might be a mirage, she came over and touched him. "I can't believe you are real. You were reported dead."

"I'm real." He let go of his stick and it clattered to the floor as he took her into his arms and kissed her.

"Ahem! I'll leave you two alone...I'll be outside if you want me." Mr. Bentley opened the parlour door and left.

After his dad closed the door, Richard pulled away and told her, "We got home late last night and I was desperate to see you. I hardly slept a wink and insisted first thing this morning that Pa hire a taxi."

May laughed and cried all at once. "If this a dream, Richard, then I never want to wake up."

Hungrily, his lips pressed against hers once more.

As they kissed, his eyes closed, she searched his face. She still couldn't believe he was here. He was gaunt, his hair in places turned grey. As they pulled apart, he rested her head against his shoulder and, hugging her tight, stroked her hair.

"Tell me—what happened?"

He hesitated in his way, forming words in his mind before he spoke.

The reality sank in, then. Richard had returned.

"I was sent to Normandy."

"I knew it."

"It was hell on earth. But it was when I moved from the beaches that I was caught up in a shell blast. I lost my memory and was blinded."

"My God. But what about your leg? You were limping."

"All fixed."

She raised her head but gently he laid it back on his chest. "Sweetheart, let me tell you how it happened."

His heart thudded in her ears.

"It wasn't me they found dead but a good friend, a medic called Charlie Oakley. He got shot. When I found him, he was in shock."

"Poor man."

"One of the first things I must do now I'm home is to get in touch with his wife. They'd just got married." His voice was heavy with sorrow. "She deserves to hear the full story."

"Why was Charlie mistaken for you?"

"I covered him with my battledress and I can only assume whoever found him discovered your picture and a couple of letters in the breast pocket."

She stood up and looked into his sightless eyes. "Someone posted the letter you wrote, that's how I found out you'd . . . died."

"Christ. That must have been terrible for you."

He found her cheek and caressed it with the back of his hand. Too late, she remembered the scar. She took his wandering hand and held it in hers.

"But what about Charlie's identification?"

"He told me he took his dog tags off when he was hot and opened his shirt because they dangled in the way when he tended the wounded. I suspect that's what happened. The raid was during the night. We dressed in a hurry and Charlie must have forgotten to put them on again." Richard shook his head in distress.

May digested what she'd heard. "Where were you found?"

"My guess is a mile or two away. Before your sharp mind thinks to ask why I wasn't wearing dog tags either: a Frenchman, Monsieur Dubois, who gave me shelter at his farm, burned my uniform and all identification in case the Germans discovered me."

He smiled. "One day in the future we'll return to thank him and his son who found me."

May marvelled at the thought that they had a future together again.

She thought of Charlie Oakley and his wife. What the poor woman would be going through was unthinkable. The emotions of the day caught up with her, and tears slid down May's cheeks.

She sniffed. "And you? What happened after that?"

"May, it's been a long day so far. You've heard all the important bits. Can we finish this later?"

In fact, May thought, she didn't want to hear any more. All that mattered was that Richard was here.

He looked tired and drawn. She snuggled up to him, savouring his unique masculine smell.

"Besides, we have a wedding to plan," he told her with a grin. "And I want to know all about this baby of ours you're carrying."

She tensed. "There is one more thing."

"I think I know. Ma told me about your accident on the train coming home."

May didn't know whether to be pleased or angry at his mother's interference.

"She also told me about the injury and how it's affected you."

He held her at arm's length. Automatically, she flounced her hair over her scar.

Gently, Richard wiped away the tears on her cheeks.

Bemused at this action, her brow wrinkled into a little frown. "I don't understand..." Her heart thumped in her chest.

"I've got something to tell you." He paused in that way she loved as he formed the words. "I've had two operations on my eyes... neither appeared to work but then I woke one morning to blurry sight in my left eye. May, I can see short distances. The specialist has high hopes for that eye."

He pushed back strands of hair and traced her scar with his fingertips. His expression softened to one of love and tenderness. "All I can see, May, is beautiful you." He kissed her scar. "Don't you dare hide that lovely face. To me you'll always be gorgeous... even when we're old and grey." He patted her bump. "If the baby is a girl and half as pretty as her mother, I'll be a proud man."

May gave a relieved sigh. She'd never felt so loved and cherished.

"I don't know about that, Richard. Wait till you meet your stepson. He's got his heart set on a boy."

ACKNOWLEDGEMENTS

Firstly, to Wal. Your help and support are invaluable. Driving me to book locations, searching out facts I'd never discover on my own, simply being there when I need reassurance—love you and thanks, I couldn't have written this book without you.

Thanks to my wonderful publisher, Bookouture, who have made my writing dreams come true. The enormous amount of help and encouragement I have received over the past year is truly amazing and I am proud to be part of the Bookouture family. Heartfelt gratitude to Kim, Peta, Ellen, Noelle, Alex, Jennie and every one of the dedicated team. Huge thanks to Vicky Blunden for the brilliant edits that improved the book and made it so much stronger. Special thanks to my fantastic editor Christina Demosthenous for her continued encouragement and belief in me and for helping to make the book better than I ever could have imagined. Working with you is a delight.

Thank you to Mary Elliott who took time to read the script and help enormously with nursing matters. I truly appreciate the advice but any errors are mine alone. Thank you to Rob Macintosh from the RAMC (Royal Army Medical Corps) for all his help and explanations.

To my amazing family, Tracy, Andrea, Joanne, Phil, Nick, Gary, Laura, Tom, Will, Gemma, Dale and Robbie. Thank you for recommending my book to people and for the support and for being proud—I'm truly blessed to have you all in my life.

Thank you to my extended family and friends for their support and delight that I've achieved my writing dream.

Lastly, to all of you who read the book and took the time to review it—and not forgetting the book bloggers—a huge thank you.

READING GROUP GUIDE

THE INSPIRATION FOR *OUR LAST GOODBYE*

(I suggest you read the book first as there are spoilers.)

First of all, I'd like to say a big thank-you for purchasing *Our Last Goodbye*. To explain where the inspiration to write the book came from, I must return to my debut novel, *The Orphan Sisters*, which took many years of polishing and drafts to become the published book it is today.

The journey to write *The Orphan Sisters* began when I read an article about a young child abandoned in an orphanage by her mother who never returned. I couldn't imagine why a mother would do such a thing and decided to explore the reason why. I became captivated by Etty, the protagonist, and followed her journey in the orphanage and later when she left and found work in a factory that made precision instruments for World War II aeroplanes.

I say I *followed* Etty's journey because I don't plan books, which would be the sensible thing to do. I have a vague notion from the outset where I'm heading and generally have a good idea of how the book will end, but the excitement for me is to see where the characters take me in their story. It would be easier research-wise if I did have a plan, but the heroine often decides on a different course and all the research I previously might have done is wasted. Hence, I research as I go along with the story.

It is at the factory where Etty meets May Robinson, who works in the canteen. From the outset I loved May's character. She was meant to play a cameo role in the book, a few paragraphs at most, but I discovered that although May appeared a timid character, she was strong underneath. As I wrote the narrative for the first book, I felt she deserved a more central role, and because May is so appealing, I gave in and allowed her to have her own way.

May became a central part of *The Orphan Sisters*, and after I'd written the closing sentence, I found I'd developed a soft spot for her and it was difficult to let go.

When, finally, *The Orphan Sisters* got published, I was thrilled and sat on my laurels, as it were, enjoying the magic of the moment. I was brought sharply back to reality when my lovely editor enquired if I had any thoughts for a second book. I didn't. My insightful editor then suggested that I take a character from *The Orphan Sisters* and write about them. Without hesitation, I knew who that person would be: May Robinson.

I decided that because of May's empathetic and caring nature I'd make her a nurse. Another reason was that, in my youth, I did nurse training and so I was familiar with the profession from all those years ago.

I wanted to explore how May's character would change from the insecure, naïve individual she was into the confident young woman who knew her own mind.

Richard's character was born out of a conversation I had with a dear friend who was (he sadly died many years ago) a devout Christian. Mark (not his real name) was always interested in my writing and asked what period of time I was tackling. I told him WWII and enquired if he went to war. He explained that because of his strong belief he could never kill his fellow man, he became a conscientious objector (a conchie). He told me he did go to war, but on the front line as a stretcher bearer. I had never had a reason to consider conscientious objectors, but one thing I did know was that Mark was no coward. That belief was reinforced when, in my research, I discovered stretcher bearers were sent out at a huge risk to their own lives.

I decided to explore the life of a conscientious objector during war time and peoples' attitudes towards him. Richard too became a favourite character of mine.

At the end of *Our Last Goodbye* I did consider having a telegram sent to say Richard was missing and then have him reappear in the final chapter to relate what happened. Then the excitement of going with him to the D-Day landings took hold of my imagination. My worry about the research I'd need for such an undertaking receded and I took myself off to the local library. I'm so glad I did because going to war gave Richard and the story more depth.

One part of the research meant getting in touch with the Royal Army Medical Corps, where a kind gentleman's explanations of medical procedures proved invaluable. I could never have written the scenes in France without his sound advice. Thank you, Mr. M. People in general are so generous with their time and sharing their expertise to answer research questions.

I endeavour to keep research as accurate as possible but sometimes I had to fabricate an event for the sake of the story, like the scene in the hospital grounds when an air raid took place as May runs past the outpatients' department.

The setting of *Our Last Goodbye* is in my hometown of South Shields in the North East of England—a lovely seaside town that unfortunately was bombed and experienced a great loss of life. The town, at that time, had a thriving shipbuilding industry situated on the River Tyne and was a target for raiders.

I no longer live in South Shields but have a familiarity with the town like one does when you grow up in a place. The Geordie people with their friendliness (stand in a bus queue and someone is bound to start up a conversation) and humour is something I tried to incorporate in the book.

I was truly sad when I finished the book and had to say goodbye to May and Richard, but I hope you'll enjoy spending time with them as much as I enjoyed writing their story.

Warmest best wishes,

Shirley

QUESTIONS FOR READERS

1. Should Etty have stayed silent about her affair with Billy? What do you think she hoped to achieve by confessing? Did she have May's welfare at heart or her own?
2. Do you think May achieved her ambition to better herself?
3. What did you think of the discipline in those days, when the matron ruled the hospital? Did you think the hospital rules were trivial? For example, having the nightdress be on show in the bedroom?
4. Should May finally, after all these years, have told Derek she was his mother? What do you think Derek would gain by being told?
5. What are your thoughts about conscientious objectors and how people treated them at the time? Were you surprised some were put in prison?
6. Do you think May was foolish to begin a relationship with Richard given all that was at stake?

ABOUT THE AUTHOR

Shirley Dickson lives under the big skies of Northumberland, United Kingdom, with her husband, family, and lucky black cat. She wrote her first short story at the age of ten for a children's magazine competition. She didn't win but was hooked on writing for a lifetime. For many years she wrote poetry and short stories and got many rejection slips. Shirley decided to get serious about writing novels when she retired, and she has now written two stirring World War II historical novels. Shirley says she is a prime example to "never give up on your dream."

YOUR
BOOK
CLUB
RESOURCE

VISIT
GCPClubCar.com

to sign up for the **GCP Club Car** newsletter, featuring exclusive promotions, info on other **Club Car** titles, and more.

 @grandcentralpub

 @grandcentralpub

 @grandcentralpub

Journey to the past with more unforgettable historical fiction. Read the *USA Today* and *Wall Street Journal* bestseller everyone is talking about!

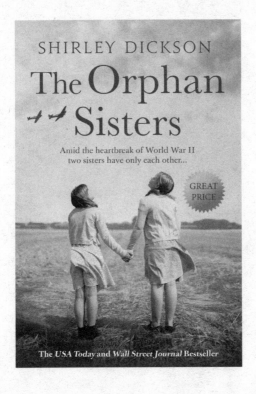

Discover bonus content and more on read-forever.com.
Find more great reads on Instagram with @ReadForeverPub

Follow @ReadForeverPub on Twitter and join the conversation using #ReadForever.

Connect with us at Facebook.com/ReadForeverPub